SARAH ANSBACHER

AYUNI

CASA MOCHA

*This novel is dedicated to the memory of
Susanne-Betty Schleimer, my beloved grandmother,
who instilled in me her passion for reading
and always encouraged me to write.*

Chapter 1

Autumn 2004

an she read my mind?

Miri sensed her mother's gaze. Sharp eyes like arrows aimed from behind, ready to penetrate her innermost thoughts. Heat rushed to her face. Miri bent low over the sink, cast about in the soapy water, and pulled out a ceramic oven dish.

Half fearful, half hopeful, her jittery hands scrubbed at the burnt remnants of supper as she braced herself for her mother's questions. A chance, at last – perhaps – to broach the unspoken subject.

Miri tried to compose her response. How would her mother react? She waited. But her mother remained silent.

Miri was mistaken to have expected otherwise. Her mother asked no questions because, from her perspective, there was nothing to discuss. Miri's future wasn't about choices. Impossible. There was a clear path her parents expected her to follow. Miri wondered whether her mother had any idea that beneath the exterior of this quiet, obedient daughter, content with her place and role in life, was a young woman

1

filled with uncertainty. And a different set of dreams.

Then what had been the meaning of her mother's stare? Maybe it was just her imagination, the needling of her conscience.

In the steamy kitchen, the only heaviness in the air was the piquant blend of paprika and garlic from the crispy schnitzels – her mother's signature dish. She prepared them every Thursday night for Shabbes. The only sound from her mother's direction, a sporadic hiss as she dropped the breaded pieces of tender chicken into a pan of sizzling oil.

I have to say something.

Miri had told herself the same thing over and over for the past three months, ever since she returned home from seminary. Time was ticking. If she didn't speak up soon, the inevitable call from the *shadchen* would seal her fate, and her horizons might never extend further than the monotonous tiled rooftops and dormers of north London that were visible from her bedroom window. Miri had tried to summon her courage several times before, but each time she did, the words would seize in her throat.

Miri turned. She was almost sure she caught her mother's surreptitious gaze before she focused again on the frying pan. She contemplated her mother, hunched over the stove, her rounded form hidden in the drapes of her green velour housecoat. Dare she say something now when her two sisters sat at the breakfast table and whispered and giggled behind their hands, ignoring their homework? When her mother might, at any minute, attend to the baby who rattled the bars of his playpen and bounced on his chubby legs in a bid for her attention? Or act as a mediator between two of her brothers, whose raised voices she heard from upstairs as they fought over a plastic building brick?

In silence, Miri rehearsed her opening sentence. *Say it*, she willed herself. She opened her mouth to speak. The phone rang. It drowned out the first syllable. Miri had lost yet another chance. With a well-practised motion, her mother lifted the receiver as she flipped the schnitzels.

'Hello, Mrs Finer. I was just thinking about you.'

Her again. Mrs Finer was an acquaintance of her mother – and the local busybody. Miri and her best friend, Raizy, did their best to stay out of her way. Whenever Mrs Finer deemed their behaviour inappropriate for a modest Chassidish girl, they could be sure she would inform their parents.

She had caused problems for Miri in the past. Like the one and only time, four years ago, when Miri and Raizy bunked off from school for the afternoon. Swapping a dull maths lesson for the tranquillity of the River Lea, they basked in the early April sunshine. They were unaware Mrs Finer had spied them as they turned off the main road at Clapton Common, onto Spring Hill. That was until they returned home to trouble from their mothers, followed by two weeks of after-school detention.

Another time, an ex-classmate stopped Miri on the high street to say hello. The headmistress had expelled the girl a month earlier after someone caught her talking to a boy in the park. The incident became the talk of the community. Mrs Finer saw fit to snitch on Miri for that too. When Miri tried to explain to her mother that she hadn't wanted to be rude to the girl by ignoring her, and they'd only spoken for a moment, her mother was still furious. Miri was guilty by association.

Then one sweltering afternoon, back in August, Miri was

heading home after doing a shop for her mother, lugging three heavy bags in each hand. Her blouse stuck to her back, and sweat trickled into her eyes. Miri set the bags on the pavement to roll up her sleeves and ran her arm across her forehead. Mrs Finer, who had witnessed her from the other side, went out of her way to cross the road and reprimand Miri right there for her lack of modesty. Miri had accidentally exposed her elbows.

Miri and Raizy laughed together in secret about Mrs Finer. Raizy once put forward a theory for Mrs Finer's constant street patrols: she considered herself Hashem's private detective. Raizy was joking, of course, but Miri wondered whether there wasn't a grain of truth to the idea.

Her mother adjusted the receiver against her ear. 'Last night at the *chasseneh,* you asked me about the Cohen boy, Tuli? … No, I hadn't heard …'

Miri rolled her eyes and blocked out the chatter by retreating into her daydreams. The many weddings that took place within their neighbourhood offered Miri's mother a steady supply of gossip, but stirred Miri's unease. Soon it would be her turn. The implication was mostly tacit, but she sensed it always and everywhere: at home, on the street, at the dreary office where she worked. Miri was living in a bell jar, under constant scrutiny both from her family and community, her every move analysed and measured. Their verdicts would help or hinder her prospects. Considered virtuous, you had the chance to be offered a *shidduch* from a prestigious family. Regarded errant, you were left with the second-rate suggestions, or worse yet, passed over and left on the shelf.

But what if you weren't sure whether you even wanted a

shidduch?

Miri found the pressure stifling. Nowhere for her to turn, no one to confide in, not even her friends. Although they were in the same position, they appeared content enough and reconciled to their future, shidduch and all. None of them would get it.

As for her mother. Especially her mother. In reality, she would react in horror to learn what was on Miri's mind. Even if Miri summoned the courage to pour out her heart, her mother wouldn't understand. Deep down, Miri knew she would have no say in the matter and no option other than to follow the same path as every other young woman in her community. Miri had always been compliant. Not a rebel. But in her mind, she was free. There, Miri could explore that side of herself she never revealed to anyone. A life she could never have.

Miri dreamt of going to college to study for a fulfilling career. The problem was, in her community, they'd consider it a disgrace. Her father would baulk at the mere suggestion. To mix with non-Jews, not to mention boys. Unthinkable!

She also dreamt of what it would be like to date someone. Long walks in the park, perhaps drinks in a hotel lobby. To get to know the person she might spend the rest of her life with. In depth. Not just meet for an hour with their parents waiting in the next room. For in her circles, they only met their future husbands through a shidduch (they were not permitted otherwise to socialise with the opposite sex). And she imagined the possibility of a different lifestyle once married – not a marriage based on separate roles, but a shared one. In a favourite scenario, she and her future husband would cook supper together and, afterwards, stand beside one another washing the dishes, sharing their innermost thoughts. Then he would say something to make her laugh. He'd lean in close, place his arm around her waist and …

The shrill chime of the doorbell cut in on the scene playing out in her mind.

'One moment, Mrs Finer. Psst!'

With a hand over the mouthpiece, her mother motioned to her. Miri replied with a placid smile, placed the tea towel on the counter and left to answer it.

'Yes, his sister is Miri's good friend.'

Halfway along the hallway, she stopped, certain she had heard her mother mention her name. The conversation continued in muffled tones. Miri strained to listen, concerned Mrs Finer had found a new excuse to cause trouble, until the incessant ring of the bell urged her onward. She opened the door and her face lit up. Raizy was standing there.

'This is a welcome surprise! Come in.'

'Want to come over to me?' said Raizy.

'Sure. You could have just called.'

'Phone was engaged.'

Raizy backed down the steps as Miri untied the strings of her floral apron. 'Give me a minute.'

'Hurry.'

'Why?'

'I'll tell you on the way.'

The whispered telephone conversation persisted in the kitchen.

'I wasn't aware they were that kind of family. What did he do?'

Her mother noticed Miri hovering in the doorway and left Mrs Finer hanging. 'What is it?'

'I'm going over to Raizy's. If that's alright.'

She dismissed Miri with a shooing gesture, eager to return to her call.

Raizy seemed in an unusual rush. She had already taken off and neared the end of the dense row of terraced houses. Miri broke into a half-run, holding down her skirt to prevent it from rising immodestly above her knees, and careful not to slide on the fallen leaves which the earlier rain had turned into a slippery mulch. Only after Miri caught up did it occur to her: they were heading the wrong way.

'I thought you said we were going back to your place.'

Raizy's mouth upturned into a sly smile. 'We're going somewhere else. I've arranged to meet someone, and I needed an alibi. So I told my mother I was coming to visit you.'

'What do you mean by an alibi?'

They turned the corner onto the busy main road which led to the high street. This was the heart of their neighbourhood where its diverse residents, from many places and communities, intersected and passed each other. Their neighbourhood of Stamford Hill was like its own little world. An intricate mosaic.

Raizy scanned from side to side but said nothing.

Miri persisted. 'Who are we meeting?'

Raizy's blue eyes sparkled with mischief, and Miri noted the unfamiliar style of her clothing. She had replaced her classic, mid-calf skirt and conservative top with a slinky, black skirt that clung to her legs, an ivory button-down shirt, and a matching cardigan which she hugged towards her against the chilly night air. What was she up to?

'Do you ever shop in Kosher Basket?' Raizy asked.

'No. My mother shops at Gold's, so that's where I go

whenever she asks me.'

'Mine sent me to Kosher Basket earlier today to shop for Shabbes. There's this good-looking Sefardi boy who works there. We got talking, and he asked me out.'

'What?' Miri stopped in her tracks, open-mouthed. 'Are you trying to tell me we're about to meet up with a boy, right now?'

'Yes.'

'We can't do that!'

Fantasies were one thing, real life with its potential repercussions, quite another.

'Why not?' asked Raizy.

'What would my parents say if they found out?'

'I won't tell them. Will you?'

'No. I'd be in such trouble. Wouldn't you?'

Raizy gave a careless shrug. 'What they don't know won't hurt them. It'll be a little harmless fun. A few hours talking to some guys. That's all. No one will ever find out.'

Miri wavered.

'If you don't want to come, you don't have to. I'm going anyway, and I'm already running late.'

Wasn't this something she'd secretly longed to do? Plus, as Raizy said, it would only be a bit of fun. She might never get another chance.

'I'll come.' Miri picked up her pace before common sense prevailed.

'Have you ever spoken to a boy before?' Raizy asked.

What sort of question was that? Raizy should have known the answer better than most. Raizy's mother was the headmistress at their old high school, the one who expelled their classmate for this very crime. Yet, Miri found herself on the defensive.

'I speak to my brothers, and even my brother-in-law.'

'That doesn't count. I mean someone who isn't family.'

'Apart from this afternoon, have you?'

'Yes.'

Miri studied Raizy's steady face for signs of jest. She found none. 'When?'

'It started when I was in sem,' Raizy said.

'That's impossible. How did you do it without getting caught?'

'There were plenty of opportunities, and I was careful.'

The revelation gave Miri a pang of resentment. Or was it envy? 'How come you never told me?'

'I couldn't write it in a letter. There were rumours that the teachers censored our post. I'm not sure if it was true, but I didn't want to take the risk.'

'You could have said something when we saw each other over the holidays. Besides, we've been out of sem since July.'

'It must have slipped my mind. It's no big deal.'

Miri found that hard to believe. She recalled all the other trivial anecdotes Raizy shared whenever they got together during breaks from their separate seminaries.

'I thought we were close friends who shared secrets.'

'We are –' Raizy paused as their old maths teacher, a colleague of Raizy's mother, walked by. They both said hello and adopted innocent smiles. Raizy waited until she had passed, then lowered her voice. 'The truth is, I was afraid to tell you in case it harmed our friendship. I worried that if you didn't approve of what I was doing, you might want nothing more to do with me, or get me into trouble by telling someone.'

The words stung. 'Raizy, you know I'd never do that.'

'I realise I made a mistake not to have trusted you before. That's why I'm telling you now. And inviting you to join me this evening.'

Miri thought about the dreams and dilemmas that occupied her mind. She had been reluctant to reveal them to Raizy for similar reasons. The major difference between them was that Raizy had been daring enough to act on what Miri had only contemplated.

'I'm sorry. Do you forgive me?'

Miri nodded. Perhaps she should confide in her friend. If anyone could relate to her, it was Raizy.

Practicality replaced sentimentality, and Raizy stopped to consult a bus timetable. 'We'll catch the 254 to Manor House and it's a short tube ride from there.'

'Oh. I didn't bring money with me. I thought –'

Raizy waved her slim leather bag. 'My treat.'

As they waited, Miri spotted a neighbour heading towards them. Heavily pregnant, she shuffled up the road, using one hand to push a toddler in a buggy and the other to grasp the hand of her tugging three-year-old who threatened to stray. Miri slipped to the back of the bus shelter and concealed herself behind a businessman reading a broadsheet. Even as she did so, she knew her actions were irrational. It wasn't a sin to wait for a bus with a friend.

Thirty minutes later, they emerged from the underground onto Upper Street in Islington. Daunted by the unknown, Miri kept close to Raizy. It was rare for Miri to venture outside their neighbourhood, and seldom at night.

Smart-suited office workers and arty students sporting an array of unconventional clothes, piercings and tattoos thronged outside the pubs and cafés. Miri caught a whiff of cigarette smoke and the fermented smell of beer. She heard laughter, the animated voices of people enjoying a night out, and from one venue, the pumping baseline of dance music, its beat so loud it seemed to reverberate through her. Miri felt a ripple of excitement at this adventure laced with danger. People like her were not supposed to visit places like this. But here, no one knew her.

Along their route, Miri glanced at the windows of the designer boutiques and trendy fashion shops. She stopped to admire the display of drawing equipment in an art shop until Raizy hurried her along.

Raizy strode with purpose, indifferent to the thrills of their surroundings. Without slowing, she yanked the tie that held her plait in place, ran her fingers through her hair and released a mass of honey-coloured, corkscrew curls that cascaded down her back. Miri watched her metamorphosis in fascination. How had Raizy learnt to adapt like that from one environment to another?

They came to a halt outside a café. Raizy checked the sign and, without hesitating, swung open the door. 'Here we are.'

Aghast, Miri remained rooted to the spot. 'What's the matter?' Raizy said.

'I can't go in there.'

'Why not?'

'It's not a kosher place.'

Raizy became impatient. 'Come on! We won't eat anything. Lighten up.'

Miri weighed up her options. Her eyes flitted between the blackness of the unfamiliar streets behind and the illuminated entrance ahead. Without waiting for further protest, Raizy grabbed her arm and propelled her inside.

The café had an inviting interior. Subdued lighting washed the mocha-painted walls and cast warm pools on the oak floorboards. The rich scent of brewed coffee filled the air, and soft jazz music played through invisible speakers. A glass candle lantern flickered on each of the rustic wooden tables, and couples sitting on wicker chairs conversed in muted tones as they enjoyed light meals and drinks.

At the far end, Miri caught sight of three young men seated together. One of them greeted Raizy with a wave. She responded likewise and wove her way towards them. Miri followed with less poise, bumping straight into a table where an older gentleman sat reading the newspaper with a glass of wine in his hand. She offered a flustered apology and slunk away.

The one who had waved welcomed Raizy with a flirtatious grin. 'Hey, you came.' Miri detected the trace of a cockney accent in his voice.

'I told you I would. And I brought my alibi. This is my friend Miri. Miri, this is Daniel.'

He turned to her with an amiable smile, his green crystalline eyes seeming to give her a once-over. 'Hi, Miri, nice to meet you.'

Unused to direct eye contact from a man with whom she wasn't acquainted, Miri lowered her head to the side and fidgeted with her sleeve. 'Nicetomeetyou,' she mumbled.

The other two at the table were engrossed in conversation and didn't appear to have noticed them.

'Oi, Moshe!' Daniel said. The one in glasses to his right gave a semi-wave. Then he pointed to the friend who sat opposite, angled towards Moshe, away from them.

'And this is Ben.'

Ben shifted around with seeming reluctance. Miri wondered whether he felt uncomfortable too. He regarded them with a serious, almost mournful expression, but his greeting was polite, if reserved.

Raizy threw them a cursory glance. 'Nice to meet you both.' She switched her attention back to Daniel with an alluring smile.

Miri was tongue-tied, unable to summon a simple hello or tear her eyes away. From his looks to his clothing, everything about Ben differed from the boys in her community. In place of the uniform white shirt and knee-length jacket, known as a *langer rekel*, he wore a simple grey t-shirt. He didn't have long *peyes* or shorn hair covered by a large, black *cappel*; instead, wavy, jet-black hair cut shorter at the sides, and a small, suede *kippah*.

A pair of striking, dark eyes looked back at her, and Miri realised she was blatantly staring. She averted her gaze and concentrated on her feet. Her hands were clammy, and her heart pounded.

'After all the effort, aren't you going to invite us to sit?' Raizy asked.

'My manners.' Daniel pulled out the seat for her next to him.

As Raizy settled herself beside Daniel, Miri noticed that the first two buttons of Raizy's blouse had come undone, exposing the top of her lacy bra, and a hint of cleavage. She suppressed a gasp. Even to display their collarbone was improper. Miri knew she ought to warn her, but that would risk drawing the others' attention. She stayed silent and hoped Raizy would soon discover the wardrobe malfunction for herself.

No one had offered Miri a seat. Standing on her own, she vacillated. There was one other vacant chair, next to – what was his name – Ben?

She tiptoed around and shrank into it. The others were talking and laughing, relaxed in each other's company. She looked at them all, dressed up for an evening out, then compared her appearance, straight out of the kitchen. A drab jumper. Pleated skirt. Brown hair tied back in a low ponytail. Mortified, she realised how dowdy she looked.

She picked up a menu from the pile and feigned absorption in its contents.

'What's everyone having?' Daniel asked.

'A cappuccino, please,' Raizy said.

'Regular coffee for me,' said Moshe.

'Same here,' Ben added.

'And for the alibi?'

Miri felt like she was standing on a stage, under a burning spotlight, on cue to deliver lines she could not recall.

'Um …'

She didn't know what to say. Was drinking out of a non-kosher cup permitted? She figured they must have been washed together with plates on which food that wasn't kosher had been served. Then there was the unsupervised milk in the coffee. In her home, they only bought milk with the rabbinical stamp of approval. Raizy wouldn't order something if it wasn't kosher, would she?

Miri examined the menu – this time for real – to give him a satisfactory answer. Her panic rose.

Americano, cappuccino, espresso, latte, macchiato. What did these words all mean?

She sensed all eyes on her and regretted having agreed to come.

'What would you like?' Ben said, his voice low and calming. 'How about herbal tea?' Miri nodded in response, grateful to him for saving her from further humiliation.

He beckoned for the waitress, a statuesque blonde who appeared with a notepad at the ready. Her black trousers were so tight they looked as if they had been painted on.

'Excuse me, do you have any herbal teas?'

'Yes, we have blackcurrant, chamomile, peppermint, and lemon with ginger.'

'What will it be?' he said to Miri.

'I think I'll try blackcurrant.'

'And would it be possible to serve hers in a paper cup instead of a regular mug, please?' he asked.

'Thank you,' Miri said to him once the waitress had taken the rest of their orders and left.

'No problem.'

She wondered about his origins. His olive complexion. High cheekbones. Deep, brown eyes framed by long lashes. There seemed to be a hint of impenetrable sadness in them. Then he gave a brief smile, and she decided she must have imagined it.

Curiosity compelled her to overcome her shyness. 'Where are you from?'

'Stamford Hill. Same as you, I think.'

They lived in the same neighbourhood? 'Are you Sefardi?'

'I'm Adeni.'

She heard the shaking in her own voice. 'What's the difference between the two? What does Adeni mean?'

'Well, the literal meaning of Sefardi is someone whose

origins are from Spain. Although it also describes those who keep the Sefardi customs. Whereas my family comes from Aden. You've heard of the country Yemen, right?'

'Isn't it somewhere in the Middle East, near Saudi Arabia?'

'Yeah, that's it. In fact, that's why we're called Mizrahi Jews.'

'What does that mean?'

'Jews from the East. And Aden is a port city that used to be a British colony, but is now part of Yemen.'

So that's who they were – those young men she would occasionally notice when returning from shul on Shabbes. They were the modern-looking ones, with dark hair and tanned skin, wearing smart suits or the simple attire of trousers and a shirt, often in colours other than white. And rather than donning a big, black hat or the fur *shtreimel* worn by married Chassidish men on Shabbes and special occasions, they covered their heads with a less conspicuous kippah.

They were the ones who walked with a carefree stride and surveyed the world around them as they passed by, sometimes catching your eye instead of casting them towards the pavement. They shared the same streets but lived in different worlds.

'That's interesting. I don't think I'd ever heard of Aden or realised there was an Adeni community in Stamford Hill. I hope I wasn't insulting.'

'Not at all.'

'How did you end up here?'

'We drove all the way from – Oh, you mean in London.' He winked.

Miri couldn't help herself and gave him a timid smile.

'My parents and grandparents were born in Aden.' His eyes locked onto hers. The rest of their group and her surroundings receded into the peripheries of her consciousness. She listened to him, captivated, and forgot her initial unease.

Ben described to her how Aden once had a small, thriving Jewish community that coexisted with their neighbours in relative harmony. 'They were close-knit, most families living side-by-side within five streets in a district of the city known as Crater. It got its name because it was built on the site of an extinct volcano. Since Aden was a British duty-free port, food was cheap and plentiful. There was a lovely beach nearby, and it was hot for most of the year. My Savta told me many stories about it.'

'Why did they want to leave?'

He grew sombre. 'They had no choice. Everything changed in 1947 when the United Nations voted in favour of the establishment of the State of Israel. Soon after, mobs of radicalised Arabs, bent on revenge, instigated a violent riot. They surrounded the Jewish quarter, and over three days, set fire to many homes, shuls, a school, and looted most of the Jewish-owned shops. And they murdered eighty-seven of us in brutal ways. They shot, stabbed or burnt them alive ...'

Miri placed a hand over her mouth, shocked at what he was telling her.

Ben broke off mid-flow. 'Oh, I'm sorry! I shouldn't have said ... it was too much ... I mean, we ... I hardly know ... it's not the sort of thing ...' He tripped over his words and struggled to form a coherent sentence. Miri remained silent and waited. She supposed it was a painful subject for him and berated herself for having caused this awkwardness. He took a breath. 'I'm sorry. I guess I must be out of practice.'

His quip confused her. 'Out of practice?'

Ben shook his head and covered it with his hand. She felt

17

stupid that she hadn't understood what he meant. What did he think of her? She couldn't read his expression. It wasn't the same as her father's face when he got exasperated with her for saying something foolish. And when Ben faced her again, she didn't see impatience, but gentleness.

He waved, implying their table. 'Like this. Socialising and stuff.' He seemed somewhat embarrassed. 'I'm sorry, I didn't mean to upset you. I shouldn't have mentioned those distressing details.'

Miri still didn't fully grasp his meaning, but his words reassured her. She'd said nothing inappropriate. A misunderstanding, that's all.

'You didn't upset me. I was just sad to hear the tragedy that happened to your community. I never heard about it before. It sounds similar to what I've read about Kristallnacht in Germany. There's no need to apologise. It's important to know and good you told me.'

He nodded and seemed relieved.

'Is it hard for you to talk about this?' Miri said.

'No, it's fine. I don't mind.'

'After the riots, did everyone leave?'

'Not all, but a lot did. They were afraid there might be more trouble to follow. Many had lost family members, their homes and businesses. Most who left settled in Israel, including a few relatives on my mother's side. The situation in Aden calmed down, so my maternal grandparents stayed. But when it deteriorated once again in the sixties, they followed the family to Israel.'

'And what about your father's side?'

'They were in Aden right until the end in 1967. When Britain announced they were about to pull out, the remaining

Jews had to flee for fear of being massacred. My dad was still a child when they left. He told me the British had to escort them to the airport with an armoured convoy for protection. The rioters were already shooting. My Saba moved the family to London – he had existing business ties there – and like most Adenim, they held British passports. So they joined the growing Adeni community, established a few years earlier. Years later, my dad met my mum when she came on a visit to London. And that's how I got here.'

'It reminds me of my grandparents coming here from Poland. Because of the war.'

A look of understanding passed between them. They could relate to one another. Both of their families had uprooted to escape persecution.

The waitress returned with their orders. Miri whispered a quiet blessing and took a sip of her drink. 'Amen,' Ben responded with a warm smile. She found once more that she couldn't prevent herself from smiling back.

'How is it?' he said.

'It's good.'

'Do you like herbal teas?'

'I don't often drink them. It's nice, though.'

'We're into them a lot at our place.'

'Really?'

'Yeah. Especially my mum. Mint tea, fennel tea. She'll almost take any leaf, stick it into a cup and turn it into a tea.'

'My mother's a coffee person.'

'My dad's like that. He likes to drink Adeni coffee.'

'What's that?'

'A strong, black, ground coffee with hawaij.'

'What is haw-a-yij?' She pronounced the exotic-sounding

name with caution as if concerned she was uttering a profanity.

Ben couldn't keep a straight face and broke into a lopsided grin. 'Hawaij,' he repeated, starting on a soft, guttural note, rolling the word through his lips and off his tongue with ease. 'It's a blend of spices for coffee. A mixture of cinnamon, cardamom, ginger and cloves –'

A shriek of laughter from Raizy interrupted their conversation. She and Daniel were engaged in an exchange of light-hearted banter. Before long, he had placed his arm around Raizy and she rested her head on his shoulder.

This was another side to her friend Miri had never seen before. It made her unsettled. They had always been close. Seminary was the first time spent apart from each other since the age of four. As Miri listened to their small talk, trying to learn the rules, she realised what a wide chasm those two years had created between them. She didn't view herself as competent enough to join this group conversation, concerned about saying something silly. Instead, a multitude of questions and emotions engulfed her.

Every so often, she would steal a glimpse at Ben. When he noticed, he replied with a lingering gaze; a silent conversation passing between them.

All too soon, Raizy announced they had to leave. Staying out late would arouse too much suspicion. The three boys escorted them as far as the station, and Raizy confirmed with Daniel that they would talk soon to arrange another date. He gave Raizy a brief kiss on the cheek.

Ben turned to Miri. 'It was lovely to meet you.'

Miri took a step back. 'You too.'

'I hope to see you again.'

'Perhaps.'

Raizy tapped her shoulder, and the two of them ran down the steps to the platform. She was excitable. 'Wasn't that fun! Did you enjoy yourself? You and Ben seemed to get on well together.'

Miri blushed. 'He's nice.'

All at once, it hit her. She'd done it. She'd actually spoken to a boy. In her community, boys would dare not look at her, let alone converse. Woven between the deep-seated guilt of her actions and the fear of discovery was a frisson of excitement. It surprised her how easy it had been to talk to Ben once she had conquered her initial shyness. Not so different from conversing with one of her friends. Well, maybe a little.

The carriage doors slammed shut. The train lurched and gathered speed, a monotonous clatter resounding from the wheels rolling along the tracks as they rushed through the gloomy tunnel.

'Do you like Daniel?' Miri said.

'He's cool, isn't he?'

'Yes, I guess so. Do you expect things will become serious?'

Raizy looked incredulous and guffawed. 'You mean between Daniel and me? Don't be ridiculous. There's no future in it.'

'Aren't you going out with him? I thought –'

'Miri.' Raizy's tone changed, and she began to address her the way a parent might speak to a child. 'We're having a laugh. A good time. Don't imagine it is anything more. It never could be. You and I both know we'll soon be offered *shidduchim*. And he knows this too.'

Miri felt the familiar prickling of fear. 'Does the idea of having a shidduch worry you?'

'No, that's how it goes. Didn't you see it with your sister, Pessie, when she got engaged last year?'

'No, I was in sem when it happened. One day, without warning, my mother phoned to tell me she'd become a *kallah*.'

'Well, I've watched it happen with all my siblings and it's worked out fine each time. Soon I'll do the same. That's why I'm having my bit of fun now, before it's too late. Then I can settle down with no regrets I missed out on anything.'

'If you had a choice – a real choice – to marry someone who wasn't Chassidish or do things another way – say, choose not to meet through a shidduch, would you?'

Raizy deliberated over the question. 'I'm not sure. I wouldn't mind if they allowed us to meet more times before getting engaged. And not restrict us on how much we can speak to each other after the engagement. But I'd prefer a husband who came from the same background as me. I don't think I'd want to marry a boy who wasn't Chassidish, with a different upbringing, who didn't know where I was coming from. I'm familiar with this lifestyle and happy surrounded by my family and friends. It makes me feel comfortable and safe.'

'Don't you ever find it –' She paused, searching for a word. 'Limiting?'

'Sometimes. I know our community may not be perfect and has its issues. But tell me one that doesn't. I bet there's not a single community where people are entirely content. Besides, do you seriously think my parents would agree for me to go out with a boy like Daniel, who – let's be honest – they wouldn't consider frum?' She stared at Miri to let the severity of the implication sink in. 'What's more, someone who isn't Chassidish. Not only that. Sefardi.'

'Adeni.'

'What?' Raizy looked puzzled.

'I think he might be Adeni.' She faltered. 'Like Ben.' Her cheeks were aflame once more.

'Whatever. No difference.'

'I think there is. His family isn't from Spain. They're from Aden.'

Raizy sighed. 'OK, Adeni.'

'What's wrong with being Adeni?'

Raizy groaned in frustration. 'Miri, what's got into you? You know how it goes. Our parents expect us to marry fine Chassidish boys with good *yichus* – and if they're well-off, that's a bonus. We'll meet them once or twice, get engaged, and then plan the chasseneh.'

'Raizy ...'

'Yes?'

'Nothing. Forget it.'

The bus approached their neighbourhood. Raizy had re-braided her plait, and the buttons on her shirt were once more fastened up to the collar.

Miri braced herself. 'It scares me.'

'What we did this evening?'

'No. The whole shidduch process. Having to get engaged to a complete stranger after meeting for only an hour. And then, not being allowed to see each other, barely allowed to talk, until the wedding. I'm no longer sure that is what I want.'

'Meeting those guys tonight has given you a few strange ideas.'

'No, this has nothing to do with them. It's been on my mind for a while.'

Raizy looked dismissive. 'Forget about it. We all get

married by a shidduch, and it's not like you have a choice. So just make the most of this time and enjoy yourself. Want to join me again for the next evening out?'

'Maybe. Can I give it some thought and let you know in the morning?'

'Sure.' Raizy rang the bell for their stop. 'Remember, not a word to anyone about this.'

Miri sneaked in through the door. The smell of fresh-baked challah wafted out to greet her. Her mother was on the phone with her sister, Pessie, and hadn't seen her. Adrenaline pumping, she darted, undetected, from the hallway to the stairs, and crept up, mindful to avoid the fourth step which creaked. She was relieved to find her two younger sisters already fast asleep in their shared bedroom.

Miri dropped onto her bed and hugged her knees to her chest. She stared out of the window to the dim street below, seeing shapes and details she'd never noticed before. Even the mundane looked different tonight.

He lives somewhere right near here.

As she thought of him, she experienced the strangest sensation, like nothing she'd ever felt before. Her stomach fluttered, and her breath came fast and shallow.

She replayed the events of that evening with a sense of amazement. He'd said he hoped to see her again …

Stop!

She was running away with herself.

Miri shuddered, envisaging the consequences if her parents were to find out she had mixed with boys. And at a non-kosher café! Her face burned hot with the shame of her wrongdoings. But was it her fault? The entire scheme had been Raizy's idea. She was the one who'd asked Miri to come along.

Still, Raizy hadn't forced her. Miri could have refused, turned back, gone home. She hadn't. She'd wanted to join Raizy. And despite her unrelenting guilt, she didn't regret her decision.

Her parents were unlikely to discover what she'd done, and she would never tell them. But the more she thought about it, the more she realised it would be too reckless to repeat. She would have to remain firm and refuse Raizy's offer next time.

Once more, Miri reflected on the encounter, trying to commit to memory each word of their conversation. The sound of his voice. His smile. His eyes.

With a low groan, she collapsed prone on her bed, head in her hands. It was futile. She couldn't lie to herself. She wanted to see him again.

Chapter 2

'Miri, I didn't hear you come in last night.'

Miri stopped in her tracks. 'Oh, I …'

The knot in her stomach tightened. She opened a kitchen cupboard and hid her face behind the door, pretending to search for something.

'I think you were on the phone when I came home. I was quite tired, so I went straight to bed.'

Miri took a furtive glance at her mother, who was placing a baking dish with two large chickens in the oven. She couldn't tell whether she suspected anything untoward.

In reality, Miri had tossed and turned for most of the night, torn by indecision. By five o'clock, she'd given up trying to sleep. Desperate to talk over the events of the night before, she planned to call Raizy around six before anyone else was awake. Miri watched the clock and waited for the minutes to pass. Her eyes became heavy, and exhaustion overcame her. When she awoke, it was after seven, and her sister, Ruchi, was monopolising the bathroom.

By the time Miri could get dressed – her parents did not permit them to appear downstairs in sleepwear – she had missed her opportunity to talk to Raizy in privacy. Her mother was already busy in the kitchen, and three of her younger siblings were sitting around the table, eating breakfast.

A shout from seven-year-old Yossi distracted her mother and put an end to any further questioning. The boys had resumed the quarrel they'd started the previous night over a plastic building brick. Yossi grabbed hold of an open carton of milk and lobbed it across at his brother, Lozi, hitting him in the face. It rebounded against the table, drenched all three children, and landed on the floor where it created a spectacular puddle.

Miri's brothers yelped. Lozi lifted his mug of hot chocolate, ready to aim in retaliation.

'Don't you dare!' Miri's mother screamed. 'Oy! As if there's not enough to do on a Friday. Lozi, Yossi, Chaim, please go upstairs and get changed at once. Put your wet clothes straight into the machine. Not in a pile in your room. Otherwise, the whole place will smell like mouldy cheese. And Miri, please clear up that mess for me.'

Grateful for the distraction, Miri retrieved a clean dishcloth from the bottom drawer. She mopped up the puddle, trying to control her trembling hands.

Am I out of my mind?

She had gone behind her parents' back. She knew what she'd done was wrong. If anyone from her community discovered her actions, it would tarnish her name. She'd be known as someone who 'mixed with boys.' She would be responsible for tainting her family's reputation. And it would affect the shidduch prospects of the rest of her siblings who were yet to be married.

For all that, she still wanted to join Raizy again. Why did it have to be so complicated?

She searched for some justification in her mind to help ease her stricken conscience. She'd met a boy through her friend Raizy, and all they had done was talk. Her parents were anyway going to introduce her to a total stranger, and she would have to sit and talk to him as part of the matchmaking process. Was there all that much difference?

Besides, her mother had never forbidden her outright from speaking to boys. It was as if she'd learnt it wasn't the 'done thing' via osmosis. Maybe it wasn't technically a sin?

Miri had to find an indirect way to determine her mother's opinion without disclosing what she'd done. She would never betray Raizy's trust.

Easier said than done. There was an unspoken rule that specific topics weren't up for discussion. If her mother deemed it a sensitive matter, she had a tendency to change the subject. (Although judging by the whispered conversations, cut short whenever she noticed Miri's presence, Miri had a hunch that her mother let down her guard further with other married women, her sister included.) It was acceptable to talk about an eventual shidduch in theoretical terms, but you didn't discuss boys per se. As for admitting feelings towards a member of the opposite sex – out of the question. That was something that came after marriage.

These powerful, new sensations confused her. A strange excitement that sent shivers down her spine and made her run hot and cold. Miri wished it were possible to confide in her mother, and for her mother to respond with a warm hug and reassurance that there was nothing the matter with her for her wayward thoughts and feelings. But that was not about to happen. Her mother had never been inclined to physical displays of affection with her children.

Miri weighed up the risks of raising such a delicate issue. Would her mother sympathise, express her disapproval, or become enraged? She feared the outcome, but the question consumed her thoughts, and she had to give voice to it.

'Mameh ...'

Her mother stood at the kitchen counter, knife in hand, poring over a handwritten list of names and numbers and chopping her way through a pile of root vegetables that would fill the massive soup pot beside her. 'Thank you,' she said, not looking up. 'Please put it in the washing machine, together with that pile over there.'

Miri gave her a quizzical look and remembered the sodden towel in her hand.

'Can I ask you a question?'

'Soon, Miri. I'm working out a meal rota. Did you hear? Baila from up the road had a baby girl yesterday.'

Now was not a good time, Miri decided.

Miri sidestepped harried pedestrians as she made her way to work. Chassidish men darted the pavements, carting shopping bags, or bearing bunches of flowers. Mothers with pushchairs, toddlers at the helm, hurried to complete their errands. In the lines of traffic, cars jostled for pole position and competed for every parking space. Such was the Friday morning rush in Stamford Hill – a weekly race before the divinely ordained calm of Shabbes, the day of rest. From sunset on Friday until nightfall the following day, there would be no work.

'Hello, Miri. How are you?' Miri gave a start. Lost in her thoughts, she hadn't noticed Mrs Finer, who now blocked her path. She gave Miri a thin-lipped smile that didn't reach her prying eyes. A dark, helmet-like wig only added to her domineering appearance.

'I'm fine, *borich Hashem*. And you?' Miri said.

'*Borich Hashem*, mustn't complain. Did you have a good evening?'

The question took Miri by surprise, but she forced herself to keep her composure and returned Mrs Finer's gaze without blinking. 'Sorry?'

'I thought I spotted you on the 254 bus last night?'

'No. It wasn't me.'

'I was sure –'

'No, definitely not me. I was at a friend's house.'

'Oh?'

Miri backed away. 'Please excuse me. I have to hurry as I'm already late for work. Have a *git Shabbes*.'

'*Git Shabbes*. Give my best to your mother.'

From a distance, she glanced back at Mrs Finer marching off in her sturdy lace-up shoes, lugging a shopping bag in each hand. Miri regretted her deceit, even if it was to Mrs Finer. And more pressing still, had her cover story sounded convincing enough? If Mrs Finer had any suspicions she was lying, she would have no hesitation to report back to her mother.

Mrs Finer turned around. Miri upped her pace and snapped her head forward. A blur of black and white flashed before her eyes. Too late to stop, she slammed straight into it. Miri looked up at the subject of her collision and recoiled. She wished she could curl up and hide.

The rabbi of her community regarded her with concern. 'My apologies, I didn't see you there.'

Miri gulped. 'I'm sorry ... I didn't mean ...'

'Are you hurt at all?'

'No. I'm fine.'

The rabbi peered over his glasses. 'You're one of the Fogel girls. Miri, isn't it?'

'Yes. I'm so sorry about this.'

'Are you sure you're OK?'

'Yes, yes. Sorry.'

'Well, have a git Shabbes.'

'Git Shabbes.'

'And please send my best to your father.'

No intention of doing so, she shrank away.

Miri debated whether she was brave enough to endure a repeat of this – the risks, deception, and excuses – all for the thrill of talking to a boy. If only she didn't have such a conscience. She wondered whether Raizy felt the same way.

Somehow, she doubted it.

'Hey!' said Daniel from behind the counter as Raizy entered Kosher Basket. She had 'forgotten' an item from the previous day's shopping. Raizy swept past without response and surveyed the other customers. She recognised a *chossid* as an acquaintance of her father. They attended the same shul. His attention focused on studying the labels on various bottles of wine he hadn't seen her. Raizy picked up a basket and slipped down the next aisle. From the opposite side, Daniel appeared by her side. He carried a box full of chocolates to stack the shelves. 'For me?' she said. 'You shouldn't have.'

Before he could reply, Raizy turned her back on him. Out of the corner of her eye, she had spotted Mrs Finer. She peeped through the window from the street outside and appeared to be watching her. Raizy feigned absorption in the snack selection and placed a few unnecessary items in her basket until Mrs Finer lost interest and continued on her way.

'Thanks for a nice evening,' she said, her eyes still darting about to ensure no one else was snooping.

'Want to go out again?'

'What do you think?'

Daniel looked amused. 'I guess I'll take that as a yes.'

'When did you have in mind?'

At the office, Mr Reich, Miri's boss, allowed her no respite. On Fridays – especially during the winter months when Shabbes came in earlier – the workday was shorter, but he didn't regard that as an excuse to do less. Rather, a reason to complete the work in half the time. There was no opportunity to call Raizy. On the few attempts she made to pick up the telephone, he would appear with another pile of paperwork to file, or letters to type. It was never-ending.

Then home again and straight into the pre-Shabbes panic, where her mother assigned her to help her youngest siblings bathe and dress, tidy the kitchen and lay the table. After last night's encounter, the domestic treadmill seemed more monotonous than ever.

All work ceased once her mother lit the candles, and an atmosphere of calm descended. The twelve candles – two for Shabbes, and ten to represent each of her children – glowed in antique silver candlesticks, buffed to a shine on the mahogany sideboard.

Like every week, her father and brothers went to shul (her

brothers leaving later than their father, much to his chagrin). It was the time of the week when Miri and her sisters got to spend quality time with their mother and converse at length. No disturbance from the phone or competing with the ceaseless demands that came with her volunteer work. They'd share stories about their week and discuss the latest neighbourhood gossip – although her mother took care to avoid topics that might lead to awkward questions. Usually, Miri appreciated her mother's undivided attention. But tonight, she resented their weekly fixation with the trivialities in other people's lives, while the real issues that concerned her were left unsaid.

For all appearances, it was a Friday night like any other. Her family sat around the table with her father at its head. It was the only night of the week they all ate together. Covered by a pristine white tablecloth and overlaid with a protective layer, Miri had laid it with their best Shabbes plates and the silver cutlery her parents had received as a wedding present. Several conversations reverberated across the table as they enjoyed the traditional Friday night meal: her mother's crusty homemade challah, followed by gefilte fish, chicken soup, then the main course of roasted chicken, schnitzel, crispy roast potatoes, a selection of hot vegetables and salads. But none of these familiar rituals eased Miri's inner turmoil.

'Miri, you're not eating. What's wrong?' her mother said.

'Nothing.'

'You look flushed. What's the matter, *shainkeit*?'

'I'm just a bit tired.'

'I thought you had an early night. Maybe you're coming down with something.'

'I had a hectic morning at work,' Miri said. 'I'll take a piece of schnitzel.'

Later, in the solitude of her bed, Miri tried to picture Ben's face. Try as she might, she could not get a clear image to form. She wished she could see him again, and she conjured up a scene in her mind of how their next meeting would play out. Next time, she would style her hair and dress in a trendier outfit. Perhaps a fitted white t-shirt and denim skirt (not that she possessed either). She would act self-assured and have the right witty comebacks. More like Raizy. Not like the night before.

She imagined how she must have appeared in his eyes: frumpy, awkward, uninteresting. She'd made a fuss over a drink, couldn't read a menu, and told him she'd never even heard of his community. He must have thought her weird and probably only acted friendly towards her in order to not appear rude. No doubt he spoke to girls all the time and hadn't given her a second thought afterwards. The conclusion filled her with humiliation.

By the following afternoon, when, at last, she had free time to visit Raizy, Miri's excitement had given way to dejection. She was beginning to think this a bad idea: not worth the potential for further embarrassment, not to mention the consequences if anyone found her out.

Miri ignored the knock at the door and let her inquisitive, fourteen-year-old sister, Ruchi, run to open it.

'Miri. It's Raizy for you.'

'Git Shabbes,' said Raizy. 'Fancy going for a walk?'

'Alright.' Miri was lackadaisical; she had all but talked herself out of another of these harebrained meetings.

Raizy waited for Miri to fetch a jacket, then the two set off together. It was a mild but overcast afternoon; rays of sunlight struggled to escape between breaks in the clouds.

'Are we actually going for a walk?' Miri said.

Raizy chuckled. 'Yes, we are. I figured it might be difficult to talk at your place, what with your sister hovering.'

'Tell me about it.'

In Springfield Park, mothers and teenage daughters gathered around the edge of the playground, where they chatted in groups while keeping an eye on their charges.

'Hi, Miri!' came a high-pitched voice from afar. Three little boys in their identical sailor outfits were suspended from the top of the climbing frame. She replied with a brief wave. They were neighbours whom she babysat once in a while.

Raizy and Miri bypassed the children's area and took the path that led down to the River Lea, where they wouldn't risk others overhearing their conversation. Heading towards them was a young woman, of similar age to Miri, who was holding the arm of an older woman and guiding her with care. Miri observed the tenderness with which the grandmother regarded her granddaughter. A white, gauzy headscarf crowned with a delicate band of flowery tassels covered the grandmother's head – a different type of head covering to that worn by married women in her community – and the young woman wore a slim-fitting skirt which stopped short of the knee. Her black, curly hair hung loose, and she had dark eyes which reminded Miri a little of Ben's. She wondered whether they too were Adeni.

All her life, their communities had lived side by side, and she'd been almost oblivious. They walked the same streets, shopped in the same shops, and passed without acknowledgement, as if invisible to each other.

Parallel lives.

Miri didn't know the reason for this norm. She'd just followed and never thought to question. Her disregard hadn't been intentional or hostile. Now, as she considered the matter further, she could think of no justification for it, and every reason to cross the invisible bridge that divided them.

'Git Shabbes,' Miri said.

They hesitated. The young woman raised her eyebrows in surprise. Did they think she meant to ridicule? Miri followed up with a heartfelt smile. Their expressions softened, and they smiled in return.

'*Shabbat shalom*,' the young woman said.

'*Shabbat shalom*. Good Shabbes,' the older lady added.

'Do you know them?' Raizy asked once they'd passed.

'No,' said Miri.

'Why did you greet them?'

'Why not?'

They found their favourite spot, a fallen tree trunk which served as a makeshift bench, secluded from the path by surrounding foliage. From their vantage point, Miri and Raizy could view the line of colourful houseboats moored on the opposite bank.

'I've arranged another date for Sunday evening. Are you interested in joining us?' Raizy said.

'I'm not sure.'

'I thought you enjoyed talking to Ben.' Raizy gave her an inquiring smile. 'He's rather good-looking, isn't he?'

Miri kept her eyes focused on the shimmering reflections of the houseboats on the water. 'Was it wrong what we did? Talking to boys, I mean.'

'No. Not exactly. There's nothing wrong in speaking to another person, including boys. Just that it's frowned upon. You know how it goes.'

'And what about deceiving our parents?'

'We're not really deceiving them. We're protecting them from disappointment. It's a different generation. They wouldn't understand.'

'When did you first talk to a boy?'

'Like I told you, when I was in sem. They gave us two afternoons off from studies each week, and once, a roommate invited me to come along to meet her brother and some of his friends from the local yeshiva. It sounded fun, so I agreed. She took me to this area in town with loads of cafés, a known hangout where the university students used to go.'

'Weren't you worried you might get caught?'

'No. More curious than anything. My friend had already been a few times and reassured me it would be fine. I had a good time that afternoon. So after that, whenever we had free afternoons, we'd meet the yeshiva boys. We were discreet. No one ever found out. And it brightened up my time in sem, I can tell you.' A sly smile crossed her face as she recalled a secret memory she didn't divulge.

'Hmm. Did you ever feel guilty about it?'

'Nah! I was away from home, and there were quite a few of us doing it.' She placed her hand on Miri's shoulder. 'Miri, enjoy it for what it is. A little adventure before we have to settle down. Don't worry, we'll be careful. This is our secret and our parents need never know. So, are you coming on Sunday night?'

The promise of another meeting beckoned.

Miri selected her moment with care. She was alone in the kitchen with her mother, helping to clear the dishes from over Shabbes. Efficient at the chore, she dried and stored them as fast as her mother stacked them on the drainer.

'Mameh,' she said.

'Yes?'

'I made plans to go over to Raizy tomorrow night. You didn't need me here for anything, did you?'

'No, that's fine.'

Miri smiled to herself as she reached for another of their best white china plates.

'Wait! I forgot. I arranged to go to a shiur with Mrs Finer tomorrow, and I need you to babysit.'

Miri blanched at the mention of her name. Typical. Trust Mrs Finer to be the one to interfere with her plans.

'Isn't there anyone else who can do it?' She tried to keep her voice measured. 'What about Ruchi?'

'Ruchi will be by Baila. She's home from the hospital and needs someone to help her tomorrow with the other children. Go Monday instead.'

'But we made plans for tomorrow.'

'What difference does it make which evening you go round to her house?'

Miri didn't respond.

Then another – more worrying – thought occurred to her. Would Mrs Finer mention anything to Miri's mother about their conversation on Friday and her suspicions of having seen Miri on the bus the night before?

Raizy didn't seem too bothered when Miri stopped by the

following morning to let her know she'd have to cancel. She stood in front of her full-length mirror, holding up her slinky skirt and a pink jumper against herself, turning this way and that.

'Not a problem. I hatched a backup plan just in case,' Raizy said.

'Sorry, it's not out of choice. I wanted to come.'

Raizy tossed the items onto her bed and rifled through her wardrobe. 'It's fine, I understand. I'll ask Chaya to come along. I'm sure she'll be up for it.'

'Chaya?'

'Why do you sound so surprised?'

'I mean, her father is a Rabbi.'

'You don't know Chaya, do you?' Raizy laughed.

What was going on here? It was as if an exclusive party had taken place, and she, the only one not invited.

Raizy gave Miri a sideways glance. 'Pot. Kettle. Black, my darling.'

Miri disregarded the comment.

Raizy held up a grey jersey dress around which she had tied a black leather belt. 'What do you think of this for tonight's date?'

'It's nice,' she said. 'Do you promise to call me as soon as you get back?'

'Mmm.' Raizy applied some fuchsia lipstick and pouted at the mirror.

'And will you invite me next time?'

'Yes, yes, sure I will.'

Miri wondered if Raizy was even listening to her.

Snap. Her pencil lead broke. Miri ripped the sheet from her sketchpad in frustration, crumpled it into a ball, and added it to the growing pile on her windowsill. She couldn't focus.

Her mother almost never went out. Why, of all nights, did it have to be this one? And what if Mrs Finer said something? She'd ruin any chance of a next time.

'Miri!' Ruchi called. She jumped at the sound of her name. 'Telephone.'

Miri ran downstairs.

'How are you? It's Devorah here. We haven't spoken for a few days. I wanted to see how you are.'

Miri smiled despite herself. Devorah had that effect on people. Quiet, refined, the epitome of goodness, she was the friend who never let you down; a person who saw the best in everyone and everything; the first to help another in need, volunteer for a communal cause, and, it would seem, an uncanny sense for sensing when something was up.

'I'm fine, borich Hashem,' Miri said.

'Have you got plans for this evening?'

If only ... She tried to brush aside thoughts of what and who she'd be missing that evening. 'No, I'll be home. Babysitting.'

'Fancy some company?'

Her mother had already left when Devorah arrived, and Miri was still putting the youngest children to bed. She showed her friend to the living room, then returned to complete her task. As she tucked the baby into his cot, her eyes wandered across to the traditional alarm clock on her mother's bedside table. Raizy would already be out, having fun with the others. How she envied Raizy, who, being the youngest of nine, was never obliged to stay at home and babysit. It was so unfair!

Her brother's angelic little face peered at her, and Miri regretted her thoughts. She stroked his downy hair. She adored her baby brother. It was the lack of freedom she resented. She kissed his soft forehead and tiptoed out of the room.

Miri found Devorah sitting on their worn, brown sofa, engrossed in a new book on the weekly Torah portion that Miri's mother had bought to read on Shabbes. Devorah glanced up from her reading and returned the book to the coffee table.

'Excellent book. I might buy a copy for my mother as a gift. I know she'd love it,' Devorah said. 'So what's news with you?'

'Not much.'

'What's the matter?'

Miri marvelled at her intuition. 'Nothing. Why do you ask?'

'It looks like something is bothering you,' said Devorah. 'Do you want to talk about it?'

'I can't.' Miri was bursting to tell her.

'That's fine.'

'Sorry.' She sat down beside Devorah.

'I understand. But I'm here for you if you want to speak to someone.'

They filled the awkwardness with small talk. The usual topics: reminiscing about their old school days, communal events, the recent engagements of mutual friends, until the conversation ran dry and there was an uncomfortable silence.

'Can I ask you a question, Devorah?'

'Anything.'

'Have you ever spoken to a boy? I mean outside your family.

Like … a friend?'

Devorah removed her glasses and fussed with the lenses, using her skirt to wipe imaginary smudges. 'No, I'd never do that. It's not the done thing.'

'Given the chance, would you want to?'

'Well, I hope I'll soon have a shidduch, and then I'll speak to my future husband.'

'Wouldn't you like to talk to a boy, just for fun?' Mindful she sounded as if she was paraphrasing Raizy, she corrected herself, 'I mean, out of curiosity?'

'No, it's not appropriate. For *me*.'

Miri studied Devorah, modest from head to toe. Her mousy hair, frizzy from over-brushing in her efforts to straighten its wayward form, braided into a low plait. She replaced her glasses and smoothed down her pleated, navy skirt. Devorah held an air of contentment about her place in the world that Miri could only admire.

'What would you say to someone else if they did?'

Devorah stared into Miri's face with her grey-blue eyes, chaste as the rest of her appearance, but infused with wisdom beyond her eighteen years. 'It's not for me to judge.' She took Miri's hand and gave it a reassuring squeeze.

On hearing the front door, Miri froze. Her mother poked her head into the living room. 'Hello, Mrs Fogel. How are you?' Devorah said.

The expression on her mother's face turned into an undisguised frown. 'Oh. Hello.'

The sudden change in mood was palpable. A gust of tension disturbed the air. 'Well, I'd better be going.' Devorah said with forced cheerfulness.

Miri saw her to the door, wishing she could leave too. She

took a few deep breaths to prepare for the grilling she dreaded was about to follow.

Miri's mother was scribbling some notes on a list as she waited for the kettle to boil. Miri hung back in the doorway.

'How was the shiur?'

'Very inspiring. How were the children?'

'Fine.'

'Good.'

Her mother poured herself a cup of coffee and stirred in some sugar. The metal spoon hit the side of her mug with a sporadic clink clink. The sound magnified, rising like a barrier between them. Miri could no longer bear the suspense.

'How is Mrs Finer?'

'Borich Hashem, she's well.'

'That's nice. Did she also enjoy the shiur?'

'I believe she did.'

Nothing.

Miri must have misread the situation, and Mrs Finer hadn't said a word after all. In which case, this was her opportunity to speak. Miri gathered her courage. 'Mameh, I have a question.'

'Yes, Miri.'

'Is it considered an *aveiro* if a girl just speaks to a boy, but they're not on a shidduch?'

Her mother flinched as if she'd received a slap. She placed her mug on the counter and gave Miri her full attention. 'And what exactly has brought on this question?' She scrutinised Miri, and all the nerve she'd summoned ebbed away. Mrs Finer must have said something.

'N–no–nothing. It was something I'd wondered, that's all.'

43

'What has Devorah been talking to you about?'

Her question bewildered Miri. 'What does Devorah have to do with this? She hasn't been talking about anything.'

'I think it would be better if you didn't mix with her.'

'What?'

'It doesn't reflect well on you if you are seen to be friendly with her.'

'Why not?'

'We don't want associations that could ruin your chances of a good shidduch.'

'Devorah?' Miri's voice rose an octave. 'I think you're mistaken.'

Her friend was the last person ever to have a bad name.

'How dare you answer me back like that!'

'I'm sorry. I didn't mean to.'

'I can already tell she's had a harmful influence on you.'

'What did she do?'

'Well, for a start, she's filled your head with strange thoughts.'

'No. I –'

'So I take it she's mixing with boys now, is she?'

'No. Devorah is *tznius* –'

Her mother made a derisory face. 'Tznius? She may dress the part but doesn't appear to act it. Mixing freely with boys? Obscene!'

'Devorah wouldn't –'

'I can't say I'm surprised, coming from the family she does. Especially that brother of hers.'

'Which brother? What did he do?'

'It doesn't matter.'

Miri's throat tightened. 'It does. She's my friend. Please

tell me what's going on.'

'We are not discussing this further. I want you to stay away from her. You have other friends. Raizy, for example. She comes from a more refined family. I'm sure she wouldn't come up with such ideas.'

'Devorah didn't come up with anything. This question came from me.' Miri felt the sting of her fingernails digging into her palms. She hadn't been aware that she had been clenching her fists.

'That may be, but it was because of her influence.'

'No. It has nothing to do with her. Will you at least answer me?'

'Enough already!'

Miri turned her back on her mother.

She retreated to her room where she sought solace under her duvet. She could no longer contain her emotions: the excitement, fear, guilt. The confusion and despair that left her at turns bursting with energy, then drained of it. And now this – her mother's surety of Raizy and instant ostracism of Devorah. No explanation.

All she had wanted was an answer which might help ease her troubled conscience.

What hurt the most was a sense of betrayal. Her mother, the one person she should have been able to turn to when she most needed advice, wasn't there for her.

Chapter 3

Mr Reich thrust the pile of correspondence across Miri's desk. The top page slid off, and she followed its silent flight as it drifted down, landing unseen next to his foot. She deliberated whether to pick it up. 'What's the matter with you today?' Miri shrunk under her boss's stern glare. His volatile temper and frequent outbursts intimidated her.

'There are mistakes in every one of these! This is unacceptable.'

'I'm sorry. I'll correct them.'

'How can we send shoddy letters like this to important clients, tell me?' Miri's face burned crimson. He stepped back and his heavy shoe landed squarely on the page. 'Have them finished by lunchtime.' He marched back to his office. 'I haven't got time for this nonsense.'

Miri bent down to retrieve the paper. Dark marks from his sole had obliterated most of the corrections he'd written in pencil. She flattened it out and returned it to the top of the pile.

She knew she wasn't working at her peak after yet another restless night. To make matters worse, Raizy still hadn't called as she'd said she would. By now, she too would be at work.

She taught in a nursery four mornings a week. Miri wouldn't be able to reach her until later that afternoon.

She was eager to hear about their evening and whether Raizy had made any further plans. Resentment had, by now, eroded her guilt. She'd been naïve. Nothing was as it appeared. While she'd been dutiful, adhering to the rules, feeling guilty for even her thoughts, and too afraid to act on them, her friends had had no such qualms and been out having fun in secret. As for hapless Devorah, where had that obedience got her? A tarnished reputation in the eyes of Miri's mother and whoever else was spreading *loshen hora*. How quick they were to judge.

For now, she had no choice other than to tackle the stack of paperwork before she further angered her boss. She worked on autopilot, amending letter after letter, alternately fighting off the exhaustion and the unwelcome thoughts that taunted her.

The telephone rang, and she answered it in a dull monotone.

'Miri, are you alright?'

'Raizy!' She shook herself out of her trance.

'I must have tried you about eight times after I got back yesterday. And again this morning. The line in your home is always engaged.'

Her explanation was reassuring for Miri. Raizy hadn't forgotten about her after all.

'Sorry.' Miri glanced up and noticed Mr Reich observing her from the doorway. He disapproved of personal telephone calls during office hours. Miri adopted a more formal tone. 'How may we assist you?'

'Pardon?'

'We offer various services related to property management.'

47

'What are you on about?'

'What are your requirements?'

'Ah! I understand. The boss hovering?'

'Correct.'

'Shall I meet you when you finish at five?'

'Yes. We're based at number twenty-six. Should I arrange a meeting for you?'

Raizy chuckled. 'OK. See you later.'

'Will do. My apologies, we can't sell your home. You'll need an estate agent for that.'

Miri put down the phone and pretended to read a letter.

'Time-wasters!' Mr Reich slammed his door shut.

She spent the rest of the afternoon clock-watching. At four fifty-five, she switched off her computer and packed her bag. Her colleagues still beavered away and eyed her with curiosity. It was rare for an employee to leave early.

'You're in a rush,' noted the bookkeeper, Mrs Klein, a serious woman in her fifties who only spoke when necessary. Her dexterous fingers glided over the keys of her calculator.

'Yes, I have to go.' Miri offered no further explanation. She grabbed her coat and skipped down the stairs. At the bottom, she pushed open the warped and faded blue door, stepped out onto the street, and secured it behind her.

'Boss keeping a close eye on you again?'

She turned around to find Raizy by her side. Miri didn't need to reply. Her expression said it all. They headed back along the high street. 'How was it yesterday?' Miri said.

'Brilliant! We all went bowling. Daniel and I teamed up against the others and we won. It was a great evening. Shame you weren't there.'

Tell me about it.

'And do you know what happened?'

'What?' Miri couldn't even hazard a guess.

'Daniel kissed me …' Raizy paused for dramatic effect. 'I mean properly. On the lips.' She giggled.

Miri gaped. She didn't know anyone who'd ever done that. It wasn't something that people did. At all. In her community. At least, not as far as she was aware. She'd never seen her parents so much as hug.

'What was it like?'

'It was … rather nice.' Raizy couldn't wipe the smile off her face.

Miri grew more thoughtful. 'So what does this mean?'

'Nothing. What were you expecting?'

'Doesn't this mean you're now serious about him?'

'No. I'm not about to marry him because we kissed. Anyway, he's not the first.'

Miri gulped at this further admission. 'What about Daniel? Do you think, perhaps, he has … feelings for you?'

'Nah! It's a thrill for him and the others to hook up with some Chassidish girls. Just like it is exciting for us to be going out with cool Sefardi guys.' She fluttered her lashes and said in a teasing voice, 'I mean, Adeni.'

Raizy hadn't yet mentioned the subject, which interested Miri the most.

'Was, er …?' Miri began, but Raizy's steady gaze unnerved her. Miri cleared her throat. 'Did you see – ' A flash of lightning ripped through the darkened sky, followed by a boom of thunder which caused them both to jump.

'Oysh, my hair!' Raizy said as heavy drops battered them. 'I just spent all afternoon straightening it.' They made a run for the nearest bus shelter and took a seat to wait it out.

A Chassidish man, concerned for his felt hat, shot open an oversized golf umbrella as he walked. He almost walked into a group of five, small boys running past, curly peyes swinging, shouting, enjoying the thrill of getting wet. A mother pushing a buggy urged on her straying toddler and pulled him away from a puddle. Across the road, a woman sporting braids and a hoodie emblazoned with a Jamaican flag tried to run, but she carried several heavy bags of shopping which slowed her down. A tall man walking behind her called her name and hurried after her. She turned around and seemed happy to see him. He took half the bags from her and together they dashed down the road. A teenage girl in a hijab rushed under the shelter to join Miri and Raizy. Miri shifted along the narrow red bench to make space for her, and she smiled in appreciation as she sat down next to them.

'How was your evening babysitting?' Raizy asked. 'I hope it wasn't too boring.'

'Not as exciting as yours. But Devorah came over to keep me company.'

'That's nice. I haven't spoken to her for a while. How is she?'

'She's fine. But I had a troubling conversation with my mother after Devorah left. She warned me I shouldn't mix with her because she has a bad name.'

Raizy sat upright. 'What? There has to be a misunderstanding. Devorah? Come on. She's goodness itself. Are you sure you didn't mishear her?'

'I agree, it sounds ridiculous, but that's what she said. She mentioned it had something to do with her brother.'

'Which one?'

'She wouldn't tell me. She refused to discuss any of the

details.'

'That is odd. Devorah's family have to be the most genuine people I know.'

'I was so upset afterwards.'

'I don't blame you. So am I. It makes me angry the way some people gossip and spread rumours around here.'

'Should I mention anything to Devorah?'

'No!' Raizy was emphatic. 'Don't say a word. We have no clue what this is about. If she were to find out your mother told you to avoid her, she'd be so hurt. I'll talk to my brother, Zalmy. He's friendly with one of Devorah's brothers. Maybe he can shed more light on this. But you're not going to ignore her, are you?'

'No. I couldn't do that. She's a good friend. Anyway, what happened to giving someone the benefit of the doubt? The more I think about it, the more ridiculous it seems. In fact, it makes me want to do the opposite and spend more time with her.'

'You're right. Try not to let it trouble you too much, though. Chances are, it's all a mistake.' She stuck her hand out of the shelter. 'Hey, look, the rain is stopping. Shall we carry on?'

They turned onto Miri's road, past the rows of terraced brick houses. Miri could almost sense countless pairs of eyes peering at them through the bay windows. When she looked up, she saw no one, just the flutter of a net curtain, and then it was still.

'Are you free this Thursday night to babysit my nieces with me?'

'Yes, should be fine.'

Raizy laughed. 'That was a joke. I mean, are you interested in another evening out using that as the excuse?'

The promise of excitement brightened her mood. 'I'd love to.'

'Great. I'll come by to get you at around seven.'

They lingered on the pavement beside Miri's gate.

'I'm looking forward to seeing you on Thursday.' Miri wanted to ask more, but held back.

Raizy smirked. There was a glint in her eye. 'Yes, I'm sure you are. I have to get going, but we'll speak before.'

She set off, then stopped, and took several steps back towards Miri. 'I almost forgot to tell you ...'

Miri held her breath as Raizy leaned across to whisper in her ear. 'Ben asked me to send you his regards. He said to tell you: sorry you couldn't make it last night, but he hopes you'll be able to come next time.'

'Thanks for the message.'

Miri turned and walked to her door, keeping her head bent to hide her face. A slow smile spread across her lips.

Chapter 4

Miri checked her reflection in the mirror, having changed for the third time. It wasn't a question of what looked the most trendy, but the least dowdy. Her black skirt was passable; preferable to the navy one. She dismissed her baggy, green jumper – too frumpy – and settled on a white long-sleeved top and black v-neck jumper. A moderate improvement.

Ruchi burst into the room. 'Why have you changed again? You're only going to babysit with Raizy. Not on a shidduch.'

Oh, for some privacy! Her sister was too close to the truth and too nosy for her own good.

'It had a stain.' Miri hoped that would put an end to the conversation, but Ruchi wasn't having any of it.

'What about that green one?'

'It has a small hole. I have to sew it.'

Miri willed her to leave, but Ruchi didn't seem in a rush to go anywhere. She perched herself on the top bunk and opened a book, a new publication, written by the Rabbi of their community, on *loshen hora*, as a ruse – but she seemed far more interested in observing Miri brush her hair than in reading.

'Ruchi!' their mother called from downstairs. 'Can you

please mind the baby? I have to pop across the road for a minute.'

Ruchi groaned as she tore herself away from her vantage point. 'Coming!'

Miri breathed a sigh of relief.

Alone again, she styled her hair and tied it back. Then she added a dab of clear lip gloss. Anything more might appear too obvious.

Fifteen minutes to go until Raizy was due to arrive. Time seemed to have slowed since she had last seen Raizy. Miri had counted down the days, the hours, and restless at work that afternoon, she'd even calculated the minutes remaining.

She posed once more in front of the mirror, pulling at the shapeless jumper. This wouldn't do. She fetched a bunch of safety pins from her cupboard, gathered the excess fabric at the seams on each side and pinned them on the reverse to give her top a more fitted appearance.

At seven o'clock on the dot, the doorbell rang. Miri sprinted down the stairs, grateful her sister was busy with the baby and her mother still out. 'Ruchi, I'm leaving now to babysit with Raizy. Tell Mameh I've gone,' she called.

At the bus stop, Miri remained on her guard, checking for sightings of Mrs Finer and anyone else she knew, but as soon as the bus left their neighbourhood, she pulled out her ponytail to leave a half updo and loose waves which tumbled over her shoulders. Raizy eyed her up and down. 'You look nice.'

Miri basked in the compliment. 'Thanks. So do you.'

Raizy had highlighted her eyes in a peachy brown hue, black eyeliner and mascara, and her lips shimmered with a brilliant pink lipstick. Miri wondered what her mother would say if she were to try something like that.

They stepped off the bus at Manor House Station and Miri's stomach flipped. She'd assumed they would take the underground like last time, but standing at the stop, waiting for them, were Daniel and Ben. For nights, she had struggled to picture his face, but here he was, greeting her with a smile.

'Hey!' Daniel hugged Raizy and gave her a brief kiss.

'How are you?' Ben asked.

A wave of shyness washed over her. 'I'm fine, borich Hashem.'

He stood almost half a head taller than her, arresting in suede boots, jeans and a grey hooded sweatshirt. Once again, she was struck by how different he was to anyone else she had ever met.

'So pleased you could make it this time.'

'Let's get going,' said Daniel. His arm was around Raizy. 'We'd better hurry or we'll miss the beginning.' He had parked his rusted, blue Vectra a short walk from the bus stop on the next street. Raizy took the passenger seat beside Daniel, leaving Miri to sit behind next to Ben. But this time she didn't mind.

'What are we seeing?' Raizy asked.

'Bride and Prejudice,' said Daniel. 'I've heard it's a girly one, so I guess you'll enjoy it.'

'So you think I'm girly then, do you?' she said, batting her eyes.

'I'd say so.'

As the bantering in the front continued, Ben said to Miri. 'It's meant to be a good one.'

Miri had already lost the thread of the conversation. 'What is?'

'Bride and Prejudice.'

'What's that?'

'The film we're seeing.'

'We're going to see a film?'

'Yeah, didn't Raizy mention?'

'In a cinema?'

'Uh-huh.'

From his laid-back answer, it was clear he considered it as natural an activity as any other for an evening out and appeared oblivious to her astonishment. 'Do you remember the classic Pride and Prejudice by Jane Austen? Perhaps you studied the book in school?' Miri had no clue what he was talking about, but nodded out of politeness. Taking it for an affirmative response, he continued, 'Well, Bride and Prejudice is a Bollywood take on the story.'

Jane Austen. Pride and Prejudice. Bollywood. Miri wasn't familiar with any of these terms, but they appeared to be part of Ben's world. She was dismayed to find the gaps in her knowledge wider than she could have imagined. She made a mental note of the author's name to search for it in a bookshop. That seemed a good starting point.

'Do you like the cinema?' Miri asked.

'Very much. I don't know if this film is my sort of thing, but Daniel reckoned the two of you will appreciate it. I tend to prefer action-adventure or historical stories. Sometimes also sci-fi and comedies. How about you, what films do you like?'

'Er ... I'm not sure.' On the spot once more, she struggled to come up with a suitable response. 'Actually, I've never been to the cinema before.'

Ben was gobsmacked. 'Are you serious? How come?'

'My parents don't approve of it, and I've never really had the opportunity.' She lowered her voice a touch. 'I have watched TV a few times,' she confessed. 'At a friend's house.'

'What do you mean?'

'My friend's parents have a television they keep hidden in a cupboard in their bedroom. No one is supposed to know about it, not even their children. But my friend found out, and sometimes, when they went out, she, Raizy and I would barricade ourselves into their room and watch a few programmes.'

'Oh. Right.'

She realised how ridiculous it must have sounded to him, but he didn't mock. 'I guess you have a TV at home?' she said.

'Yeah, we do.'

'Do your parents mind you watching it?'

'Not at all. It's in the living room, for the family.'

'You keep it downstairs?'

'Uh-huh.'

'What happens when people visit your home and see a television there?'

'Nothing. Sometimes friends come over to watch a film.'

'You don't get a bad name?'

'No.'

'You're so lucky you can watch whenever you want.'

'Do you know what, I hardly do.'

'I think if I had a TV, I would all the time.'

'You would get bored after a while, believe me. Most of the stuff on isn't that exciting. Besides, what with studying and stuff, there isn't much time.'

They had arrived at the enormous, glass-fronted multiplex. Daniel took Raizy's hand, and as Miri watched them, she experienced an inexplicable and unfamiliar pang. Was it envy, perhaps? She wasn't sure and did not wish to delve too deep into her thoughts either.

Tickets purchased, they followed the throngs of people through a blue-carpeted foyer that glowed from neon-blue mood lighting. A sweet popcorn scent filled the air, and the hum of conversations, pierced by occasional laughter, lent the atmosphere a sense of celebration. It was as if they were about to attend a party. Miri gazed around, trying to imprint every detail to memory. This might be the only chance she ever got to visit a cinema.

They passed a kiosk where lines of cinemagoers queued for soft drinks served in oversized cups, and giant cardboard buckets filled with popcorn. She had never seen such large serving sizes.

'Did you want a drink or anything?' Ben asked. Miri shook her head, her senses too overloaded to speak. Her eyes now focused on a bank of screens advertising future releases.

Daniel handed their tickets to a waiting attendant, and they entered the auditorium. She gaped when she saw the size of the screen which reached the ceiling.

The trailers ended as they found their seats, and the film began. It transported her to Amritsar in India, with its wide-open expanses of farmland and city streets filled with a melee of swerving cars, mopeds, pedestrians and bicycles stopping for nothing except cows crossing the road. A glimpse into a place so exotic compared to London. The sights, colourful clothes, the singing and dancing – even boys and girls together. It was an eye-opener for Miri. Fascinating and surreal and beautiful.

Then there was the sound that immersed her into the story.

At one point, she heard a voice coming from behind. Her natural reaction was to turn around, half-expecting to find someone standing there. Miri could sense Ben smiling at her in the dark.

Listening to the conversation between a group of mothers who sat and discussed the suitability of two eligible men as potential husbands for their daughters gave Miri a taste of home. Mothers in her community were always talking about shidduchim. She had seen Indian people around her neighbourhood. Who would have thought they had so much in common?

She followed the journey of Lalita, the heroine, through sadness and despair to happiness, finding it remarkable that Lalita's parents could rejoice at their daughter's marriage to William Darcy, whose background was worlds away from theirs.

Miri was swept up in the heady escapism and sheer joy generated by the energy of a feel-good musical, and she loved every minute. She stared at the screen until the final credits rolled and the lights came on. It was then she realised she and Ben were the last two sitting there.

'Did you enjoy that?' he asked.

'It was amazing!'

Still entranced, she stood up, forgetting that her small shoulder bag had been resting on her lap.

'Here, you dropped this.'

He held the bag out to her. She reached for it. A sudden jolt. A current. For a moment, their hands met. She looked at him. He stared at her.

'We … had better go,' Ben said. 'Daniel and Raizy will be waiting for us.'

They left the cinema in silence and walked back to Daniel's car. A snake of cars were queuing to leave the exit, and the car park was almost deserted. But no sign of their friends.

'I hope they come soon,' said Ben. 'It's getting late. I don't want you to miss the bus and I want to try to get up early tomorrow for *Shacharit*.'

'What's that?'

'You know, Shacharit, the morning prayers.'

Miri considered it further and then had a flash of recognition. 'Oh! You mean *Shacheris*.'

Ben chuckled. 'Yes. But we pronounce it *Sha-cha-rit*.' The 'r' rolled off his tongue with a trill.

'You go to shul, to the synagogue, on weekday mornings?'

'You sound surprised.'

'It's just that –'

'You didn't think I was religious enough to go to shul?'

His teasing was light-hearted, but Miri lowered her eyes. 'Sorry, I didn't mean it like that. I didn't mean to offend you.'

'Absolutely no offence taken. And in answer to your question, I try to go. Sometimes.' He ran a hand through his hair. 'But I don't always get up on time.'

She returned his smile.

'Miri …?' It was the first time she'd heard him say her name. It sounded euphonious to her ears.

'Yes?'

'Can I call you sometime?'

Such a simple request. Yet significant. And impossible to accept.

She shook her head sadly.

'Your parents?' he asked.

'I'm sorry.'

60

The sound of laughter cut through the night air and they saw Daniel and Raizy approaching. They walked close together, hand in hand.

'You ready guys?' Daniel asked them.

'Yeah,' Ben said.

A sense of regret gnawed at Miri as she sat at the back of the car, staring absently out of the window at the passing streetlights. What was he thinking? Was he insulted by her rebuff? If only she could have agreed.

'When shall we go out next?' Daniel asked.

'Wednesday works for me,' Raizy said. 'My parents will be out at a wedding.'

'Sounds good. Ben?'

Ben turned to Miri with an expectant look on his face that heartened her. 'Is Wednesday OK for you?'

'I think so.'

'Wednesday it is then,' Daniel said. 'Let's meet seven-thirty, at Manor House.'

Chapter 5

They watched the bus pull away, then walked back to the car. Daniel lit a cigarette. There was a smirk on his face as he inhaled, but Ben suspected the reason wasn't that it was his first smoke in several hours.

'Raizy looked happy this evening. What's going on between you two?'

Daniel chuckled. 'Never you mind.'

'Does this mean you and her are an item?'

'Nah! Nothing like that.'

'She seems quite into you.'

'It's just some fun before she settles down to become a respectable Chassidic housewife.'

'You're having me on, right?'

Daniel exhaled the smoke from his mouth. 'She hasn't told me outright, but I get the impression her parents will soon find a shidduch for her.'

'I had her down as one of those rebels who wants to leave the community.'

'I don't think so. She might have a rebellious streak, but she's not unhappy.'

'Then why is she going out with you?'

Daniel furrowed his brows, affecting an exaggerated, smouldering look. 'Because forbidden fruit tastes sweeter?'

Ben shook his head in mock exasperation and gave him a friendly jab.

Daniel's mouth tightened into a more serious line. 'It's not something we've discussed much. Perhaps it's out of curiosity, or the thrill of dating someone from "the other side."' Daniel curled his fingers like speech marks. 'So what she's doing is probably unusual. I think most of them are dutiful, innocent girls who'd never look twice at me. Probably not even once. I suppose they'd consider me a *shaigetz*.'

'What's that?'

'A guy who isn't Jewish or doesn't appear to be.'

'Yiddish, I presume?'

'No shit, Sherlock.' Daniel continued, 'Even Raizy, once she gets engaged, she'll act all modest, as if she's never so much as looked at another guy. This interlude will remain her little secret. It may give her a kick to remember the "naughty" things she did. But you can be almost certain, once married, Raizy will raise her children the same way her parents brought her up.'

'Hypocritical much?'

'Who am I to judge? If my mum knew half the things I got up to, I think she'd be none too pleased either.'

'If she found out you were having a fling with a Chassidic girl, she'd probably give you a *kuff*!' Ben moved his hand through the air mimicking a slap.

'Hey! My mum isn't that bad.' Daniel laughed. 'Alright, she'd probably go ballistic.'

Daniel settled himself beside Ben, leaning against the side of the car. 'You could look at Raizy's attitude from another perspective. After seeing different lifestyles other than her own, she is choosing to remain of her own free will.'

'Wouldn't it make it hard for her to settle back in afterwards, with *this* forbidden, *that* forbidden?'

'I imagine if you're brought up that way, you're used to it. There are also positive aspects. Raizy mentioned her mum does volunteer work, and cooks for new mothers or those sitting shiva. A bit like your mum. She often helps with stuff like that, doesn't she?'

'Yeah, she does.'

'Then there's the charitable organisations, taking care of those in need, which are also such an important part of their community. Within the fold, there's a sense of security they will be taken care of even if they fall on hard times. You know how it is when you're a part of such a community. It creates togetherness. The downside is that they have established so many rules in their efforts to prevent the outside world from seeping in. But I suppose there's a logic to it. No one can deny there's lots of dodgy stuff going on out there. Hey, who knows?'

Daniel shifted on his feet and took another puff. 'I'm getting too philosophical here. All I'm saying is that she is almost certain to go back and settle down with a boy from her own community. A family like hers wouldn't consider anyone who wasn't Chassidish for their daughter. They want yichus. Pedigree. God help Raizy, or me for that matter, if her parents ever found out we were dating.'

'Then why are you doing this?'

'I've got nothing else going on right now. She's sweet enough, attractive. We have a laugh together. We're both consenting adults. So why not? We too exist in a kind of bubble. It's intriguing to learn more about her background. But

I understand the rules of the game and know my limits. I'm quite aware there could never be anything serious between us.'

'You talk like a man of experience.'

'Well, it's not the first time I've done this.'

'Oh yeah?'

'Yeah. Don't you remember when Moshe and I hooked up with those other two Chassidic girls a while back?'

'No. When was that?'

'Last winter, during the holidays. Ah yes! You were in Israel, preoccupying yourself with a certain Yael,' he chaffed.

Ben folded his arms. 'Well, that's finished now.'

'Right. I've heard that one before.'

'No, this time I mean it. We haven't been in touch for about six months.'

'I thought you two had something.'

'It would never have worked out long-term between us. We're very different. Yael's into that whole partying scene. Great to have a good time with, but not much more. We weren't compatible. And long-distance relationships are hard.'

'Will you see her again in December when you go for your brother's wedding?'

'I have no plans to contact her, but I'm sure she'll be there. She's a good friend of my future sister-in-law.'

'Won't you find it awkward?'

'No, I've moved on, and so has she. I hear she's seeing someone else.'

'I guess she was a distraction for a while, to take your mind off what happened …?'

'Yeah, maybe.'

'I get how tough things were for you last year.' Daniel's voice softened. 'And I understand why you've kept to yourself a lot the past few months and not wanted to go out much.'

Ben felt like he had a fist pressed against his chest. Daniel had always avoided the subject. This was the closest he'd gone to broaching what Ben had locked away and never discussed. Ben didn't speak, afraid that his voice might betray him, and focused on the red taillights of the passing cars, blinking back a few times until he regained control.

Daniel stubbed out his cigarette and patted him on the shoulder. 'Sorry for bringing it up.'

'No worries. I'm fine about everything.' The instant had passed as if it had never happened. But the darkness masked a trace of his lingering pain.

'It's good to see you more like your old self.'

'Thanks for dragging me out. It's been more fun than I expected.'

'I hardly had to drag you. Well, except that first time to the café. But since then, you seem to be more than willing to come. It has nothing to do with Miri by any chance?' Daniel shot him a side-glance. 'Don't think I haven't noticed.'

A hint of a smile spread across Ben's face, which he tried in vain to suppress. 'I don't know what you're talking about.'

'Oh no? I saw your disappointment the night we went bowling, and she didn't show. And this evening, you were rather attentive to her. Though I have to hand it to you mate, she's not a bad looker.'

Ben held up his hands in surrender. 'Alright, I admit it. I quite like her. There's more to her than first meets the eye. She's interesting to talk to. And yeah, she's not a bad looker.'

Daniel slapped him on the back. 'It's alright, you don't have to justify yourself. I'm glad you're finally smiling and getting back into circulation. But a word of advice. Don't get too emotionally involved, mate, or you'll get burnt.'

Chapter 6

Miri simmered with excitement. An unfamiliar euphoria she could barely contain. All she could think of was him.

When she wasn't replaying scenes in her mind of their last meet-up, she was planning for Wednesday night. And she'd concluded that nothing in her wardrobe was suitable. She needed some new clothes.

There was a rare period of quiet in Miri's home that Sunday afternoon. Her Aunt Esty had offered to mind the little ones for a few hours, and her mother was taking full advantage of the break from duties with an afternoon nap. Which meant Miri had the phone to herself and could call Raizy, undisturbed, to plan a shopping trip. But all she got from Raizy's end was an engaged tone. She had another idea.

'Miri, I was about to call you. I have some exciting news to share.' Devorah sounded exuberant. 'My brother Tuli got engaged last night!'

'Mazel tov. Who to?'

'Shoshi Muller. She was the year below us in school. Do you remember her?'

'I think I remember the name. What wonderful news!'

'Thank you.' She paused, concern edging into her voice.

'How are you? Is everything alright?'

Miri recalled their last conversation and their awkward parting. 'Yes, borich Hashem, I'm fine. I wondered if you'd be interested to come shopping with me for clothes tomorrow evening? I'd welcome the company, but understand if you're too busy.'

'Yes, I'd love to. Perhaps I'll be able to find an outfit for the *vort*. It's next Sunday night at our home at seven-thirty, *im yirtze Hashem*, and you're invited.'

No sooner had she hung up than Raizy called. 'Did you hear Devorah's brother, Tuli, got engaged?'

'Yes. I just spoke to her.'

'Isn't it great? By the way, I asked my brother if he knew of any gossip about Devorah's family. He wasn't aware of anything. He agreed it must be a mistake. But now, with the engagement, I'm certain it will give people better things to talk about.'

'I hope so.'

'I also spoke to Chaya earlier. She suggested going to eat out at Café Liat in Hendon tomorrow evening. Fancy joining us?'

'I'd have loved to. But I already made plans to go shopping with Devorah.'

'No worries. I'll see you Wednesday, anyway.'

'Definitely.'

Alone and unseen, Miri pirouetted around the kitchen.

Devorah's enthusiasm was waning. It showed in her disinterested expression and the way she lagged as Miri raced from one shop to another. She couldn't disguise her relief when, at last, after over two hours of Miri flicking through endless racks of clothing, she picked out several items and headed off to try them on.

Miri studied herself in the mirror, stunned by the reflection. Staring back at her was an elegant young woman, almost unrecognisable. She felt like the ugly duckling transformed into a graceful swan.

Miri emerged from the changing room wearing a fitted, pale blue jumper and a black jersey cotton skirt, cut on the bias so it flowed in soft drapes to her ankles. She gave a balletic twirl. 'What do you think?'

Devorah wrinkled her nose. 'It's kind of ... modern-looking.'

That wasn't a compliment, rather a euphemism for clothing that, while not immodest, didn't conform to their conservative standards. Miri's shoulders slumped, weighed down by the familiar load of shame. Maybe this was a bad idea after all. Then she paused in front of the full-length mirror outside the changing room and took a good look at herself. Her style may not be to Devorah's taste, but it was the truest reflection she'd ever seen of herself. Miri liked what she saw. She reminded herself that 'modern' was the look for which she'd been aiming. Like Raizy's trendy outfits, or the young woman she'd greeted on Shabbes who had been walking with her grandmother near the River Lea.

'You look nice, though.' Devorah appeared in the mirror behind her. 'It suits you.'

At the cosmetics counters, Miri pondered over the dizzying selection of pots and palettes. Devorah, who only ever went bare-faced, observed from the sidelines as Miri selected a peachy eyeshadow and blusher, black mascara and tinted lip gloss. If Devorah had any misgivings or wondered about this sudden desire for self-reinvention, she kept her thoughts to herself, and Miri did not explain.

'Anywhere else you want to go?' Miri said.

'No, I can't find anything suitable. I might try Mrs Levy who sells lovely outfits from her house, which she imports from Antwerp.'

Miri kept a diplomatic silence. The overpriced, shapeless suits Mrs Levy offered did not impress her.

Before they left, Miri made one final detour – the bookshop – where she bought a copy of Pride and Prejudice by Jane Austen.

Miri opened her cupboard for another quick peek at her purchases. She held the beautiful skirt against her, tested out the lip gloss, checked her reflection and smiled. Tomorrow night...

'Miri, telephone!' The summons from the kitchen stopped her in her tracks. She buried her bag beneath the pile of clothes she'd deemed to frumpy to wear, away from the prying eyes of her inquisitive sister, and ran downstairs to take the call.

'I hate him!' said the furious voice on the line.

She had caught Miri off-guard. 'Raizy, what's up?'

'Daniel.'

'What about –?' Her mother slowed the stirring of her cake mixture. 'What about Mrs Levy?'

'You can't speak?'

'No. I've never found a *simcha* outfit there either.'

'Can you come over?'

71

'Yes. Let's go through the stuff you have in your wardrobe. See you soon.'

Miri replaced the receiver, her heart thumping. Her mother poured the mixture into a loaf tin. 'Is anything the matter?'

She tried to appear nonchalant. 'No, everything is fine. Raizy wants help figuring out what to wear for a simcha. I'm popping over there for a few minutes.'

She didn't linger for a response and hoped she hadn't aroused her mother's suspicions. But of greater concern to her was Raizy's sudden outburst.

Raizy was already waiting by the front door when Miri arrived and beckoned her to come upstairs.

Raizy's bedroom never failed to impress. It was the same size as Miri's, her bed even positioned in the same spot, beside the window. Except Raizy had the entire space for herself. A row of built-in oak cupboards spanned the length of one wall, and both her dressing and bedside tables were of the same wood. The soft furnishings coordinated too, the pink rose design on her bedspread repeating itself on the draped curtains and lampshade. In contrast, Miri had to contend with her two sisters, their bunk bed squeezed beside her bed with just enough space to pass between them, each covered in mismatched bedding. And their storage comprised three, time-worn cupboards – inherited from the previous owners who first moved into the house in the thirties.

'Sorry if I put you in an awkward position earlier.' Raizy flopped onto the plush, cream carpet and patted it, inviting Miri to join her. There was an enormous bowl of crisps on her bedside table. Raizy reached for it, took a handful and began chomping her way through them, before sliding the bowl across to Miri who took one.

'What happened between you and Daniel?' Miri said.

'Last night, while Chaya and I were waiting to order, Chaya's mobile rang. She has a secret phone. She whispered, "Hello, Daniel," then placed her hand over her mouth and turned around to speak and I overheard her say, "I can't speak now, I'll call you later." After she put down the phone, I asked her, "Were you speaking to Daniel?" and she couldn't look me in the eye.'

'What did you do?'

'I walked out while she just sat there. She couldn't say anything. She had guilt written all over her face.'

Raizy scooped up another handful from the bowl.

'Is it possible you made a mistake, and it was a different Daniel?'

Raizy snorted. 'Yes, right! Earlier this afternoon, I went over to Kosher Basket and confronted him.'

'What did he say?'

'I asked him straight if he phoned Chaya last night and he said he did. Not even embarrassed enough to deny it.'

Miri had a creeping sense of foreboding. 'What happened next?'

'He called after me to wait. I guess he wanted to "explain". But what's there to explain? It's obvious there is something going on between them. So I told him, "You can forget about tomorrow night." Then I turned around and stormed out. To think the guy I was seeing and one of my closest friends would go behind my back.'

'You must have misunderstood. Perhaps there is a good explanation.'

Raizy carried on as if she hadn't been listening. 'I can't believe those two!'

'But you said there was nothing serious between you and Daniel.'

'That doesn't give him the right to see someone else when he's meant to be dating me.'

'Why don't you call Chaya and ask her what's going on?'

'I'm not calling her! She should contact me to apologise and explain.'

'Does that mean it's …' Miri had difficulty swallowing. 'Over?'

'I'm sorry. I know you quite liked Ben. But don't worry, there will be others. As the saying goes, there are plenty more fish in the sea.' Miri had never heard the saying – and had no interest in others.

'Aren't you upset about Daniel?'

'No, I'm not upset. I'm angry at being cheated on by a supposed boyfriend and a good friend. But why should I care? Give it another couple of weeks, he'll have found a more exciting conquest, and he'll dump her too. Easy come, easy go.'

There were still some rules of this game Miri hadn't grasped.

Returning home later that evening, all Miri wanted to do was to hide under her duvet and wallow in self-pity. But before she could retreat to her room, her mother cornered her. 'Devorah phoned while you were out and asked if you could call her.' Her mother made her disapproval clear. 'She says it's important. Please don't make it too long. I've got to sort out a food rota. Mrs Woolf is sitting shiva for her father.'

Miri dialled her number, wondering if perhaps Devorah

had good news of her own to announce. That notion was dispelled as soon as Devorah answered. 'Th-thanks for calling back.' Devorah sounded tearful. 'I have a bit of bad news. Tuli's engagement has been called off.'

'Oh no! I'm sorry to hear that. What happened? Sorry, I shouldn't have asked. You don't need to tell me.'

'There isn't much to say. Even we don't know the exact reason. The shadchen rang my mother and told her the other side wanted to break it off. She gave no explanation. Tuli is devastated.'

'I'm so sorry,' Miri repeated, unable to find adequate words to convey her sympathy.

She wondered whether there was a connection to the rumours circulating to which her mother had alluded, but there was nothing she could say.

Wednesday night, seven o'clock. She should have been dressed in her new clothes, ready to head out with Raizy to meet Daniel and Ben. Instead, Miri sat on the floor, staring at her new purchases with a sense of regret. The rare happiness she had experienced for that brief time had evaporated. It was over. If only she could have given Ben her number when he had asked.

Why did it seem her fate always depended on someone else? Just because Raizy had fallen out with Daniel and Chaya, she might never see Ben again. But if not for Raizy, she would never have met him.

Logic told her to forget him. It was pointless to mope. She stuffed the clothes back in the bag. She had no use for them now. But meeting him had awoken something within her and she didn't want to let go.

Miri thought about all the choices she'd ever made. Or rather, all the choices made for her. In her eagerness to please, never wanting to be a source of disappointment, she had let others sweep her along and never said no. What if she were to start taking a measure of control over her life? The concept was both liberating and daunting.

Like the first brush strokes on a fresh sheet of paper, an idea began to form. What if she went to the station for the scheduled meeting time? She knew it was a crazy idea. It probably wouldn't achieve anything and it was doubtful he would show – he had no reason to – but at least it would satisfy her mind.

Miri changed into her new top and skirt, rolling it up at the waistband to make it appear a more conventional calf length, and applied a touch of makeup. She slipped across the landing, past her mother, who was bathing the baby. From the foot of the stairs, she called, 'Mameh! I'm going over to Raizy's.'

'OK. Don't be too late.'

Miri grabbed her jacket and opened the door to find Raizy standing there.

'Hi, Miri. Were you on your way out?'

'Yes. No. I mean yes.' She couldn't tell Raizy what she'd been about to do. She'd think her ridiculous. 'I was about to head over to you.'

'We must be telepathic. I've got amazing news to tell you!' Raizy hurried Miri out of the door. For an instant, it raised her hopes. Perhaps Raizy had reconciled with Daniel, and the date was back on?

'You'll never guess what. I'm going on a shidduch tomorrow

evening. My parents think the boy suggested will be very suitable. He comes from a family with good yichus, they're well off, and he's …'

Why hadn't she plucked up the courage to tell Raizy what she had intended to do. Once more, she'd allowed yet another opportunity to slip away. Now she felt obliged to accompany Raizy. It wouldn't be fair to desert her best friend when it was clear how eager she was to share this monumental rite of passage in all its detail.

Eight o'clock. He took one last look outside the station, no longer sure what he had been expecting. He didn't even understand what had made him come. Who was he kidding? Did he honestly think she'd show?

Ben returned to his car and started the engine.

Chapter 7

Miri awoke with a start and looked at the clock. That couldn't be the right time. She checked her watch. It was.

Miri leapt out of bed in a panic, knocking over the cup of water for *negel vasser* across the floor. She flung open her wardrobe, grabbed the first clothes within reach, dashed to the bathroom, washed her hands, splashed water on her face, and ran a toothbrush around her mouth at a terrifying speed which made her gag. Hands fumbling, she dressed, tied her hair into a haphazard ponytail, and sped out of the house before rushing back to get her bag.

Everything was going wrong. Everything!

Try as she might, she couldn't get thoughts of Ben out of her head. Though, she knew it was pointless to dwell on a person she'd met twice and be unlikely ever to see again.

Then there was Devorah. Miri felt awful for the hurt and confusion her family was going through over Tuli's broken engagement, unaware of the gossip behind their backs. She wondered whether she had done the right thing by not warning Devorah, but until she had the facts, she might risk causing further upset.

And now Raizy's bombshell.

Miri marvelled at Raizy's ability to move on with such ease. Daniel had already become a mere footnote in her history. She seemed excited to go on the shidduch. Miri had spent the evening listening to Raizy talk about nothing else. Most of the discussion centred on what she'd wear and how she would style her hair and do her makeup.

Miri knew she ought to be happy for her friend if this was what she really wanted. She only hoped her motives were genuine and not a misguided intention to get back at Daniel. Perhaps Raizy's parents had given her no say in the matter, and she was making the best of the situation. Or maybe Raizy considered herself ready at last for this new stage of her life. After all, she'd confided in Miri that she never thought of Daniel in serious terms and wanted to marry someone from a similar background. The only way to do that was by accepting shidduch suggestions.

If Miri was honest, she feared that if Raizy got engaged, it would change the status of their friendship and they'd lose a degree of closeness between them. Miri would miss that. Their daring evenings out together would end when they had only just begun.

Above all, Raizy's shidduch served as a sober reminder that Miri's turn was imminent. It filled her with dread. She had little faith in her parent's ability to introduce her to someone compatible. How could they? They didn't know the real Miri. Even if she summoned the courage and admitted the truth to her mother, she wouldn't listen. Less likely agree. As for her father, he'd lose his temper and shut her down before giving her a chance to explain herself.

Miri checked her watch as she hurried along the high street in as dignified a manner as possible. To top it all off, she was over an hour late for work. There would be a harsh reprimand from Mr Reich waiting for her when she arrived. She tried to come up with a suitable excuse that would mollify him. Wrapped up in her concerns, she didn't notice the car that drew up alongside her.

But he had seen her. Like a vision, there she was, walking with an energetic stride along the high street. Her hair, styled in a casual pony, tumbled down her back in thick, glossy waves, and her cheeks glowed from the crisp, early morning air. He understood it was rash to stop her right here, in the centre of everything, when she appeared to be in a hurry. He wasn't sure how she would react, but this might be his one opportunity. If he let it go, he would kick himself. He wound down his window.

'Miri!'

Miri searched for the source of the male voice and did a double-take. There, regarding her with his deep, warm eyes, was Ben. He had pulled up beside her in his small silver Peugeot.

Miri scanned the vicinity to check no one else had spotted her. Then she remembered her dishevelled appearance, having dressed in such a rush, and cringed inwardly.

'Hi, Miri,' he said. 'It's nice to see you again.'

Her eyes darted around. She seemed awkward. Ben couldn't figure out whether speaking to him in public was making her uneasy, or had he misread the signals and she had no interest in him at all.

'How are you?'

'Fine, borich Hashem. How are you?'

She had replied to his question and hadn't walked off. That had to be a positive sign. Or was she being polite?

'I'm good too, thanks.' He had no idea what to say next. 'Where are you going?'

'To work. I'm running late. What about you?'

'To university. I'm early, for once. My first lecture isn't for another twenty-five minutes.'

They opened their mouths to speak. 'Sorry.' And they both laughed.

'Listen,' he said, 'I'm sorry for whatever took place between Raizy and Daniel. I don't understand the whole thing. But there's no reason we can't still see each other, is there?'

Miri stared at him without a response. Before his nerves betrayed him, he continued, 'Can I meet you this evening after work? What time do you finish?'

'At five, but –'

'Where do you work?'

She looked horrified. 'I couldn't possibly meet you there!'

Thinking fast, he tried once more. 'OK. How about Manor House Station, five-thirty? I can wait for you there. What do you say?'

The sound of rapid footsteps punctured the space between his question and her answer. Miri glanced behind, and her face clouded over. 'Oh no!'

'What is it?'

'It's –'

She broke off to address a severe-looking woman who had

appeared by her side. 'Hello, Mrs Finer.'

The enthusiasm in her voice sounded forced. Ben got the distinct impression Miri wasn't in the least pleased to see her.

'Do you know the way to … Shoreditch? This, er … car stopped to ask for directions, but I'm not sure where that is.'

The woman leaned towards his open window, and Ben experienced an uncomfortable sensation of being sized up. 'You do realise you're heading in the complete opposite direction, don't you?' Her accusation suddenly made him feel guilty, for he knew not what. 'You need to turn around, drive down that road and go right at the next junction.'

'Thanks,' said Ben. 'I got rather lost. I'm not from around these parts.'

Miri backed away. He was desperate to get her attention, but the crone continued to bark instructions at him. Ben was powerless to do anything but pretend to listen, frustration rising, as he watched Miri slink off.

Then she turned around. Fleetingly. Her eyes met his. She gave a brief nod and walked on.

The brisk footsteps gained on her from behind. She groaned to herself.

'You should be more cautious about talking to strangers.'

Miri summoned all her self-control to face Mrs I'm-Finer-Than-You with a serene expression. 'I was just trying to be helpful and give directions when asked.'

'All the same, be careful who you speak to.'

'I always am.'

'I'd also advise you to take care with whom you mix.'

'What do you mean?'

'I noticed you with that Cohen girl the other day.'

'Devorah?'

'Yes. She's not the sort of friend you want to be hanging around with.'

Once Miri would have held her tongue, but not only had Mrs Finer hit a sore point, she might have also just thwarted her chance to meet Ben again. 'What rubbish! There's nothing wrong with Devorah.'

'Excuse me? That's not the way a refined girl speaks to her elders.'

'I'm sorry, I didn't mean for it to sound the way it came out.'

'I'm not one to talk. But with a brother like that ... and I understand his shidduch has broken off ...' She gave Miri a look as if to say she knew more than she was willing to reveal.

Chapter 8

Ben checked his watch: five-thirty. Any minute now, he told himself. A bus pulled up at the stop and he watched all the passengers alight. Then it sped away. She had not been on it.

5:37 pm

Would she show? Had he imagined that nod?

5:42 pm

Another bus passed, still no sign of her. Ben paced back and forth. Perhaps she had a long walk to the bus stop or got held up in traffic.

5:49 pm

Did she say she finished work at five or five-thirty? Had he misunderstood?

5:58 pm

He had made a mistake asking her to meet him at the station. She could have been nervous coming there on her own after dark. He should have suggested somewhere else.

I'll give her five more minutes.

6:05 pm

He had blown it! She wasn't coming.

OK, just another five minutes.

6:12 pm

Did he say Manor House Station? He ran through the conversation in his mind. Yes, he had. Then it occurred to him there were five separate entrances. Would she remember this was the place they had met last time or was she waiting outside another? Should he check or would he miss her? Had she already left, thinking he'd stood her up?

Five more minutes. If she's not here by then, she has no intention of coming.

6:16 pm

Had she been happy to see him that morning or just tried not to appear rude? Perhaps she hadn't given him a second thought afterwards and forgotten about their conversation.

'Sorry I'm late!'

He shook his head slowly, as if he couldn't believe his eyes, and greeted Miri with a broad smile. She was out of breath and her brown hair fell loose over her shoulders. She looked … beautiful.

He steadied his voice. 'No problem. I only got here myself a few minutes ago.' She smiled with relief. 'My car is right over there.'

He held the door open for her and she sat down in the passenger seat, still panting. 'My boss made me stay an extra half an hour because I arrived late this morning. Then I had to find a phone box to ring my mother to make an excuse where I was going after work.'

'What did you tell her?'

'A good friend from sem is here for a visit and I'm meeting up with her this evening.'

'Right. How long will she be staying?'

Miri lowered her eyes. 'I don't know if she's booked her return flight yet.'

Ben gave her an impish smile. 'Okaaay ...'

She couldn't keep a straight face.

'Fancy a bite to eat?' he said. 'I thought maybe we could go to a place in Hendon.'

'Thank you. That sounds lovely.'

Sitting beside Ben in the car felt surreal. She could hardly believe this was happening. He navigated the rush hour traffic, eyes focused on the road. She caught the subtle citrus and woodsy notes of his aftershave and stole surreptitious glances in his direction. He was wearing a pale blue shirt, the top two buttons open to reveal a white T-shirt underneath, and she noticed something glisten against his neck – a chain of some sort. In her circles, it was unheard of for men to wear jewellery, except perhaps a watch. It wasn't considered the 'done thing'. But she found it thrilling that Ben did.

Half an hour later, they arrived in Hendon. Ben located a parking space and they set off together down Brent Street. At first glance, the street didn't have any notable features. The parade of shops included the usual estate agents, charity shops, hairdressers, newsagents and a pub. But what set it apart for outsiders like them was the broad offering of kosher eateries absent from Stamford Hill where casual socialising was discouraged.

Here, people didn't just walk with a hurried sense of purpose but also came together for entertainment. And lit by the burnished amber street lamps and colourful shop-front illuminations, the harsh edges of its blocky, post-war buildings were lent the convivial atmosphere of a street fair.

For Miri, it was the contrast between the more tolerant

attitudes of this community compared with her own that left a deeper impression than the aesthetics. She might almost have been in a different country. She passed two girls in their late teens, dressed in the modern ensemble of ankle-length denim skirts and trainers. They stopped to greet a boy clad in faded jeans and a knitted kippah, his tzitzit hanging out from under his shirt. She observed a religious man in a black hat shake hands and converse in Hebrew with a bareheaded man sporting an earring. In this foreign land of Hendon, no one paid heed that she was walking with a boy, or threatened to damage her reputation because of it.

Together they strolled the length of the street, enjoying the luxury of being able to choose from a selection of establishments. It was a corner café that ultimately enticed them with a delicious aroma of fresh herbs and hot pastries wafting from its entrance. For Miri, the prospect of eating out was an additional delight. It was an activity she'd done only twice before with friends. She'd never been to a restaurant with her family – both for financial reasons and their sense of propriety. Miri was fascinated by the other young people who sat there and seemed to take this for granted.

A waitress showed them to a table and handed them menus. It reminded Miri of her awkwardness the first evening they'd met. But how different the situation was this time, without their friends. Just the two of them. Ben smiled at her as if he'd read her thoughts.

'By the way, how's your friend Raizy?'

'She's fine.'

Raizy was, in fact, anything but. She was a nervous wreck. She had called Miri on three separate occasions that day for advice on whether she should stay with her original choice of outfit or change it. Each time she called, Mr Reich hovered around her desk as if he had a sixth sense, forcing Miri to cut short her conversation with the excuse of a wrong number.

'It's a shame about her and Daniel. I didn't get the entire story, but I heard she had an outburst in Kosher Basket and wouldn't let him get a word in edgeways. She got the wrong end of the stick, though.'

'What do you mean?'

'About Daniel and Chaya.'

'Weren't they seeing each other behind Raizy's back?'

'No. It seems she jumped to that conclusion without letting either of them explain. They weren't going out at all.'

'But didn't he call Chaya on her mobile? And from what Raizy said, Chaya was very secretive with him.'

'I believe that part is true. From what I understand, the night we went bowling – when Raizy brought Chaya along – she took a liking to Moshe. The following day, Chaya went into Kosher Basket to speak to Daniel in confidence. Daniel promised he'd find out on her behalf whether Moshe was interested in her too. That's why he called. Unfortunately for Chaya, the answer was no. But it's a pity Raizy wouldn't hear Daniel out.'

Miri raised a hand to her temple and shook her head.

'Why don't you tell Raizy? It's a shame for them to fall out for no reason,' he said.

'There might not be much point now. Raizy is going on a shidduch this evening.'

'Wow! That was quick.'

A look of shared understanding passed from one to the other.

'I know,' said Miri.

The waitress returned with a pad and a pen to take their order.

'What would you like?' Ben asked.

She studied the menu, once again overwhelmed by all the options. 'A pizza?' she ventured.

'Sounds good. Wanna share a large one?'

So here she was, sharing a plate of food with Ben. It should have felt strange, uncomfortable even. But it didn't. Right there and then, eating together like that seemed the most natural thing in the world.

'You mentioned earlier that you got hassle at work for coming late. Sorry if that was my fault because I delayed you,' he said.

'No, it's fine. I was running late anyway.'

'What do you do?'

'I'm a secretary at a property management company.'

'Do you enjoy it?'

'To tell you the truth,' she said, 'I can't stand it. My boss is strict, and the work is dull.'

'Have you thought about leaving to do something else?'

'I've got no proper qualifications. It would just be another boring secretarial job. I suppose there's always teaching, but that doesn't interest me either.'

'What interests you?'

She shifted in her chair. 'I'm not sure.'

'Come on, you must have an idea,' he said. 'If you had the choice to do anything at all, what would it be?'

'You'll probably laugh at me if I tell you.'

'No, I won't. I promise.'

She saw the sincerity in his eyes and knew she could trust him with her secret.

'I know it sounds silly, but I'd love to study to become an architect or an interior designer. Or else, something art-related. I love drawing.'

'That's not silly at all. The opposite! I think those are amazing choices. Why don't you study one of those then?'

She looked downcast. 'My parents would never let me do that.'

'Have you discussed it with them?'

'There's no point in even bringing it up. Girls in our community, we don't attend secular colleges. Very few of the boys do either. If my parents had any idea how much time I spend drawing, I think they'd consider it a complete waste of my time.'

'What do you draw?'

'It varies. Buildings, landscapes, people ...'

'I'd be interested to see some of your work. If you're willing to show me.'

Miri remained noncommittal. She'd never shown her pictures to anyone.

'What do you do? You mentioned this morning you were on your way to university.'

'Yeah, I'm in my final year, studying computers at Metropolitan.'

'That sounds so interesting,' she said, no clue what Metropolitan meant. 'What will you do afterwards?'

'I'm considering web design.'

She could have talked to him for hours, but before she knew it, they were already on their way back.

'I don't want to leave you at Manor House on your own this late. It can be a dodgy area, especially at night. Would it be alright if I dropped you outside your door?' he said.

Miri hadn't given the logistics much thought until that point. 'Not really. I can't risk being seen with you.' Ben was looking at her. Was he hurt? 'Sorry, I didn't mean it in that way.'

'I understand. But I'm worried for you to go home by yourself. What if I left you a few streets away and then followed you in the car, would that work?'

'I think so.'

'Can I see you again?'

'I'd like that.'

'Are you free this *Motzei Shabbat?*'

'*Motzei* – oh, *Moitzei Shabbes* – I should be. I must just check my mother doesn't need me for anything.'

'How can we speak to confirm? Do you have a mobile phone, perhaps?'

'No, I don't.'

Ben tapped the steering wheel with the tips of his fingers, his head tilted sideways. 'How about if I give you my number, and you call me?'

'Is it alright to call you at home? I mean, what if your parents answer?'

Ben laughed. 'It's alright. They won't mind.'

'They don't mind if you talk to girls?'

'No. Not as long as I come home with a nice Jewish girl. Eventually.'

'Even if she's not Adeni?'

'Yeah, sure. Why not?'

'By us, it has to be a shidduch, a chossid, yichus …' Miri stopped mid-flow as Ben drew up to the kerb and parked beside the open, green common that traversed their neighbourhood. He reached into the small storage compartment beneath the radio, rummaged for a pen, settling for an old petrol receipt to write on, and jotted down his number.

He passed it to her, and as she took it, their fingers brushed. They stared at each other, fixated, held in the connection of that light touch.

'Call me?' he murmured.

She nodded.

Miri walked the path to her door, patting her ponytail to check it was in place. A familiar silver car drove past, slowed down for a moment to ensure she was home safe, then accelerated. She hugged her shoulders, feeling a warm glow course through her.

Chapter 9

Miri's mother bustled from the kitchen, her hands covered in flour. 'Where have you been all this time?'

Miri tried to keep her composure. 'I told you, I was meeting Malka Brocha.'

'Never mind,' she said, dismissing Miri's excuse with a wave of her hand. 'Raizy has been trying to reach you.' That's when she noticed her mother trying to conceal a smile. 'She says it's urgent. Go call her!'

She ushered Miri into the kitchen.

The line was busy, and it took several attempts to get through. This could only mean one thing.

'Miri!' Raizy yelled. 'I became a kallah!'

Despite half-expecting it, Raizy's announcement still took her by surprise. 'Mazel tov.'

'We're having a *l'chaim* right now. Please come over. See you soon!'

Her mother stood over her shoulder and prompted her. 'Nu? So what was her urgent news?'

Stunned, Miri was still staring at the phone. 'Raizy's engaged.'

Mrs Fogel clapped her hands, though Miri suspected her

mother already knew. 'Mazel tov! Who to?'

'I didn't have time to ask, but I'm sure he comes from a *chosheve* family.'

'I'm certain. The Zilbergs would take nothing less.'

'She invited me to come over for the *l'chaim*.'

'Yes, you must go. Your best friend is a kallah. *Im yirze Hashem* by you!'

Miri hovered by the doorway, observing the chattering female relatives who surrounded Raizy. She was reluctant to push herself forward, but Raizy spotted her and bounded across to pull her into the party.

Miri hugged her. 'Mazel tov! I can't believe it.'

Raizy was breathless. 'Neither can I. Isn't it amazing? I'm getting married! The vort is on Sunday evening at eight o'clock. Tomorrow, my mother's taking me to buy a new outfit and shoes. I want to get a manicure too, but not sure if I'll have enough time. Being *erev Shabbes*, it will be such a rush.'

Raizy wore a subdued yet stylish navy blue suit, and she'd had her hair cut to a chic, shoulder length. Her face glowed, though a hint of light makeup may have contributed to her dewy complexion. Raizy wasn't her usual self. She appeared distracted, almost dazed, and every so often, her eyes wandered to the gap between the double doors, to the men's side in the dining room.

'Tell me about your *chosson*.' Miri said.

'His name is Naftoli Fischer. He's rather tall and good-looking, his family is well-to-do and he's the best boy in yeshiva. Everything I wanted. He's also descended from several renowned *Rabbonim,* which delights my parents.'

'But what's he like?'

Raizy beckoned her over to the small opening between the dividing doors, and Miri studied the sea of men. Most wore a black hat and a langer rekel over a pair of black trousers and a white shirt.

'Which one is he?'

'He's over there.' She pointed to a group of four men standing by the back door, deep in discussion. One of them stood a few inches taller than the rest, with a straight posture and a neat, dark beard. He glanced at them as they peeped through the gap and gave Raizy a discreet wink. She answered with a coy smile.

'I'm choosing a design for my engagement ring next week. Isn't that amazing?'

'Yes.'

'And I'm also going to look at wedding dresses –'

'Raizy, how did you know he was the one for you?'

'I just knew.'

'But how?'

'When the time comes, you will too. You'll see. Im yirtze Hashem by you soon.'

Please Hashem, not in this way, Miri prayed.

The circumstances were as she imagined: they would remain close, but the status of their friendship would surely change. Raizy's central focus had shifted to becoming a married woman, leaving Miri behind, her still-single friend.

But it wasn't just Raizy who had moved onto a new chapter. So had Miri.

That Friday, Miri spent a restless morning at work, her thoughts concentrated on the meaningful deed she was about to do. From the office, Miri made a covert detour to the phone box. She withdrew the old receipt with Ben's number, tucked away in her purse. Her hand shook as she dialled. After three rings, a soft-spoken woman with a faint accent answered.

'Hello … can I speak to … Ben, please?'

'Yes, sure. One moment, please.'

Despite Ben's assurance that there would be no problem calling him at home, his mother's unruffled response still astonished Miri. She didn't seem bothered in the slightest that a girl had rung, asking to speak to her son. If it had been the other way round, and Ben had called Miri at home … it didn't bear contemplation.

'Ben, telephone!'

She heard the hurried footsteps of someone running down the stairs.

'Hello?' he said.

'Hi, Ben. It's –'

'Hi, Miri! So good to hear from you. How are you doing?'

'I can make it tomorrow night.'

'That's great! What time shall I meet you, and where?'

'I'm meant to be babysitting a few roads away. How about the place where you dropped me off last time, at eight o'clock?'

'Perfect. I'll be there.'

'I have to go as I'm on a payphone.'

'No problem. I'm looking forward to seeing you. Shabbat shalom.'

Miri felt her way around the unfamiliar Shabbes greeting. 'Shabb-at shalom.'

As soon as Shabbat ended, Miri washed and dried and put away all the dishes as fast as possible. Then she showered, changed into her new skirt and jumper, applied some peachy eyeshadow, a coat of mascara, and tinted lip-gloss. Her mother was feeding the baby, so she slipped out unseen.

True to his word, Ben was already waiting for her at their prearranged rendezvous. After a cursory glance to check no one was watching, she climbed into Ben's car and he sped away.

'How about going to Hampstead Village for a drink this evening?' he said.

'I'm not sure if I've ever been there.'

'I think you'll like it.'

'Come on, one more spoon,' Mrs Fogel urged the stubborn toddler who had clamped his mouth shut. She nudged the spoon against his lips, but he wasn't having any of it. He turned his head from side to side, refusing the leftover cholent. A brown mush of beans, potatoes, and shreds of meat made its way down his chin. She scooped up another spoonful, ready for one more attempt when the phone rang. On instinct, she got up to answer it.

As she lifted the receiver, she turned to find the baby had immersed both hands into the contents, grabbed hold of the bowl and placed it on his head like his father's hat. He clapped his hands in joy as the sticky goo ran down his face. She wanted to shriek but fixed a smile on her face before she spoke, as if all was under control in her household.

'Hello Mrs Fogel, it's Raizy here. Can I speak to Miri, please?'

'Mazel tov, Raizy. We're excited for your vort tomorrow evening.'

'Thank you. Can I speak to Miri, please?'

'No, you missed her. She already left.'

'Where has she gone?'

'To do your babysitting job for you.'

'I'm sorry, did you say she's gone babysitting?'

'Yes. Miri explained it would have been difficult for you to do it the night before your vort. She was glad to help.'

What on earth was Miri's mother talking about? She'd never asked Miri to babysit for her. Unless … was it possible Miri had used her as an alibi? It was out of character for Miri to pull a stunt like that, but she decided she had better cover for her, just in case.

'Yes, Miri's such a wonderful friend. She's always so helpful. I was calling to make sure she'd remembered she was babysitting for me this evening. But it seems she did. Well, I have to go, lots to do. See you tomorrow.'

Raizy deliberated at length between the two outfits laid out on her bed, undecided whether to opt for the oyster-pink suit or the salmon-pink one. Where was her best friend when she needed her most? Stranger still, it was clear Miri wasn't babysitting. So where was she?

Hampstead Village was as Ben had described it to her on the drive over. Like being in the countryside without having left the city. Wrought-iron street lamps lit up the

98

leafy avenues and narrow, cobbled lanes. Miri admired the contrasting architectural styles: Victorian red brick houses, rows of quaint mews homes, and minimalist houses with large expanses of glass.

They reached a stylish high street lined with trendy boutiques and restaurants and paused every so often to look at things of interest that attracted their eye. They walked close to one another. Several times, their arms brushed by accident. But Miri didn't step away.

'It's so pretty here. I didn't realise such a place existed in London,' she said.

'I thought you'd appreciate it.'

'How did you find out about this –?' She didn't finish her question.

Ben tentatively took her hand and linked his fingers with hers.

Miri caught her breath. Her stomach flipped. Through the haze, Ben explained something about having gone there with friends for drinks.

We're holding hands!

She'd dreamt of a moment like this so many times, supposing it was unattainable. Nothing like that would ever happen to her. But here she was, dressed in her new clothes, walking in this picturesque setting, hand in hand with Ben. It was real. And it was perfect.

Ben found an intimate little café with a wood-burning fireplace. They chose the table situated nearest to enjoy its radiant heat, and they ordered hot drinks.

'I've been meaning to tell you,' Miri said. 'Raizy got engaged on Thursday night.'

Ben spluttered and almost choked on his coffee. 'You're having me on?'

'No, I'm serious.'

'But wasn't that the first time they ever met?'

'Yes, it was.'

'He proposed on their first date?'

'It's not a proper date where you go out. It's called a *beshow*. He came to her home and they spoke to each other. Then, they agreed to get married.'

'Unbelievable. I've never heard of anyone getting engaged the first time they meet.'

'It's normal by us to do it that way.'

'But how do they decide in such a short time?'

'The parents make all the enquiries and meet each other to find out if the families are compatible before they agree to the shidduch. Then it is up to the boy and girl to say yes.'

'And does it always work out?'

'I suppose there are exceptions to the rule. But in most cases, it does. Perhaps it's because they go into it with a different attitude and expectations.'

Ben tried to pick his words with care. 'Is that … are you expected to do the same?'

'Maybe.' Her face fell. 'I mean, yes.'

'You don't seem happy about the idea.'

'No. I'm not.'

Miri stared into the fire, watching the crackling flames.

'Do you want to talk about it?' he said.

'I've never spoken to anyone about this. I tried to discuss it with Raizy, but she didn't listen. I don't think she took me seriously.'

'I promise I'll listen.'

She picked up a sachet from the bowl on their table and nervously fidgeted with it. 'For the past few months, ever since I finished sem, knowing that soon, my parents will expect me to go on a shidduch, I have given the matter a lot of consideration. I've decided it's not what I want. The problem is, I don't have a choice. I'm trapped.'

'You're not trapped. It's your life. There are always choices. Why don't you tell your parents how you feel?'

'You don't understand. I can't speak to them. They won't accept it. For them, there is no other way. I'm different from the rest of my family. Even to Raizy. Although she may have appeared … well … not like a Chassidish girl when she was with Daniel. But she told me she viewed going out with him as a bit of fun. She didn't see him as anything more. When it came time to settle down, she knew what she wanted – a shidduch with someone from the community.' Miri's voice wavered. 'Unlike her, I couldn't say yes to an almost stranger. And I don't want the exact same lifestyle as my parents. I want … something else.'

'Miri, what would you like?'

She looked at him, hesitant to continue. Ben nodded his encouragement.

'I would like to be with someone who I could be myself with and feel comfortable enough to talk about anything. Share my innermost thoughts and not have to worry that they'd think any less of me.'

Her fingers continued to twist around the sachet, wearing it away at the edges until brown granules trickled onto the table.

'It's not that I want to rebel against my parents. Just that I wish I had a little more freedom. I'd like to do something more interesting than a secretarial job. I wish they had allowed me to study. I'd like to learn and to see more of the world. Not made to feel guilty for watching TV, or going to the cinema, or reading secular books. There's a lot I appreciate about my upbringing and community. I don't want to abandon my way of life in every respect. Only that I'd like to have more of a balance. Does that make sense?'

'Yes, it does.'

'This system can work when parents understand their child and what they need. The problem is, my parents don't know the real me. And I'm afraid to tell them.' She looked fearful. 'I've never shared this with anyone. No one can know.'

'Don't worry. Your secret is safe.' He reached across the table and placed his hand over hers. 'And I don't think any less of you.'

Then, suddenly, something became clear to him. Unlike Daniel and Raizy, neither of them were playing games.

Chapter 10

Naftoli raised the *gartel* – a black woven belt – before the assembled gathering of family and friends to signify he agreed to the marriage. With his head lowered, he winked at Raizy. Next, it was her turn to lift it. She bit her lip as she tried, and failed, to contain her giggles.

Then the Rabbi took centre stage to say a few words. It was the standard address for these occasions. He extolled both families and their prestigious backgrounds, and he blessed the happy couple who stood at a modest distance from each other. He reminded them of the importance of building a virtuous Jewish home, safe from the dangers of the outside world, where Torah learning was the priority.

To conclude the ceremony, Raizy and Naftoli's mothers stepped forward. There was a palpable silence as they held aloft a cloth bag containing a china plate. With a nod to one another, they hurled it to the floor – an ancient custom serving as a reminder that a measure of sadness tempered even the most joyous celebrations. For after two thousand years, the Holy Temple in Jerusalem had yet to be rebuilt. The plate gave a satisfying smash and there followed resounding shouts of 'Mazel tov!' by all those present.

Raizy accepted kisses from her mother and future mother-in-law. Then the two mothers held each other in a stiff embrace.

Raizy looked demure in her oyster-pink suit made from silk taffeta. She wore a new pair of pearl studs in her ears and a gold chain around her neck: gifts from her future husband and in-laws. She received the cluster of well-wishers with grace and smiles, but as soon as the initial excitement had simmered down, she made a beeline for Miri.

Raizy presented her with a shard of the broken plate – a *segula*, or good luck charm, for her own swift engagement.

'Im yirtze Hashem by you,' she said. 'And where were you last night? Who is Malka Brocha? I call to tell you I'm engaged and you're out with this mysterious friend I've never heard of. Then, when I'm trying to reach you because I'm having a what-to-wear crisis the night before my engagement party, your mother tells me you're out doing a babysitting job – for me! What's going on?'

Raizy's grilling ought to have elicited her guilt, but Miri couldn't help feeling an unfamiliar sense of bliss at being reminded about the night before.

Before Miri could explain, a well-wisher interrupted them.

'Mazel tov, Raizy! Such wonderful news. When's the chasseneh?'

The woman was in her late-twenties but appeared a decade older. The strains of life were already visible on her face. Her black suit was immaculate, though there were frays on the cuffs, and her polished shoes were well-worn. Miri knew her by sight from around the area. She might have been a friend, colleague, or a fellow volunteer of Raizy's mother, Mrs Zilberg.

Everyone knew the powerhouse Mrs Gittel Zilberg: high

school headmistress, popular Torah lecturer for the community's women, star volunteer for several charitable organisations, not to mention an effortlessly glamorous wife, mother and grandmother. Most women in the community admired her. Many secretly aspired to be like her (Miri suspected, her mother included).

Miri drifted away to the buffet tables laid out against the back wall. Mrs Zilberg had organised an impressive spread. Bridge rolls, cut vegetables with a selection of dips, small cakes on mirrored trays, and a remarkable fruit display in the shape of a swan. She noticed Devorah standing alone in the corner, drinking a cup of orange juice, and went over to join her. Tonight should have been her brother's engagement party.

'Isn't it wonderful that Raizy has become a kallah?' said Devorah. If she was upset, she didn't let it show. She had put on a brave face to celebrate with Raizy.

'Yes, it is. I can't quite believe it.' She squeezed Devorah's arm. 'How are you doing?'

'I'm fine, borich Hashem.'

'Are you sure?'

'Yes, really I am. It was hard at first, especially for Tuli. Then we realised, if this shidduch wasn't meant to be, it's better that it ended sooner rather than later. And im yirtze Hashem, Tuli should find his *beshert* soon.'

'I'm sure when he does, she'll be someone special.'

Miri felt a tap on her shoulder. It was Raizy, itching to talk to her. Then she noticed Devorah and hugged her. 'Thanks so much for coming. I appreciate it. I can imagine it's been a difficult few days for you.'

'It hasn't been easy. But borich Hashem I have a wonderful

family and we have supported one another.'

Raizy pressed two pieces of the smashed plate into Devorah's hand. 'Im yirtze Hashem may both you and your brother find a shidduch soon.'

'*Omein*. I treasure your friendship, both of you. And I hope we'll always be able to celebrate *simches* together. I must apologise that I have to leave so soon. I promised my mother I would go back to watch the baby so she could also come and wish you mazel tov. I'll try to speak to you during the week.'

As soon as Devorah left, Raizy probed once more. 'Well?'

Miri lowered her gaze. 'It's Ben,' she whispered. 'I've been meeting up with him.'

'What? B–!' Raizy shrieked.

'Shh!' Miri glanced around to find that several people were giving them curious stares.

Raizy continued in an undertone. 'How did this happen?'

'Raizele!' Mrs Baum patted Raizy's shoulder affectionately, leaning heavily on her walking stick with the other. The kindly woman must have been over eighty by now, but her short wig was still jet-black. Only her eyebrows and wrinkles gave her away.

Mrs Baum was everyone's favourite 'aunty', a woman who had suffered a great deal of tragedy. Her whole family, including her young husband and child, had been murdered in the Holocaust. Despite her personal circumstances, she was never without a smile or a kind word to say to everyone, and she spent her days volunteering for charitable causes in the area.

'Such a fine *kallah maidele* you have become. Such *naches* for your dear parents. I remember when you were born.'

Raizy clasped Mrs Baum's hand in hers. 'Thank you for coming.'

Miri wandered over to the swan display, wanting to sample some exotic fruits, only to find her mother and Mrs Finer already there, engaged in conversation. She did an about-turn.

'I didn't know you had kept in touch with him.' Raizy sidled up to her. 'Why didn't you tell me?'

'I'm sorry. There wasn't an opportunity. I met him by chance last Thursday, the day of your shidduch, and he asked me if I would like to go out with him that evening. So I had to invent a friend from sem who was visiting.'

'Then you went out with him again on *moitzei Shabbes* and told your mother you were babysitting on my behalf?'

Miri was contrite. 'Yes.'

'Listen, I don't mind if you want to use me as an alibi, but for goodness' sake, will you please warn me first? I didn't realise what you were up to and almost got you in trouble.'

'You're right. I'm sorry.'

'Raizy!' Hinda squealed. 'I can't believe it. You're getting married!' Their former classmate gave Raizy an air kiss on both cheeks. 'Miri, what do you say to your best friend becoming a kallah?'

Hinda, who had married over the summer, was coiffed to perfection in a custom-made wig. She wore a fitted, cream suit with a daring, shorter skirt that skimmed her knees and she tottered on six-inch heels. Although they were the same age, she appeared the epitome of a sophisticated married woman.

Raizy and Miri had never been close with Hinda. She was the type who strived to outdo everyone and was friendly when it proved beneficial to her.

'It's lovely,' Miri said.

'I bet you'll be next.'

Miri didn't answer. She had no desire to swap places with Raizy. Instead, she savoured her little secret.

'Raizy, when's your chasseneh?' Hinda asked.

'My parents are still trying to book a hall. We're hoping either the end of January or early February.'

'Wow, that's so soon, about three months away. Are you going to have your dress made?'

'I'm not sure, we haven't decided.'

'Have you got your ring?'

'No, not yet. I'm having it made.'

'So was mine.' She flashed her ring at them. 'It's two carat.'

Raizy and Miri pretended to study it, though they had seen it before.

'Oh, there's Baila with her new baby. Look how thin she is already.' Hinda sauntered over to her without giving Raizy or Miri another glance.

Raizy nudged Miri and they laughed.

'You like him a lot, don't you?'

Miri felt a tingle travel down her spine.

'Has he kissed you?' Her eyes sparkled with mischief, the old Raizy revealing herself again.

Miri looked mortified. 'No!'

'Have you held hands?'

Miri's cheeks burned.

'I knew it!' Raizy smiled in satisfaction. 'Just don't get in too deep. You know what I'm saying? But hey, enjoy yourself, I suppose. While it lasts.'

Raizy's mother stepped in with a shy girl in her early teens.

'Raizy, this is Chavele, Naftoli's first cousin. She's come down from Manchester.'

The girl stood beside Raizy's mother, head down, arms wrapped across her body and feet turned in. She said nothing.

'Hi, Chavele!' Raizy shocked the timid cousin with a hug. 'It's so nice to meet you.'

Miri caught sight of Yocheved, another close friend from school days. She was the one whose parents had a secret television in their room that they liked to watch when circumstances permitted.

'Hi, Miri. Long time no see. Don't you find it hard when a close friend gets engaged? It makes me nervous about whether my turn will come soon. Then I feel added pressure when people wish me that I should be next.'

'No, I'm fine, not stressing about it. I'm just happy for Raizy.'

'Really? Do you remember Shprintzy Schwartz from the year below us in school? I heard she got engaged last week.'

'That's nice.'

'And there are already nine people from our class who are engaged or married.'

'I'm sure it won't be long until someone suggests a shidduch for you too.'

'I hope so. I'm getting worried I might be left on the shelf.'

'Never! The best is yet to come for you.'

As the guests dwindled, Miri caught up with Raizy again. 'Did you invite Chaya?'

'No, she refuses to speak to me since that episode. I left her a message, but I doubt she'll come.'

'She wasn't seeing Daniel, you know.'

109

Raizy was taken aback. 'But I thought –'

'No. She wanted to go out with Moshe so asked Daniel if he could find out for her whether he was interested in her. That was all.'

'Oh.'

Miri detected a slight wistful note in her voice. She recognised her mistake at once. This had not been the right time to bring it up.

'It doesn't matter, anyway,' Miri added. 'Like you said, there was nothing serious in it. Borich Hashem, you have a special chosson who is everything you wanted. And you've got your chasseneh to look forward to.'

Raizy's face brightened at the reminder. 'Yes, it's so exciting. Can you believe I'm getting married? My mother has already booked so many appointments for me this week.'

Miri only hoped that Raizy was truly content with her choices.

All evening Miri had dreaded the possibility. She'd tried her best to avoid it. But the inevitable happened, and she was cornered.

'Miri, how nice that your best friend is engaged.' Mrs Finer smiled, but her eyes remained cold and fixed. 'Such a chosheve family they are too.'

'Yes, borich Hashem.'

'I don't suppose she'll have much time to go shopping in Kosher Basket anymore.'

'I'm sure she will be busy.' Miri tried to stop the shaking in her voice. 'There's a lot to plan before a chasseneh.'

'Well, im yirtze Hashem by you.'

Raizy found Miri hiding in the corner. 'What's the matter? You seem on edge.'

'I got accosted by Mrs Finer.'

'Not that *yachne* again. Now that her last child has left home, she has nothing to worry about, so she's hassling everyone else. She keeps going on and on about how her darling son, Pinny, is doing so well in yeshiva in *Eretz Yisroel*.'

'I'm worried Mrs Finer may be onto us.'

'What do you mean?'

'She made a remark that you won't have as much time to go to Kosher Basket anymore.'

'What?'

'Also, I haven't yet told you what happened when I first met Ben on Thursday morning. I was walking on the high street on my way to work and he was in the car on his way to university when he stopped to talk. And just then Mrs Finer came by.'

'Oh, my gosh! Are you crazy, talking to him in the middle of Stamford Hill. What did you do?'

'I pretended I didn't know him. I made out he was a stranger who had stopped to ask for directions.'

'That was quick thinking.'

Except afterwards she caught up with me. She made a comment about how I should be careful who I spoke to and warned me about who I mix with. Then she mentioned Devorah, saying she wasn't a good influence with, in her words, "a brother like that."'

'I bet she's the one behind those odd rumours!'

'The thought crossed my mind.'

'I hope she doesn't cause trouble for me. It's the last thing I need right now. And you had better be careful too. If word gets out about what you've been doing, it will ruin your shidduch chances.'

111

Raizy glanced across the room to where Naftoli stood trying to catch her eye, and she forced a dazzling smile.

Chapter 11

'I can make it tonight,' Miri said.

'Great!' Ben's delight was unmistakable. 'What time and where?'

'Only from eight. I need to sort out the laundry and do the ironing for my mother first.'

'No problem. Shall I meet you at the usual place?'

'That would be perfect.'

'Dress warm.'

'Why, where are we going?'

'It's a surprise. All I'll say is that it's outdoors, so it will be cold.'

Miri returned to work after her lunch break. Even the tedious paperwork Mr Reich had piled on her desk was a less daunting prospect now that she had an evening out to look forward to.

As promised, Ben was already waiting in the car when she arrived. He was bundled in a thick, grey, ribbed jumper and a black, puffy jacket.

'Hi!' He gave her hand a light squeeze as they drove off, sending a charge through her. 'How was the engagement party?'

'It was nice. I saw a few friends. But it's still kind of strange that Raizy is engaged.'

'So what is her fiancé like? Did you speak to him?'

Miri looked aghast. 'No! Of course not.'

Then she noticed his teasing smile and laughed.

'Somehow, I didn't think so,' he said.

Then she grew serious. 'Mrs Finer spoke to me, though.'

'Who's she?'

'Do you remember that woman who gave you directions the day we met when I was on my way to work?'

'Oh yeah, her. She's rather intimidating.'

'You can say that again. She remarked Raizy would no longer have time to go to Kosher Basket.'

'That's an odd comment.'

'I think she was referring to how Raizy visited Daniel there. I don't know how much she knows, but she seems to have her eyes everywhere. That day we met, she gave me a warning about being careful who I speak to, and mentioned Devorah, another of my friends, saying she's a bad influence.'

'What's it her business who you hang around with?'

'It isn't.'

'Then why let it bother you what she thinks?'

'Because I'm worried about her spreading rumours that could damage my reputation and those of my friends. Or worse, for my parents to find out.'

'That's well out of order. What have you ever done to her?'

'Nothing I can think of.'

'I wish I could tell you to ignore her and not care about other people's opinions. But I understand it's not that simple. My guess, though, is that she should first get her own house in order before worrying about everyone else.'

'What do you mean?'

'There must be something in her own life that she's not comfortable with.'

'I'm not aware of anything.'

'People often find faults with others when they share a similar character weakness, and that's the reason it bothers them.' Almost as an afterthought, he added, 'I heard it at a shiur once.' Miri looked at him with renewed admiration.

'I hope Raizy is happy.'

'It sounds like you don't think she is.'

'Well, yesterday evening, I made the mistake of telling her the truth about the misunderstanding with Daniel and Chaya. I realised straight afterwards I shouldn't have. She seemed surprised. I pray she is doing the right thing and her reasons are genuine. I'm torn between whether to discuss it with her.'

'Being realistic, was there ever a chance of something serious developing between her and Daniel?'

'No, I doubt it. She always knew she would go for a shidduch of her parents' choice.'

'Then she has made her decision. It's not surprising she has the jitters when she hardly knows her fiancé. But this is how she intended to find a husband. If not this guy, it would have been a similar story with another. And you mentioned he's from a prestigious family, so hopefully everything will work out fine. It might be better not to raise the subject again. But if she brings it up, be there for her as a friend. Support her. Whatever she chooses. It's her future, and she needs to commit to it.'

'I think you're right. Thanks for your advice.'

'Sure.'

'I really appreciate it.'

'Pleasure. I didn't do much.'

'You did. You listened to me.' Her voice trembled and the unexpected wave of emotion took her by surprise.

'Anytime. I'm here for you whenever you want to talk. OK?'

She nodded in reply.

They left the main road and were now driving up an incline. Ben turned up the volume on the stereo. An ambient piece was playing. Its synthesised, cosmic sounds echoed the clear, star-filled sky and the soaring melody rose in octaves the higher they ascended.

'That's lovely music,' Miri said. 'What is it?'

'It's a chill-out compilation from Ibiza.'

'Who's Ibiza?'

Ben looked amused but didn't belittle her lack of knowledge. He never did. 'A place, an island off the coast of Spain, famous for its clubs. People go there for holidays to dance and party. There's a well-known café by the beach where a DJ plays music like this while people sit and drink, watching the sunset over the Mediterranean.'

'And a DJ is …?'

'Ah, right. That's someone who arranges and mixes the music.'

'That place sounds beautiful. Have you ever been?'

'No. I'm not so into that dance club scene. But I like the music.'

'I do too.'

As they neared the top of the hill, Miri could see that ahead was a palatial building with broad, arched windows. Ben pulled up into a parking space. 'Isn't this Alexandra Palace?' she asked.

'That's right.'

'I came here with my family a few times as a child. We went to the park and boating on the lake. Why are we here?'

'There's something I want to show you.'

He took her hand as they climbed the stairs to reach the highest point, their breath forming clouds of vapour in the still air. The only audible sounds were their footsteps and the occasional vehicle passing by on the road below. At the summit was an observation terrace. Ben pointed ahead. 'Look over there.'

Miri gasped. Spread out before them was a sweeping panorama of London, lit up under the night sky. 'It's breathtaking!'

Ben's smile was wide. 'Isn't it awesome?'

She pointed to a tall tower in the distance with a triangular point and flashing light on it. 'Isn't that Canary Wharf?'

'Yes, it is.'

Then she caught sight of a small wheel glowing on the horizon. 'And that's the London Eye?'

'Uh-huh.'

'It's an incredible structure, designed by a husband and wife architect duo.'

'Really? I never knew.'

'Yes, they drew the first designs at their kitchen table. The project took about six years to complete and it involved around one thousand seven hundred people.'

Ben looked at her in wonder. 'How do you know all that?'

She shrugged. 'I once saw a TV program about it. I watched it in secret at my friend's house.' She gazed out over the skyline. 'This must be the same view you'd see from an aeroplane.'

'You've never been on a plane?'

'No. I haven't travelled outside England. My passport is unused. I've never been on a proper holiday. Well, except for Bournemouth, Manchester and Gateshead.'

'They count too.' He paused in thought. 'Miri, are you free tomorrow?'

'No, sorry. I meant to tell you. My mother has to pay a shiva visit tomorrow evening so I have to babysit.'

'How about Wednesday?'

'That should be fine.' She tipped her head towards her shoulder as if embarrassed to tell him. 'Actually, Wednesday is my birthday.'

'Are you serious? Then we must do something extra special to celebrate. Let's spend the entire day together!'

Miri considered his suggestion. 'I'd like to. But I have to be at work.'

'Take a day's holiday. Or call in sick.'

'Don't you have university?'

'I'll skip lectures for a day, too. What do you say?'

His ebullience was infectious.

'I guess I could as a one-off ... OK.'

'Brilliant! I'll plan something special for you,' he said. 'But now, do you fancy a hot drink?'

Miri took one more lingering look at the magnificent view. 'It's so amazing.' She faced him, eyes glowing with happiness. 'Thank you for bringing me here.'

'You're amazing,' he whispered.

Then he drew her towards him and wrapped his arms around her in a gentle hug. Cautiously, she placed her arms around him and rested her head on his shoulder. Held in the warmth of his embrace, she had never felt as cared for in her life or realised she could feel this way towards another person.

The small voice of her conscience told her this should be wrong. But it felt so right.

Chapter 12

'What's happened, you're at home?' Raizy teased on the other end of the telephone.

Miri sighed. 'Yes. I'm babysitting. My mother's gone to the Berger shiva.'

'You sound thrilled.'

'Yes, well ...'

'Boy, you've got it bad.'

'What do you mean?'

'Don't pretend you don't understand what I'm talking about. You know.' Miri smiled to herself at the hint of a mention of Ben but didn't reply. 'Since you're home for the evening, can I come over? I fancy a chat.'

Raizy rested against the kitchen counter and fiddled with her hair, uncharacteristically quiet as she watched Miri prepare two mugs of tea.

The rattle of a key in the lock caught Miri's attention. She set down the sugar bowl and left the kitchen to investigate.

'Ruchi, what are you doing back so soon? I thought you were babysitting.'

'I was, but the baby wouldn't settle so they sent me home.'

'Oh.'

It wouldn't have been too late to meet Ben after all. Then she glanced at Raizy, whose restless demeanour told her she hadn't come for small talk. Miri brushed aside the fleeting regret. Tomorrow, she would have the entire day to spend with Ben, but right now her best friend needed her. Except, Ruchi hovered in the doorway, making a private conversation impossible.

'Don't you have homework to do?' Miri said.

'I did most before I left.'

'You should finish the rest.'

'I can do it later.'

'Please do it straight away.'

'Can't I sit with you and Raizy?'

'No.'

Ruchi screwed up her freckled nose and scowled at Miri, but showed no intention of leaving.

Miri gave her a firm glare. 'Go!'

'You're such a pain!' Ruchi stomped up to her room.

The kettle clicked off, and she poured boiling water into the mugs. Miri raised hers. 'To younger sisters,' she said before making a quick blessing and taking a sip. 'Shall we sit in the lounge or stay here?'

'Here's fine.' Raizy said.

Miri placed their drinks on the table and sat down. Raizy took a seat opposite and hugged the mug in her hands.

'How are the wedding preparations going?'

Raizy forced a smile. 'Fantastic.'

'Have you got your ring yet?'

'We're organising that on Thursday.'

'And what about your dress?'

121

'We've decided I'm having it made. I spoke to the dress-maker this afternoon and we are meeting next Monday.'

'That's exciting.'

They both took a sip of their drinks.

'Miri ...?'

'Yes.'

'I'm a little nervous. I hope I'm making the right choice. Do you think I am?'

Miri rested her chin on her hand. Remembering Ben's advice, she considered her words with care. She reminded herself this was about Raizy, not her personal thoughts. 'It's not for me to say. This has to be your decision.'

'But what do you think?'

'I don't know. I'm not in your position and I've never spoken to your chosson. Do you like him?'

'Yes, I do. We seemed to click when we spoke. Our families are similar. We have a lot in common.'

'Do you feel ready to get married?'

'I think so.'

'So what's bothering you?'

'Maybe it's –' Raizy twisted one of her pearl engagement earrings. 'To tell you the truth, I'm envious of you.'

'Why?'

'You're off seeing Ben the whole time and enjoying yourself while I'm now engaged, but I can't see Naftoli until the wedding.'

This was a concern that had long preyed on Miri's mind. 'Didn't you realise this was how it would be?'

'Yes, but I didn't expect it would be this difficult. I wish they allowed us to speak more, so I could get to know him better before we get married. We're only meant to talk about once a month. And although I can speak to my future mother-in-law and pass on messages, it's not the same at all.'

Miri patted Raizy's arm. 'I can understand that.'

'If only it didn't have to be this way.'

'I imagine it's not something you could even bring up with your mother.'

'As a matter of fact, I did.'

'Really? I don't think I could with mine.'

'My mother doesn't get that shocked about matters like this. Obviously, I'd never tell her about stuff I did before I got engaged. That's different. But she's got a lot of experience with engagements. She's been through it several times before with my older siblings.'

'What did she say?'

'My mother understood how I felt but told me it's not the done thing. She explained that by limiting our conversations we make each one far more meaningful and adds to the anticipation of the wedding. She may be right, but I'm finding it hard enough we can't see each other, never mind not speak. There are things I'd like to discuss with him, questions I'd like to ask, and because I can't, I have all kinds of doubts and worries. I asked my mother whether she'd be prepared to speak to his parents and see what they say about us being able to speak more often, but she's not willing to raise it with them. Perhaps she doesn't want to add any complications and jeopardise the shidduch.'

'I doubt they would call off an engagement over something that minor.'

'I'm not so sure. Look at what happened to Devorah's brother, Tuli.'

'We don't know the real reason for that, but this is not the same situation at all.'

'Either way, if my mother won't discuss it with his parents, I'm stuck.'

'No, you're not. When will you next be speaking to Naftoli?'

'On Sunday night.'

'Then you discuss it with him.'

Raizy's sat upright. 'Me?'

'Yes, you. If you're planning to spend your life with Naftoli, you need to be comfortable talking to him about the issues that matter to you. This is for the two of you to decide. No one else.'

'But even if he agrees …' Raizy rested her chin on her hand. 'How can we speak more often without his parents, or mine, finding out?'

'You're resourceful. You'll figure out a way.'

'Thank you for listening, and for all your advice.' Her dark moment had passed. 'I sketched some ideas for my wedding dress this afternoon. Would you like to see them?'

'I'd love to.'

Raizy was pulling the drawings out of her bag when the chime of the doorbell interrupted them.

Miri went to answer it, only to return seconds later. 'Just someone delivering a package for my mother. Let's see your sketches.'

But Raizy seemed to have forgotten about them. 'Miri, what are you going to do when it's time to end it?'

Miri stared into the depths of her tea as if the answer lay there.

The vibrations from a heavy bass beat startled them. And the sound of a deep male voice rapping over the rhythm in a language that sounded like Hebrew reverberated through the house.

'What the –?'

Miri shot up the stairs like an arrow before Raizy could finish her question.

The music came to an abrupt end, and there followed the muffled sounds of a heated argument. When Miri reappeared, she looked shamefaced with a stack of CDs in her hand.

'What on earth was that?'

'Subliminal,' she mumbled.

'Who, or what is Subliminal?'

'Israeli hip hop.'

Raizy gave her a playful nudge. 'I don't suppose I need to guess where that came from?'

'Ben lent me a few of his CDs.' She fanned out the selection. 'Subliminal, Eyal Golan, an Ibiza chill-out compilation. I had them hidden under my bed, but Ruchi's been going through my stuff.'

'No clue what any of that means. All I can say is someone has been influencing your music taste.'

They regarded one another, neither able to hold a straight face. Raizy snorted with laughter.

'Not quite Chassidish music, is it?'

Miri shook her head, unable to speak for her giggles, and wiped the tears from her eyes.

The click of a key turning in the lock sobered them at once. Miri froze, still holding the CDs. Her eyes darted about.

'Quick! Give them to me.'

Miri thrust them at Raizy who stuffed them in her bag right before Miri's mother walked in.

'Hi, Miri. Hello, Raizy. How are your chasseneh preparations going?'

Raizy affected a demure smile. 'Borich Hashem, everything is going well, thank you.'

'How is your mother?'

'Borich Hashem, she is well too. Very busy right now.'

'I'm sure. Please send her my best.'

Ruchi thundered down the stairs. 'Mameh! Miri's got CDs of *goyishe* music.'

Mrs Fogel fixed a glare on her daughter. 'Miri, is this true?'

Miri hesitated. 'I – I have no clue what she's talking about.'

'It's true, I saw them.'

Mrs Fogel faced her again. 'Miri?'

'I haven't got CDs like that.'

'Yes, you do.' She turned to her mother. 'They were under her bed.'

Mrs Fogel's eyes passed between her daughters, weighing up the validity of their stories. 'Ruchi, please bring them to me.'

'I can't. She took them.'

Miri held up her hands. 'I haven't taken anything.'

'You must have hidden them,' Ruchi said, her credibility ebbing away.

'If they were under my bed like you say they were, how could I hide them when I was sitting downstairs with Raizy?'

'Yes, I've been here the whole time,' said Raizy.

'Anyway, who gave you permission to go through my stuff?' Miri said.

Ruchi wasn't surrendering without a fight. 'She's also got a CD of Jewish music that sounds like what you hear booming out of those cars with tinted windows.'

Mrs Fogel looked exasperated. 'Now you are talking nonsense. There's no *Yiddishe* music that sounds like that.'

Defeated, Ruchi glowered. Miri shrugged her innocence. And as soon as her mother turned her back, she gave Ruchi an impish wink.

Chapter 13

Miri stepped off the bus at Manor House station. And her stomach fluttered to catch sight of Ben. He was leaning against the car door, hands inside his jacket pockets, eyes lowered. His face broke into a wide smile as he spotted her and strode across. '

'Happy birthday!' he said, giving her a hug.

She decided her nineteenth was already her best birthday ever.

'You'll never guess who I saw getting off the bus before yours.'

'Tell me.'

'Mrs Finer.'

'No, you're joking.'

'I'm serious. She keeps turning up like a bad penny, doesn't she?' He looked amused.

'Are you sure?'

'Yeah. She had her shopping bags in hand and marched down into the station.'

'Did she see you?'

'Nah. I pretended to be checking the car tyres. I doubt she recognised me.'

His comment triggered a Pavlovian response and Miri's

eyes darted around. 'Is she still about?'

'Relax, she's long gone. Don't worry about her. Today, just enjoy yourself. I've planned something special for your birthday. We're going on "holiday" for the day, right here in the city. But first, have you eaten breakfast?'

'Not yet. I was in too much of a rush to leave the house earlier so I could call work and make my excuses.'

'All sorted?'

'Yes.'

It gave her a kick to be skipping work. Miri hadn't done anything like this since bunking school for the day with Raizy. Thankfully, this time, she'd evaded Mrs Finer.

They returned to the same café on Brent Street, which this time enticed them with the delicious scents of brewing coffee and fresh-baked croissants. She'd never been out for breakfast, and spending a leisurely morning with Ben, on what should have been an ordinary workday, made the experience more precious still.

From there, they took the tube into the centre and wandered around Covent Garden. It wasn't hard to slip into holiday mode as they milled with the other tourists. They stopped to enjoy a string quartet in the piazza, and further along, under the colonnade, joined a crowd to watch a street performer who juggled three skittles while balancing on a unicycle three metres high.

Miri soaked up the atmosphere, relishing these new experiences, sharing them with Ben, talking and laughing together. She had never felt so content. They browsed the old-fashioned stalls selling handmade art and design, as well as the little boutique stores, and she studied the architectural details of the building's structure. Her eyes followed the contours of the wrought-iron support arch under the glazed roof. Beams of sunlight filtered through the glass onto the piazza below.

'Thinking about drawing it?' Ben said.

'How did you know?'

'I figured.'

She was surprised at how well he had read her thoughts.

'By the way, how are you enjoying the CDs I lent you?' he asked.

'I like them a lot. I've been listening to them whenever I have the chance – when no one is around, or with headphones while my sisters are asleep. But last night—'

'What happened?'

'My fourteen-year-old sister, Ruchi, found them under my bed and played Subliminal at full blast.' She rolled her eyes for comic effect.

'Oh no!' Ben looked like he was fighting to hold a serious expression.

'It gets worse. I ran up to get them. Then, my mother arrived while I was still holding them. Luckily, Raizy was with me and she hid them in her bag. Except, Ruchi came running in and blabbed I had Jewish music that sounded like the stuff people blare out of those cars with tinted windows.'

'What did your mother say?'

'She said, "No Yiddishe music sounds like that." I denied all knowledge of the CDs. Thanks to Raizy, my mother was convinced Ruchi had made it up.'

Ben could no longer contain himself. 'Sorry, I shouldn't laugh. It must have been awkward, what with your younger sister putting on Subliminal. Oof.' He winced.

Miri nodded in agreement as she recalled some of the more obscene lyrics in English.

'It was hilarious. All the same, I wish I didn't always have to creep around and hide stuff. It's even more challenging when you have a nosy sister who rummages through your things. I'm constantly making excuses and I hate feeling guilty.'

'Yeah, I can imagine that's tough. Are you the oldest in your family?'

'No, I have an older sister, Pessie, who's twenty. But she's married with a baby and lives in Manchester. I'm next. Below me, I have two brothers, Duvid and Efraim. Then there's Ruchi. After her comes Bruchi, Lozi, Yossi, Chaim and Eli, the baby who's fifteen months.'

'Wow! So that's ... how many in total?'

'Ten of us.'

'Your mum must always be busy.'

'She is. And if she's not occupied with the younger children or doing housework, then she is helping people in the community. She organises food rotas, cooks for new mothers, those sitting shiva or who are unwell.'

'My mum does something similar in our community. She makes and delivers meals for those in need.'

'Really?'

'Yeah.'

The similitude delighted her.

'Miri, what would have happened if your mum had caught you with the CDs. Would it have been so terrible?'

'Yes, it would.'

'She wouldn't be sympathetic if you talked it over with her?'

'No. I can't speak to her about things like that. I've tried before but it didn't work out too well.' The last disastrous attempt was still fresh in her mind. 'She can never find out about the CDs. Or where they came from.'

'What about your father? Do you find it easier to speak to him?'

'No, it's even more difficult with him. He's ... distant. I think he has a better connection with my brothers. I suppose because they're boys and he can discuss Torah learning with them. While with me, he'll sometimes ask how I'm doing or how work is going, but that's about it. We have little to say to each other.'

Ben took her hand as they walked between the stalls.

Miri envied Ben's upbringing. From the few details he had mentioned, his home life seemed way more carefree, almost idyllic. Though it occurred to her, she knew little about his family.

'How many siblings do you have?' she said.

'There are four ... I mean, three of us. My brother Davidi is twenty-six. He lives in Israel and is getting married next month. Then there's me, followed by my sister Natalie, who's eighteen. She's in Israel for the year too, studying in sem.'

The revelation of his sister being in sem, like she had been, was something she never would have expected. Perhaps their families had more in common than Miri realised.

'What are your parents like?'

'What?' Ben appeared distracted. 'Oh, they're great. My mum is thoughtful, loving, and always fussing about us all. My dad is hardworking and devoted. But ... shall we go for a walk by the River Thames next?'

'That sounds nice.'

Something wasn't right. Miri could sense it. He had been on the verge of saying more, but then changed the subject. What just happened?

They walked across Waterloo Bridge which granted them a

magnificent view of some of London's most iconic landmarks. It was one of those rare, halcyon November days with a cloudless, blue sky, the afternoon sunlight casting shimmers on the water. But rather than admiring the sights, Miri focused her attention on Ben. He had become so withdrawn in the last few minutes and stared vacantly into the distance. It made her anxious. Had she said something inappropriate? Was he angry with her, or just deep in thought? She wished she could read his thoughts as well as he seemed to be able to read hers.

On the South Bank, they followed the path beside the river. He still hadn't said a word.

'Ben?' she said. 'Are you upset with me?'

He stopped walking and faced her. 'No, of course not.' His tone was gentle, sincere, but she saw that same haunting look in his eyes she'd noticed the first time they'd met.

'I hope I didn't say anything wrong.'

'No. It's nothing you said.'

'But something is troubling you.'

'Yeah.' His face had taken on a pained expression.

'Do you want to talk about it? I mean, you don't have to if you don't want to. But if you do. I'm here. I'll listen.'

'There is something,' he said. 'I've been meaning to tell you. It's just … kind of hard for me to talk about. I tend not to discuss it. But I want you to know.'

He exhaled deeply. 'You asked me earlier about my family. There used to be four of us.'

An icy shiver ran through Miri.

'My brother Natan. He was fifteen months older than me. We were very close.' He gave a wan smile. 'Natan was everything you could wish for in a brother. Kind, caring, always smiling. Smart. He dreamt of becoming a doctor. He had a wicked sense of humour and was a brilliant mimic. Shabbat meals with the family were the best. He'd have us all in stitches.'

Ben's eyes were distant as if he was elsewhere. 'He looked out for me. When I got bullied in school, he was the one who taught me how to stand up for myself.'

'How come you were bullied?'

He shrugged. 'It happened when I started high school. Some kids can be unkind if they consider you different. And they could tell I was. My features, my skin tone. It was written on my face. There were differences in my upbringing, my interests, customs, the way I prayed. While it didn't matter to most of my classmates who were friendly towards me, a few singled me out for ridicule. I guess they regarded me as strange, or my heritage as less authentic. There were times I got embarrassed about my background and wished I could be the same as everyone else.

'When Natan found out about the bullying, he faced down those kids. He had charisma, never needed to resort to physical violence. He taught me not to cower and to remain proud of who and what I was. The bullying stopped after that.'

'He must have been such a special person.'

'He was. It was impossible not to love him. We were inseparable as kids. As teenagers, we always hung out. There was a group of us, siblings, cousins, friends, including Daniel and Moshe. We had great times together. We'd go out for the evening … Although, like I told you, I'm not into clubbing now, I once was, for a time. You know, with the others.' He stopped to check her reaction. 'I hope you don't think less of me.'

His honesty endeared Miri. She was touched that her opinion even mattered to him. 'No, I don't. Not at all.'

He nodded, reassured. 'Natan grew more serious towards the end of high school and opted to spend his gap year studying in a yeshiva in Israel. Encouraged by him, I did the same. He loved being in Israel and chose to stay. I too considered the idea but then returned to London to complete my studies. My intention was to go back after I finished university, like Davidi, my older brother. There are times I wonder if I should have remained there. I'm not sure ...' He folded his arms across his body and bent his head. 'Natan enlisted in the army and became a paramedic. He only had a few months left until he finished his national service. He was planning to study medicine afterwards and become a doctor ...' His voice cracked. 'I'm sorry.'

Ben turned away and grasped the railing that ran alongside the river, his hands paling under the strain. Miri stood beside him and waited. He seemed to have retreated into a dark place inside of himself, his eyes shut tight. Heavy minutes ticked past. Perhaps five minutes or so, but it felt far longer. Held in limbo, frozen in that state, she didn't know how to navigate the void that now separated them. A pleasure boat sailed past. The waves of music and laughter in its wake pierced the strained silence.

She reached out her hand, hesitated, pulled away, then reached out again and placed her hand over his. 'It's OK.'

The tension in his hands released. He turned to her. His eyes were red. 'A little over a year ago, on a Thursday morning, Natan called to say hi. He mentioned he was unsure whether he'd get leave that Shabbat or have to remain on base. We spoke about his recent visit to London over Sukkot, a few weeks before that, and how nice it had been spending time together again as a family. "I miss you," Natan said, and I reminded him I'd soon see him over the winter holiday. "I can't wait. Don't forget that I love you, bro," was his reply. That was the last conversation we ever had …'

Miri took his hands in hers. 'Natan got leave for the weekend. But we only found that out later. That evening, he went to a café in Jerusalem with a few friends for a night out. He wasn't even on active duty.'

He shook his head as if he couldn't believe it. Didn't want to believe it. His shoulders slumped, and he grasped her hands as if she was an anchor and all that held him from sinking. 'While they were sitting there … a terrorist … a suicide bomber burst in. He blew himself up, in that café. Back in London, we were sitting at home, in the kitchen, and heard on the radio the awful news that there had been a suicide bombing at a café in Jerusalem, killing at least ten and injuring many others. We didn't yet make any connection or realise he'd been there when it happened …'

Ben tipped his head upwards, breath trembling as his raw tears flowed. 'And then … we got a call telling us … Natan had been there. In that café … Oh God …!'

Miri placed her arms around him. He pulled her close.

'My brother's dead.' He let out a low, heart-rending moan. 'Oh God! Natan is gone. He's gone.'

She held him tight as his body racked with sobs. Silent tears rolled down her cheeks.

It was as if a dam had broken within him. All the memories

he had tried to suppress overran his thoughts.

Ben had been the one to take the call and break the news to his family about Natan. As his parents and sister fell apart, he had tried to keep a level head to support them and make the arrangements. Hours later, they were on a night flight. He hardly noticed landing for their rush to the funeral. Together with his father and Davidi, he recited kaddish for the first time, with news cameras focused on them. None of it seemed real. He was too shocked to cry.

He went through the ritual of sitting shiva. But it was as if he was observing himself from the outside. He couldn't believe he was sitting there, with his family, mourning for his brother, watching their lives unravel.

Then he met Yael.

She was a close friend of Keren, his brother Davidi's girlfriend, and she'd come along to pay them a shiva visit.

Yael had been a way to forget.

They started going out. There were parties, drinking. For a short period, the alcohol worked to dull his emotions. But he got tired of pretending.

He tried to confide in her – an attempt to deal with what had happened – but she brushed him off. She told him he shouldn't dwell on it, but try to move on and focus on more positive things. So he never brought it up again.

When his family returned to London, he continued to comfort them as they struggled to come to terms with their loss. But he didn't want to burden them with his own pain, so pretended he was coping. He was fine. Whenever his mother or his father brought it up, he evaded the subject. No, he didn't need to speak to anyone or get outside help. He was fine.

For several months, he travelled back and forth, picking up where he left off with Yael each time. But he couldn't find contentment or fill the emptiness. Their relationship was based on having fun. In-depth conversations were rare. And he realised when the distance separated them, they would drift apart. Until the next visit.

When Davidi and Keren got engaged six months later, it prompted Ben to consider his own relationship with Yael. He attempted to salvage what he had with her, but they both realised they didn't have enough in common for a long-term future together and split on amicable terms. She soon found someone else. It didn't bother him.

And though friends were aware of what he had been through, they tried not to raise the subject. Perhaps they were uncomfortable because they weren't sure what to say. Or else they assumed he preferred not to speak about it. Maybe that was true. Like a vicious circle. The longer he bottled it up, the harder it became to talk about.

None of them had any idea about the melancholic thoughts that haunted him every day. That he could barely utter his brother's name or acknowledge the truth.

Until now.

Natan was gone. The loss was searing. Grief poured from his eyes, pain escaped from his throat. He would never see his brother again.

He found himself in Miri's arms. For how long had he cried? She continued to hug him, saying nothing.

Drained of energy, he staggered to the stone bench behind them and collapsed onto the seat. She sat beside him, holding his hand, and as they watched the undulating currents of the Thames, his breathing evened, and a calmness descended that he hadn't experienced for a long time. An acceptance.

He had consoled his parents and siblings. Now Miri was doing the same for him. She had given him the space – a space he didn't realise he had needed – to mourn.

He withdrew his wallet, pulled out a photo and passed it to her. She studied the picture of Natan in uniform, leaning against a truck, and smiled. 'I can see the resemblance.'

'They told us he was probably killed instantly. That he didn't suffer. At least that ...'

Her eyes met his. 'Ben, no one can ever take away your memories and the good times you shared. Or his love. All that he gave you will stay with you forever. Natan will never stop being your brother. It's natural to be sad and miss him. And whenever you need to talk, I'll be here for you. I'll always listen.'

Overcome with a fresh wave of emotions, he nodded and hugged her towards him. He couldn't comprehend how he'd been able to hold it in for all this time with no one to turn to.

Until now.

With Miri.

A girl he'd only known for a few weeks.

But she 'got' him.

The peal of bells from Big Ben attracted their attention. He checked his watch as four chimes rang out.

'Oh!' I lost track of the time. We'll be late.' He sprang up. 'For what?'

'A surprise.' He became awkward. 'And I'm sorry about ... I mean, it's your birthday and everything.'

'No, this was more important. Please don't apologise.'

'Thank you.' The words sounded so small and didn't convey what he wanted to express. He kissed her lightly on the forehead.

They continued along the path they had started. He felt ... alive. For months he had drifted from one day to the next, going through the motions, doing what was necessary. He'd eat, sleep, study. Sometimes, he forced himself to socialise. Plaster on a smile. But inside, he had been numb, carrying a constant heaviness.

Since meeting Miri, something within him had changed. He had begun to smile more. Even laugh. He enjoyed being with her. And it was strange, but sometimes, when they were apart, he missed her. He'd let her in, more than he ever had with any of his closest friends; even his family. With her, he felt he could be himself, no need to pretend. He had allowed her to see him at his most vulnerable. But instead of feeling exposed, he found it had strengthened him.

The iconic wheel, the London Eye, materialised ahead of them. 'Wow! I didn't realise how big it is up close,' said Miri.

'Would you like to check out the view from the inside?'

'You mean, ride on the wheel?'

'Yeah.'

'I'd love to!'

Her face shone and he basked in its reflection.

The timing was perfect as they entered a pod, with the sun setting. Miri looked in awe at the sights from above. From Tower Bridge, the river looked like a ribbon of molten gold flowing towards Big Ben and the Houses of Parliament. And he watched her in wonderment.

Ben knew he'd never stop missing his brother. There would always be a sense of loss. But she had come into his life. Unexpected. And she was filling the cracks in his heart.

'What do you think?' Miri's voice penetrated his thoughts.

'Er ... yes?'

She looked at him with concern. 'Ben?' He hadn't noticed the golden flecks in her eyes before. They were the same shade as the sunset. 'Are you OK?' He sensed the light touch of her hand on his arm through the fabric of his thick jacket.

Ben smiled. 'Yeah, I'm fine. Tell me more about what we can see down there.' He observed the expression of pure joy on her face as she pointed out the OXO Tower and Buckingham Palace to him.

It was twilight when the ride ended and the lights had come on across the city. They strolled back along the pathway. The tide lapped against the shore, and even the brutalist architecture of the South Bank appeared enchanting. She was speaking about all they had seen. He listened, smiled and responded, taking pleasure from her enthusiasm. But he knew afterwards, he wouldn't be able to recall much of their conversation.

They reached the Millennium Bridge, its illuminated steel suspensions stretched across the river. 'Isn't this the one they called the wobbly bridge?' Miri asked.

'Yeah, that's right. I'm sure it's stable now, though. Shall we try it?'

Ben was unsteady on his feet, even though the bridge was firm. They stopped halfway to admire the view and he shivered as he watched her take in the cityscape silhouetted against a purple sky. He could no longer deny it.

'Miri,' he whispered. She met his gaze and his voice shook. 'I think ... I've fallen in love with you.'

She continued to stare into his eyes. 'I think I've fallen in love with you, too.'

Ben placed his arms around Miri, placed his lips on hers

and tenderly kissed her.

Miri shut her eyes for a second, reliving the scene on the bridge. When she opened them, Ben was smiling at her from across the table and he put his hand over hers. They'd returned to Hendon to retrieve his car and stopped at a restaurant for supper. Miri savoured this newfound serenity. It was as if a barrier had lifted between them and everything made sense.

'Can I invite you to come to us for lunch this Shabbat? My mum would love to meet you.'

'She knows about me?'

'Not too much. But she's figured I'm seeing someone and is rather curious.'

'I'd like to, but we don't go out on Shabbat. It would be difficult to make excuses and my parents would become suspicious straight away.'

'How about one night during the week?'

'That could work. How about Sunday evening?'

'Yeah, Sunday is great because my parents are going away to Israel the day after, for a quick visit, to sort out the last arrangements for Davidi's wedding. And also to visit my Savta who lives there. She isn't too well at the moment.'

'I'm sorry to hear that. I wish her a *refuah sheleima*.'

'Thanks. We worry for her. But *b'ezrat Hashem*, we hope she'll be well enough to attend the wedding.'

'When is it?'

'First week in December.'

'Oh.'

So he'd be leaving soon. Unbidden, Raizy's question came

back to her.

Ben inclined his head. 'Don't look so worried. I'll be away for less than two weeks and be back before you know it.'

She gave him a smile and buried it in the back of her mind. She had no answers. Better not to mull. Savour the moment. 'You must be looking forward.'

'I am. But it will also be emotional. The first wedding in our family, but the first celebration after … everything.'

'Do you often visit Israel?'

'Usually once or twice a year to see the family, sometimes more.'

'What is it like?'

'It's beautiful. Exciting, dynamic, crazy. Never boring. It's home. You discover the most amazing things in the most unexpected places. One day, you'll go too and see it for yourself. I think you'll love it.'

A young couple passed by on the way to their table. The woman wore a denim skirt and a blue cotton scarf which covered most of her blonde hair; her husband, a tanned complexion, and a close-shaved beard. He noticed Ben and stopped at their table.

'Ben! I don't believe it. How are you doing?'

'Jonny!' Ben stood up and the two clasped each other's hands and slapped each other on the back. 'Good to see you. How come you're here?'

'We came for a week to visit my parents.'

'I didn't hear you were coming.'

'It was all last minute. I had a few days' holiday due, and we found a cheap flight so thought we'd grab the opportunity. You've met my wife, Dafna?'

'Yes, but only briefly at your wedding. It's nice to meet you again.'

He turned to Miri. 'This is Jonny, a good friend of Davidi. We all grew up together. And this is his wife, Dafna.' She gave Miri a friendly smile. 'And this is Miri. My girlfriend.'

Miri glowed at her introduction.

'Nice to meet you,' they both said to her.

'Well, it was so great bumping into you guys like this. I might see you at shul on Shabbat. Otherwise, I guess at the wedding.'

'For sure.'

Ben waited until they were out of earshot. 'Now you must come to our home on Sunday and meet my parents before the whole community hears.'

'People gossip in your community too?'

He chuckled. 'They might be discreet and polite about it. But there are always some people who love to talk.'

They sat in the car, wanting to prolong their time together. They had rounded off their evening in a bar off Brick Lane, listening to chill-out music mixed by a DJ at the decks while lounging on a blue, velvet sofa and sipping mint tea. With his arm around her and her head resting on his shoulder, Miri wished their day together would never end, but knew her mother would start asking questions if she didn't get back soon from her supposed babysitting.

'Before we go, I have a little gift for you.' He reached into the glove compartment and produced a gift-wrapped package. 'Happy birthday.'

She opened it with care and gasped. 'A mobile phone.'

'Now it will be easier for us to keep in touch.'

He showed her all the functions: how to make calls, send and receive messages, and turn on silent mode so no one else would hear it ring.

'I've already charged it up for you so it's ready to go.'

'This is the best present anyone has ever given me. Thank you.'

'My pleasure.'

He leaned across and gave her a lingering, passionate kiss.

Miri was on a high; too wound up to sleep. She paced barefoot across the confined space of her bedroom, arms wrapped around her shoulders. 'I love him!' she whispered to herself. 'I really love him.'

She climbed into bed, hid her head under the covers and took out her new phone. There was already a message waiting for her.

Happy birthday. I love you. Speak soon x

Chapter 14

Torrential rain was fast creating puddles on the pavement. Ahead stood a white-painted terrace with a low stone wall and trimmed hedge which partially screened the house from the street. Who would have guessed that this was where Ben had grown up, just a few roads away from her? A black gate hung ajar, beckoning them to enter and walk the paved path through the small garden to the oak front door. But Miri was having second thoughts.

'It doesn't seem like it's stopping,' he said as the heavy rain pounded the roof. 'Shall we make a run for it?'

It had seemed like a good idea when Ben first suggested she come over for a meal at his place. Now, she wasn't so sure. Would his parents approve of her? She considered her new, knee-length denim skirt, just on the edge of daring, which she'd concealed beneath her long winter coat. Perhaps it wasn't appropriate for a first meeting. She should have worn something smarter, less trendy.

'Miri, what's wrong?'

'Are you sure your parents don't mind me coming over?'

'Quite the opposite. They're looking forward to meeting you.' He stroked her hair. 'There's nothing to worry about.'

They dashed through the downpour to the shelter of the

open porch, wiping their feet on the coir mat. Ben unlocked the front door and stood aside to let her in. She hung back at the entrance. The interior was modern and light, with off-white walls and oak laminate floor. To the right, next to the stairs, was an ornate picture of a *hamsa*, an upturned hand with a blessing for the home written in Hebrew, in shades of green and turquoise with illuminated gold. The scent of delicious cooking wafted through the house and Miri inhaled a blend of unfamiliar spices.

Ben spread his arms. 'Welcome.'

At the sound of his voice, a petite woman emerged from the kitchen to greet them. 'Hi! I'm Ben's mum. You must be Miri. It's lovely to meet you.' Miri recognised her voice from the few occasions she'd answered the phone. To her surprise, his mother gave her a kiss on both cheeks.

She had the same warm smile and olive complexion as Ben. Her shoulder-length hair was uncovered, unlike that of Miri's own mother, whose short hair was always hidden from view.

'Nice to meet you, Mrs Aharoni. Thank you for inviting me.'

'It's a pleasure to have you. Please, call me Mazal. Come inside and take your coat off. If you'll excuse me for a few minutes while I finish up in the kitchen, and then I'll be right with you.'

'Can I help you with anything?'

'Thank you, darling, but no, I'm fine. Why don't you go into the living room with Ben and make yourself at home.'

Ben took her coat, hung it in the cupboard under the stairs, and led her inside.

The living room, which led into the dining area, contained two, tan leather sofas arranged in an L-shape. Spanning the opposite wall was a fitted display cabinet filled with books, Judaica, decorative objects, photographs, and on the low shelf in the centre, a television. Although Ben had mentioned that was where they kept their TV, its blatant position was a startling sight for Miri. In exceptional cases of families she knew who had one, it was always a guarded secret and hidden away in a bedroom cupboard. Miri liked the honesty and openness in Ben's home, their sense of balance.

Miri drew nearer to the unit to study the pictures, admiring a sepia photograph of a bride wearing an elegant, fifties-style wedding dress, a crown of white flowers encircling her hair.

'My Savta,' he said.

'Was this taken in Aden?'

'Uh-huh.'

'Your Savta's dress is stunning.'

'Her sister made it for her.'

'Wow! She must have been talented.'

'They often sewed their own clothes because they wanted to copy the latest fashions, but there wasn't much choice available in the shops. What they had, though, was access to beautiful fabrics. Aden was a trading post between India and England, and many families worked in the business.'

She moved on to the next photo. Three small boys sitting on a beach, making a large sandcastle, and Ben's mother standing behind them holding a tiny baby.

'Which one are you?' Miri asked.

'Guess.'

She pointed to the smallest, who had a head of tight, dark curls and was showing off his red spade. 'Him?'

He grinned.

'You were so sweet.'

Ben gave her a sideways glance and raised an eyebrow. 'So what you're saying is, I'm not anymore?'

Miri laughed. 'I didn't say that.'

There was a more recent picture of the four siblings, dressed in formal wear, their arms around each other. 'That's from my cousin's wedding two years ago. There's Davidi, Natan, me and Natalie.'

So this was the sister whom he had mentioned was studying in a seminary in Israel. In her easy pose alongside her brothers, Miri thought she looked elegant in a figure-hugging, black evening dress and silver hoop earrings with her hair swept over one shoulder. Her smile was wide and her posture relaxed. It conveyed the self-assuredness of someone comfortable in their own skin. Miri experienced a curious sense of longing to be part of a family like this.

Beside it was a photo of Natan in his uniform. She recognised it as a larger version of the one Ben had shown her.

She continued on to a picture of an ecstatic couple standing cheek to cheek in front of a table decorated with balloons and laden with platters of food.

'That's Davidi with his fiancée Keren at their engagement party.'

On the sideboard in Miri's dining room was a similar photograph of her sister Pessie from when she and Yitzchok got engaged. Except in their one, the young couple stood on either side of the table, staring towards the camera with nervous smiles on their faces.

Miri noticed a guitar case propped against the wall beside the sofa. 'Who plays that?'

'I used to. A little.'

149

'I'd love to hear you play.'

'I'm probably rusty by now.' He glanced from her to the guitar case. Miri didn't need an explanation to understand how long it had been since he had last played. 'My fingers must have softened after all this time. I'm not sure if I could sound clear notes anymore.'

Her voice was gentle. 'Why don't you try it and see?'

With near reverence, he uncased the guitar and embraced it like a long-lost friend. He settled himself on the corner of the sofa and beckoned Miri to join him. As she did so, he regarded her with a tender expression but couldn't mask his grief just below the surface.

Resting the guitar on his thigh, he drew it close. He concentrated on positioning his fingers on its neck, and with the thumb of his right hand, teased the strings. He tightened and adjusted each one. Then he tried again. Melodious notes reverberated from the instrument. He wavered as if startled by the sounds that emerged.

Gaining confidence, he strummed and picked the strings while the fingers of his left hand slid up and down the frets. Miri sat spellbound as she listened to the haunting, beautiful piece he played.

From the kitchen, Mazal Aharoni set down her knife on the board where she had been chopping vegetables, and listened. She smiled to hear her son play again and wiped away a bittersweet tear.

Miri exhaled as the last notes faded. 'That was gorgeous.' She spoke in a low voice, not wanting to break the spell. 'What is the name of that piece?'

'A song called Fragile.'

She could have almost guessed its title.

He laid down the guitar and drew her towards him. 'I'd forgotten how much I missed it. Thank you for encouraging me.'

'Where did you learn to play?'

'My mum. She's very musical. Taught all of us kids how to play. And my dad can play the oud.'

He answered Miri's confusion by pointing to a pear-shaped instrument on a lower shelf, that resembled a guitar but with a series of double strings and a shorter neck. 'A kind of ancient, Middle-Eastern guitar. But I haven't mastered that one yet. We used to sometimes play together. My dad on the oud, my mum, Natalie and I on the guitar, and Davidi and Natan each on the tabla, a hand drum. Good times ...'

'It must be such an incredible feeling to pick up an instrument and play music.'

'Would you like me to teach you how to play sometime?'

They both turned at the sound of the door.

'Must be my dad.'

Ben untangled himself, but seemed at ease as he prepared to meet his father.

The man who walked in was a fraction shorter than Ben, a little stockier, but had the same dark eyes. He noticed the guitar on the sofa and beamed at them.

'Hi, Abba.' Ben embraced him. 'I'd like you to meet Miri.'

Miri rose too. His father bowed his head and extended his hand. 'Hello, Miri. A pleasure to meet you.'

She hesitated. Never had a man offered his hand to her in

formal greeting. She reciprocated and he gave it a friendly shake.

Mazal reappeared carrying plates and bowls. 'Just in time,' she said to her husband.

She followed Ben and his father to the kitchen to do the ritual washing of hands, three times on the right hand followed by three times on the left, before eating bread. Out of habit, Miri helped his mother carry the abundant dishes she had prepared into the dining room.

His mother had laid the table for four. Ben's father took his seat at the top, his mother to the right, Ben to his left and Miri beside him. It struck her was how relaxed they were in each other's company. The conversation was mostly small-talk, and it flowed with ease back and forth. None of them seemed uptight, or felt the need to watch what they said, or to veer away from a topic in case it was inappropriate. His father oh-so-casually mentioned a TV programme he'd watched the night before. Then Ben mentioned one of the actors who played in it reminded him of Mansoor. A second cousin, Ben explained to Miri. Did they know, his mother said, that Ben's aunt used to fancy Mansoor? Instead of reacting in shock to the comment, his father laughed. Yes, he remembered. Ben said he never knew that. It was well before he was born, his mother said. Apparently, this Mansoor was quite popular with the ladies when he was younger.

Miri had little experience of what went on in different households when they sat around the table since her family tended not to go out to eat. She didn't realise other families could relate to each other in this way and hadn't expected to feel as comfortable.

Ben reached for her hand under the table. She still couldn't quite believe she was sitting here beside him, in his home, having a meal with his parents.

Ben's mother passed around the serving bowls and encouraged Miri to fill her plate. She had never seen such a spread for a Sunday night supper. There was an aromatic meat stew with bulgur wheat and a hint of coriander, which Mazal introduced as *haris*. This was followed by a dish named *tukreesha*, a tasty blend of potatoes, coloured peppers and strips of meat. There was a big bowl of rice, assorted dishes filled with salads, a pile of spongy pancake-type bread called *lachuch*, pitta bread, and several dips. One of them had an almost jelly-like consistency. 'That's *hilba*,' Ben said. 'It's made from fenugreek.' Then he pointed to another that was leaf-green. 'Careful with that one. It's *bisbus*. You might find it quite spicy. That's why it's called *bisbus*. You take a small *bis*, a small piece. And *bus*, enough."

'What is it made of?'

'Coriander blended with garlic and hot chilli peppers. Try a bit, to begin with.' He scooped a small amount onto a teaspoon and fed it to her. Miri noticed a covert smile pass between his parents. 'How is it?'

'A little hot. But it's good.'

Ben seemed impressed. She reached for the jug and poured herself a tall glass of water.

'So how did you and Ben meet?' his father asked.

Miri looked to Ben, uncertain how to respond, but his smile encouraged her.

'Through friends,' Miri said. 'My best friend was meeting up with Ben's friend, Daniel, and she invited me to join for the evening. Daniel had brought two friends along, including Ben, and we got talking.'

'How lovely,' he said. 'Now I understand why he's never home these days.' He winked at Ben, causing the faint hint of a blush to colour his cheeks.

As swift as the focus had turned to her, it moved on to the subject of Davidi and Keren's wedding. They didn't seem concerned to find out every detail of her family or who she was related to.

Mazal offered her the bowl of *tukreesha*. 'Please help yourself to more.'

'Thank you, but I'm full. Everything was so delicious.'

'You're welcome, darling.'

'Do you always have such amazing suppers like this?' she asked Ben. Mazal Aharoni beamed at the compliment.

'Tonight was extra special. My mum pulled out all the stops because you were coming.' And with a mischievous smile, Ben whispered conspiratorially in Miri's ear (but still loud enough for his mother to catch), 'We'd be having pasta otherwise.'

'Ben!'

He grinned as she wagged a finger at him with mock seriousness, and Miri could see she took the joke with the good humour that he intended. 'Just you wait till later, my dear. You'll get one kuff from me!'

Ben burst out laughing. And before long, they all were. Ben got up, stood behind his mother's chair, and gave her an affectionate hug, kissing the top of her head.

She reached across and gave his hand a loving pat. '*Ya ayuni.*'

'You should see what she makes on Shabbat,' he said to Miri pointing to some of the dishes on the table. 'Bisbus, hilba, haris. Also *fasoolia*, the most delicious beans you will ever taste; *ka'adid*, a round flatbread; sometimes homemade *gachnun*, a flaky pastry which we love to have for breakfast with jam or honey. Oh, and *hudra mudra*, a kind of vegetable stew we cook with fish. Even to smell the hudra mudra while my mum is making it is enough to make your mouth water.'

Miri wasn't familiar with all these exotic-sounding dishes, but judging by the food she had sampled that evening, she decided that she already liked them. How she wished she could spend a Shabbat with Ben and his family.

'She's an incredible cook. Isn't that right, Abba?'

'Indeed. She's incredible altogether.' He gazed adoringly at his wife. 'Miri, you must join us for *Shabboth* when we return from Israel. Ben, please arrange it.'

A look passed from Ben to Miri. 'Yeah. We must figure something out.'

She couldn't imagine such a scene taking place in her house. If only the situation were different and she could invite Ben home for a meal to meet her parents … But that would never happen.

The sound of the telephone interrupted them, and Mazal rose from her seat. 'Excuse me, please.'

Ben and his father rose to clear the table. Miri joined them. From the hallway, she overheard Mazal conversing in an unfamiliar language with a few words of English sprinkled in here and there.

'What language is your mother speaking?'

'Hebrew, English, and Adeni, which is like a dialect of Arabic.'

'What, all three together?'

Ben was unfazed. 'Uh-huh.'

'Does she often speak to people like that?'

'When she talks to other Adenim, the older generation in particular.'

They carried the plates into the kitchen. 'Do you speak that way between yourselves too?'

'Nah! English, or sometimes Hebrew. My mum grew up in Israel until her early twenties.'

'Do you also know Adeni?'

'I can't speak it but know a few words.'

'Tell me some?'

'There's *ayuni*. That is what we kids are to our parents.'

'Oh yes. She said that to you before. What does it mean?'

'It means my eyes. It's like your most precious thing, because eyes are so precious.'

'Is it similar to calling someone "the apple of my eye"?'

'Yeah, that's it.' He smiled. 'Another is *ya albi*.'

'What's that?'

'What you are to me.' He rubbed the back of his neck out of shyness. 'It means, you are my heart.'

He leaned in towards her, then heard his mother's returning footsteps. He turned around, busied himself stacking a pile of plates, then left the kitchen.

'It's a long time since I've seen Ben look this happy and content,' Mazal said. 'I think much of that might be because of you.' She smiled, but Miri read the scars of loss etched on her face. She placed her hand over Miri's with tenderness. 'It's wonderful to see. I am so pleased that we've finally met. I hope you'll feel at home now and come around more often.'

Ben returned with the last of the dishes from the table.

'Abba and I are popping out for a while to visit Aunty Rachel. She wants us to take a package for her grandchildren in Israel. Are you staying here or going out?' Mazal said.

'Not sure,' said Ben. 'The weather is so lousy outside. Miri, shall we stay here a while and watch some TV?'

156

The idea sounded perfect.

The door shut behind his parents. They relaxed on the sofa and Ben put his arm around her. 'What do you want to watch?'

'What's on?'

'Let's see.' He picked up the remote control and flicked through the channels. 'We have a soap opera with miserable people who argue a lot. A documentary about the effects of an oil spillage on seabirds. Here's a program about parents who can't control their children. On this channel a supermodel giving her intelligent view of the world. Or a moody French film about a group of morose people sitting together in a bar, philosophising about life.' He flicked back to a text display on the screen. 'Oh, here's something you'll like. The soap opera ends in a few minutes, and after, there will be an interior design makeover show.'

Miri's eyes sparkled. 'Yes, please!'

'I thought that might be up your street.'

She spent the next half hour transfixed, but her enthusiasm waned five minutes into the crime drama that followed. 'You were right when you told me that time it's all rather boring.' He raised his hand in a mock gesture of triumph, and she laughed. Then he stared at her, his expression changed, and he leaned in to kiss her, all thoughts of the TV forgotten.

She lay enveloped in his arms, his lips on hers. She wrapped her arms around him. He caressed the nape of her neck, running his hand down the length of her spine and tracing the outline of her body. A key turned in the lock.

'Hi, I'm back.' Mazal called out. They sat bolt upright, feigning absorption in a documentary about a donkey sanctuary in East Anglia. Miri smoothed down her skirt. Mazal entered the living room. 'Have you had a good evening?' She looked at what they were watching with a quizzical expression and gave a shrug.

'Yeah, it's been fine. Nothing much on TV, though,' Ben said, trying to sound offhand.

'Like usual.' At the sound of a braying donkey, she glanced again at the screen. 'Aunty Rachel sends her love. Her son Shimon came by, so Abba stayed on to talk to him. She gave us a beautiful wedding present for Davidi and Keren.' She showed them a leather canteen of silver cutlery.

'Pshhh! Very nice,' Ben said, then turned to Miri. 'Aunty Rachel is not an aunt but a good friend of the family, so we call her aunty. Although she's sort of related to us, isn't she, Ima?'

'Yes, somehow. A third cousin, I think.'

'I guess it's getting late. I'd better take you home.' He went to fetch her coat.

'Thank you so much for having me,' Miri said, 'and for a lovely supper.'

'A great pleasure.' She kissed her on both cheeks. 'We're back later next week, so I look forward to seeing you again soon.'

Ben drove her to their usual drop-off point. 'I think my parents really like you,' he said.

Miri glowed with happiness. 'Do you think so?'

'Definitely.'

'I really like your parents too.'

'I'm so pleased. Will I see you tomorrow after work? My parents are leaving tomorrow afternoon. We can have the house to ourselves.'

'That sounds lovely. I should be able to make it. I'll text you soon, anyway.'

Ben's gift to her had made all the difference. When they were apart, they messaged each other at every opportunity. And at night, hidden under the covers, Miri texted him until she drifted off to sleep.

Mazal reflected on the evening as she washed up. Seeing Ben with Miri had been heartwarming. She was well aware he had been through a rough time, and it had been eating him up inside. She had tried to broach the subject with him many times. Whenever she mentioned Natan, he comforted her, though wouldn't speak about him and seemed unable to open up. But over the past few weeks, he had become more like his old self.

It wasn't hard to tell that he and Miri were smitten with each other. And Mazal had taken an instant liking to her. There was a lot she wanted to ask, but it wouldn't have been polite for their first meeting and she didn't want to make Miri feel uncomfortable. Mazal wondered about her background. She didn't come from their community; of that she was certain. She was also different to Yael, his previous girlfriend (who she'd never been keen on, though she had kept quiet about this, hoping the relationship would run its course, and relieved when it did), and the other girls he'd hung around with in the past. Miri seemed ideal for him in many respects. It's true, they were still young, but they could go out for a while and, in time, who knew … She'd make a lovely daughter-in-law, one day.

But something didn't seem right. Mazal couldn't put her

finger on what it was, and it niggled her. Not that Miri had come over on a Sunday night instead of Shabbat. Perhaps she lived too far to walk. It was when her husband, Shalom, had again suggested the idea of her coming to them for Shabbat. A strange look had passed between Ben and Miri. Maybe she wasn't from a religious family. But the clothes she had worn were modest. Had she dressed that way out of respect? She couldn't work it out. Mazal decided that even if Miri wasn't observant, she would have to leave her own feelings out of it and not interfere. Ben's happiness was the priority here. He deserved it, and Miri seemed good for him. The rest would take care of itself, *b'ezrat Hashem*. Mazal would get to know her better. One day soon, hopefully, she would feel comfortable enough to join them over Shabbat.

'So what do you think?' Mazal glanced up to find Ben leaning against the doorway. She had been so deep in thought she hadn't heard him come in.

'She's lovely, Ben. A sweet, sweet girl.'

'I know.' His smile was dreamy. She found it adorable.

'You like her a lot, don't you?'

'Yes. I do.'

'So, are you serious about her?'

'Hmm,' was his noncommittal reply.

'What does that mean?'

'Might be.'

'It's good to see you looking so happy.'

'Thanks, Ima.' He strode over to her to give her a quick kiss on the cheek and grabbed a cloth to help dry the dishes.

'So where is she from?'

'Round here.'

Vague, she thought. 'I don't recognise her. She's not from our community.'

'No.'

'She doesn't look Persian or Moroccan either.'

'No, she isn't.'

'Then?'

'Chassidic.'

Ben's mother stiffened and turned around to face him. Her mouth opened and closed, but no sound came out. The plate she was holding slipped out of her grasp and smashed to the floor.

Ben hurried for a broom.

Jolted by the clank of the china fragments, she found her voice. 'What do you think you are doing?'

'I'm sweeping up.'

'I'm not talking about the plate!'

'Hang on. A minute ago you were saying how much you liked her. What's the problem?'

'A Chassidic girl! Are you out of your mind?'

'What do you have against her for being Chassidic?'

'Nothing. I haven't got a problem with her. I think she is wonderful. But do her parents know she is seeing you?'

Ben shifted on his feet. 'No.'

'*Fahgarek fahgara!*' Her voice rose to a panic. 'What are her parents going to say when they find out? They will make such trouble for her. And for you. *Inta magnoon!*' She held onto the counter for support. 'What were you *thinking*? Her parents will expect her to have a shidduch and marry someone from their own community.'

'But she doesn't want that.'

'I don't think it matters to them what she wants. That's what they'll make her do anyway. They will never agree to a family like us.'

'And what's wrong with us?'

His wounded expression broke her heart. 'Nothing.' She put her hand on his shoulder to placate him.

'Our customs are just as valid as theirs,' he said.

'This is not about customs. You know how it is. Maybe they regard us as being second rate or less religious because we come from the Middle East and not Europe. It's not right but –'

'So what is it? Love your fellow Jew as yourself. Unless they're Adeni? Aren't we all supposed to be one people who originated from the same place?'

She let out a drawn-out sigh. 'It's not me you have to convince. It's her parents. Her community. I know you like her, but you have to forget it. This will not happen.'

'But I love her.'

Mazal shook her head. She couldn't bear to look at his doleful eyes. Inside, she was crying. She had never heard him express himself like this before.

Why?

Why did the one person who'd brought so much joy back into his life be a girl he could never have?

'I wish it didn't have to be this way, but I think it is impossible. You will both wind up getting hurt. You have to end it. As soon as possible. The longer this continues, the harder it is going to be.'

His eyes were downcast. 'I can't. She's the best thing that's ever happened to me.'

'Then what will you do?'

'I don't know,' he said. 'But I don't want to let her go.'

Chapter 15

With his parents away and the house to themselves, Ben and Miri settled into an idyllic routine.

Each day after work, Miri went straight to Ben's house. Together, they prepared supper, which they ate at the breakfast bar sitting on high stools. Later they would stand side by side doing the dishes, sharing amusing stories about their day.

They savoured their taste of domestic bliss and hardly ventured out. Instead, they lounged on the sofa. He taught her to play the guitar. They watched films. But they were most content to talk for hours, lie in each other's arms, discover and delight in one another, their love and passion intensifying with each passing day.

But all too soon, their escape from reality was coming to a close.

Ben's parents were due to fly back the following morning, and he needed to do a shop on his way back from university to stock the refrigerator. Since Miri couldn't be seen out shopping with him in the neighbourhood, they arranged he would message her once he got back. And for the first time in many days, she came straight home from work.

She knew all wasn't as it should be the moment she came

through the door. The house was quieter than usual. No activity in the kitchen. Instead, both her parents were sitting and talking in the dining room.

Her father never came home that early.

'Miri, can you please come in here for a minute?' her mother said. 'There is something we want to talk to you about.'

Miri's mind raced. Somehow they must have found out about her and Ben. Mrs Finer?

Miri stumbled into the dining room. Her heart pounded loud in her ears and she was sure her parents could hear it too. Her mother got up and closed the door to give the three of them privacy. Miri's stomach lurched as she sat down at the table opposite them.

But then she noticed they didn't seem angry. In fact, her mother was smiling.

'Miri, we have some important news to tell you,' she said. 'A shidduch has been suggested for you.'

'What?' said Miri.

Miri felt like she'd had the wind knocked out of her.

'Isn't that wonderful? The Blochs are a fine family. We met the parents this afternoon. Their son Lipa is in yeshiva in America. We've been told he is the best boy in yeshiva.'

'His father is also a great *talmid chochom*,' Miri's father said. 'How special for Tateh to have a son-in-law like that.'

Her father stroked his beard and nodded in agreement.

'Tomorrow, he is returning to England for his brother's chasseneh which takes place in Manchester next Tuesday,' her mother continued. 'How exciting to think by that time, im yirtze Hashem, you will have become a kallah!'

Miri gulped. 'Why, when am I supposed to be meeting him?'

'Sunday night.'

'This Sunday night?'

'Yes.'

'I can't meet him.'

Her mother narrowed her eyes. 'Why not?'

'I … um … promised to … help Raizy with her wedding dress design that evening.'

'Raizy's wedding dress can wait a day or two. Sunday you have a shidduch and then you'll have your own wedding to prepare for.'

'I'm not sure that I'm ready to meet someone yet.'

'Of course you are. You're already nineteen years old. Do you want to be left on the shelf like our neighbour Bluma? Twenty-three and still not married.'

'No, but –'

'Look at your friend, Raizy. See how excited she is for her chasseneh? I'm sure she did not tell her parents she wasn't ready when they told her about that excellent shidduch. Don't you want to be a kallah like Raizy?'

'Yes, but –'

'What a privilege to be offered a shidduch with such a prestigious family.'

She couldn't shake off her parents' expectations or mask her rising anxiety. 'I can't do it! I can't see him.'

'Yes, you can. I think you are maybe a little nervous, that's all. A lot of girls are before a shidduch. It's natural. But you have nothing to worry about. From such fine parents can only come a good boy who will make you a suitable husband.' She sighed dreamily. 'Ah! To think our Miri will soon be engaged.'

She had to broach the subject. Now!

'I don't want to go on a shidduch,' she blurted out.

Her mother frowned in puzzlement. 'How do you expect to get engaged then?'

'A different way?' she ventured.

Her father shook his head and gave her a withering look. It was clear he regarded her reply as the ridiculous idea of a foolish young girl.

Her mother took a deep breath. Her patient smile was forced. 'There isn't another way. This is how it is done.'

'Do I have to see him?'

'Yes, you must. It's all arranged.'

'Can't you cancel or postpone it?'

Her father gave her an impatient glare and raised his voice. 'Enough of this nonsense now! You will meet him on Sunday. That is final.'

The walls felt like they were closing in and suffocating her. 'I have to go.'

'Where to?' said her mother. 'You're always running out these days. To Raizy's home, babysitting, this friend's house, that friend's house, meeting sem friends, shopping. Well, once you are engaged, you'll be too busy for all of that and will have more important things to worry about.'

'I'm going out for a walk. I have to think.' Miri rose to leave before either of them could stop her, and as soon as she was out of the house, broke out into a run, not stopping until she reached Ben's home.

She rang the doorbell and waited. Moments passed with no answer. She tried again.

'Coming!' he called.

He opened the door, his hair dripping wet, half-dressed in jeans with a shirt he'd thrown on in haste but not had time to fasten. The gold Magen David pendant he always wore glistened on his chest.

He welcomed her inside with a quick kiss. 'You got here fast. I messaged you, like, three minutes ago, before I jumped in the shower. I didn't expect you'd be this quick.' She pulled out her phone and found the message he'd sent:

Home. Come over! x

Ben's eyes travelled upwards. She heard a tap running and water splashing on tiles.

'Oh! The hand-washing –' He darted up the stairs. 'Come up for a minute if you like.'

She trudged up to find him mopping up a puddle from the overflowing sink.

'Just give me two minutes and I'm done.'

He wrung out a pair of tzitzit and hung them on the bathroom radiator. Then he ran into another room. Miri followed. She realised this must be his room. His bed was set against the far wall with a load of folded washing piled on top. Beneath the window was a desk, set up with a laptop and a tower of books beside it.

He gathered a stack of laundry and carried it out to the cupboard on the landing. Back to his room for a pile of towels. Back into the bathroom. She trailed after him.

He turned to her with an apologetic smile, mistaking her silence for irritation. 'Sorry about this. Almost there.'

He scooped up the last pile, stuffing it onto a shelf in his wardrobe.

'Alright, I'm finished. Now, tell me about your day.'

She faced him, and he saw the torment in her eyes.

'Miri, what's wrong?'

'It's my parents. They've found a shidduch for me.'

Ben went still. He blinked slowly. 'Can't you get out of it?'

'I tried, but they wouldn't listen. They're forcing me to see him.'

'When?'

'Sunday night.'

He let out a long exhale.

'There's no way out and I don't know what to do,' she said.

'Is this – Is this the end for us? Is this goodbye?'

The words pierced like a jagged shard of glass.

'I don't want to end it.' Her voice broke. 'But I'm trapped.'

'Oh, God! What are we going to do? I don't want to lose you.'

A tear rolled down her cheek. 'I don't want to go through with this, but I have no choice.'

'I've never felt this way about anyone before. I love you and I want to spend the rest of my life with you.'

She stared at him.

'I mean it,' he whispered.

She emitted a cry. 'I wish I could. More than anything. I love you too. I don't want this to be goodbye.'

He hugged her tight. She shut her eyes, trying to block out her heartbreak and the imminent loss of him. She clung to him, not wanting to let go.

He kissed her. Softly at first. She responded. Their kisses became more passionate, more urgent.

They sank back onto his bed. She answered to his touch and his caresses.

And then she gave herself to him. And he to her.

In love and despair. In pleasure and in pain.

Chapter 16

He held her in his arms, their faces streaked with tears.

'I'm sorry.' His words tumbled out in a choked voice. 'I didn't mean to … I hope I didn't hurt you … It was my first time too. Please forgive me?'

'It's not your fault. I'm as much to blame.' Miri rested her head on his chest. He stroked her hair. Knowing their time together was ending and they would have to break up tore her apart.

'I know we should have been more careful, I'm sorry. I wasn't thinking straight. But I meant every word I said. I love you and I don't want to lose you.'

'I love you too. It's so unfair. If only things were different. I don't want this shidduch.'

'There has to be a way out of it,' he said. 'What if I were to speak to your parents and tell them how I feel about you?'

The idea did nothing to ease Miri's despair. 'They would go mad if they found out we'd been seeing each other behind their backs. And the shidduch is all arranged. They won't cancel it. When I asked my father, he lost his patience with me.'

Ben groaned. 'Alright, so you can't get out of this shidduch.

But do you have to marry the guy? Surely they must give you a choice on that. Can't you say no?'

'I don't know ...' Miri considered it. 'What would I say?'

'Tell them he's not for you. Make up a reason. Say you have nothing in common, that he's ugly or boring. It doesn't matter, you just have to convince them to let you reject the shidduch.'

Miri gave a weak smile. 'I suppose I could try. But what would it help? They'll only line up another one soon and we'll face the same situation all over again.'

'Miri, what do you want? I'll respect your decision, whatever it is. If you decide you must follow your parents' wishes, and ask me to back out of your life, I will. I won't hassle you. I'll be discreet and no one will ever find out what happened between us. You mean everything to me, but I won't force you into anything against your will.'

'I want to be with you.'

'Then let me speak to your parents.'

Her face turned ashen. 'No, you can't do that.'

'But we can't continue like this. Eventually, they'll find out and it will be far worse. If we are honest with them and explain how much we care about one another, they will have to agree.'

'I'm not so sure.'

'OK, what if I become Chassidish?'

She stifled a giggle.

He raised an eyebrow. 'I am trying to be serious here.'

'You couldn't do that.'

'Why not? Course I can. I'll get the clothes, grow my *peyot* ... Sorted!'

Miri facepalmed at the ridiculousness of the proposition.

'I wouldn't want you to do that.'

'You don't fancy me in a long black jacket?' he teased.

'Langer rekel.'

'Whatever.'

'It's not you. I like you as you are.'

'Then this is what we will do. Play along with this shidduch. See the boy to please your parents. Afterwards, make your excuses and stand your ground. They can't force you to marry him. We'll wait a few days to let it blow over, and then I'll go with you to speak to them. They don't need to know we've been going out all this time. We can pretend we've just met. I realise it may not be easy to convince your parents, but if we want to be together, we have no choice but to be brave and do this the correct way. And I'm not about to give up on you.'

Her eyes welled up again.

'Be strong, my love. In a few more days, we'll sort this. No more creeping around, no more lies.'

Miri smiled through her tears.

'Don't be afraid, he said. 'Somehow it will all work out. You'll see.'

Chapter 17

Ben checked his watch for the umpteenth time. How was it only five o'clock? It felt like the longest day of his life. Ever. Still another hour until Miri's shidduch was scheduled. Ben tried working on an overdue assignment but couldn't focus. He pulled out his mobile to check for any new messages from Miri. Her last text had been fifteen minutes ago after her mother had nagged her about getting ready. From their ongoing communication, he understood her mother was buzzing with excitement, convinced they would announce an engagement that evening. Meanwhile, Miri was a nervous wreck.

He reminded her, as he had done many times over the past few days, to stay calm, remain steadfast, and he reassured her he was there for her. Ben only hoped she'd be able to withstand the pressure.

He drifted into the living room, picked up his guitar and strummed a few chords, but his heart wasn't in it. He returned the instrument to its case. Then he sent Miri another message. He tried reading the weekend paper but found it impossible to get through a paragraph without his mind wandering. Even the sports supplement could not hold his attention.

'Miri, what are you wearing?'

Startled by her mother's outburst, Miri appraised her appearance. Her clothes were modest and she had tied back her hair.

'What's with this skirt?'

Miri blinked rapidly. She had slipped up with her more modern-looking, ankle-length skirt. She wasn't thinking straight.

'You can't go down in those scruffy clothes. Get changed into something smarter. What will he think of you if he sees you in that?'

It never bothered Ben, she thought. In fact, he had been complimentary about her clothes as she experimented with her individual style.

Miri scanned the clothes in her wardrobe for a suitable alternative, too overwhelmed to make even such a simple choice. She wished she could escape ... straight into Ben's arms. Right now, anything seemed preferable to going through with this shidduch: cleaning the bathroom, a dentist appointment. Heck! She'd agree to have tea with Mrs Finer if it meant avoiding this. To steel herself, she ran through the plan she and Ben had discussed.

Her mother returned to find her still staring at her wardrobe. 'Hurry! It's already twenty to six. He'll be here soon.'

Miri made a half-hearted attempt to leaf through her clothes.

Mrs Fogel softened. 'I understand you're nervous, Miri. It is a big step to get engaged. But there's nothing to worry about. Look how happy Raizy is.'

Her mother rummaged through her wardrobe and withdrew a formal navy suit with large gold buttons down the front. 'This is perfect!'

Miri hid her grimace as her mother handed her the outfit. It wasn't worth making a fuss. She would put up with this charade for one evening. Her mother bustled out of the room, leaving Miri to change. She slipped on the suit and seized the moments alone to check for messages.

It's been a long day. Can't concentrate on anything. Miss u. x

Miri hugged the phone to her chest, then fired back a reply.

Miss u too x. Mum made me change into something hideous.

Seconds later, the phone flashed a notification.

Maybe the outfit will put him off LOL!

PS You and hideous don't belong in the same sentence.

It made her smile. But at the sound of the doorbell, she flinched.

Must go. He's here!

Her mother knocked on the door. 'Miri, are you ready?'

She dived for her underwear drawer and concealed her mobile in a pair of thick, black tights. 'Yes, please give me a minute and I'll be down.'

Miri closed her eyes, praying for the strength to get through this. She finished by lifting her hands in a gesture of supplication and kissed the tips of her fingers. It was an action she'd seen Ben do. She did not know if it would help, but it couldn't hurt.

She felt like a prisoner awaiting her fate as she made her way down the stairs. But she was going to free herself. Her mother was waiting for her at the bottom. She, too, wore a smart outfit in anticipation of the celebration Miri was intent on preventing.

This is it, Ben told himself.

He took several deep breaths to slow his racing heart. 'Miri, please be strong enough to say no. I don't want to lose you,' he prayed.

He paced the floor, waiting, helpless.

With slow steps on shaky legs, Miri entered the dining room. The familiar space felt alien and forbidding. Her mother had laid the table with their best white tablecloth and set out snacks and drinks. On the opposite side sat a boy, not much older than her, dressed in traditional Chassidish clothes. A sandy beard framed his face – a sliver of maturity on his delicate complexion, which spoke of hours spent in the study hall, out of the sunlight. With eyes downcast, he twirled one of his curly peyes, but as she took a seat opposite, he glanced up and regarded her with curiosity.

'I'm Lipa.'

She faced him. 'Hi, I'm Miri.'

His cheeks coloured, and he turned to the untouched drink in front of him. 'It's nice to meet you.'

'You too.'

'So. Um ...' He smiled. 'What do you do?'

'I work in a property management company.'

'That's ... er ... very nice. What do you do there?'

'I'm a secretary. I do admin, type up letters and answer the phone. That kind of thing.'

'Oh.' He nodded. 'Do you like it?'

'It's OK.'

'So, how long have you been by this company?'

'About four months.'

'Very nice.'

Miri was finding the stilted conversation stressful. Her mind wandered to thoughts of Ben. She pictured his sultry eyes as they would stare into hers. She remembered the first time they had met at the café and how he had put her at ease. Right from the start, the conversation had flowed much easier between them.

' … sem …?'

'Sorry?' Miri asked.

She realised she had blanked out for a moment and lost track of what he was saying.

He cleared his throat. 'Er … how long were you in sem for?'

'Two years.'

'Very nice. Did you enjoy it?'

'It had its moments.' Miri smiled.

'Pardon?'

She pulled herself together and adopted a more serious tone. 'Sorry. I meant I learnt a lot.'

'That's good.'

Lipa had a self-conscious smile as his eyes shifted from side to side, desperate to come up with something else to ask her. Miri couldn't help feeling sorry for him and came to his aid. 'I understand you're in yeshiva?'

'Yes.'

'In America?'

'Yes.'

'What's America like?'

'Very nice.'

'Do you enjoy learning in yeshiva?'

His face brightened at the question and he expounded on what he was learning, going into such great detail, so all Miri had to do was give him a polite nod every so often to make out as if she was paying attention. But at least she didn't have to answer a stream of questions.

She didn't find him unpleasant. There was an endearing quality to his shyness and she could relate to his predicament. He seemed gentle and kind, eager to engage her in conversation, but hampered by his inability to discuss much that wasn't in his own bubble.

There was no doubt his family background was more similar to her own than Ben's. He was everything her parents wanted for her. But no one would ever touch her heart and soul the way Ben had. Now she understood what Raizy meant when she said, you know when it's right.

Lipa was trying so hard to make a good impression. None of this was his fault. She felt awful that he was being misled and a level of culpability that she had helped put him in this situation.

'What are your thoughts about educating children?'

'Huh?' She sat a little straighter in her chair.

'In the future, after marriage?'

Miri coughed. 'Er … I'm not sure. What do you think?' He gave a keen smile, as if ready to give his opinion, and she suspected this was why he asked in the first place.

Ben went to the kitchen to make coffee as a distraction to pass the time. As he waited for the kettle to boil, troubling thoughts gnawed away at his confidence in the outcome of this evening. He held a teaspoon in his hand and tapped it back and forth on the granite counter.

What if her love for him wasn't strong enough?

Tap, tap, tap.

What if she changed her mind about approaching her parents because she was too afraid to deal with the reaction to their relationship?

Tap, tap, tap.

What if she found the boy pleasant enough and convinced herself it might be less trouble to settle down with him and lead the life mapped out for her, like Raizy had done?

Tap, tap, tap.

'Is everything alright?' his mother said.

Clink. He dropped the spoon.

'Sure, everything's fine.'

'You're not seeing Miri tonight?'

'No. She's got something on this evening.'

'You seem worried. Did something happen between the two of you? Have you had an argument?'

A fleeting image of her lying in his arms appeared in his mind. He shut his eyes for a second. 'No. Everything is great.'

'Have you given any more thought to what we discussed?'

'Yeah.'

'And?'

'I'm still thinking about it.'

'Ben, you can't carry on like this with her. It's not fair on either of you.'

He sighed. 'I know.'

This isn't right, she thought as Lipa put forward his ideas on how he'd like to run his home once married. He already seemed to be under the assumption she would agree to their engagement. But she only wanted Ben. Her parents thought they were doing their best for her but had no clue what was going on. Waves of guilt surged against her conscience. Ben was right. They had to end this secrecy and bring it into the open. It wasn't fair to anyone. If they explained to her parents how much they cared for one another, they would have to agree. Wouldn't they?

The hour was up. Ben fixated on his phone with bated breath.

Please tell me the shidduch is off.

Each second that passed was torturous. He prayed he and Miri still had a future together.

'Well?' Her mother couldn't disguise her anticipation. She closed the kitchen door while Lipa and his parents remained in the living room. 'Do we have a mazel tov?'

Miri shook her head. 'No. He's not for me.'

Her mother's disappointment was evident. 'Why not?'

'We had nothing to say to one another.'

Her mother sat down next to her at the kitchen table, resting her chin on her hand. 'I suppose this was only your first meeting, and the first time you have ever spoken to a boy. Sometimes it is hard at the beginning.'

Miri wished she could laugh out loud, but kept a straight face. 'Also, we have nothing in common.'

'Yes, you do. Your backgrounds are very similar. Not only that, he's the second oldest in his family too. And were you aware his Zeide went to the same school as yours in Poland?'

'No, I didn't.'

'And he comes from an excellent family. It's a fine shidduch.'

'But we don't share any of the same interests.'

'He is a boy in learning. What do you want that he should discuss? Shopping? When you marry, you will have what to say about your home and then, im yirtze Hashem, the children.'

'But I don't want to marry him. I don't like him.'

'What's not to like? He is polite, no?'

'Yes,' she said in a resigned voice.

'And friendly?'

'I suppose so.'

'There you are! An excellent start.'

'I could never love him.'

'Love?' Her mother looked horrified, as if Miri had just uttered an expletive. 'What do you know from love? When you get married, have a life together, and children, these things grow. This is not how we talk. You shouldn't be thinking about that now.'

Ten minutes passed.

Nothing.

Twenty minutes.

Still no word.

What is going on?

Was it possible she had agreed to it …?

Please, no!

Miri was getting desperate. 'I don't like the way he looks.'

'What's wrong with his appearance?'

'It's not for me.'

'What do you expect him to look like?'

Miri pictured Lipa's reserved expression in contrast to Ben's fine features and alluring smile. Just thinking about him gave her butterflies. She loved his thoughtful nature. The way he made her laugh. How they talked for hours about anything and everything and still never ran out of things to say. His grandfather may not have gone to the same school as hers, but what did it matter? They understood each other so well. It was Ben she wanted. Only him.

Miri lost her patience and sprang from the chair. 'I don't want to marry Lipa!'

'It's alright. Calm down.' Her mother tried to soothe her. 'I'm sure it will be better when you see him a second time.'

'What? I don't want to see him again.'

'Well, you must. Sometimes it takes a second meeting in order to make up your mind.'

'I've already made my decision.'

'Miri, you have no experience in these matters. Next time will be different.'

'It won't.'

'Sometimes the first meeting isn't so easy. But then, the second time, it works out. That's why you have to give it another chance before you decide. I'll speak to the shadchen right away to find out how soon we can arrange it.'

Miri was frantic. 'Can we wait a while before we meet again?'

'How long do you want to wait?'

'A month or two, perhaps?'

'A month? In a month, he might be engaged to someone else and then you would have lost out.' Her mother reached for the phone and began to dial the number. 'No, we must arrange it, as soon as possible, once he's back from his brother's chasseneh.'

His phone buzzed. A message from Miri.

Not engaged.

Ben exhaled. Then a second one came through.

But mum says I have to see him again. Arranged for next Mon. So upset.

'Damn!' he muttered under his breath, then tapped a reply.

Disappointed but I guess no choice. See him next week, say no, then I speak to your parents.

I'm sorry. Are u angry with me?

No. I feel bad for u. It's not your fault.

Don't know how I'll cope with stress till next week.

Hang in there. Just a few more days and we'll sort it. I love u.

Chapter 18

Mrs Fogel glanced at the still-sealed bottle of whisky and shook her head, unable to hide her disappointment. 'I don't understand it, Miri!'

Miri busied herself putting away the snacks her mother had on standby for the expected engagement announcement. She decided it was the least she could do.

'He was everything we could have wished for. A perfect shidduch suggestion and you are ready to throw it away?'

'I told you, he's not for me.'

'But what if he is your beshert?'

'He isn't.'

'Are you sure?'

'You said I had to see him a second time. I did. My answer is still no.'

'I suppose I'd better call the shadchen and tell her.' Mrs Fogel's hand hovered over the telephone. 'Are you sure you shouldn't give it more thought? Perhaps consider it for a day or two? Maybe we should speak to the rabbi first and ask for his advice?'

Stand your ground, Miri reminded herself. 'No, my mind's made up. I don't want to marry him.'

'Shidduchim like this don't come up every day. I hope you

won't regret it.'

Miri hopped up on the kitchen stool to store the pack of plastic shot glasses in a high cupboard. 'I won't.'

'What is it you want?' She sounded desperate. 'Tell me and I'll pass it on to the shadchen so she can make a more suitable suggestion next time.'

This was Miri's chance to speak to her. The ideal opportunity. She stepped off the stool. 'Well, the thing is, I don't think the shadchen could find what I'm looking for.'

'What do you mean?'

'I'm not sure I want to marry someone Chassidish.'

There was a sharp intake of breath. 'This is our way of life. What else do you know from? You want that we find for you some non-frum boy from somewhere that we have no details of his background, where he is coming from or his yichus? Now you are talking nonsense, Miri!'

She'd been wrong. This wasn't the ideal opportunity to discuss it.

'I'm so nervous,' Miri said.

Ben hugged her. 'I'll be there with you.'

He'd parked on a quiet street, a few minutes away from their neighbourhood, as they prepared themselves to face her parents.

'I wonder if it would be better for me to talk to them first and then call you to come in after?' Miri said.

'I don't know what they're like. If you think it's the best way, I'll go along with it. Whatever you think is better.'

'I'm worried that if we walk in together, with no warning, it will shock them. They'll get angry and dismiss the suggestion out of hand. I mean, they assumed Lipa Bloch was the first boy I'd ever spoken to.'

Ben smiled at her flirtatiously. It made Miri laugh and eased the tension.

'Picture the scene. My mother is in the kitchen, my father learning in the dining room, and we walk in with no warning. My mother stares, open-mouthed, and drops whatever it was she was doing. Then my father looks up in horror. Their daughter, Miri, together with … a man? Not only that, he isn't Chassidish. Not even dressed in a suit and hat. Worse than that, he's wearing modern clothes like jeans.

'"Miri?" he asks, "Who is this?"

'And I reply, "This is Ben. We're going out." At this point, my father's face would turn an angry red. He would cut me off and shout, "What do you think you are doing? Have you gone mad?"

'You wouldn't get a chance to say anything.'

Ben looked alarmed. 'I wasn't expecting it to be as bad as that. I thought, OK, at first it would come as a shock to them to learn we were going out. Maybe they'd find me a disappointment because I wasn't what they'd hoped for you. But afterwards, they would calm down, I'd introduce myself properly. Then we could explain the position, apologise for not telling them sooner, and reach an understanding with them.'

Miri's was sceptical.

'That won't work, will it?'

'You haven't met my father.'

'Oh God, I can't wait to get this over with.'

'Tell me about it.'

'Alright then. I'll wait in the car at the end of your road, and you call me as soon as you're ready for me to come.'

He dropped her off at their usual place, and she was a bundle of nerves as she prepared to leave him.

'I wish there was an easier way to do this,' he said.

'So do I.'

'Good luck. Be strong. I'll be waiting for you.'

The setting was almost the same as she had described to Ben. Her mother was in the kitchen, cooking with her ear to the phone. Her father sat at the table in the dining room, immersed in his learning and stroking his greying beard.

She entered with timid steps and approached him. 'Tateh ...?'

'Mmm.'

'Can I speak to you about something?'

'What is it?' His eyes were still on the book in front of him.

'I wanted to discuss with you about finding the person I'd like to marry.'

'So now you regret turning down such a good shidduch?'

'No, he wasn't the right one for me. I was wondering ... what if, I happened to find my own shidduch?'

Her father sat up, folded his arms and gave her his full attention. 'How would you do that?'

'Like if I went out and ... met someone.'

'Where would you meet *someone*?'

How would she explain this without implicating Raizy? 'Um ...'

'Miri, what are you trying to say?'

'If I met people –'

'What *people*?'

186

'Young people. My age. And we went out together.'

'Are you saying you want to go out with boys?'

'Er …'

'Like a *shiksa*?' He stressed the last word with disgust.

Miri winced. This wasn't going well.

'You want to mix with that *drek* that hangs around the streets of Golders Green and Hendon?'

Miri's voice quivered. 'They're not drek.'

His face reddened. 'Miri! How dare you answer back and contradict me!'

'I'm sorry.' Miri couldn't raise her head to look at him. 'But that wasn't exactly what I was thinking of. What if I was to meet someone closer to home, from our own neighbourhood?'

'Our boys don't go out looking for their own shidduchim! They don't go around talking to girls! They conduct themselves the right way.'

'What if he didn't come from a Chassidish family?'

Her father threw his hands in the air. He was fast losing patience with her. 'Then from where?'

Her mouth was as dry as if she'd swallowed a spoonful of sand. 'The … um … Adeni community?'

'Adeni?' He looked at her as though she was crazy. 'Adeni!'

'Y-yes.'

He pushed back from his chair and stood up. 'Adeni?' he shouted. 'Have you gone mad? Are you out of your mind? They're not even frum!'

Her voice trembled. 'They are. It's just –'

'And how would you know?'

'There's something I –'

He thumped the table with his hand. Miri gave a start and

stepped back.

'Enough of this already! I'm not interested in hearing more of your foolish talk! You'll do what we expect of you. You will have a proper shidduch with a Chassidish boy from a decent family and let this be the end of it! I don't want to hear you bring this up again. If word gets out about the *meshuggener* ideas you have, no one will want to marry you! Now go to your room!'

Miri fled the room, ran upstairs and locked herself in the bathroom. Her hands shook so much she struggled to pull her phone out of her bag. There was a message from Ben.

How's it going?

She placed her hand over her mouth to stifle her sobs.

I failed!

Through blurry eyes, she related the disastrous conversation.

I should just go speak to him tomorrow evening when he has calmed down a little. We have no other option.

But you are going away the day after.

Yeah, I know.

If it goes wrong, I will have to face them on my own. What if they don't let me see you again?

There was an extended pause. *You're right. Don't want to risk that. Wish we didn't have to wait to sort this out until I get back. But sounds like we have no choice. I'm away for less than two weeks. Will you wait for me?*

Yes. I will!

I'll go straight from the airport to your home and speak to your parents. You have my word.

I'll be counting the days.

My parents already leave for Israel tomorrow. Come over and

I'll make you a nice supper. And we'll make the most of our last evening alone together.

I'd love that x

Chapter 19

The past few weeks had taken their toll on Miri. She appeared on Ben's doorstep looking pale and drained. He melted in sympathy and wrapped his arms around her.

'Oh, Miri! I know it's been tough. At least that whole shidduch business is over. I'll only be away for a few days, and then we'll get this all sorted. I promise.'

'But it will be lonely without you. I'll miss you so much!'

'I'm going to miss you too. It's exciting going to the wedding and all, but I wish I could bring you with me.'

'If only.'

'Hey! What if …'

She seemed to toy with the idea for a moment. 'I wish. But doing something so reckless might ruin everything. I must be careful about how I tread right now.'

'I know, you're right. It would be irresponsible to pull a stunt like that. One day soon, though, I hope I can take you there.'

'I can't tell you how much I'd love that.'

'Come into the kitchen. I'm almost done.'

He pulled out a stool for her and she sat beside him at the counter, watching as he peeled and chopped an array of colourful exotic fruits. She pointed to one.'What is that?'

'Papaya.'

'I don't think I've ever eaten it.'

He sliced the fruit in half and scooped out the large clump of seeds in the centre. He cut a tender slice and offered it to her. She took a cautious nibble.

'It's good, no?'

'Mmm.' She bit into it again, much to his delight.

Miri helped him carry the food through to the dining room. He'd spent all afternoon preparing a feast for her: pitta bread with homemade dips, grilled chicken, rice and salads.

The room glowed by the light of many candles that he had placed around the room. A single rose in a crystal vase sat at the centre of the table, and he had laid the table for two.

'This is beautiful!' she said.

It pleased him that his efforts had touched her. He was intent on making this, their last evening together, a special one.

'More fruit salad?' he said.

'No, I'm stuffed! Thank you, it was all so delicious.'

'My pleasure.' He placed his arm around her and leaned his forehead against hers.

An unwelcome ring on the doorbell interrupted the moment.

'Are you expecting anyone?' said Miri.

'No.' The bell gave another impatient ring. 'I wonder who it could be. I'll be right back.'

Ben peered through the peephole and blanched when he discovered Daniel and Moshe standing outside. Should he ignore them and pretend he wasn't home? But they would have already noticed his car parked outside and the light from the kitchen. He opened the door a crack, keeping his smile polite.

'Hey, stranger! Where have you been these past few weeks? Hardly seen you or heard from you. Thought we'd drop by to see you before you fly off tomorrow. I also want to give you a wedding gift for Davidi, from the family.' Daniel pushed the door open wider, dropped a gift-wrapped package into Ben's hands, then sauntered past him down the hall.

'Thanks. I've just got company with me right now ...'

'Oh yeah?'

Too late. They had already walked into the dining room. Ben followed behind them and mouthed a discreet 'Sorry.' Miri gave him a look that said it was fine.

Daniel took in the intimate scene in the dining room. Candles on the table, a vase with a single rose and ... Miri.

He couldn't believe his eyes. *Miri?*

'You remember Miri, don't you?' Ben asked.

'Yeah, sure I do,' he said. 'Hi, Miri!'

'Hi, Daniel, Moshe. Nice to see you both again.' She greeted them without a hint of self-effacement. What had happened to the shy, awkward girl he'd last seen several weeks ago when they went out for the evening to the cinema? In her place sat an attractive young woman with poise and confidence. And the two of them seemed very much an item. He shot Ben a questioning stare, desperate to ask what was going on, frustrated he could not.

Ben looked awkward as he rejoined Miri at the table, and

Daniel realised it had been a mistake to barge in unannounced, plainly ruining their romantic evening. An uncomfortable silence settled, uneasy smiles all round.

'So,' Moshe said. 'What time do you leave tomorrow?'

'My flight's around ten in the evening,' Ben said.

'And what's the schedule once you get there?' Daniel asked.

'I arrive in the early hours of Friday morning. Davidi will meet me at the airport and drive me over to my aunt and uncle's place, where I'll be staying together with Natalie and my parents. We have the *hinnah* on Sunday night, followed by the wedding on Monday, *sheva brachot* the rest of the week and the *Shabbat Chatan* the next weekend. Then I fly back on Monday.'

'You're gonna have a busy few days,' Moshe said.

'Yeah, quite a whirlwind. I'm really looking forward to the wedding and seeing all the family, but also looking forward to getting back again.'

Daniel noticed Ben's surreptitious glance towards Miri.

'Can I get either of you something to drink, perhaps?' Ben said.

'Cup of coffee would be great,' Daniel said.

'Same here,' said Moshe.

Daniel rose together with Ben. 'I'll give you a hand.'

'No need, I'm good.'

'I'll come and help all the same.'

Once in the kitchen, Daniel cornered Ben as he filled the kettle and prepared two mugs with coffee and sugar.

'You're a dark horse, aren't you? What's going on? You mentioned in passing that you met Miri again, by chance, and that you'd seen her a few times. But I didn't figure it was like this. What's with this candle-lit dinner?'

Ben's smile was bashful. 'We're going out.'

'I can see that. But this isn't just casual going out. Looks like quite a serious relationship.'

'Yeah, I guess you could call it that.'

'How did this happen?'

'It just did.'

'And her parents are OK with all of this?'

Ben concentrated at a point on the floor. 'They don't actually know yet.'

'You're crazy! Ben, what are you playing at?' he said in an urgent whisper. 'You are both going to be in such deep shit if they find out. Do you realise that?'

Ben gave a helpless shrug.

'Does your mum have any idea that you're dating a Chassidic girl?'

'Yeah.'

'And she's happy about it?'

'Not exactly.'

'I bet not. What does she say?'

'She thinks I need to finish with her.'

'She's right. This is insane! You should listen to your mum and end it.'

'I'm not going to do that.'

'So what the hell are you going to do?'

'I'm planning on speaking to her parents when I get back.'

Daniel snorted and took his cup of coffee. 'Good luck, mate.'

Ben carried one of the mugs into the dining room for Moshe. Daniel quickly emptied the contents of his own while still standing, then checked his watch.

'Didn't realise that was the time already.'

Moshe had only taken his first sip when Daniel dragged him from his seat. 'What's the rush?' he asked.

'Hurry, or we're gonna miss the game.'

'What game?' said Moshe as Daniel ushered him out.

Ben returned from seeing them to the door. 'Sorry about that.'

'It's fine, don't worry,' said Miri. 'Ben, what is a hinnah?'

'Ah! A hinnah is a party that usually takes place a few days before the wedding for family and close friends of the bride and groom. The family of Davidi's fiancée, Keren, originate from Morocco so they also have this custom.'

'What, they'll both be there, Davidi and Keren, right before their wedding?'

'Uh-huh.'

'Wow! With us, they don't even see each other after the engagement party.'

'So it's a little different.' Ben smiled. 'They dress up in traditional, ornate costumes and look stunning. The bride will often wear lots of jewellery too. At this party, they, and all the guests, get their hands printed with henna dye. That's why they call it a hinnah, Hebrew for henna. Hinnah, henna – same word. There is food, and music, and dancing – lots of dancing. It's great fun!'

Ben walked over to the display cabinet in the living room, flicked through a row of CDs, then inserted one into the stereo system. An up-tempo Mizrahi dance song burst through the speakers. He clapped his hands to the beat and shook his hips in an exaggerated fashion. Miri raised her eyebrows in amusement. It was good to see her looking happy

195

again.

He held out his hands to her. '*Habibti?*'

Unsure of what to do, she remained rooted to the spot. Ben took her hands, one by one, and led her into a dance.

'Next time, it will be our turn,' he said.

Miri laughed as he spun her around the room, and they danced to the music until they were breathless, forgetting everything else.

Chapter 20

An unending flow of passengers streamed towards departures, pushing luggage trolleys, suitcases on wheels, and pushchairs, and lugging backpacks, skiing equipment, and instruments. Their animated chatter was interrupted every so often by the sound of a chime, followed by a flight announcement that cut over the sibilation. Soon, Ben's flight would be called, but for now, he and Miri sat in the café area, snatching these last few minutes together.

'It's going to cost a fortune for either of us to send messages or call each other,' Ben said. 'So I spoke to my brother last night and asked him to get me an Israeli mobile. He's going to charge it first and bring it with him when he comes to fetch me. As soon as I meet him at the arrivals gate on the other side, I'll text you my new number.'

Miri nodded, trying to hold her emotions in check.

'Hey, don't get upset. We can keep in touch all the time, just as we do now,' he said. He handed her a slip of paper. 'And these are the details of my return flight.'

She scanned the note and slipped it into the pocket of her coat. 'I'll be there.'

'If it's too much hassle for you to come to the airport, I can always meet you back at home, after you finish work.'

'No, I want to come. I'll make an excuse for why I have to leave early like I have a dentist appointment.'

'Only if it doesn't put you out.' Ben gave an appreciative smile. 'I can't deny, it will be great to see you as soon as I arrive.'

Miri reached into her bag. 'I have something for you.' She handed him a flat package, gift-wrapped with purple tissue paper and a matching ribbon. 'I hope you like it.'

He untied the ribbon and carefully peeled off the paper. In his hands was a framed painting of two figures, standing in silhouette on the Millennium Bridge, locked in an embrace under a purple sky, with the River Thames, Big Ben and London Eye in the background.

'Wow, Miri, this is incredible! You painted this?'

'Yes.'

'I'm speechless. It's beautiful. You've got serious talent.'

Miri blushed at his praise. It was the first time anyone had ever seen her art.

Ben leaned over and kissed her. 'Thank you. I'll treasure this – always.'

He re-wrapped the paper around the picture and made space for it in his backpack. There was another chime, and an announcement that the passengers on Ben's flight were to make their way to check-in and security.

Reluctantly, he stood up. 'I guess it's time I got going.'

He took her hand and she walked with him to the gate. Miri studied his face, trying to imprint every detail to memory. How lucky she was to be with this incredible person. Why was she letting herself get so emotional? Twelve days wasn't a lot to ask for a promise of forever. The time would soon pass.

They stood facing each other at the departure gate, neither of them willing to be the first to say goodbye. Ben gazed at her, towards the gate, and back to her. 'Come with me for a minute.'

He led her to the side, away from the rush of passengers. Then he reached for the gold chain around his neck and unclipped it.

'This belonged to my brother, Natan. It's very precious to me.'

He held it out to her.

'But –'

'Look after it for me until I return.' He fastened it around her neck. 'Until I can give you something else.'

She looked down and touched the Magen David pendant. 'Ayuni,' she whispered.

He nodded. 'Ayuni.'

Then he kissed her, his lips expressing the emotions for which he had no words.

At the departure gate, he hugged her once more. 'I love you.'

'I love you too. Mazal tov for the wedding.'

'Thanks. Take care of yourself and *b'ezrat Hashem*, I will see you soon.'

Miri climbed the stairs at Manor House Station, carried along by the tide of passengers. Darkness, ice-cold air, and the rumble of city traffic met her as she surfaced onto the main road. There was no warm car beckoning, or loving company to escort her home. She felt a pang of emptiness.

She hunched against the bitter wind, drawing the collar

of her coat tighter. In the surge of headlights, she saw her bus approaching, but it sped away before she could think of running for it.

With a few minutes until the next one, Miri paused on the side of the pavement and checked her phone for messages. She found Ben had sent her a string of texts while she had been underground with no network. He'd been updating her on his progress through the airport. He'd sent the last one ten minutes earlier.

Waiting to board. Miss you x

Miri sent a quick reply. *Miss you too. Just got off the tube x*

Her ears pricked up. Rapid footsteps in the distance, behind her. She slipped the phone back into her bag and started walking. The footsteps grew louder, closer. Menacing in the way they echoed hers. She stiffened and upped her pace. Her heart raced. She dared not turn.

There was no one at the bus stop. Should she continue walking? Cross the road?

A heavy blow landed on her back. Miri lurched forward. She gasped, winded, and lost her balance. Her hands splayed out in front of her, trying to stop her fall. But she continued hurling forwards. Her hands met the pavement, scraped across the rough surface, and she hit the ground.

An unseen hand grabbed her arm and yanked at it. Miri cried out in pain and terror.

'Oi!' A male voice shouted. Then she heard footsteps running away.

Sprawled on the pavement, she raised her head to see two hooded youths make off down the road at a sprint. The white trainers and baggy trousers of a third figure passed in front of her eyes.

She whimpered and lifted her raw, grazed hands. They stung in pain. A trickle of blood oozed from her mouth. She sat up, panic rising, and felt around her mouth, checking her teeth one by one, relieved to find none of them were missing.

Her eyes followed the direction her attackers had taken. She caught sight of the third figure. He had stopped in front of the housing estate. He looked this way and that. Then he turned around and ran back towards her.

Terrified, she tried to lift herself in order to get away, but he was too fast.

She stared up at the tall black man who now loomed over her, and froze in fear.

He knelt beside her.

'Are you OK?' His accent was cockney with a slight Jamaican lilt. 'I saw what happened, but they was too quick. Gone before I could catch 'em. What scum!'

She looked at him wide-eyed.

'Are you alright? Did they hurt you?'

Her chin trembled. 'I d-don't think so.'

'Here, let me help you up.' He held out his hands and helped her to her feet. She gazed up at the towering figure. She didn't even reach his shoulders.

Miri sensed something missing. She patted her coat. 'Oh no!'

She crouched on the ground and checked the surrounding pavement in frenzy.

'Oh no! Please, no.'

Hand over her mouth, she stared down the dark street and stumbled to her feet. 'They stole my bag!'

'D'you wanna to go to the police and report it? I can come with. I saw the whole thing and I'm willing to give a statement.'

She shrunk away. 'No! Please don't call the police. I can't
–'

'I understand. You not supposed to be here right now or something?'

Miri felt ashamed at having been found out by this stranger. 'No.'

'Which hood are you from?'

'Hood?'

'Yeah, which area?'

'Oh. Stamford Hill.'

'Are you Hassidic?'

She nodded.

'Thought you might be. I've met some of your bros in the club where I DJ.'

Her brothers? Miri couldn't make sense of what he was saying.

'Are you heading back to your crib now?'

'Sorry, what's that?'

'Your house?'

'Yes.'

'Me too. I live in the same hood. I'll make sure you get home safe.'

Miri was wary but felt too vulnerable to dissuade him. He smiled at her as they stood together at the bus stop. It seemed he was only trying to be helpful. She hoped his intentions were genuine. She also prayed that she wouldn't bump into anyone from her community.

'My name's Simon, by the way. What's yours?'

'Miri,' she said without thinking. She wondered whether she should have just done that. Perhaps it was dangerous to have given him her name.

'So you was somewhere you shouldn't?   With your boyfriend or something?'

'Something like that.'

'Is he not Jewish then?'

'No, he is.'

He shrugged. 'So what's wrong with that?'

'He's not from the same community.'

'Is that a problem?'

'Kind of.'

She felt odd discussing her personal life with this total stranger. He must have sensed her unease because he changed the subject. 'So, anyway, like I said earlier, I DJ part-time in a local garage club, and I also teach sports in a high school. What d'you do?'

'I work as a secretary at a property company.'

'That's cool.'

Their bus was approaching. Simon put out his hand for it to stop. 'Here we are.'

Miri reached for her purse, then remembered. It was gone.

'It's alright. I got it.' he said and paid the driver for her ticket as well.

'Thank you so much.'

'No problem.'

She moved to the back of the bus to find a seat. Like a bodyguard, he followed and sat beside her. Miri began to warm to this caring stranger. She was curious about an earlier comment he'd made. 'What did you mean before about my brothers at your club?'

'Oh yeah! A couple of them come to the club.'

'Are you certain? My brothers?' She couldn't imagine they'd

ever set foot in such a place.

'Yeah, your bros, as in, your crowd.'

Who could he mean? She doubted it was Ben. He wasn't much into the clubbing scene anymore. Though she guessed he'd like the music. Raizy? Improbable. Then again … what else she had she got up to and 'forgotten to mention' before getting engaged? It was more likely to be someone like Daniel or Moshe. But how would Simon have any idea she knew them?

'How do you know my crowd?'

'You said you're Hassidic. They're about your age, so I guess they might be friends of yours.'

'Chassidish?' Her voice rose in pitch.

'Yeah.'

'I doubt it. Chassidish boys wouldn't go to a club.'

'Well, they are. One of them told me. A young guy called Sruli.'

The name indeed sounded like it could be genuine. 'What's his family name?'

'Dunno.'

'It doesn't matter. I doubt I know him, anyway. We don't mix with the boys much.'

'There was another. Nice guy called Pinny. Pinny Finer.'

'No, doesn't sound familiar.'

'He used to come quite often. Until the one night he got wasted. That's how I found out his full name was Pinny Finer.'

'Sorry?' Miri broke in. 'Did you say his surname was Finer?'

'Yeah. Know him?'

'I think I might.'

'Friendly guy. Had a tough life, though. No dad. Could relate, as I also lost mine when I was young. He told me he didn't get on that well with his mum. Very strict, always on his back. He liked to come to the club to escape from things.'

'What did you say happened to him? What does wasted mean?'

'Collapsed like. You know, drugs. Like I said, I got on well with him and didn't wanna cause him trouble. So I checked his wallet for his full name and called a friend off his mobile to ask if he could take care of him. This guy arrived, I think his name was Tuli Cohen. Something like that. At least that's how he was listed on his phone. He seemed out of place and frightened. First time in a club, I reckon. Devout looking, know what I mean?'

Miri thought if her jaw opened any further, it would hit the floor.

'That's the last time I saw Pinny. But he messaged after to thank me for my help. He went off to rehab in Israel after that. Drugs is bad news.'

'Thank you,' she said.

'What for?'

'For helping me this evening. I appreciate it.'

'No problem. You alright now? You got a real fright.'

'I'll be alright. I get off at the next stop.'

'I can get off here too. It's only a short walk to my crib.'

She hesitated as he stood beside her at the stop. It was clear he intended to accompany her all the way home. How would she explain that to her parents? She was already getting curious stares from passersby. They must have appeared as an incongruous pair.

'Thanks once again for all your help. I'll be OK from here,' Miri said.

'Maybe I should walk you to your door to make sure you

get home alright and don't have no more trouble.'

Out of the corner of her eye, she noticed two young Chassidish boys in their early teens, staring and pointing at her from the other side of the road. 'I'll be fine. My parents, they might have questions if they see … you know …'

He gave a good-natured laugh. 'Yeah, yeah, I get it. Hassidic daughter arrives home with a guy like me. Might have some 'splaining to do. Alright, if you're certain. Well, take care of yourself, Miri.' He extended his hand. She glanced about before giving it a discreet shake.

'And next time, get your boyfriend to escort you. Manor House ain't a good place to hang out on your own at night.'

'How will I repay you for the bus fare?'

'Don't worry about it. See ya around!' He strode off down the street with a relaxed bounce and turned around to wave at her. Miri waved back.

Alone again, the shock of what had just happened caught up with her. She couldn't tell Ben. She couldn't face going home. She needed a friend.

Raizy opened the door to Miri with a smile, but it faded as she took in her pale, dishevelled appearance, a split lip and a bruise on her forehead.

'Oysh! Miri, are you OK?' She took her arm. 'My mother is giving a shiur in the dining room. Come upstairs.'

She shut the bedroom door behind them. Miri sank to the floor, curled her knees to her chest, wrapping her arms around them.

Raizy put her arm around Miri. 'What happened?'

She let out a shaky breath.

'Did you see Ben off at the airport?'

Miri shut her eyes and the tears poured out.

Raizy ran downstairs, returning with a glass of water. 'Drink this.' She held the glass to her lips and encouraged her to take sips.

'Now, please tell me, what happened to you?'

'When I got back to Manor House I was … attacked … by two men.' Her face crumpled in anguish.

Raizy offered the glass to her, coaxing her to drink more.

'What did they do to you?'

'They stole my bag!'

'Oh no! Did they hurt you at all?'

'They pushed me, I fell on the pavement and cut my lip. But everything's gone! My purse. My phone. Now I have no way of getting in touch with Ben!'

Raizy sat next to Miri, who heaved with sobs, and tried to comfort her. Bile rose to Miri's throat. She placed a hand over her mouth. 'I'm going to be sick –'

She struggled to her feet, fled to the bathroom and lowered her head over the toilet bowl just in time.

Miri returned after several minutes looking drained, but she'd washed the caked blood off her face and was a little calmer.

'Are you feeling any better?'

'A bit. But what am I going to do? Ben said he would text me when he got to Israel with his new number, but now he won't be able to.'

'Call or message him on his regular phone and explain what happened.'

'I can't! His number was in my purse. And that's also gone! I never learnt it by heart.'

'Did he tell you where he's staying?'

'With his aunt and uncle, but I don't remember their names or where they live.' Her eyes welled again, and she put her head in her hands.

'Don't panic. I'm sure we'll figure out a solution. Anyway, it's just a few days and it will go fast, you'll see. He'll be back soon.'

'But I can't bear not speaking to him for so long!'

Raizy hugged her. 'You're tired and in shock. You've had a scary ordeal. Tomorrow, after a good night's sleep, you'll think of something.'

'I hope so.' Miri swallowed hard. 'Do you think Hashem is punishing me?'

'No. Why would you think that?'

'Because of –'

'You mean because you're going out with Ben?'

She didn't answer.

'Of course you're not being punished. So you're dating a guy. Big deal. Not much difference to when I was seeing Daniel and the other guys. You've done nothing terrible. Manor House is a dodgy place at night. In fact, I should have thought about it before and come with you. I'm just relieved you weren't seriously hurt.'

Raizy walked over to the dressing table, rummaged through her cosmetics and returned with a beige tube. 'I better apply some concealer to your face. If your mum sees you coming home in this state, you'll get a lot of questions.'

'Thanks, Raizy. It feels like a nightmare. First having to say goodbye to Ben, then the attack and having my phone stolen.'

'I know. But don't worry, everything is going to be alright.' Raizy dabbed on the concealer and stepped back to admire her work. 'Hang on. If they stole your bag, how did you get back from Manor House?'

'I took the bus.'

'I thought you said your purse was in your bag.'

'It was. But a kind man who lives somewhere nearby helped me.'

'A chossid?'

'No, he was black. His name was Simon. He tried to chase after the men who attacked me, but they got away. He stayed with me and paid for my bus fare.'

'Wow!'

'But it gets more interesting. He told me he works as a DJ in a garage club.'

'You've lost me. What's a DJ and what's a garage club?'

'Garage is a style of music. You know the kind you hear from those cars when they go past with the fast beat and deep bass? It sounds like that. And a DJ is someone who plays the music in a dance club.'

Raizy chuckled. 'Ben's taught you well, hasn't he?'

The mention of his name induced a weak smile. 'Anyway, he told me a few of the Chassidish boys from our neighbourhood have been there.'

'No! That can't be true. He must have been joking.'

'That's what I thought at first.' She fixed Raizy with a meaningful look. 'Then he mentioned a name I recognised.'

'Who?'

'Pinny Finer.'

'As in, Pinny Finer, Mrs Finer's son?'

'Yes, the very same.'

'Her precious son who she was going on about at my engagement, bragging how he's gone off to yeshiva in *Eretz*

209

Yisroel blah blah blah.'

'Except, he didn't.'

'What do you mean?'

'From what Simon the DJ told me, it sounded as if he had been taking drugs and is in a rehabilitation place somewhere in Israel.'

Raizy drew in a sharp breath. 'Oh. My. Word!'

'And there's more. One night Pinny sort of collapsed in the club. I think he overdosed or something. They took his mobile to call someone to fetch him. And the person they called was Tuli Cohen.'

'Devorah's brother?'

'Exactly.'

Raizy looked sceptical. 'You think he's into all of that too?'

'No, I'm almost certain he isn't. From what I understand, they called a random friend from his contacts to come and help him, and that happened to be Tuli. Simon told me he didn't look comfortable being there. He didn't think he'd ever been into a club before.'

Raizy clapped her hands together. 'This explains everything! That's why Mrs Finer has it in for Devorah and her family. I guess she's worried the story would get out.'

'Yes. You could be right.'

'And that may be why she's been hounding us. Mrs Finer knows you're close with Devorah. Maybe she was afraid Devorah would blab and that word would spread. As if Devorah would ever do that.'

'When I first told Ben about Mrs Finer, he said there must be something wrong in her own life which was why she was giving us hassle.'

Raizy looked impressed. 'Clever guy. He was right.'

Miri basked in pride. 'Yes, he was.'

'How should we confront her?'

'Mrs Finer?'

'Who else? Now that we've discovered the truth, we can't let her continue ruining the name of Devorah's family, or threaten us, in order to protect herself.'

'I'm not all that good at confrontations. I'd be afraid to approach her. Especially if she figures out how I heard. I don't want to risk it.'

'Leave it to me. She's bound to be out and about shopping for Shabbes tomorrow morning and I'll have words with her.' Raizy rubbed her hands in glee. 'I'm looking forward to this.'

'What will you say?'

'I'll prepare something.'

'Please don't mention me. I can do without further trouble right now.'

'Don't worry. I'll be discreet.'

Ben emerged through the sliding doors and heard someone shout his name. He studied the sea of faces gathered around the barriers in the arrivals hall and spotted Davidi standing opposite and waving to him. Ben dashed forward with his trolley. His brother met him halfway with a firm hug. 'Hello, bro! How was your flight?'

'Good.' He looked expectantly at Davidi. 'Did you bring it?'

'What?'

'The mobile.'

'What mobile?' Davidi's eyes were the picture of innocence and he only just managed to hold back his playful smile.

'The phone I asked you to get me.' The corners of Ben's

mouth tightened in exasperation.

'Oh!' He pulled it out of his backpack and waved it in the air. 'You mean this one?'

'Yes, that one.' Ben tried to grab it but Davidi whisked it away, laughing.

'Can I have it, please?'

With mock reluctance, Davidi handed it over to him. Ben checked the number and immediately thumbed a text.

Davidi grinned. 'She must be special. You couldn't wait, could you?'

Chapter 21

Miri awoke, and her heart sank as the chilling memories of the night before overwhelmed her again. She heaved herself out of bed, feeling drained, as if she hadn't slept at all.

She did not look forward to facing a morning in the office with Mr Reich. Her one solace was that it was Friday – a shorter workday before the weekend.

But her most pressing concern, still, was how to contact Ben. She'd wracked her brains late into the night until falling into a fitful sleep. No closer to finding a solution.

Miri clasped Ben's necklace, which hung around her neck, and brought the pendant to her lips. She missed him so much. She didn't know how she was going to get through the next few days.

Nothing else for it, Miri grabbed her clothes and Raizy's tube of concealer and headed for the bathroom. She didn't need another telling off from Mr Reich for coming late again.

Raizy had awoken earlier than usual that morning, leaping out of bed with rare enthusiasm. Today she was going to confront Mrs Finer.

She surprised her mother by offering to do the last-minute shopping for Shabbes, but was still giving Kosher Basket a wide berth. Raizy hadn't set foot in there ever since her engagement.

Her first stop was the bakery where she bought a chocolate cake and three loaves of crusty, fresh challah, still warm from the oven and exuding a divine aroma. She left the welcoming heat of the shop for the bustling high street and raw cold that stung her ears and ankles. Raizy plunged her hands deep into the pockets of her quilted coat and hoped she wouldn't have to wander the streets for too long.

As if on cue, there she was, marching with a determined stride, her eyes sweeping the street like a security camera on the lookout for anything untoward. Raizy was ready and rehearsed. If Mrs Finer thought she could make trouble for others to protect her precious son, she had another thing coming. Raizy strolled towards her and pretended to be daydreaming.

'Raizy!' Mrs Finer said.

'Hello, Mrs Finer! Sorry, I was miles away. I didn't see you there.'

'I suppose you were thinking about your chasseneh.'

'Yes, of course. It's almost all I think about. There's a lot to organise.'

'You probably don't have time these days for much else, not least seeing your friends?'

'I still try to make time to see my close friends.'

'Close friends like Miri?'

'Indeed.'

'Perhaps your dear friend should take a leaf out of your book and settle for a decent shidduch rather than hanging around

214

with undesirables.' Mrs Finer pursed her lips in disapproval.

'I'm not sure I understand. What undesirables?'

'The other day, I spotted her in a car with some Sefardi-looking boy.'

'Oh! Fancy that.'

'I wonder if her parents are aware of her antics.'

'I wouldn't know. By the way, how is your son, Pinny, doing?'

'Borich Hashem, he's making excellent progress in yeshiva.'

'How interesting. Is that what they call rehab these days?'

Mrs Finer stiffened. Her eyes blinked rapidly. 'I–I don't know what you mean.'

'Really?' Raizy faced down her prey with folded arms. 'I understand he's been frequenting rather undesirable places himself. Garage clubs perhaps? I hear he also developed a bit of a drug problem.'

'Who told you that?' she snapped. 'Was it that Cohen girl?'

'No, it wasn't Devorah, she's too good to tell tales. Besides, I doubt she would have the faintest clue what a garage club is. She'd probably assume it was a kind of *gemach* to help people if their car broke down. No, I have other sources.'

Mrs Finer shrank back. 'It's n-not true.'

'Ah, but it is. Because I also went to that club a few times.'

'You?'

'Oh yeah!' Raizy assumed a cool pose. She was settling into her role and rather enjoying herself. 'Before I was engaged, I made a few mistakes and did things I shouldn't have. But then I did *teshuvah*.'

'You're lying.'

Raizy smirked. 'I got to know the DJ, and he filled me in on the story about how your son overdosed, and they had to call a friend to help him.'

'Who else knows?'

'No one. At least, not yet.'

'He isn't a bad boy,' she said, on the verge of pleading.

'And are any of us so terrible? We're all human. None of us are perfect, and sometimes we make mistakes. But you see fit to pass judgement, spread rumours and give people bad names.'

'I have no clue what you are talking about.'

'I think you do. And if you don't want your little secret to get out, I suggest you start giving more thought to what you say about others.'

Flustered, Mrs Finer swayed from side to side.

'If you dare breathe one word about Miri. To anyone. And I mean anyone, including her parents, I'll make sure that the entire community knows about your son before the day is out. I would also suggest you try to fix the damage you've done to the Cohen family. I'll be keeping a close eye on you from now on.' Raizy gave her a self-satisfied smile. 'Have a git Shabbes.'

She turned on her heels and sashayed away, leaving Mrs Finer standing there, shopping bags on the floor and mouth agape.

A misty rain descended, dampening the pages of Ben's siddur. Even the grey Jerusalem morning seemed to reflect the sombre mood. Ben stood with his family around the grave, a heavy silence hanging over them. It seemed to carry the weight of their collective pain. Once more, the gaping loss hit him like a sharp blow. Ben's jaw strained from the tension as he watched his father finish his prayers and wipe away the tears. They formed a circle. Ben, his father, mother, his sister and brother, in a family embrace, drawing strength from each other.

His mother was the first to pull away. 'We'd better get going. We still have to visit Savta.'

'Please give me a couple more minutes and I'll be right with you,' Ben said.

'Sure.' His father placed an affectionate hand on his shoulder. 'We'll be in the car.'

Ben waited until his parents and siblings were out of sight. He bent down and kissed the headstone.

'Hi Natan,' he said. 'Mazal tov on our brother Davidi's wedding. We are so going to miss you. It won't be the same without you.'

He traced his brother's name on the grave with his finger and tears streamed unchecked from his eyes. 'I suppose you will celebrate with us wherever you are.'

Ben shivered as he recalled the day they buried his brother. Everyone wrapped up in their shock and sorrow. Ben had felt an emptiness, as if a little piece of himself died with him. Since then, he had drifted, sometimes merely existing, wondering whether he'd ever experience happiness again. Until the day he saw the rays of sunlight break through the bleak, grey clouds that had enclosed him. And for the first time since his world shattered, he looked forward to the future with hope.

'I have something to tell you. I've met someone too. She's like no one else I have ever known.' He wrapped his arms around his shoulders and hugged them towards himself. 'Her name is Miri. She's kind, talented, and beautiful. She gets me, I get her, and she's so easy to talk to. We can talk for hours and hours. I want to spend the rest of my life with her.'

He smiled through his tears. 'But I guess you knew all that already.'

Somehow, Miri made it through the morning at work and straggled home. From the minute she got in, there would not be a moment's peace until Shabbat began. She wondered whether Raizy had spoken to Mrs Finer and was eager to hear what had happened. Miri had to admire Raizy: she had guts. Getting engaged hadn't quenched her fiery spirit. The same daring she displayed the night she invited her along to meet …

Miri stopped in her tracks, hand over mouth. Yes. Why hadn't she thought of it before? It was so obvious.

She checked the time on her watch. It was after one o'clock. Maybe a slim chance he would still be there.

She sped through the streets. As she had suspected, Kosher Basket was already shuttered for the day.

But she'd found the solution. If anyone had Ben's number, it was Daniel. As soon as they opened on Sunday morning, she would be there to ask him for it.

Chapter 22

The telltale signs of concealer hid Miri's bruises but couldn't disguise her drawn face. Raizy was hesitant to mention Miri's recent ordeal. Instead, sitting on the floor with their backs against her bed, she held Miri's attention with an account of her confrontation with Mrs Finer.

'"Is that what they call rehab these days?"'

'What! You didn't actually say that, did you?' Miri said.

'Oh yes, I did!'

'How on earth did you explain how you knew what had happened to Pinny?'

'I confessed I'd also visited that club, got to know the DJ, and that he was the one who told me all about it.'

'You're daring,' said Miri. 'More than that. You're brilliant.'

Raizy gave a little bow. 'Why, thank you. But what else could I do? It was the only way she would believe me without letting on I'd heard it from you.'

'Aren't you worried she might spread rumours about you clubbing?'

'Not a chance. She wouldn't risk it. And you can rest easy, she won't say a word to anyone about your "undesirable Sefardi-looking boy" either.' She gave Miri a playful dig in the ribs.

'Thanks, Raizy, I appreciate you doing that for me.'

'It was a pleasure. I mean it. I thoroughly enjoyed myself.' She giggled at the recollection. 'But Miri, you'd better be careful. You can't carry on like this. Someone else might spot you with Ben and cause trouble.'

'You're right. As soon as he gets back, we're planning to approach my parents together and speak to them.'

Raizy remained unconvinced but chose not to voice her misgivings. Instead, she returned to a safer subject. 'Mrs Finer is such a hypocrite. Can you believe she had the nerve to tell me he "isn't a bad boy," even though she knows full well what he was involved in?'

'Simon told me he was a nice guy. Perhaps he is. I kind of feel sorry for him. And even Mrs Finer to an extent.'

Raizy threw up her hands. 'Why? He took drugs, hung out in nightclubs and got up to who knows what else. As for Mrs Finer, she went around gossiping and giving others a bad name when her son got up to far worse than any of us.'

'He lost his dad when he was young. It couldn't have been easy for him growing up without a father figure around. And it seems he also had a complicated relationship with his mother, which I totally understand. If she gave us hassle, imagine how much worse it was for him. At some point, it probably got a bit too much. The club was his way to escape, but then he fell in with some interesting company. It couldn't have been easy for Mrs Finer either, losing her husband and then struggling to raise her children on her own. Maybe she worried what would happen if people discovered the truth about her son, so put on this "holier than thou" attitude as a defence.'

'That doesn't give her the right to do what she did.'

'Which is why I'm glad you put her in her place once and for all. Let's hope that puts an end to her trouble-making. Although, we should be careful to keep the information about Pinny confidential and not let it go further.'

'Agreed. It ends here and we never mention it to anyone else.' Raizy fingered a corkscrew curl and grinned. 'But I must admit, I did enjoy making her squirm a little.'

'I would *love* to have seen the look on her face when you confronted her.'

'It was a picture! And all thanks to your meeting Simon the DJ. At least something good came of it. Not only that, but had this not happened, Mrs Finer would have blabbed to your parents before long, and we wouldn't have been able to stop her.'

'It was beshert.'

Raizy studied her. 'How are you doing?'

'Much better. The bruises and scratches are healing. And most important, I figured out a way to get in contact with Ben.'

'That's great. How?'

'I'll ask Daniel for Ben's English mobile number.'

'Yes, of course! Why didn't I think of that before?'

'I'm planning to go into Kosher Basket on Sunday to talk to him.'

'See? I said you'd figure something out. It's all going to be OK. And at least we get to spend more time together this week.'

'I'm sorry if I've been neglecting you.'

'It's fine. I'd probably be the same if it was the other way round. Anyway, the chasseneh preparations have been keeping me busy.'

'How are things coming along?'

She flashed her sparkling diamond solitaire. 'Well, as you can see, I've got my ring. I have my first wedding dress fitting on Wednesday. My parents have found a lovely three-bedroom house about five minutes away from our place. We've got a viewing arranged for Monday morning. And, big news: I started kallah classes.'

But Miri had not heard her.

'Miri!'

She jolted awake. 'What were you saying?'

'Am I that boring? You fell asleep.'

'Sorry. No, you aren't. Not at all. I'm just tired. I guess I haven't been sleeping well the past few nights.'

The sound of laughter echoed through the Jerusalem night as the brothers, cousins and close friends sat at a café on a pedestrianised lane off Ben Yehuda Street. Outdoor umbrella heaters kept the chill at bay while they enjoyed their beer and light-hearted banter.

'Is it true that in England, before a guy gets married, his friends tie him up to a lamppost?' asked Ilan, one of Davidi's friends.

'There are no set rules,' said Davidi. 'But they do lots of crazy things on stag nights such as putting the grooms on trains when they're drunk and fast asleep, and they wake up several hours later, with no money, not knowing where they are.'

'Ben,' said Ilan, a suggestive glint in his eye. 'What do you say we give your brother a proper stag night, eh?'

'Hey! Don't get ideas,' said Davidi, and he shook a castigatory finger.

'You keep out of this,' Ilan said, waving away the finger. He was grinning now. 'Ben, you in?'

Ben didn't reply. He was studying something under the table. Ilan reached across to tap him on the shoulder, and Ben glanced up. 'Sorry, what did you say?'

'Shall we send your brother on a train somewhere this evening?'

Davidi chuckled. 'Don't listen to him!'

Ben's expression showed no hint of humour. 'Where to? I doubt you'll find any trains still running this evening.'

'It. Was. A. Joke. Ben.' Ilan shook his head.

'Oh.'

Davidi leaned over and whispered into Ben's ear. 'Something's bugging you. What's going on?'

'I'm not sure. I haven't had a reply from Miri yet, though I've sent her several texts. It's not like her.'

'Have you got the right number?'

'Yeah, I checked a few times.'

'What about the correct dialling code for the UK?'

'I double-checked that too.'

'Well, you know how rushed Fridays can be. And remember, they are two hours behind, so Shabbat only finished in London a short while ago. Give her a chance.'

'You're right.'

Davidi gave him an affectionate pat on the back. 'Lighten up and try to enjoy yourself.'

Ben forced a smile, but couldn't shake off his unease.

Chapter 23

The frigid, early-morning air seeped through her thick winter coat. Miri hopped from foot to foot as she waited outside the still-shuttered entrance to Kosher Basket. Daniel should have been here by now.

She was just about to leave when a jangle of keys caught her attention. She spun around. But it wasn't Daniel.

'Sorry,' said the ginger-bearded young man with an apologetic smile. 'The car wouldn't start this morning.' He unlocked the shop and invited her inside.

Miri wandered the aisles, now feeling obliged to make a purchase. The shop had the sour odour of herring mixed with chemical floor cleaner; it made her feel queasy. She grabbed a packet of crackers and quickly paid for them. Deflated, she returned home.

Later that afternoon, Miri sauntered into the kitchen. Her mother sat at the table immersed in planning another food rota, and Miri casually opened the fridge to inspect the contents. 'We're low on milk. Would you like me to get more?'

'Thanks, Miri.' Without lifting her eyes from her list, she pointed to her bag on the counter. 'Please get me a loaf of bread and a box of eggs, too. There should be a five-pound note in my purse.'

Her second visit proved just as futile.

Maybe he doesn't work over the weekend.

Miri's frustration was mounting. She'd now have to wait until Monday afternoon to try again.

Her workday dragged. She watched the clock, her mind elsewhere. Was Ben worried, upset – even angry – with her for not keeping in touch? Or was he too preoccupied in the excitement for his brother's wedding, taking place that evening, to care? She was desperate to get Ben's number from Daniel to smooth over any misunderstandings and explain her silence.

But to her disappointment, it was the same worker from the previous day who greeted her. With bile rising from her stomach, Miri did a sweep of the aisles and peeked into the stockroom at the back, but there was no sign of Daniel. It left her with no alternative.

She cautiously approached the cashier. 'Excuse me. When does Daniel come in?'

He inclined his head. 'Who's Daniel?'

'He works here.'

'I don't know of anyone by that name.'

'Are you sure?'

'Well, I've been working here for three weeks and done the various shifts but never met him. He might be the guy I replaced.'

'Would you, by any chance, have contact details for him?'

'No, sorry.'

'Oh.'

'But the boss may have it. He'll be in around eight if you want to check with him.'

That wasn't an option. The owner was an acquaintance of her father; they attended the same shul. She couldn't risk word getting back to her parents she was asking for a boy's phone number.

'No, it's OK,' she mumbled. 'It's not important.'

Raizy opened the door to find Miri hunched on her doorstep.

'What happened?' Raizy said.

Miri's eyes were red, and she was too distraught to answer.

Raizy ushered her upstairs, her fears mounting with every step. Dreadful scenarios ran through her mind. Miri's parents had found out about Ben. Or she'd spoken to him, and he told her he wanted to break up. Or perhaps her parents were forcing her into another shidduch.

In the privacy of Raizy's room, Miri sagged to the floor and broke down.

The dread tightened in Raizy's stomach. 'You haven't been attacked again …?'

She shook her head.

It had to be something awful. An accident or else someone had died.

'He … wasn't … there!' Miri said in between sobs.

'Who?'

'Daniel! He no longer works at Kosher Basket.'

'Oh.' Raizy breathed an inward sigh of relief. It was an inconvenience, to be sure. But she was thankful it wasn't any of the more serious possibilities she'd considered. 'Are you certain?'

'Yes. Another worker who's new and started there three weeks ago told me he's never seen Daniel.'

'Sorry, I didn't realise. I haven't been in there for a while.'

Miri placed her head in her hands. 'What do I do now?'

Raizy placed a sympathetic arm around her shoulders. Miri was taking all of this far too seriously.

'I'm not sure if there's anything else you can do but wait until he returns. It's only another week to go, that's all. Spare a thought for me. I have to wait for much longer than that to see my chosson –'

'A whole week! I can't wait that long. He probably thinks I don't want to speak to him anymore.'

'I'm sure he doesn't. He's bound to realise something has happened to your phone.'

Miri sprang up. The colour had drained from her face. She covered her mouth and fled into the bathroom, heaving.

It was several minutes before she returned. But as soon as she settled back beside Raizy, the tears flowed again.

'Miri, what's got into you? I know you're missing Ben, but it's just a week to wait. That's all. It's not like you to get this upset over something. You keep working yourself into a state. You're constantly exhausted. You keep throwing up. If I didn't know better, I'd say you almost remind me of my sister Dassie, who burst into tears at the slightest thing, when she was … having her first …' She drew a sharp breath.

No! It can't be.

Raizy fixed Miri with a stare. It was several seconds before she next spoke.

'Miri … um … did …' Raizy felt unbearably hot. 'Did you … er …'

Bewildered, Miri asked 'What is it?'

Raizy squirmed and lowered her voice. 'Did … you … sleep with Ben?'

Miri averted her eyes.

'Miri?' There was an urgency in her voice. 'Did you go to bed with him?'

Miri shrugged.

'Answer me!' Raizy put her hands on Miri's shoulders, forcing her to face Raizy.

'Er …'

'Did you, or didn't you? Yes, or no?'

'Yes,' she whispered.

'Shit!' Raizy said.

Miri's eyes flew open.

'This is important. I need you to give me a truthful answer. Have you missed a period?'

'I'm not sure. It might be a little late this month.'

Raizy got to her feet. Her breathing came fast and shallow. She pressed her hands to the wall, trying to steady herself.

'What's wrong?' Miri said.

Raizy turned to face her. 'I think you may be … pregnant.'

'But how can I be? I'm not married yet.'

'Bloody hell!' Raizy blew. 'Don't you know the facts of life?'

Miri shrank back and curled her arms around her knees. 'I think so. I'm not certain. I'm so confused.'

'Miri, what were you thinking? More to the point, what the hell was he thinking? Did you even use protection?' Raizy studied her face. 'No, I guess not.'

Raizy paced the floor, charged with nervous energy. But alongside her fears, another emotion struck her: envy.

One burning question came to mind, but she didn't dare ask.

She couldn't ask. Not right now.

Miri looked petrified. 'What do I do?'

'First, we need to make sure.'

'How?'

'By taking a test. You can buy them at the pharmacy, off the shelf. Go tomorrow morning and get one. But for goodness' sake, whatever you do, don't go to the pharmacy on the high street. If anyone should see you ... oh my God! Take the bus down to Finsbury Park, or Stoke Newington. Bring it back here and we'll do it together.'

'What if I am?'

The question hovered between them like an impending storm cloud.

'I could be wrong. Stress can mess with your cycle. What with that shidduch and the attack. It could be a shock reaction.'

The hypothesis seemed to placate Miri. But Raizy's insides churned, and she prayed for a false alarm.

Davidi's foot stamped hard on the glass with a satisfying crunch.

'Mazal tov!' The cheer rang out from the wedding guests, and the band struck up. Family members from both sides embraced, and Ben hugged his brother. It filled him with joy to see the look of unbridled happiness on Davidi's face as he took his bride's hand and they walked down from the chuppah, beaming at one another.

But he missed her. The miles between them had opened a void of silence and unanswered questions.

Family and friends followed the couple, singing and clapping. Ilan put a hand on Ben's shoulder and drew him into the lively group. Ben pushed his worries to the back of his mind as they sang and danced the newlyweds down the aisle.

'Mazal tov!' Ben heard a familiar voice greet him.

And he turned around to see his ex-girlfriend, Yael, with a broad smile across her bright, red-painted lips.

Chapter 24

'Did you get it?' Raizy asked.

Miri's was tense as she pulled out the pharmacy bag from her pocket. She clutched the bag tight. As long as she didn't open it, none of this was real.

How had they arrived at this point from an evening that had only ever intended to be some harmless fun? But Raizy had been the catalyst for what followed, and it weighed on her. If her involvement became known, she risked her engagement being called off, just like Devorah's brother. Miri would be disgraced, and Raizy, branded with a bad name. It would affect any further shidduch prospects for both of them – and in Miri's case, for her younger siblings too. With their reputations ruined, their lives within the community would effectively be over.

Raizy couldn't let that happen. If the test proved positive, there was only one solution.

It wasn't hard to find her work number. Ben regretted he hadn't thought of the idea sooner. But even as he dialled, he had misgivings. He didn't want to cause her any trouble. He cancelled the call before anyone picked up. Then he reconsidered. He had no other option.

'Can I help you?' said the brusque woman on the other end.

'Uh, yeah, hi …' he said. 'May I please speak to … Miss Miri Fogel?'

'She's not in the office.'

'When will she be back?'

'Who is this?'

He thought fast. 'Oh, I'm calling from … her bank.'

'She called in sick today. Try tomorrow.'

'Thank you. I'll do that.'

Disappointed, he hung up. Something was awry. He sensed it.

While his family slept off the late night of the wedding, he grabbed his jacket and crept out for a walk.

Ben wandered the residential streets of Ramat Gan, the winter sun warming his back. He walked with no fixed destination, eventually finding himself at a flight of stone steps that led to a park, built on the side of a hill and split into three different levels. Miri would love it here. He climbed the further two flights to find a tranquil seating area bordered by trees and vibrant, purple bougainvillea.

He couldn't understand why she hadn't responded to any of his messages. Their relationship had seemed solid before he left. They'd had an understanding between them and promised to stay in touch.

Was she really unwell as the woman claimed? Had something else happened that prevented her from calling?

Was it possible her parents – or her nosy sister – had discovered her phone and taken it from her?

Where are you, Ayuni?

Raizy read through the instructions. 'One line means the test has worked. Two lines, it's positive.'

They watched the stick as a cloud of pink swirled its way across the indicator panel.

One line appeared in the window.

'Alright,' Raizy said in a shaky voice. 'It worked.'

Seconds passed.

They looked to one another, an unspoken prayer passing between them. Maybe Miri would be alright …

They looked back at the stick.

Then there was another. A second, strong, pink line.

'No. It can't be possible. It can't be.' Miri let out a low moan. 'What am I going to do?'

Raizy gripped Miri's hands in hers. 'I don't think you have a choice but to make it go away.'

'I don't understand. How can I do that?'

'I've heard of clinics where you can go. They have proper doctors who can do it safely. I'll find out more and come with you.'

'I should speak to Ben first.' Her legs buckled, and she dropped to the floor. 'I can't even reach him. What am I going to do?'

Miri stared at the test stick as if it held the answers.

Raizy crouched beside her. 'Even if you could call him, I'm not sure it would be a good idea to break news like this to him over the phone. Can you imagine how shocked he'll be? And you need to act fast. Each day you wait puts you at risk of discovery.'

'I want to discuss this with him.'

'Perhaps it's better if he finds out afterwards. It's not as if he can do anything.'

'But –'

'Do you think the two of you can approach your parents and announce you're pregnant?'

'No.' The gravity of the situation descended on Miri. 'But, maybe if he tells them we're getting engaged.'

'Even *if* they agree – and that's an enormous if – they'll set a date for the wedding in a few months. By which time you'll be showing. How are you going to explain that?'

'I still feel I should speak to him about it.'

'Has Ben actually spoken to you about getting engaged?'

'Not in so many words, but we spoke about being together.'

'That's not a commitment. I get the impression that in his community, they usually date for much longer and get engaged a few years later than us. He may have intentions to be with you but not want to settle down for a while yet. His older brother who just got married, how old is he?'

'Twenty-six.'

'And Ben is how old?'

'Twenty-two,' said Miri in a choked voice.

'What if he doesn't feel ready to get married? How will he react when he finds out you're pregnant? He may want to run a mile in the opposite direction.' Raizy's voice softened. 'I know how difficult this is, but it might be easier if he never knows.'

'I won't do that. No matter what his reaction, I want him to know. He has a right to know. He's back in less than a week. A few more days shouldn't make much difference.'

Raizy hadn't anticipated Miri's vehemence. Never before had she seen her display such determination.

'In the end, it's your choice, I suppose,' Raizy said. 'But please, be careful.'

Miri crawled out of bed. Her stomach churned. She rushed for the bathroom, but Ruchi was already occupying it. She sat outside on the worn patch of carpet next to the door and lowered her head between her knees, trying to stop herself from throwing up.

Her mother appeared at the top of the stairs. 'Miri! What's wrong?'

'I'm not feeling too good.'

'You look terrible. Your face is almost green. Do you think you should see a doctor?'

'No!' Miri shouted. Her mother was taken aback. 'I mean, there's no need. It's probably one of those twenty-four-hour bugs.'

'OK. But I think you should stay at home for a day or two. You can't go to work in that state.'

Her mother banged on the bathroom door. 'Come on, Ruchi! You've spent enough time in there. Other people need to use the bathroom too.'

As soon as Ruchi emerged, Miri barged past, slamming the door in her face. She barely reached the toilet bowl in time.

Raizy was right. Each passing day put her in a more precarious situation.

Ben excused himself from the café where his family were having a late breakfast and stood outside, on the street, away from the noise of conversation and background music. He called the number again.

'Good morning, is Miss Miri Fogel there please?'

'Sorry, she's not in today. Is there a message?'

'No, it's all right.'

235

Ben stared at the phone. *Miri, what's happened?*

He was beginning to wonder whether to change his ticket and fly back earlier. He missed her so much. But if he did that, he'd miss the rest of the celebrations with his family; and he knew that wouldn't be fair to them. He was torn between the people he loved most.

Fresh fears infiltrated his thoughts. Had Miri's parents found out about them? What if they had pressured her into another shidduch and she had submitted?

Chapter 25

Time crawled. One hand in front of the other, edging forward. Uneasy minutes interrupted by pangs of visceral fear. If Raizy had read the signs, how long would it take Miri's mother, a veteran of ten pregnancies, to become suspicious?

Finally, Monday had arrived. Miri had tossed and turned most of the night, and it was still dark when she gave up on the idea of sleep altogether.

Today she would be reunited with Ben. Though it wouldn't change her predicament, at least she would no longer be alone. She felt sure Ben would have a better grasp on how to deal with the situation. There was only a three-year age gap between them, but a chasm in terms of worldly experience.

The rest of the household was still asleep when Miri crept into the bathroom. There, in privacy, she peeled off her voluminous, pink nightdress and climbed onto the edge of the bath. From that precarious vantage point, she studied her naked body in the mirror that hung above the sink. She examined her shape from the front and side and tentatively stroked her hands across her stomach. It still looked flat. No one would suspect anything. Yet.

Then she dressed with care. A fitted, grey top; a baggy

cardigan to hide its shape until she left the office; her new denim skirt (which had led to some disapproving looks from her mother the last time she wore it), and her favourite black suede boots. She wanted to look her best to meet Ben at the airport later that afternoon.

It was a struggle for her to get through the day at work, both from excitement and the two dashes to the bathroom to throw up, but she had to show her face. She had taken off too many sick days already. It made it a little more bearable to know she would see Ben in a few hours and picturing him holding her in his arms again sent a delicious tingle down her spine.

'Are you feeling better?' said Mrs Klein.

Miri wiped the dreamy smile off her face and assumed a sober expression. 'Yes, thanks, borich Hashem. I came down with something like the flu or a virus. I've got a doctor's appointment this afternoon for a checkup, so I'll be leaving a little earlier.'

The bookkeeper continued working her way through a pile of invoices without looking up. 'Perhaps you should have gone earlier, instead of taking extended amounts of sick leave and giving the rest of us double the amount of work.'

'I'm sorry.' Miri hoped this would close the discussion.

'Oh, and someone rang for you a few times while you were away. I think they said they were from the bank.'

With all the turmoil, Miri had almost forgotten about the theft of her bag. She assumed it was to do with her replacement debit card. She made a mental note to call her branch as soon as she had sorted through the mountain of paperwork dumped on her desk. That, or when the assiduous bookkeeper took a rare break. Whichever happened sooner.

Mrs Klein huffed in annoyance when the phone rang later that afternoon in the middle of her calculations.

'Can I help you?'

'Uh … hello …' The voice on the other end sounded strained. 'Is Miss Miri Fogel there, please?'

'Sorry, you missed her. She left about ten minutes ago. Did you want to leave her a message?'

'Yes. Could you please tell her Mr Aharoni called and ask her to call back as soon as possible? Here's my number …'

Miri bounded through the arrivals hall and checked the details from the note in her pocket with the information on the flight board. His flight was early and expected to land in five minutes. She squeezed herself with delight and joined the crowd gathered around the barriers.

A rush of passengers emerged through the double doors. Miri kept herself occupied, trying to guess who they were and where they were coming from. Some appeared to be first-time visitors who stared at everything in wonder. Travellers returning from overseas holidays sported fresh tans and bright, summery clothes that looked conspicuous for a murky winter's day in London. The business travellers were a different breed altogether in their conservative suits, wheeling carry-on bags. They strode with purpose, scanning for their names on signs held up by drivers congregating near the exit.

A young family emerged: identical twin girls wearing pink satin dresses, with netted underskirts like little princesses. Their father pushed the trolley, and their mother held their hands. All at once, they broke away from her grip and ran.

Instead of looking alarmed, she smiled. They raced towards an older couple and their outstretched arms.

The flight information on the screen was refreshed. Ben's flight had landed.

Not long now ...

To pass the time Miri looked for clues to figure out passengers' country of origin: duty-free bags bearing the name of the departure airport, and luggage tags with their flight information. The latest arrivals seemed to have come off a flight from Madrid that had arrived twenty minutes earlier.

A woman with waist-length hair searched the waiting faces. She paused, smiled in delight, and rushed straight into the arms of a man meeting her who held a single red rose.

Miri hadn't given consideration to how she would react when she saw Ben again. Unlike that woman, she had to be careful in case someone from her neighbourhood was on the flight and saw her.

But that was a minor detail. She had a far more significant concern weighing on her mind: the confrontation with her parents later that evening when they would break the news to them about their relationship. She was dreading it.

Miri prayed they would give their blessing, or at least be willing to accept it. Though chances of that happening were remote. But she had made up her mind. She wanted to be with Ben, and if her parents forbade it, she would have no choice but to go against their wishes. With Ben by her side, she would have the courage to face the inevitable consequences.

A bearded man in a black hat and dark suit came through carrying a bag with Hebrew writing on it. This had to be the first of the passengers off Ben's flight. Her pulse quickened.

Any minute now, he too would appear through the sliding doors. She hoped he wouldn't be too upset with her for her lack of communication while he was away. She was sure that after she explained, he'd understand. But what if he'd got used to not being in touch all the time? What if he was losing interest?

He'd told her he wanted to be with her, but had he meant it, or was that an impetuous comment blurted out in a moment's passion when he feared she would have to marry another?

No. He'd made his intentions clear.

Then again ... they'd never actually discussed getting engaged. Did he intend for them to marry soon or only after he had finished his degree and found a job? Raizy was correct in her assessment. In his circles, it was acceptable to date for an extended period. Not so in hers. It wasn't the 'done thing'. Supposing – in the unlikely event – her parents agreed, they would insist on an immediate engagement. There was no way they would allow her to go out with Ben otherwise. (And even then, they would object to them seeing each other during the engagement period.) What if Ben wasn't ready to make that commitment? Where would that leave her?

And this was all before taking the pregnancy into account.

The trickle of people from Ben's flight had grown into a flood. Miri kept her eyes peeled.

What if Raizy was right? Would he back off when he learnt about her condition?

Perhaps she should have listened to Raizy and gone to the clinic. He need never know what had happened.

Enough!

Why was she doing this to herself now and ruining the moment for which she'd waited for so long?

Any minute now ...

Passengers who had arrived off later flights from Istanbul and Frankfurt were emerging. But she hadn't yet spotted him.

Miri tried to ignore the knot in her stomach. She double-checked the details. They were correct.

She studied the tags of each passenger as they passed. There didn't appear to be any more from his flight.

Maybe he was still waiting for his luggage?

She would wait another five minutes and then decide what to do next.

Five minutes became ten, fifteen, thirty ...

A whole hour passed and still no sign of him.

She headed for the information desk, constantly looking back to the arrivals gate to ensure she didn't miss him. A woman sat behind the counter staring into the middle distance, her long, manicured fingernails wrapped around a mug of tea.

'Excuse me,' Miri said.

The woman adjusted her focus and looked at her blankly.

'I've been waiting for someone to come off a flight from Israel, which landed over two hours ago. Would it be possible for you to check a name on the passenger list?'

'Sorry, can't. Not allowed to. Security.'

'Is there anyone else I can speak to?'

'No. Sorry, love. There ain't.'

Miri headed back to the arrivals gate, though she knew it was pointless.

He wouldn't be coming.

Lost in a sea of anonymous people, endless faces flashed in front of her eyes, becoming a blur.

Her feet carried her down the escalator, from the airport into the tube station. She made the return journey in a haze and found herself at Raizy's door.

'You're the last person I expected to see tonight,' Raizy teased. Then her expression froze. 'Where is he?'

Miri shook her head. Raizy took her by the hand and led her upstairs.

'I waited and waited, but he never showed.'

'Did you get the right day and flight?'

She handed the note to Raizy, who took a quick glance. 'Miri, I'm so sorry.'

'I don't understand what happened. I don't know what to do now or which way to turn.'

'Think hard. Did you ever meet any other friends, or members of his family?'

'I once met a friend of Ben's brother along with his wife. Except, they live in Israel and I can't even remember his name. The only other one is Daniel.'

She remembered the last time she saw Daniel, at Ben's place, the night before he left, when he cooked supper for her. How adorable he looked mouthing 'sorry' to her as Daniel waltzed in uninvited, followed by ...

'Moshe!' She sprang up. 'Moshe! Daniel's friend.'

'You have his number?'

'No. But don't you remember when Chaya wanted to go out with him, and then Daniel called her that evening when the two of you were out, and you thought ...?'

Raizy nodded, comprehending.

'Do you have Chaya's number?'

'Yes, I do. But there's a good chance she'll slam the phone down on me again. We fell out, remember?'

243

'Please!' Miri begged. 'Can you at least try?'

Raizy rocked her head from side to side, weighing it up. 'I'll do it.'

She withdrew a floral-covered book from her bedside table and leafed through the pages. Then she locked the door and reached into her handbag. To Miri's surprise, Raizy pulled out a mobile phone. It seemed she and Naftoli had figured out a discreet way to keep in touch during their engagement.

Raizy dialled the number.

Miri's heart pounded.

'Hi Chaya,' she said. 'Please don't hang up on me. It's Raizy, and I'm calling you about something important. First, I want to apologise for what happened between us. I was in the wrong and I hope you can forgive me.'

There was a long pause. Miri tried to read her expression.

'Yes ... Thank you ... I need to ask you for a favour. It's not for me, but someone else. I can't explain right now, but it's extremely urgent. Do you still have Daniel's phone number?'

There was another pause. 'Thank you, Chaya! Thanks so much! And please, don't mention this to anyone else.'

Miri hovered, waiting for her to hang up. 'Well? What did she say?'

'She's going to text it right now.'

Her phone buzzed.

'Got it!'

Miri let out a breath.

Raizy put the phone on speaker to make the next call. 'Hi, Daniel,' she said, her voice wavering. 'It's Raizy here.'

'Oh ... hi, Raizy.'

'Is this a good time to speak?'

'Er ... yeah. Fine. I understand congratulations are in order.

Your recent engagement?'

'Yes, thank you. I'll get straight to the point. I'm calling on behalf of Miri. Ben was supposed to return from Israel this evening, but he wasn't on the flight. Has he called you at all?'

'No, sorry. I thought he was coming back today, but we haven't spoken since he left. Isn't Miri in touch with him?'

'No, she had her phone stolen so hasn't been able to speak to him.'

'Oh.'

'Do you have any idea what might have happened to him?'

'No, I don't. Last time this happened –'

'He's done this before?'

Daniel cleared his throat. 'Well, yeah.'

'And what was the reason last time?'

'That occasion, he stayed on to spend more time with Yael.'

Miri tapped Raizy's shoulder. 'Who is Yael?' she mouthed.

'Who's Yael?' Raizy said.

'She was his … old girlfriend. Look, I'm just saying what happened last time. The situation was different back then.'

'Do you have any way to contact him?'

'All I have is his English number. But it's rather late there.'

'Please, call him now!'

'Alright. Give me a few minutes.'

They waited in tense silence. Miri stared at the phone. She crossed her arms and held her shoulders, walking in circles.

The phone rang.

'Hi, Raizy. I tried, but he's switched off his phone. I'm sorry. It's past midnight there, too late to contact anyone else now. But I'll make a few calls in the morning and see if I can find out what happened and get a number for him.'

'Thanks, Daniel, I appreciate it. Please call me as soon as

245

you have an update. I often have to keep this phone on silent mode because no one knows I have it. So if I don't pick up, leave me a message.'

'Sure, no problem. I understand. And Raizy, I'm sorry for how things turned out.'

Miri let out a wail, and she doubled over. She felt like such a fool. Raizy had warned her from the beginning not to get too serious. Having not heard from her in all this time, had he decided to drop her? And why had he never mentioned Yael?

Raizy held Miri's shoulders to prevent her from falling. 'You heard what he said, he doesn't know anything. Hopefully, he'll be able to find out more tomorrow.'

'It's over, isn't it?' Miri said through anguished sobs. She searched Raizy's eyes but could find no signs of hope there. 'Do you think he got back together with his old girlfriend?'

'I don't know. It seems strange that he never told you about her. Maybe, Daniel's got it wrong, though.' she said. 'But no matter what, I don't think you have any choice but to go to the clinic tomorrow.'

Miri slumped to the floor. There was no way out.

She nodded in acceptance.

And defeat.

Chapter 26

Ben shut his eyes, willing, hoping. Please be there, Miri. Please pick up the phone.

The woman on the other end sounded irritable. 'She's not here!'

'I called yesterday afternoon and left a message for her. Did she get –?'

He didn't finish his sentence. She had already disconnected the call.

Ben leaned back against the wall and slid to the floor. His life was unravelling in front of his eyes all over again. He'd exhausted every option.

Unless …

He checked directory inquiries for the number and dialled.

'Hello?'

The line was unclear.

'Hello?'

Was it her?

'Hello?'

One way to find out. 'Hello … Is that Mrs … Finer?' he bluffed.

'No, it's Mrs Fogel.'

'Sorry, wrong number.' He hung up.

There was a light tap on the bedroom door and Davidi peered in. 'How are you doing?' Ben didn't need to reply. His brother placed a supportive arm around him and brought him to his feet. 'We need to go.'

He couldn't leave things as they were, but how else to get word to her? Then it came to him. Daniel.

Perhaps Daniel could figure a way to contact Miri. But he would have to be careful. Could he trust Daniel to be discreet? Did he have any other alternative?

'Come on, Ben,' said Davidi.

'I need to make a quick call.'

'There isn't time. Everyone's here.'

Later. He'd do it as soon as they returned.

Ben composed himself and followed his brother.

From the gate, Raizy watched the shattered figure of her friend approach his front door. The outcome was inevitable, but she had agreed to this slight detour to placate Miri.

She rang the bell and knocked on the door. But Ben's family home remained dark and silent, and provided no answers. Raizy's heart ached to see her friend's anguish. She led Miri away, still casting glances back at his house.

'Have you heard back from Daniel?'

'Nothing yet.'

Raizy checked her watch. They had a few minutes to spare. She beckoned Miri, and they ducked into a small side alley.

'Hi, Daniel. Any news?'

'Not yet. I've tried his UK number several times, but it's still switched off. I sent him a text too, just in case. And I've also called a few people who I'm waiting to hear back from.'

'Thanks for trying. Please call me the minute you find out anything.'

'Will do.'

Before they entered the low, brick building, Raizy checked her phone once more.

'Anything?' Miri asked.

'I'm sorry.' Raizy switched the handset to vibrate and dropped it into her bag.

A buxom woman sitting at the reception desk acknowledged them with a cordial smile. 'May I help you?'

'My friend has an appointment,' Raizy said.

'Can I have your name, please?'

'M-Mir –' Miri's eyes darted around. 'Will anyone find out about this?'

'No, don't worry,' she said. 'Everything here is confidential.'

'Miri Fogel,' she mumbled.

The receptionist handed Miri a booklet and directed them to a waiting room. The cheerful interior was unexpected. Padded, lilac chairs surrounded a coffee table piled with magazines. Raizy and Miri found two empty seats at the far end, next to a window framed by flowery, purple curtains.

Raizy looked around at the others seated there. The cross-section of ages and backgrounds surprised her.

A couple in their late thirties with their heads bent close together conversed in hushed tones. Her face was tear-stained, and he held her hand. 'Nothing else we could have done …' Raizy overheard him say. 'Abnormalities … this for the best …'

A bored-looking twenty-something and her friend browsed fashion magazines as if waiting for a manicure appointment. Opposite, a woman dressed in an abaya sat alone, eyes downcast, twisting her hands in her lap. A young woman, around their age, with cornrow braids glanced up. She and Raizy acknowledged each other with grim smiles.

Raizy watched Miri leaf vacantly through the booklet. 'I'm right here with you. It's going to be alright.'

Miri seemed to have retreated into herself and continued to flip absently through the pages.

For all Raizy's pretence of calm, inwardly, she felt scared and out of her depth. She had no experience with anything like this either, but she knew they had no choice. It would be impossible for Miri to remain in the community, pregnant and unmarried. They would ostracise her. Her life would be ruined. A termination was the only solution. She only hoped that, in time, Miri would recover from this traumatic ordeal, be willing to accept a shidduch and try to make a life for herself.

As for Ben. Raizy had to admit, he seemed more serious than most of the boys she'd ever met and must have had genuine feelings for Miri. But separated from each other, with no means of communication, perhaps he assumed she wanted to break up. His family may also have encouraged him to finish with her, knowing that Miri's parents would never accept him. A relationship like theirs wasn't sustainable. Then, on the rebound, Ben had probably returned to what was familiar: his old girlfriend. Raizy could understand him.

All the same, she resented Ben for the hurt he'd caused Miri. It had been careless of him to leave her in this position. Miri was too sensitive. She didn't understand the rules of the game.

A middle-aged woman with greying hair appeared at the doorway. 'Miri, please!'

The cushioned carpet absorbed the sound of their footsteps as they crossed the room to meet the consultant. It was as if they had designed the place to muffle thoughts and emotions and make them lose track of time.

'Is it alright if I see you by yourself?' the woman said. She turned to Raizy. 'It won't be long.'

Raizy watched Miri trail behind, her posture sagging, chin to her chest. She looked so fragile.

The consultant sat opposite Miri, poised with pen in hand. She consulted her file.

'So, Miri, you're here to see me about an unplanned pregnancy.' She had no qualms to say aloud what Miri and Raizy had been afraid to whisper. 'Have you reached a decision about it?'

Miri's reply was toneless. 'Yes.'

The consultant continued with further questions, taking notes along the way. Miri heard herself answering, but her voice sounded hollow to her ears as if it belonged to someone else, her mind and body in different places. She'd become trapped in a living nightmare.

Miri focused on a crack in the green-painted wall behind the consultant. She followed its trail from the ceiling to a shelf stacked with ring binder files in blue and red. Then she returned her attention to the consultant to nod in the affirmative. Miri noticed how she fiddled with her pen and that her nails were the same shade of bright pink as her lips.

A drawn-out, detailed explanation followed. The consultant's words sounded far away. Miri feigned attention but found it hard to absorb much. Through the fog, she picked out

251

the words: choices, abortion, adoption, process, termination.

'Do you have any further questions?'

'No,' said Miri.

'Before we finish, one last point to make.' She regarded Miri with compassion in her eyes. 'If you decide to change your mind, you can stop this process whenever you want. Remember, you're in control all the way through. Now, if you return to the waiting room, the nurse will call you soon.'

Ben excused himself and retreated to the privacy of the bedroom. His mind drew a blank on Daniel's number, so he switched on his other phone. A new message alert flashed. A surge of expectation. But it was only from Daniel.

Call me as soon as you can!

'Ben! Thanks for calling back. What happened mate?' Daniel said.

'I'll explain, but first –'

'Weren't you supposed to come back yesterday?'

'I got delayed because –'

'Did you hook up with Yael again or something?'

'What?' Irritation crept into Ben's voice. 'No! Why would you even suggest that?'

'I thought –'

'Can you please let me get a word in to explain?'

A petite, blue-uniformed nurse entered the waiting room.

'Miri, please come this way.'

Miri dragged her feet and stopped before she reached the nurse. 'Can my friend come with me, please?'

'Yes, alright.'

The nurse walked at a confident pace, leading them through a maze of corridors, into a dimly lit room, and shut the door behind her. Turning to Raizy, she pointed to a spare chair resting against the wall. 'You can sit there.'

Raizy took a seat and placed her bag beneath her feet.

'Please go behind the curtain and remove the garments from your lower half,' the nurse said to Miri. 'Then pop yourself onto the bed and cover yourself with the sheet.'

The examination bed was partially screened by a pale blue curtain suspended from a ceiling track. Through the opening, Miri glimpsed an unusual support device, on either side, at the foot of the bed. At first, she wondered why a bed would need armrests, and why in that unusual place. Then she realised they weren't for her arms at all. Placing her feet into the stirrups would prise her legs apart, trapping her onto the bed in a vulnerable position.

An abrupt snap made her look around. The nurse had moved across to the side of the bed, poised in front of a stand that held a computer monitor, and was slipping on a pair of tight rubber gloves. Then she withdrew a long, plastic stick.

What kind of torturous medical procedure was this?

Her stomach tied in knots, Miri broke out in a cold sweat. She backed away but collided with the closed door that barred her way.

'What are you going to do to me?'

Miri tried to turn the handle in desperation, but her clammy hands couldn't get a grip.

'It's alright,' said the nurse, trying to calm Miri in her anxious state. 'We're only doing the ultrasound. It may be slightly uncomfortable, but it won't hurt.'

Raisy rose from her chair, took Miri by the arm and led her to the bed. She gave her a little nod as if meaning to echo the nurse's reassurance. Hemmed in behind the curtain, Miri trembled and struggled to remove her clothes.

The nurse urged her onward. 'Just let me know when you're ready.'

Raizy's phone rang, but no one answered. After three attempts, Daniel waited for the line to transfer to voicemail and left a message as she had asked.

'Hi, it's Daniel. First, I want to apologise. I may have caused a slight misunderstanding …'

Miri lay down as instructed and placed her feet into the stirrups. Her breath came fast and shallow.

'Try to relax,' the nurse said.

Miri shut her eyes, clenched her fists, and winced as the nurse inserted the wand.

'What are you doing?'

'We need to see what's there before we go ahead with the procedure.'

Miri cautiously opened her eyes. The nurse's attention was fixed on her monitor. Miri wondered what she was viewing and peeked around. Monochrome particles she couldn't decipher moved across the grainy screen. The image paused, focusing on a small, flickering, white dot. Miri pointed towards it.

'What's that?'

The nurse kept her eyes focused on the screen. 'A heartbeat.'

Blip. Blip.

A heartbeat.

The fog lifted. She saw it.

This wasn't just a pregnancy.

She was carrying the start of a child.

A child created out of love.

And it was hers.

And Ben's.

Our child.

The realisation hit her like a slap to the face. She was in an impossible situation.

Her hand felt for his necklace.

Look after it for me until I return. That's what Ben had said when he placed it around her neck. He had given her his precious possession to look after. He had been planning to come back. Whoever this Yael was, Miri was almost certain she wasn't the reason for his delay. Ben hadn't left her. Something serious must have happened to delay him.

Her heart pounded; it thudded in her ears.

Once done, there would be no going back. No way to change her mind. Miri had to be absolutely certain before she went ahead. Is this what she really wanted, or just what Raizy thought would be the best solution for her?

She was no longer sure.

What if she didn't go ahead with the abortion? Would she have the strength to face the consequences: her parents, her community, her reputation? Was she prepared to lose everything?

The thought terrified her.

A termination would be a quick fix and solve the problem. Except, she would have to live with it. This baby was a part of them both.

But then, how might Ben react to the news? Raizy had warned it might frighten him away. She would be taking an enormous risk. What if he left her, and she had to do this all alone?

Wouldn't it just be easier to end it now? He'd never have to know …

But didn't he have a right to know? Could she forgive herself if she did this to him?

Miri was in a spin, but one fact was becoming clear: the only person who could make this decision was her.

Not Raizy. Not the nurse. Not her parents.

Not even Ben.

If there was ever a moment in her life where she had to take control, that time was now.

This had to be her choice alone.

Her eyes shifted from the screen, to the nurse, to Raizy, and back to the grainy image on the screen.

'Stop,' Miri said.

'What is it?' the nurse asked.

'Stop!' she shouted.

Momentarily disconcerted, the nurse removed the wand. 'Is everything OK?'

Miri took her feet out of the stirrups, adjusted the covering over her lower half and sat up.

'I've changed my mind. I'm not doing this.'

A powerful urge to escape overwhelmed Miri. She yanked the curtain shut and flung on her clothes.

'Miri, what's going on?' Raizy said.

Miri fled from the room and rushed through the corridors, losing her way several times until, at last, she found the exit and the cold light of day. She looked up at the overcast sky and inhaled the fume-filled air of the traffic-clogged inner city. No purple flowers. But this was her reality. She set off once more and broke into a run.

'Miri, wait!' Raizy called.

Out of breath halfway to the bus stop, Raizy caught up with her.

'What's got into you?'

'The consultant told me I could stop the process any time I wanted. She said I would be in control the whole way. So I took control,' Miri said.

'This is crazy!'

They boarded the bus and ensconced themselves in the row right at the back.

Miri lowered her voice. 'Raizy, I'm expecting a baby.'

'Yes, I think I'm well aware of that by now,' Raizy said.

'Don't you see? All this time, I was so overwhelmed by the idea of being pregnant, I never stopped to think what it meant. This is our child. It's mine and Ben's.'

'Then what exactly are you planning to do?'

'I haven't decided yet. All I know is that I'm not ready to go through with this today.'

Miri's voice was gentle but assertive and left no room for argument. 'All my life I've kept quiet and done as I was told because I didn't want to cause trouble. I moulded myself into the expectations of me and buried my dreams. Then I finished sem, and I saw my life mapped out. I'm no rebel, but I realised it wasn't exactly what I wanted and I couldn't find my place. I was confused, unhappy, but whenever I tried to express myself or ask questions, I was shut down.'

She gave a weak smile. 'Then I met Ben and found in

him someone who understood me. He encouraged me to be myself. When pressured to go on that shidduch, I feared we would have to break up and I'd be forced into a marriage against my will. I wasn't thinking straight. Neither of us were. And this situation is as much my doing as his.'

'What will you do?'

'I don't know. I hope our relationship will work out. Whatever happens, my life is infinitely better for having met him and I don't regret it. He is good and kind and genuine and comes from such a loving family.'

Miri shook her head, still reeling from the shock. 'And I'm expecting our baby.'

'You can't seriously be thinking of going ahead with the pregnancy?'

'I have to think things through.'

'What's going to happen to you? They'll throw you out of here. Where will you go? What will you do?' Raizy's voice tightened. 'And what's going to happen to me when they find out I played a part in all of this? My shidduch will be called off. My life will be ruined.'

'Please don't be afraid. You aren't responsible for what happened and no one ever needs to know of your involvement.' She put her hand on Raizy's arm. 'Whether I go ahead with the pregnancy or abort, there are enormous implications either way and only I can decide which choice to make. Please don't be angry with me.'

'Of course I'm not angry with you. And you're right. I'm not in your position. This has to be your choice.'

They stepped off the bus and lingered at the stop.

'I'm sorry I put pressure on you. But I was also scared. I hope you're not angry with me either.' Raizy said.

'No, on the contrary. I'm grateful,' Miri said. 'Thank you for being there for me. I couldn't have got through these past few days without your help.'

'Shall we go for a walk by the river and talk everything over?'

'I'd love to. But first, I need some time on my own. My siblings aren't back from school yet, so I'll have some quiet time in my room to sit and think for a while.'

'Shall I call you in a couple of hours?'

'Yes, that would be great.'

Miri shut her eyes and took a few breaths.

'Miri, are you sure you're OK?' Raizy said.

'I won't lie. I'm terrified. But I have to take responsibility and try to figure this out.'

Raizy hugged her. 'Look after yourself. And please be careful.'

'Thanks. I'll speak to you later.'

Miri set off for home, a newfound strength and quiet resilience growing within her.

Chapter 27

Raizy flung her bag onto the kitchen counter and rested her head against the cool, marble surface as she caught her breath. Wound up like a coil, she didn't dare to even consider what would happen next. A question mark hung over both of them. And yet, she felt a curious sense of relief about Miri's decision. As wayward as it was. What a morning!

She filled up the kettle and pulled out her phone as she waited for it to boil. With the dramatic turn of events, she'd almost forgotten about Daniel. She'd had her doubts anyway about whether he'd get back to her. But true to his word, he had, and she found a voicemail waiting for her.

'First, I want to apologise. I may have caused a slight misunderstanding. I finally reached Ben. It was nothing to do with Yael …'

Raizy drew up a chair and sat down to take it in.

'His grandmother has been ill for a while. Last Saturday night, she took a turn for the worst. Sadly, she passed away yesterday evening. That's the reason Ben had to delay his flight. When I spoke to him, he'd only just returned from the funeral. He's also been anxious about Miri. He told me he tried calling her several times at work, but she hasn't been there. Anyway, please be in touch when you get this message.'

Raizy stared at her phone.

He really loves her.

Miri's siblings may not have been home, but if she assumed she could slip past her mother unnoticed, she was mistaken.

Her mother sat at the kitchen table with the phone pressed to her ear, but as soon as she saw Miri, her eyes bore into her. 'I'll call you back.'

Miri headed for the stairs, but her mother followed close on her heels. 'What are you doing here at this time of the day?'

'I didn't feel well, so I left early,' she said. 'I think I'll have a little lie-down.'

'So you've just come back from work, have you?'

'Yes.' Miri tried to keep her calm.

'You've been there all this time?'

'Uh-huh.'

'Mr Reich, your boss, rang earlier.'

Miri stopped in her tracks.

'He asked where you were. I told him at work. He said you weren't.'

Miri began to panic. She had slipped up and forgotten to call in sick that morning.

'He was furious that you've been taking so much time off. He said you left early again yesterday. And this morning, not only did you not bother showing up, but you didn't even have the courtesy to call and tell him. Miri, what is going on?'

Miri desperately racked her brains for a plausible excuse. She considered saying she'd been helping Raizy with wedding

261

preparations. No. She would not risk mentioning her name.

'I'm waiting for your answer. I've had your boss on the phone yelling at me about you not showing up for work. You lied to me about being there when you weren't. Tell me where you've been!'

'Nowhere. Um –'

'What were you doing?'

'Nothing.'

'It's not "nothing". It's something. If you weren't in the office, where were you?'

Miri was burning up as if she had a fever. She wished the interrogation would end.

'I want an answer.'

'I told you already.'

'No, you didn't. This strange behaviour has been going on for a while. Something isn't right and I'm getting worried. I think it's time I took you to see the doctor. I'll check if I can get a last-minute appointment for you for this evening.'

Miri's head reeled. 'No!'

'What has got into you, Miri? I want answers and I want the truth.'

Her mother had her cornered.

No more creeping around. No more lies. She was tired of it all.

'I know what it is,' she said in a cracked voice.

'So tell me.'

Miri lowered her gaze.

Her mother grew impatient. 'What is it?'

'I'm ... pregnant,' she whispered.

Her mother took a sharp intake of breath. 'Miri! Don't talk such nonsense!'

'It's not,' she said. 'I am.'

'No, you're not. That's impossible! Tell me the truth.'

'I am telling the truth.'

'You're talking rubbish. How can you be pregnant? You're not even married!'

Miri slumped down on the landing. 'I did one of those tests. The result was positive.'

The colour drained out of her mother's face. She grabbed the banister for support. 'Were you ... attacked?'

'No. It wasn't an attack.'

She shook her head. 'No! It can't be true.'

'It's the truth.'

She shook Miri by the shoulders. 'Who did this to you?'

She had to stay strong. She wouldn't betray Ben. Or Raizy. 'You don't know him.'

Her mother let out a scream.

'No! It's impossible!'

Her mother dashed into her bedroom, Miri heard her rummaging through a drawer and she returned with a pregnancy test stick. The same kind Miri had used when she took the test a week before. She held it to her face.

'Do it.' Her voice had a threatening edge. She pointed towards the bathroom. 'Go in there right now and do it again. Then show me.'

'Hi Daniel! I got your message. Thanks for getting in touch with Ben. I can't tell you how grateful and relieved I am. Where is he now?' Raizy said.

'They're at his grandmother's apartment in Ramat Gan where his mum, uncles and aunts are sitting shiva. He told me he's feeling cut in two. He wants to come back, but also needs to be there for his family.'

'I can understand that. I'll call Miri straight away and get her to come over. Then perhaps we can arrange for them to speak. In the meantime, would you be able to update Ben?'

'Yeah, sure.'

Miri emerged from the bathroom and showed her mother the irrefutable result: Two. Strong. Pink. Lines.

She recoiled in horror. 'No!'

Downstairs, the phone rang. And in her mother's bedroom, disturbed from his nap, the baby cried. She ignored both.

'What have you done?' she screamed.

Miri jumped at her ferocity.

'You have ruined yourself! How will you ever get a shidduch now? What are people going to say about us?'

She turned away from Miri and examined the test again. 'No, this can't be right!' she said. 'No. No. No. It's not possible.'

She had never seen her mother in such a distraught state. Not even when her grandfather died. Miri had no words to make this better. Something shifted in Miri, and for the first time, she saw her mother through different eyes: as a person thrown into a situation without any forewarning and for which she had no experience. In her role as a mother, she was expected to have the answers and know what to do. But she didn't. Beneath her mother's anger, there was fear. Miri thought of the life growing inside her. Soon, she too would become a mother. And Miri's heart went out to her.

'This will ruin the shidduchim for all the children. This

will ruin us. I have to tell Tateh! What do I say? *Reboine shel oilom*! What do we do with you?'

The baby's cries continued. Mrs Fogel rushed down the stairs. The phone rang again. She returned with a bottle of milk for Eli. The phone went unanswered.

Ben checked the display and answered his mobile. 'Hi! He spoke in a hushed voice. 'Give me a minute.'

He excused himself from his family and the visitors gathered in the living room and escaped to the bedroom.

'Sorry about that. What's happening?'

'I got off the phone to Raizy a few minutes ago. She's calling Miri to come over to her place so the two of you can speak.'

'Oh, thank God!' he said. 'Daniel, I owe you one. Thanks, mate!'

'I'll hold you to that. Raizy said she'll call back soon. Stay close to your phone and I'll keep you posted.'

Raizy paced the tiled floor with mounting impatience as she dialled Miri's number over and over. It continued to ring without being answered.

'Come on. Pick up!' She tapped on the floor and muttered to herself. 'For days you've been driving me mad. We've been through one crisis after another. Now I have Ben waiting to speak to you, and you don't answer! Enough thinking already. Will you please pick up the bloody phone!'

Her mother stood over Miri's bed and clasped her head in

her hands.

'How did this happen?'

Miri stared back.

'Who was it?'

'It doesn't matter.'

'What do you mean it doesn't matter?' She pointed at Miri's stomach. 'Look what he's done to you.'

Miri edged away to the wall, trying to envelope herself into the corner

'Tell me his name!'

'It's not anyone you know.'

'Was it a Chassidish boy?'

In her nervousness, Miri had the urge to laugh, but she stifled it. 'No.'

'When did this happen? How?'

She shrugged.

'Where is this boy?'

'He's gone and I'm not sure where he is.' Miri placed a hand to her throat and felt his necklace beneath her top. She ached with emptiness.

'So he ruined your life and then he left you?'

'It wasn't like that.'

'So how was it? What happened to you, Miri? We raised you as a good *bas Yisroel*. We taught you to be tznius. Not to even talk to boys. How has it come to this? We find you a wonderful shidduch. A fine boy from an excellent family. A shidduch many families would wish for. But you turn that down. And instead, this is how you repay us? By deceiving us and ruining not only your life but the entire family!'

Miri shut her eyes. 'I'm sorry. I never meant for it to be this way.'

'Is this what you learn from hanging around friends like Devorah, with that brother of hers? Now we'll get a bad name worse than her family. Perhaps this was all her doing?'

A burning rage bubbled up inside her. 'Devorah has no connection to this! None! And her brother did nothing wrong either.'

'And how would you know that? Mrs Finer told me –'

'Mrs Finer is a *yachne* and a busybody and –' Miri was balancing on a fine line. If she revealed what she'd discovered about Pinny Finer, she would have to explain how she'd found out. And implicate Raizy.

'And what?'

'Forget it.'

'What are we going to do? Hashem, give me strength!' She paced the room, frantic, still clutching the test stick. 'Perhaps we could find out from a Rabbi whether he would permit you to have a procedure, to have it removed.'

'I already looked into that. I went to a clinic. And I've decided against it.'

Her mother gave a strangled cry that sounded barely human. She raced back down the steps. Her moans pierced Miri's conscience, filling her with guilt and shame. But Miri's resolve remained firm.

'It's an emergency!' She heard her mother shouting down the phone. 'You need to come home now.'

Despite her trepidation, a wave of exhaustion overwhelmed her, and she drifted off to sleep. She was shocked back into wakefulness by a heated conversation between her parents in the kitchen that became louder and angrier, with her mother crying.

The heavy footsteps of her father rumbled up the stairs,

coming ever closer. He flung open her door with a force that crashed the handle against the wall, causing a tremor throughout the house. Crumbling pieces of plaster fell to the floor. Miri cowered as he loomed in the doorway. His face was puce with rage.

'*Pruste shiksa*! *Zoinah!*'

She covered her face with her hands.

'What have you done? Your immoral behaviour has brought disgrace not just on yourself but all of us! You are repulsive! You disgust me! I can hardly bring myself to look at you. You stay here in your room. You don't leave here, and you do not speak to anyone!'

He grabbed the handle and slammed her door shut. Another tremor.

Miri collapsed face down on her pillow and sobbed.

It had been over six hours since they parted at the bus stop. Raizy's optimism that there would be a happy resolution for Miri had been short-lived. First, the phone had rung unanswered, now the line was constantly busy. She debated whether to go around to Miri's house, but resisted. Something was wrong; she sensed it.

Her mother hadn't found out about Miri's pregnancy, or Ben, had she?

No! Raizy dismissed the thought.

Even though Miri had reassured her, maybe she was still angry with her. She had every right to be. Raizy regretted her hasty response from the outset and for pressuring Miri to go ahead with an abortion.

She also couldn't wait to tell Miri the news: Ben was

desperate to speak to her. He had never considered breaking up. Nothing had happened with Yael.

Daniel had rung three times so far to find out if there was a further update. And now he was on the phone again.

'Raizy, is something the matter?'

'To be honest, there might be. We planned to meet up again this afternoon, but she hasn't been in touch and I can't get hold of her.'

'What do you think has happened?'

'It's possible her parents discovered she's been dating someone behind their backs.'

'You sound worried.'

'Well, if they have, it could have repercussions for me too.'

'How?'

'It could threaten my engagement.'

'What has any of this got to do with your engagement?'

'If they found out about how this all began …'

Daniel was quiet for a moment. 'You mean because of us?'

His words gave her an unexpected twinge. 'Yes.'

There was a short silence.

'I might be mistaken,' she said. 'Until I know what's going on, please don't let on to Ben that something might have happened to Miri. Make up an excuse. Tell him she's stuck at home helping her mother and I'm still working on it.'

'Yeah, no problem. I think Ben's had enough of a roller-coaster today as it is, what with the funeral and everything else.'

And he has no idea what's still to come, Raizy thought.

It was another two hours until Mrs Fogel answered. 'Could I speak to Miri, please?'

'Who is this?'

'It's Raizy.'

'Oh, yes! Sorry I didn't recognise your voice for a second there. Hello Raizy. How are you? How are all your chasseneh preparations coming along? You must be very busy?' Her words came too fast and unnaturally cheerful.

'I'm fine thanks, borich Hashem. Can I please speak to Miri?'

'Oh, Miri! Well, she's … she wasn't feeling too good. She's gone to bed early.'

'I'm sorry to hear that. Please wish her better for me.'

'I will! Have a good night!'

The call disconnected.

Mrs Fogel was lying. She knew something.

But how much?

Chapter 28

A clatter of crockery stirred Miri as her mother entered with a tray of food. It was daylight outside. She sat up, disorientated, to find herself on top of her bed, still fully clothed. She wondered where her sisters had slept that night.

'Get up, eat, and then start packing.'

'What?' Miri must have misheard.

'You cannot stay here with that!' She gestured towards Miri's abdomen with a look of disgust. 'We have arranged for you to go somewhere else for the meantime.'

'Where are you sending me?'

But an impatient ring on the doorbell summoned her downstairs before she was able – or willing – to answer.

Raizy persisted with the bell until Mrs Fogel appeared beside the jamb, her smile clearly strained.

Raizy replied with a dazzling one. 'Good morning, Mrs Fogel! Is Miri in?'

'Sorry, she's not available at the moment. I'll tell her you came by.'

With that, she shut the door in her face.

Raizy stood there, astounded. Then she primed herself and did something a young woman like her would never normally do.

She ran.

She sprinted through those familiar streets in her patent leather slip-ons and calf-length skirt, gulping mouthfuls of icy morning air as she dodged pedestrians who obstructed her path.

And crashed straight into Mrs Finer.

'Sorry, so sorry.' Raizy gathered three oranges that rolled across the pavement and handed them to the dumbstruck woman before she bolted off again.

She wrestled with the lock as the world tilted back into focus, and charged up the stairs like an ignited fuse.

Panting, she snatched her phone. 'Daniel. Please give me Ben's number. This is urgent. I need to speak to him. Now!'

The unfamiliar number with a UK dialling code caught his attention. He dashed from the living room where his mother sat on a low chair beside her siblings, to a quieter spot in the corridor.

'Hello? Hello?' All he could hear was heavy breathing. 'Hello. Is anyone there?'

'Is … that … Ben?' said a female voice.

'Yes. Who is this?'

'It's Raizy!'

'Oh, hi! Is everything alright?'

'No. I think Miri is in serious trouble. If you love her, please come back. Please!'

His forehead creased in concern as he withdrew to his room

to continue the conversation behind a closed door. 'What's wrong?'

'I haven't been able to reach her since yesterday when we parted at the bus stop and she said she was going home and we'd talk and meet again later but she never called and I couldn't get through for ages and when I did her mother didn't let me speak to her so I went round there this morning but her mother made an excuse and said that she wasn't available and almost slammed the door on me and I'm sure she's hiding something and she's found out about the two of you!'

'Raizy, please slow down. I don't understand. Start from the beginning. What happened yesterday?'

There was a heavy silence on the other end of the line.

'Raizy, are you there?'

'Yes. I'm still here.'

'Raizy?'

'Yes.'

'What happened yesterday?' His chest tightened. He placed his hand over it, feeling for his necklace. It wasn't there.

'I'm not sure how to say this –'

'Please, just tell me!'

'Miri is … pregnant.'

Ben fell back against the wall with a thud.

'Hello …?' she said.

He felt as if he'd been winded and fought for breath.

'Ben, are you still there?'

He opened his mouth to speak, but all that came out was a wheeze.

'Did you hear what I said?'

'Yes.' The room was rotating. He kept a hand on the wall for support as he moved across to sit on his bed. 'Are you certain?'

'I'm certain. I was with her when she did the test.'

Raizy waited on the line. Ben's heart beat rapidly. He felt it marking time like a metronome.

His mind was a tumult of conflicting thoughts. He shut his eyes for a moment to try and calm his breathing.

'I'm coming,' he said. 'I'll leave for the airport right now and see when I can get on a flight. Once I know more, I will be in touch.'

He grabbed his backpack, stuffed it with essentials, flung on his jacket and slung the bag over one shoulder.

When Ben returned to the living room, his mother looked confused. He had dressed for a cold winter's day while a mild breeze and bright sunshine streamed in through the windows of his late grandmother's apartment. 'Where are you going?'

He approached his mother and gently placed his hands on her shoulders. 'I'm sorry I have to leave you. I have to fly back to London,' he said in an undertone.

'What, right now? Why? Is it to do with Miri?'

He leaned over and gave her a quick kiss on the cheek. 'I'll call you as soon as I can. I love you, Ima.'

'Wait, Ben,' he heard her say. But he was already out of the door. He didn't turn around.

Ben slouched down in a quiet corner of the departure lounge next to a window. He rubbed his sweaty palms against his jeans and returned a call to the last number on his phone.

'It took some time and a lot of persuading, but I changed my ticket and got a seat on the afternoon flight,' Ben said. 'I'll be arriving this evening.'

'Borich Hashem! Thank you!'

'I should be the one thanking you. I appreciate you doing this. If Miri calls or if you reach her somehow, please tell her I'm coming.' He lowered his voice, and somewhat embarrassed, said, 'And that I love her.'

Ben heard an indistinct sound on the other end, like a whimper. 'I will.'

He watched the taxiing planes and service vehicles, still trying to come to terms with his new reality, and what lay ahead of this flight. So many unknowns, so many fears. Then he made the next call.

'What's up, mate? Raizy called me earlier this morning. She was in a right state –'

'Daniel, I have a big favour to ask of you. I'm about to catch a flight back to London and will arrive at Heathrow at eight this evening. Are you able to fetch me from the airport? I won't have any luggage, so I will come through right away. And from there I need you to take me straight to Miri's home.'

'Yeah, no problem. What's going on?'

'I'll explain when I get there.'

Miri took a last look around her room. Night had already fallen. She was leaving the house under cover of darkness, like a fugitive, so as not to arouse attention from their neighbours. Her parents were waiting in the hallway. As she came down the stairs, her father turned his back on her. He retreated to the dining room. Not even a simple goodbye. Her mother remained dressed in her housecoat and turban. Her eyes were red and puffy.

'I'm sorry for everything,' Miri said in a quivering voice.

275

'I hope one day you'll be able to forgive me. Please know, I never meant to hurt either of you.'

'So why did you do it?'

Miri shook her head. 'I don't think you'd understand.'

Her mother folded her arms. 'The taxi is waiting for you outside.'

Miri faced her mother, eyes brimming, too much left unspoken between them. The taxi driver met her at the gate and carried her case into the car. She took the backseat and stared back at her home until they turned the corner.

Ben rushed through the airport passageways, an urgency in his stride. He leapt onto the travelator, overtaking other passengers with luggage who stood on the right-hand side, content to let the moving walkway transport them at its own speed.

To his left, a thick layer of glass separated them from the stream of departing passengers. He glanced through at the travellers heading in the opposite direction. He was drawn to a young woman in the crowd. For a moment he thought it was Miri. Same height, same long wavy hair, same profile. She seemed lost. On instinct, he turned around and started walking the travelator in reverse, trying to follow her in the line of people.

'Oi! Watch where you're going, mate,' said a heavy-set man as Ben collided with his travel crate containing a white poodle.

'Sorry,' said Ben.

'Excuse me!' An impatient man in a pinstriped suit pushed past, forcing Ben to the side. He craned his neck, trying once more to find the young woman again. But she had disappeared in the dense crowd somewhere ahead.

His mind was playing tricks. He allowed the travelator to carry him forward.

Daniel was waiting for him as promised. 'Hi, mate.' He greeted him with a brief hug and slap on the back.

Daniel took one look at him and led him straight to the car. Ben was thankful he drove in silence.

They had reached their own familiar neighbourhood, but suddenly the area felt foreign.

'What's the address?' Daniel asked.

'I'll recognise it by sight. I used to drop her off nearby and follow her in the car to check she got home safe.'

Daniel raised an eyebrow. 'So are you going to tell me what all this drama is about?'

'After I've been over to her place.'

'You're killing me with all this suspense, do you know that?'

'Daniel, please ...' he said with no hint of jest.

Ben rehearsed himself for the meeting as he directed Daniel down a street lined with near-identical terraced houses. He pointed to one. 'There.'

Daniel slowed the car and reversed into a parking space opposite the house.

'Do you want me to wait for you?'

Ben considered it. 'It might take a while.'

'I don't mind.'

'Thanks, I appreciate it.'

It was the first time he'd ever stood at the entrance to Miri's home. He hesitated then rang the doorbell. A light came on above him.

Miri's mother hadn't been thinking straight when she opened the door to a stranger.

'Mrs Fogel?' he said.

She was facing a twenty-something-year-old man with striking brown eyes, dark, wavy hair, and a hint of stubble on his olive-skinned face. She gave him a once-over, trying to recall if she knew him. Perhaps he was there to read the gas or electricity meter, or on some other official business, since he asked for her by name. But he wore casual attire: an anorak, jeans, and the type of boots you might wear for hiking or manual work. Then she noticed an inconspicuous suede kippah on his head.

It was curious. She couldn't place him, but with his soft-spoken voice, fine features, and those eyes … There was something vaguely familiar about him. For a moment, it disarmed her.

'Yes?'

'My name is Ben.'

'Can I help you?'

He shifted his weight from one foot to the other. 'Is Miri here? I'm not sure if she has told you about me.'

At the mention of her daughter's name, it clicked. This had to be the young man in question. The one whose identity Miri had refused to divulge and had been meeting behind their backs. The one who had defiled her and ruined her life.

Her face hardened, and her resolve strengthened. 'She's not here.'

'When will she return?'

'She won't be back. She's gone. Please don't come here again.'

Miri's mother closed the door.

Ruchi peered into the hall. 'Who was that?'

'No one. If anyone else comes to the door, you are not to open it without checking with me first. Do you understand?'

She escaped upstairs for the solace of her bedroom. She passed Miri's room, where Miri had slept since she was a baby. There was a dull ache in the pit of her stomach.

Zissy Fogel stood by the window and watched a car drive away, consumed by a mixture of emotions.

So much confusion. A grief without definition. Disbelief. Out of nowhere, a fault line had opened and it was tearing her family apart.

But there was another underlying sensation. Almost like déjà vu, and it unsettled her.

Why had he looked familiar? She didn't remember ever having met him. It was near impossible she ever would have: she didn't mix with other men.

Had it been in a shop, perhaps? There was that helpful young Sefardi boy who had served her once or twice when she had popped into Kosher Basket for items out of stock at Gold's, her usual shop. He also had quite a striking appearance, but she was sure it wasn't the same person.

Those eyes. Somehow, they reminded her of someone. But who and why?

The glimmer of a recollection flickered like an old ciné film, taking her back to the girl she had been at sixteen. Memories she had done her best to forget.

She had been returning from shul with her parents on Shabbes morning when they passed another shul. It was unlike the others in their neighbourhood and always made her curious. She knew little about the people who went there because her family didn't associate with this quiet, Middle

Eastern community who had moved to the area several years before from a place called Aden. They were different in every conceivable way: looks, dress, customs. But they fascinated her.

The members of this mysterious congregation were just leaving. Zissy stole a glance in their direction, and as she did so, noticed a boy who must have been about eighteen or nineteen. With his dark eyes, high cheekbones and honey-toned face framed by short, curly hair, she thought him the most handsome boy she'd ever seen. He caught her staring and smiled. She blushed and lowered her gaze but couldn't prevent her mouth from turning at the corners.

Oblivious, her family continued onward. She turned around. So did he. And their eyes met again.

Each week after that, she looked forward to the walk home in case she saw him. And on the occasions she did, it filled her with an unfamiliar joy.

She even offered to run errands for her mother at every opportunity in the vain hope she might meet him.

Then one day it happened.

Zissy had just finished shopping at Gold's, and on the pavement outside, she juggled the heavy carrier bags while trying to put her purse back in her handbag. The purse slipped from her grasp and she bent to retrieve it. But someone else got there first. And as he stood up, she found herself face to face with the boy with the beautiful eyes. He smiled, and she smiled back. He handed her the purse with a smile, and as she accepted it, their hands brushed.

'Th-thank you.'

'You're welcome,' he said in an accented English that told the story of a faraway land. To her ears, it sounded as beautiful as his eyes. Then he gave her another warm smile and walked on.

Less than thirty seconds. That was the extent of their encounter. But it remained in her mind as she replayed it over and over. Each tiny detail. The way his eyes locked onto hers. His smile. She could hear his voice saying those two simple words: *You're welcome.* But most of all, she tried to relive the feeling of that slight touch. It gave her butterflies every single time.

After that, whenever they passed each other returning from shul, he always smiled, a shared little secret. And if no one was watching, so did she. But they never had a chance to speak again.

Four months after their encounter outside Gold's, Zissy left for seminary. From what they taught her there, she came to realise that she had transgressed. She shouldn't have been thinking about boys in that way. It was wrong to do so if not for marriage purposes. Certainly not to talk to them. Never to touch. Racked with guilt, she tried to repent, purge her thoughts, and worked on herself to become a more virtuous person. A refined Chassidish girl.

Six months after she finished seminary, her parents found her a suitable shidduch. Following the path her parents had laid out for her, Zissy married and learned to care for her husband. During those early years, maybe she even grew to love him. Then the children arrived. Life became busier. It ticked along in a routine, punctuated by Shabbes and festivals, celebrations, tragedies, and obligations of communal life.

Most of the time, Zissy didn't reflect on her past or the direction her life had taken. She was too busy with her responsibilities. Now, as she stopped to consider, she wasn't sure whether she would describe herself as happy. But content enough. Borich Hashem, she had a lot to be grateful for. She was a dutiful wife and mother and did her best to keep an ordered home. Their children were healthy, she always made sure they were well-fed and dressed. They were considered a respected family, and she had her own standing through her volunteer work. Zissy had found her place within the community.

Perhaps the boy had also married at some point and had children of his own. She never learned his name or saw him again. In all these years, she hadn't given him much thought. And if she did, tried to expunge them as fast as possible. The guilt instilled in her had become deep-seated.

She had never, ever dared to mention a word about him to anyone. Especially not her parents. They wouldn't have understood. They probably would have reacted in horror to learn what was on her teenage mind.

And Miri's mother began to understand.

Chapter 29

Ben yanked open the car door and flung himself into the passenger seat.

Good God! What happened during that brief exchange on the doorstep? Daniel wondered. Ben was shaking. Daniel drove him home without saying a word.

Ben was still quiet as he dug into his pocket for the key and let them into his dark house. Daniel wasn't certain whether he wanted him there, but Ben didn't protest. And Daniel sure as hell wasn't about to leave him alone in this state. Besides, he was curious.

The house had the faint musty smell of absence: traces of cooking mixed with stale air. Ben flicked on the light, and as they made their way through the hallway, Daniel glimpsed a solitary vase, holding a wilted rose, left on the dining room table. Ben unlocked the kitchen door, and despite the biting cold, he slumped down on the back step, running his fingers through his hair.

Daniel followed and stood at a short distance, observing him. He lit a cigarette, blowing smoke into the frosty night.

'Give me one.' said Ben.

'But you don't smoke.'

'Can you give me one!'

'Alright. OK.' He fished another out of the packet, lit it, and handed it over, hoping to calm Ben's uncharacteristic ire.

Ben took a puff, coughed, regarded the cigarette with disdain, then crushed it underfoot. 'You're right. I don't.'

Daniel stopped short of saying, *told you so,* and shook his head. 'Can you please explain what's going on here?'

Ben looked at Daniel with doleful eyes. 'Miri is pregnant.'

Daniel's eyes widened. The cigarette he was holding fell from his fingers. 'Holy crap!'

Ben replied with a helpless shrug.

'Is that what Raizy was in such a panic to tell you this morning?'

'Yes.' Ben conveyed all his anguish in the single-syllable.

'Is it ... yours?'

Ben exploded. 'What do you think? Yeah. It's mine.'

Daniel retreated and raised his hands in a gesture of surrender.

'Wow!' He fixed his attention on Ben with a look that held a trace of admiration. 'You and her ...? What was it like?'

Ben glowered back at him. His eyes burned like flames. They conveyed a message. *Don't go there.*

'Sorry. Bad time to ask.'

He sat down next to Ben in companionable silence to let the news sink in.

'Wow,' he muttered to himself once more. 'What happened over at Miri's place just now?'

'Her mum opened the door. At first, she didn't have a clue who I was. Not even after I told her my name. Only when I asked for Miri did she seem to realise who I was. And when she did ... let's put it this way, I didn't get the warmest welcome. She told me not to come round again and closed the door on me.'

'Mate, what did you expect? You knocked up their good Chassidic daughter. They would hardly welcome you in with open arms.'

Ben cringed. 'Oh my God, Daniel! Do you have to make it sound so crude?'

'Sorry, it's the truth. At least, how they see it,' he said. 'Let me put it another way for you. They've just discovered their daughter, whom they assumed was an innocent girl waiting to get set up on a shidduch, who had never so much as spoken to a boy outside the family, has been creeping around meeting some guy behind their backs. But more than that, he's got her pregnant. Then, out of the blue, he shows up unannounced on their doorstep. Those are not the most ideal circumstances in which to meet your future mother-in-law, ya know?'

Ben rolled his eyes to mask his discomfort.

'Remember what I warned you once, early on? Don't get too involved. You went past the point of fun. If they had found out she had been talking to a guy, even gone out a few times, they might have forgiven her. As for you …' He made a dismissive gesture with his hand. 'I imagine they'd still have told you to get lost. But this is something else. You've ruined their daughter. Their whole family. This is never, ever supposed to happen. In their eyes, it's unforgivable.'

Another thought struck him. 'Never mind in their eyes; have you told your mother yet?'

Ben shivered. 'No.'

'Oh, dear.' He whistled. 'You've still got that to look forward to.'

'Why don't you rub it in further?'

Daniel lit another cigarette.

285

'Miri's mum told me she's gone away and won't be coming back. Do you think she was telling the truth?' said Ben.

'It's possible. Before long, it will become obvious what's happened, so they won't want her hanging around.'

'Where would they send her?'

'That I couldn't tell you.'

He exhaled and watched the smoke curl in the night air. 'You won't like what I'm about to say. But I'm going to say it, anyway. You've had a stressful few days, what with your Savta and all, and now this. You're feeling lousy, perhaps even a little guilty.' Daniel's eyes shot him an icy, emerald stare. 'But so you should. You *should* feel guilty. You've messed up her life. It was such an irresponsible thing to do. I don't get what you were playing at. You could have been more careful. I mean, really, what were you thinking?'

Ben's torment was unmistakable; he had no comeback. Daniel wondered what was going through his mind. Was this infatuation, a game gone too far, or were his feelings genuine? Was he remorseful, would he try to extricate himself given the right get-out clause, or was he prepared to face up to what he had done? Time to play devil's advocate, he decided.

'Saying all that, it happened. You can't rewind or change anything. I understand you liked her a lot. But the kindest thing now may be to let her go.'

Ben straightened up. 'Pardon?'

'Her parents would never agree to this relationship. They want a shidduch for her with a boy from their own community. That's just how it is, and you knew that from the start. Once upon a time, it was the same for our grandparents and great-grandparents back in Aden. They didn't date as we do now. The family arranged marriages in much the same way. It might take a while, but you will get over this and find someone else.'

'Daniel, don't you get it? I don't want anyone else.'

'You're hanging on to something that can't ever be, and it will eat you up inside. But can you imagine how much harder this is on Miri, and what hell her parents must have given her when they found out? She won't have any option now other than to follow their wishes. I reckon they'll make an excuse why she's gone away for a few months and try to hush up the episode. Afterwards, they'll possibly bring her back and try to find her a shidduch. She may never forget, but perhaps she'll be able to move on and make a life for herself. Don't make this harder for her. Let her go, Ben. Let her go.'

Daniel put a hand on his shoulder. 'Ben, it's the only life she's ever known. I don't see how this can work out for the two of you.'

'It's not only the two of us anymore.' His voice was straining. 'There's also a baby.'

'There's no way they'll let her keep it.'

'They're going to put the baby up for adoption?'

'I imagine so, but I'm certain they'll make sure it goes to a loving family –'

'This is our child. Hers and mine. No one other than us should decide what happens.'

'I understand this is tough for you, but don't let guilt cloud your judgement.'

'This isn't about guilt. I don't want to give her up or to let the baby go either. It's part of us.'

'You realise it would mean becoming a father and a husband.'

'I do.'

'And that brings responsibilities, not just sneaking off for fun dates together.'

'Yes, I'm aware.'

'Are you ready for that?'

'Yes, I think I am.'

Daniel regarded him anew. 'You're serious, aren't you?'

'More serious than I've ever been about anything.'

'Let me ask you something else, and I want an honest answer. If it wasn't for the pregnancy, would you still be as keen to do this?'

'Remember before I left, I told you we'd planned to speak to her father when I got back from Israel?'

'Do you mean you'd been planning on getting married?'

'I hadn't formally asked her because I wanted to do things right. I realised her parents wouldn't agree to us dating on a long-term basis, but perhaps they may have accepted an extended engagement until I finished my studies in the summer. Although, that's no longer an option. I never meant to drive a wedge between her and her parents. I know I'm not what they had intended for her, but ... I hoped ... if they knew how we felt about one another, maybe they'd agree.' He shook his head. 'What an idiot I was to even think they would consider someone like me! And look what I've done now – I've messed up big time.'

Daniel adopted a commanding tone. 'Alright, hold it right there. What's with this "someone like me" business?'

'You said it before, they'd have told me to get lost –'

'Forget what I said earlier, alright? And stop with this pity party. Yeah, you screwed up. You both did, and now you're in this together. But you're not second rate. You come from a wonderful family. The best I know. You're a good guy, Ben, and honourable. Most parents would praise the skies if their daughter found such a great guy like you. And if her parents took off their blinkers, perhaps they'd realise it too.'

'I can never be what they want.'

'But it seems you're everything that Miri wants,' he said. 'Do you want to be with her, no matter what?'

'Yes. She's the one I want to spend the rest of my life with.'

'Then you go after her mate. And you don't take no for an answer.'

'I doubt they'll ever open the door to me again.'

'If you're that determined, you'll find a way. This doesn't have to be the end. Use the one thing you've got.'

'What's that?'

'You.'

He raised his eyebrows. 'I don't understand.'

'Do you have the courage to face her parents and fight for her?'

'I'll do anything.'

'Then I have an idea that might just work.' Daniel got up and stubbed out the cigarette. 'But can we please go inside before we carry on? It's bloody freezing out here!'

Chapter 30

Daniel parked a short distance from the Fogels' home and faced Ben. 'Are you ready?'

'As ready as I'll ever be.'

He clasped Ben's hand. 'Go for it! You fight for her.'

Ben stepped out of the car and strode towards Miri's home through the misty rain. Two young Chassidic boys, aged around ten, stood on the pavement and gawped with unreserved fascination. Ben responded with a brief smile. At this, they turned their heads and scooted off.

He marched up to the front door and rang the bell. A teenage girl peeked out from behind a net curtain in the bay window. She reminded him of a younger version of Miri, but with more freckles. He guessed it had to be Ruchi, the sister who had found his CDs under Miri's bed.

She disappeared from the window and opened the door a crack.

'Hi,' Ben said. 'I'm a friend of your sister, Miri. Are your parents home?'

'Ruchi, who is that?' Miri's mother called from inside.

The girl's expression switched from curiosity to fear. She tried to slam the door. But it wouldn't close. Her second frantic attempt was unsuccessful too. She glanced down in alarm. Ben had been too quick for her and had wedged the gap with his boot.

'Ruchi, what did I tell you about not opening the door?'

Miri's horrified mother pulled her aside and appeared in the space. She opened her mouth, but Ben preempted before she could speak. 'Mrs Fogel, I don't mean any harm but I am not leaving here until you either let me know where Miri is or allow me to talk to your husband.'

'My husband isn't here.'

'When will he be back?'

'He has already left for shul.'

'OK. I'll wait.'

'He's not returning after.'

'When can I talk to him?'

'Can you please step away from the door?'

'Please, don't worry, that's what I'm about to do.' Her face relaxed through the slit. 'But, I'm not leaving. I plan on waiting outside your door – all day if I have to – until you either tell me where I can find Miri or when I can meet with your husband.'

The young man before her raised an eyebrow. He didn't need to say anything more. Dressed in his jeans, standing outside her house, on display for all the neighbours to see, his ultimatum mortified her. If any of them were to see him it would be sure to set their tongues wagging. Instinctively, she glanced across to the houses opposite. Was that the twitch of a curtain?

She recalled the exchange she'd had with her husband in the kitchen earlier that morning, having summoned the courage to tell him how Ben had shown up at their door the night before.

'The boy probably just wanted to try his luck again. To meet her again, for more … fun!' He spat out the last word.

'Ben. His name is Ben.'

'Whoever.' He dismissed this insignificant detail with a wave of his hand. 'I doubt he realised the background she comes from or the damage he has caused.'

'What if he comes back?'

'Didn't you tell him not to?'

'I did.'

'Then he won't.'

'But what if he does? Perhaps we should discuss the situation with him? Maybe he doesn't realise –'

Her husband's face darkened. 'So he can brag to all his friends? And then word gets out and soon everyone in the town knows. It will be the ruin of our family!'

'What if he is more genuine?'

He gave a derisory snort. 'That type?'

'Could there be a chance he is … serious about her?'

'He is not "serious". Do you not get it? They aren't like our boys. His type only messes around. I bet Miri was the latest in his long line of conquests. Look what he's done to her. That lot don't come from good backgrounds and they don't know how to behave.'

'Do you think we should ask the Rav for advice on the matter?'

'Have you lost your mind?' he shouted. 'What is the Rav going to think of us? Do you want that none of our children ever get shidduchim?'

Zissy Fogel sank back into a kitchen chair and placed her

head in her hands.

'No one is to find out about this. No one! I don't want to hear about this again. Or speak about it. He won't come back. And this discussion is over!' He stormed out of the house and slammed the door behind him.

Ben was still standing on the doorstep in front of her, waiting for a response. 'Mrs Fogel,' he said, his eyes imploring. 'I'm sorry for all the trouble I've caused. It was never my intention. I realise I'm not what you hoped for your daughter, but I'm serious about Miri and I care for her. Let me make things right. Please tell me where Miri has gone. Please?'

She stood back from the door, her hand grasping the lock, regretting the words before they left her mouth. 'My husband will be home from seven o'clock this evening.'

'Thank you. I appreciate your help. I'll come back then.'

True to his word, Ben walked away without further protest. But it was only a temporary reprieve. The worst was yet to come. What would she tell her husband?

'Well?' Daniel prompted him the moment he opened the passenger door.

'She told me her husband returns at seven.'

Daniel raised a fist in victory. 'Told you so! The last thing she'd want would be to have you hanging around outside their door.'

Ben gave a wan smile. 'Thanks, Daniel.'

'What do you want to do now?'

'No idea. If I go home, I'll be climbing the walls until this evening.'

'Shall we go for a walk to pass some time?'

'Yeah, why not?'

They found themselves beside the bank of the River Lea. The rain had abated and a weak sun was trying to force its way through the clouds. Bundled up against the cold in thick jackets and beanie hats, they leaned against the railings, gazing at the line of houseboats on the opposite bank. The ripples on the surface of the water shimmered like crystal as the river flowed downstream.

'What's this? *Tashlich?*' a voice called to them.

They turned towards its source, and Daniel did a double-take. 'Hey Raizy! Yeah, it is rather. What are you doing here?'

'Same as you, I guess.'

She settled in line beside them and turned to Ben. 'I'm so relieved to see you back! I wanted to call you and find out what was happening but didn't want to bug you too much. Have you gone around to Miri's yet?'

'Yeah, I went straight over there last night, but Miri isn't there. Her mother told me she's gone away.'

'What? I didn't realise. Where have they sent her? Could you get any more information out of her mother?'

'That's all she told me. Then she asked me to leave. I returned this morning, but she still wouldn't tell me anything. I'll be speaking to her father this evening. Perhaps I can get further with him.'

'I take it you've never met her father? To put it mildly, he's not the warmest of characters. I wish you luck.'

'Thanks.' His smile was grim. 'I also want to thank you again for everything you've done to help Miri.'

'That's what friends are for.'

'And I'm sorry for everything she's gone through because of me. The past few days can't have been easy for her.'

'No, they haven't. She's had a rough time. First, there was the mugging –'

'What mugging?'

'Outside Manor House Station when she returned from seeing you off at the airport. That's how her phone got stolen. It was in her bag and they grabbed it off her.'

'Oh my God! I didn't know. Is she alright? Was she hurt?'

'She's alright. More of a fright than anything. They pushed her over, and she got a few scrapes. Nothing serious. It was the loss of her phone, and the connection to you, that upset her more than anything.' She turned towards Daniel. 'She had the idea to ask you for Ben's details, but when she went into Kosher Basket, a new employee told her you no longer worked there.'

'Yeah, I left a few weeks ago for another part-time job with better pay.'

'Then we found out about –' She looked from Ben to Daniel.

'It's alright,' Ben said. 'Daniel knows.'

'It came as a massive shock, and she needed to talk to you about it. She was counting the days until your return. Except, you didn't. With my friend Chaya's help, we got Daniel's number, at last. Though, that conversation left Miri quite distraught.'

'Why?' Ben asked.

Daniel cleared his throat. 'I think I owe you both an apology. Your call was so unexpected, and when Raizy asked if I had any idea why you hadn't returned, I wasn't thinking straight. The first thought that came to mind was perhaps you and Yael –'

'Miri had never heard of her and was heartbroken that you might have left her,' Raizy said.

Ben cupped a hand over his mouth.

'I didn't yet understand the seriousness of your relationship,' said Daniel. 'But it was a thoughtless comment to make all the same. I'm sorry, mate.'

'You weren't to know. I can see how you jumped to that conclusion. It was the reason I delayed my flight a couple of times in the past.'

'Why did you never mention anything about her to Miri?' said Raizy.

'It wasn't intentional. I had planned to, but hadn't found the right time to tell her. When I was going out with Yael, I wasn't in a good place. We broke up several months ago and I promise nothing happened while I was away.' Ben raked a hand through his hair. 'I should have said something to Miri. But I never expected all this would happen in the meantime.'

'Just so you know, Miri still cares for you a great deal. Even though she was upset, she was never angry with you.'

'Thank you for telling me. It means a lot.'

'I hope I didn't cause too much harm with my stupid remark,' Daniel said.

Raizy bowed her head. 'I also owe you a huge apology. There's something else I have to tell you.'

'What is it?' Ben said.

She fiddled with a lock of hair. 'Like Daniel, I didn't realise quite how serious you were about Miri. We were both shocked to discover she was pregnant. I didn't know how to deal with it. I was concerned it might frighten you off, and perhaps it would be better if you never found out. And I have to confess, there was also some selfishness involved on my part.'

'I'm not sure I understand.'

'When you didn't return, and I spoke to Daniel –' she turned to him. 'And now I have the chance to say it, I'm sorry about the misunderstanding with Chaya. It would seem we're both guilty of jumping to conclusions too fast.'

He gave her a look of reassurance. 'Water under the bridge, Raizy.'

'Thank you.' She returned her attention to Ben. 'I made a terrible mistake. Miri was in a state. I thought it was possible you had left her. I worried about how she would face her parents with this alone. And I was afraid it might also threaten my shidduch if word got out that I was the one responsible for the two of you getting together.' Raizy shut her eyes. 'I encouraged her to go for an abortion.'

'Did she …?'

'I even took her to the clinic.'

Ben paled.

'She started the appointment. Then she did the ultrasound scan. And she saw a heartbeat. Her baby's beating heart. She couldn't go through with it,' her voice choked with emotion. 'Miri said, "This is our child. It's mine and Ben's." And she ran out.'

Ben backed away. 'I need a moment.'

'Please forgive me for what I did,' Raizy called after him. 'I'm sorry.'

He carried on along the path and turned off behind a clump of trees. When he returned a few minutes later, he had collected himself, but his eyes were bloodshot.

'You did what you thought would be best for Miri under the circumstances. You were only trying to help,' he said. 'I understand how much pressure you were under. It must have been frightening for you to have to cope with the situation all

297

on your own. I forgive you. I'm just so relieved she changed her mind and didn't go ahead.'

Raizy dabbed her mascara-smudged eyes. 'Thank you.'

'And I am almost sure, you have nothing to worry about regarding your engagement. I don't think she revealed your involvement because she never even told her parents my name.'

'In the end, I think she's the strongest of us all,' Raizy said.

'Yes, she is,' Ben said and Daniel murmured his agreement. Then they faced the water, contemplating in silence, each with their own thoughts meandering like the course of the river. Three friends inextricably linked.

Chapter 31

The shrill scream of a siren fading into the distance ripped her from her sleep. Miri inhaled traces of a bleachy odour; it turned her stomach.

Something wasn't right.

She rolled over to burrow beneath her duvet. Instead, her hand chafed against a coarse blanket.

She forced herself to open her eyes. It hadn't been a bad dream. She felt a wave of loneliness.

A heavy window shutter blocked out the light. Miri didn't know what time of day it was, or for how long she'd slept. In the semi-darkness, the unfamiliar room came into focus. Apart from the creaky, metal-framed bed, the only other pieces of furniture were a small wardrobe that listed to one side, and a bentwood chair piled with her clothes. There were no extraneous, decorative touches. Not even a mirror. Her suitcase rested on the mottled, stone floor beside the splintering door.

Miri had arrived in the early hours of that morning while it was still dark. Vulnerable and alone, she'd taken a taxi, showing the driver a paper with the address of her destination. Rather than leave her on the street by herself, the considerate man carried her luggage up two flights of stairs to the front door and refused a tip.

If she could, she would have fled and asked him to take her elsewhere. Only, she had nowhere else to go. At least, not yet. Miri comforted herself with the thought she would soon try to plan her escape. But until then, it seemed her best option would be to comply without protest.

She had been about to knock when a stern old woman wearing a black headscarf low on her forehead opened the door. The woman was a great-aunt on her father's side, a widow for many years and a semi-recluse. Miri had never met her before. She scrutinised Miri through her thick-rimmed glasses, her facial expression one of disdain. It was clear Miri's parents had informed her of Miri's circumstances, and she'd only agreed to have her out of a sense of family obligation.

'You must be Miri.' She addressed her in Yiddish. 'You'd better come in.'

Miri trundled her suitcase and followed her as she shuffled through the bleak apartment in thick stockings and slippers. Her great-aunt showed her to the spare room and returned with a glass of water for her. She told Miri to get a few hours' sleep after her journey, and said she would contact her parents to let them know she had arrived safely. While staying with her, Miri would be her home help, doing light housework and cooking. Once a week, on Friday, she would let her call her parents for five minutes to wish them a git Shabbes.

This, she realised, might be her lifeline. If she were to make a quick call to Raizy and get a 'wrong number' before then phoning her parents, her aunt would be none the wiser as she spoke almost no English. Miri hadn't spoken to Raizy since they parted at the bus stop. She'd made an attempt from a public phone, but the line was busy and she then needed to hang up and leave. She could have kicked herself for not having thought to ask Raizy for her new mobile number. By now, Raizy must have figured something had happened to her.

Miri wondered whether Daniel had contacted Raizy again and if he'd been successful in reaching Ben. Her gut instinct told her that Raizy wouldn't rest until she found out what had happened. Miri hoped that with her and Daniel's help, she could get a message through to Ben.

Meanwhile, she would have to wait for the right opportunity.

I will not cry. I will stay strong, Miri reminded herself. And by the time she climbed into bed, she was so fatigued from the strain that she fell into an exhausted sleep.

Now, she sat up slowly, feeling lightheaded and queasy. She lowered her legs off the side of the bed, shuddering as her left foot touched something cold and wet. Miri looked down to find she had tipped over the cup designated for *negel vasser* into the washbowl in which it stood.

Unable to locate a towel, she dried her foot using a corner of the blanket. Then, she walked over to the window and hoisted up the shutter. Sunlight burst through. Shading her eyes in the crook of her arm, she adjusted her vision and peered outside.

A bus careened past, its brakes screeching, followed by a motorcycle which attempted to pull out and only just avoided a collision with a car heading in the opposite direction. Groups of girls wearing navy blue uniforms and backpacks made their way home from school, talking and giggling among themselves as they ambled along. A harassed mother in a turban pushed a double buggy, its handles weighed down with shopping bags, while leading two small children from the pavement's edge. Across the road, a bearded man wearing a black hat and long coat hurried past rows of near-identical, concrete apartment blocks which continued down the street as far as she could see.

Opposite the apartment block, there was an open space between the buildings. Filled with low overhanging trees and shrubs, it provided a patch of oasis in an otherwise relentless, urban view. Through the gap, she studied a parade of shops on a parallel street, storing their details to memory in case they proved useful later. Perhaps soon, she could gain her great-aunt's trust enough that she would allow Miri to go shopping for her. Then, while out, she would ask a shopkeeper if they'd let her make a quick phone call.

This wasn't the way things were supposed to have worked out. Her life had been turned on its head. She knew her situation wouldn't be permanent, but in the meantime, she was a virtual prisoner.

Overcome by misery, she clasped Ben's necklace and brought it to her lips.

A loud rap on the door gave Miri a start. Her aunt was calling her to get up. It was Thursday, already late in the day. They had to start preparations for Shabbes.

Miri hid the necklace, dressed, and regained her composure. She wouldn't display any emotion in front of her great-aunt.

Chapter 32

Ben edged his way into the dining room. His limbs tingled and his courage ebbed with every step. Not even a summons to the headmaster's office had ever been as daunting. This was the most significant confrontation he'd ever faced. He prayed he would succeed and present a persuasive case for himself and on Miri's behalf. He couldn't fail her.

He doubted it was possible to have started off on a worse footing. Miri's parents already had preconceived notions about him. From what he'd overhead as he waited in the hallway, her father had, at first, refused to see him. He sounded furious when Mrs Fogel told him that Ben had threatened to remain outside their front door until they met. It was only after much persuasion on her part that he agreed a meeting may prevent further embarrassment.

A mahogany table with curved legs dominated the room's centre. Miri's father sat at its head, illuminated by a suspended pendant light. From the shadows where Ben hung back, Mr Fogel cut an imposing figure with his full, greying beard and long, Chassidic coat, which Miri had called a langer rekel. He studied the heavy volume which lay open in front of him, and if he had noticed Ben's entrance, he'd chosen to ignore him.

'Mr Fogel ... er, Rabbi Fogel ...?' He took a few steps forward and wavered. Should he offer to shake hands? Was he expected to take a seat or remain standing? 'Thank you for agreeing to meet me.'

Miri's father looked up. Trapped in his unyielding glare, Ben froze. 'What do you want?'

Ben coughed. 'Your daughter, Miri ... and I ... we've been seeing each other for a while.'

'Seeing each other?'

'Yes. We've been going out.'

'You mean you have been meeting my daughter behind my back?'

He would not make this easy.

'I want to apologise. We never intended to deceive you. We wanted to speak to you earlier, but we were waiting to find the right time. Miri worried you might not agree to us –'

'Of course I wouldn't agree!' he snapped. 'This is not the way we behave. Our girls don't talk with boys. They don't go out like *shiksas!*'

Ben recoiled, it hurt to hear her father allude to Miri in that manner.

'Were you aware an ideal shidduch was suggested for her? A wonderful boy; polite, an excellent family, good yichus. A learned boy in yeshiva. A chossid, who dressed like a chossid. Not like a –' He waved his hand in Ben's general direction. He didn't need to say more. Ben understood the connotation. 'But she refused the shidduch. I couldn't understand it. Why should she turn down such a good boy? We brought her up with expectations to marry such a person. Why give up all we wished for her?'

He tapped the table and then threw his hands in the air. 'She couldn't even give me a proper reason. She made excuses, claiming he's not for her, she has nothing to say to him, she doesn't like the way he looks, they have nothing in common. It made no sense. But now, I understand the reason she said those things. Because of you. She lost out on the opportunity because, without our knowledge or permission, she was seeing you.'

Miri's father sat back in his chair and sized him up. 'So tell me, who are you? What are you? Where do you come from?'

Mrs Fogel stood in the hallway, straining to listen through a crack in the door as he spoke low. 'My full name is Ben Aharoni. I'm twenty-two years old, in my last year of university. Before that, I was in a yeshiva for a year in Israel …'

'Who's in there talking to Tateh?'

Ruffled that her daughter had caught her eavesdropping, Mrs Fogel straightened up and adjusted her turban. 'Shh!'

'Is it that man who came to the house this morning who said he was a friend of Miri?'

'Ruchi, can you please go to your room!' she hissed.

'Where is Miri? Why won't you tell me what's going on?'

'I will not ask you again. This is not for your ears. Upstairs this instant!'

Ruchi scowled before doing as instructed. Mrs Fogel chose not to admonish her daughter for her lack of respect – just this once – and resumed her position outside the door.

' … I realise we didn't go about things the right way,' she heard Ben say.

'No, not "we". It was you who went about things the wrong way!'

'OK, I admit what I did was not appropriate. And I'm sorry.'

'Do you understand what you've done? Do you have any idea? You crept around with Miri behind our backs. You made her deceive us. You used her. You ruined her. You've ruined *our* lives. And you *think* saying sorry makes it all OK?'

'I didn't mean for it to happen like this.'

'No, I'm sure you didn't. You thought you could use her and get away with it. That no one would find out!'

'That's not what I meant.'

He had Ben trapped at every turn. No matter what he said, he kept finding himself at a dead-end.

'So what *do* you mean?'

'I'm trying to say I regret my actions.'

'Yes, perhaps now you do. After you've caused the damage. We raised Miri to be a good girl. Before going out with you, she was pure and innocent. She had never so much as looked at a boy, never mind speak to one. You took advantage of her.'

Ben shook his head. 'I didn't take advantage of her.'

'Do you expect me to believe that she agreed with no coercion? That my daughter would do that?'

'Yes. Even before we met, she had given it a lot of thought and decided she didn't want to go on a shidduch.'

'And how would you know?'

'She confided in me that this wasn't the life she wanted, but she couldn't tell anyone because no one would listen. And when she tried, she got shouted at and silenced.'

'You're lying.'

'I'm not lying. Did you speak to her? Did you ever ask her what she wanted? Or does that not matter to you?'

'How dare you! She is my daughter and I know what is best for her. Before she met you, she was happy to do what we expected of her.'

'That's not true. She wasn't happy.'

His voice rose. 'You are talking rubbish. You used her. And you treated her like a common prostitute!'

The words stung Ben to the core. His mouth ran dry. 'I didn't … *use* her.'

His words came at Ben punch after punch, as if they were in a boxing ring. When Ben attempted to defend one area, the blow came from a different angle. And each time he attempted to rise, he hit him again and left him staggering.

'You thought you'd have your way with my daughter, before moving on to your next conquest.'

'No. That wasn't it at all.'

'She was just a plaything to you, wasn't she? Someone to brag to your friends about.'

'No.'

'She meant nothing to you.'

Ben straightened his posture, readying himself for another round. 'Miri means everything to me. I love her and I want to marry her.'

'Love? What do you know about love? Love is something that grows later. It's not something you take before!'

Mr Fogel banged his fist down hard on the table.

Ben took a step back.

'This is not our way. We go by a shidduch. Our girls don't mix with boys or "date" and you know why? Because it leads to this!'

He rose from his chair and his eyes bored into Ben's. 'By your actions, you have ruined her and her chances of a good shidduch. Your actions forced us to send her away. We now have to make excuses to our family, friends and neighbours. And once this is over, we will need to arrange a secret adoption.' He pointed a finger of accusation at Ben. 'All because of you!'

'Don't I have a say in this?'

'You?' Mr Fogel's expression spoke of his derision. 'Are you *meshugge*? Out of your mind?'

'I should be allowed to have a say too.'

'Who are you to have a say?'

He summoned the last of his resolve. 'Because Miri is carrying our child.'

Ben's words sent Miri's father into a blind rage. 'No, you have no say! You walk in here, a stranger who has taken advantage of my daughter. How dare you come into my home and speak to me like this!'

'I am the father of the baby.'

'And I am her father. I have the say. You are nothing.' He pointed to the door. 'Now get out!'

Ben hung his head in defeat, the strength sucked out of him, and he slunk out. They would not see him break down. He kept his eyes focused straight ahead.

Ben opened the door.

He was done here.

He slammed it shut behind him.

Miri's mother watched him leave, but he didn't notice her standing by the stairs as he passed. She saw the anguish on his face. His heart ripped out. She flinched at the slam and waited for her husband to come thundering out. But he didn't follow. She glanced between the dining room and the door.

This was it. It was now or never. She made up her mind.

Chapter 33

Who does he think he is, coming in here and speaking to me like that?

Miri's father was livid.

The door slammed. A tremor ran through the walls.

How dare he!

He should go after that *chutzpadik* young man. He took a determined stride, then paused and reconsidered. Let him go. He wouldn't lower himself by chasing after him.

He sat back down to continue his learning, but the letters jumped across the page. He shut the volume, pushed back his chair and smacked his hand on the table.

What chutzpah to even enter my house, after all the devastation he's caused!

He gritted his teeth and clenched his fists. The room was too small to contain his seething anger. He needed to get out. Away from everyone and everything.

He headed for the door – and barged straight into his wife, who stood in front of it. She seemed flustered. 'W-where are you going?'

He expected she wanted him to give her a full report, but he was in no mood to talk. Ignoring her question, he grabbed his hat and stormed out.

He marched through the streets with no set destination, his head bent low to evade attention.

A few weeks ago, he'd been so hopeful about the imminent engagement of their second daughter. By now, they should have been busy preparing for her wedding. Instead, he found himself yelling at an uninvited stranger who'd sauntered into their lives – out of nowhere – undermined the foundations of his family, and then assumed entitlement to a say in their affairs!

Where had it all gone wrong? So spectacularly wrong!

The structure of his family was collapsing like a house of cards in front of his eyes.

He made a left as he reached the end of Spring Hill, onto a footpath running alongside the River Lea. The lights from the street barely penetrated beyond the windswept trees, their branches reaching towards the black sky like crooked fingers. But the darkness provided a haven, and he welcomed it.

The nervous energy that had pushed him onward was waning, and a wave of tiredness overcame him. He chanced on a fallen trunk beside a cluster of trees and sat down to rest, enveloped by the silence.

Where did I slip up?

All his life, Zelig Fogel had followed a set path, never veering from it, and had taken every precaution to shelter his family from the negative influences of the outside world. He'd been careful about what reading materials he allowed into their home; never owned a television and limited use of the radio to news programs and classical music. Miri only socialised with girls from suitable families in the area. They'd sent her to the finest schools and then seminary as was befitting a frum, Chassidish girl. When she received a job offer after sem, he even checked out the office before allowing her to accept the position to make sure the environment would be appropriate. The inevitable next step was a shidduch and to settle down in the neighbourhood surrounded by her family and friends.

Why would she want anything different? This was all she'd ever known.

In his opinion, Lipa Bloch would have made the ideal husband. He possessed all the attributes required of a spouse for his daughter. He would have been proud to call Lipa his son-in-law. A boy who dressed and behaved like a chossid. Not this one, who looked like a ... *shaigetz*!

Miri. He shook his head in disbelief. Never in his wildest imaginings would it have occurred to him that out of all his children, she would be the source of such a calamity.

How often had he stood by her cot when she was a baby to watch her sleep and marvel at her? His beautiful Miri. What a sweet girl. So obedient, never any trouble.

How had it come to this?

The boy was mistaken. She had always appeared content. At least, she never complained. She had a decent job, a little circle of friends, a stable home. It had to have been Ben's disruptive influence that introduced her to these inappropriate ideas.

He knew what was best for his own daughter. It was obvious.

Yet, what did he know of her?

Did she enjoy her work? What were her interests? What did she think about when she stood at the sink washing dishes with that faraway look in her eyes? Where did her mind wander as she sat at the table on Friday night while he learnt

Torah with his sons?

To his dismay, he had no answers. Could this young man be telling the truth? Did Ben understand Miri better than he, her father?

Zelig Fogel tried to remember the last time they'd spoken at length. The most recent conversation he could recall was when she made the outlandish suggestion that instead of having a conventional shidduch, she wanted to meet a boy from the Adeni community. Adeni, of all things! He had thought it ridiculous and wondered how she'd come up with such an outrageous idea. Now it all made sense. She must have been attempting to broach the subject of Ben. And he'd been blind to it. He'd shut her down.

How did this happen? Where did they meet? What did she see in him?

Grudgingly, he had to admit, though only to himself, that despite Ben's major lapse, he seemed to be sincere. Serious. His bearing almost regal. Is that what Miri saw?

Ben's words still haunted him. Like a scratched vinyl record, the conversation replayed itself over and over in his mind.

'Who are you? What are you? Where do you come from?'

'My name is Ben Aharoni. I'm twenty-two years old, in my last year of university. Before that, I was in a yeshiva for a year in Israel. I am an Adeni Jew. My parents were born in Aden, in the Middle East, where my ancestors lived for generations. But I was born here in London because the threat of a massacre forced my parents to flee their birthplace. Similar to the way your family fled Eastern Europe because of the war.

'And so, I grew up in this neighbourhood. Just like you. I share the same heritage, collective history, and the same

Torah as you. I observe the same Shabbat and festivals. And when I pray, I face east, *mizrach*, just like you.'

Just like you.

It was true. Zelig Fogel's parents had been forced to uproot and rebuild the remnants of their shattered lives in a new community in London. Just like Ben's.

Zelig's knowledge of his family's background from before and during the war in Poland was vague. His father refused to discuss it. But he knew that most of their family, and their community, had been annihilated and their way of life destroyed. From as far back as he remembered, his father always stressed the need to 'rebuild'.

He must have been young, maybe five or six, when he first considered it: if only he learnt how to build, it would stop his father's anger and make everything right. It would put an end to the beatings when his father deemed him disrespectful, if he answered back or he got poor marks in school. He tried so hard to behave, but more often than not, he failed. Perhaps he was a bad child. As his father explained, it was his duty to punish him, to keep him on the correct path. Now he was a father himself, with a responsibility to discipline his children. But much to his own father's displeasure, he couldn't agree with the practice of striking them to keep them in line. His father often chastised him for being too soft with his children. Well, here was another failure to add to that long list.

As a child, Zelig had tried every which way to gain his father's approval and make him happy. Once, when aged eleven and doing his homework, he caught sight of his younger brother's wooden blocks and they gave him an idea. He thought at last he'd found the answer. He'd teach himself to build a tall tower and show his father how he'd mastered the art of building. But when his father discovered his school books abandoned and Zelig sitting under the table playing with childish building blocks, his father became angrier than he'd ever seen him. In one exasperated swipe, he kicked them down shouting, '*Bittul zman!*'

Though it happened many years ago, the memory still made him shudder. He'd cowered in terror and shut his eyes as his father administered the belt. The first of many occasions.

With his childish logic, Zelig figured he'd disappointed his father because his demonstration had been too basic. By now he should have progressed to more advanced techniques. So, by the same means with which they learned much about their insular world – books – he discovered there was a wider world, outside their community, and taught himself how to build.

Whenever he found an opportunity, Zelig made furtive trips to the public library. He read everything he could find about architecture and he learnt that when designing a structure, the first step was to make a drawing, known as a draft. He realised he would first need to teach himself how to draw buildings in order to rebuild.

In secret, he spent every quiet moment honing his skills.

Zelig was fourteen years old and had drawn a masterpiece: a picture of the London skyline with the Thames in the foreground. Rendered in meticulous detail were some of its most famous landmarks, including St Paul's Cathedral, the Palace of Westminster and Big Ben. He'd worked on it for countless hours to get it perfect. At long last, he would make his father proud.

Filled with anticipation, Zelig approached his father, who was sitting at the dining room table and showed it to him.

His father took one glance at his painstaking work and became enraged. He swiped the paper out of his hands, and with an excruciating rip, tore it across the middle. Then again. And again. Until his picture lay in a pile of tiny shreds on the table.

Zelig never drew again.

In time, he understood that to rebuild meant to restore what the Nazis had destroyed, and the way to do this was by learning Torah and doing good deeds, and later, to marry and have children, helping to replace the six million slaughtered. In fact, they named Pessie after his wife's grandmother and Miri for his paternal grandmother, both of whom perished in the Holocaust.

How he loved his daughters.

Zelig had tried to block out the memory of the day the dynamics of his family changed, but he couldn't forget.

He had been looking after his girls while his wife took a nap. Two-year-old Miri wanted to make a tea party for him and her older sister, Pessie. So he sat down with them as she laid out her tea set and poured him a pretend cup of tea. His Miri, such a delight, so sweet and clever. He kissed the top of her head as he took the cup from her.

At that precise moment, his parents entered his home unannounced. They found him sitting on the floor in the living room, making an exaggerated demonstration of drinking, pretending to take noisy sips from the toy cup, resulting in peals of laughter from his delighted little daughters. Zelig's father gave him a withering look and uttered two words: *'Past nicht!'*

Even as a grown man, Zelig Fogel remained a disappointment. No matter what he did, he could never be the son his father expected him to be.

Having realised his mistake, Zelig got up at once. He felt ashamed at having demeaned himself. It wasn't becoming for him as a father to behave in that manner. He needed to present himself as a figure of respect and authority. The girls were to be under their mother's care, the trivial games left to her. He never played on the floor with his children again.

After that, Zelig Fogel's relationship with his family changed. He repressed his emotions, which remained hidden behind a sober facade, as did his secret passion for buildings and architecture.

Occasionally, he would take his family on an outing to Alexandra Palace. There, he would leave his wife in the play area to take care of children while he walked to the summit of the south slope to study and admire the London skyline. From a distance, Zelig also watched his wife and children, filled with undisclosed pride and love. His wife, who gave all her energy to the family, the community. To him. She put up with his irritable moods with infinite patience and kindness. He hadn't told her enough over the years how much he appreciated her.

Did Miri understand how much he cared for her? That she was a light of his life? How could she?

In his quest for approval as a son to transform himself into the father he thought he was meant to be, he'd shut out his daughter.

As an adult, Zelig understood his father still suffered from the unspeakable traumas he'd experienced during the Holocaust. He wasn't able to be the loving father he himself needed and longed for. He had to accept that in his own way, his father cared, and that would have to be enough.

But regret plagued Zelig. He had repeated many of the same mistakes of his upbringing. There was no excuse.

Who was his daughter, Miri? What had she become? And who was this Ben?

One thing was clear: he cared for her, and it seemed she cared for him a great deal too.

But this pairing couldn't work. She came from a refined Chassidish family. She was meant to marry a chossid. He might be a nice boy, but he was Adeni. Surely he should marry a girl from his own community.

Shouldn't he?

Ben's words kept echoing in his mind. *Just like you.*

But they were different in every way: their backgrounds, customs, nuances, even their pronunciations.

Or were they?

Were there more differences that divided them or similarities that united them?

Did they both speak the same language – only with distinctive accents?

Were Miri and Ben meant to be together? Was he Miri's beshert?

No! He couldn't reconcile it.

It was inappropriate. Not the *done thing*. And what they did – sinful. It should never have come to this! She shouldn't have so much as spoken to a boy before going on a shidduch. Never mind what came after ...

Could it have happened any other way?

But look where it had ended. With Miri's downfall, and their family's reputation at risk.

Yes, he had been justified to send Miri away for her actions. He was right to be incensed and throw this young man out of his house.

As Ben turned to leave, Miri's father saw the immense hurt in his eyes. Yet, he still retained that quiet dignity he'd noticed when Ben first walked in.

Had he wronged his daughter, his dear Miri?

From his earliest constructions to his family, all he had ever wanted to do was build. But whatever he built came tumbling down.

Every. Single. Time.

He was a failure.

Like that first rip across his picture, something tore deep within his soul. Out of the depths came his raw cry. A sound that pierced the night, swept away with the current down the river. He could no longer hold back the tears he had suppressed for so many years.

For all his hopes and dreams lost along the way.

For the approval he could never get, no matter how hard he tried.

For each time he attempted to build, only to watch his efforts destroyed.

For the little girl that was no more.

For the daughter he didn't know.

For the love he never showed her.

For the attention he should have paid.

For the times he didn't listen.

For the woman she had become.

For Ben, because he hadn't met the expectations he wanted for his daughter.

For the callous way in which he had spoken to the young man.

For disparaging him and his community.

For the sin he wasn't able to forgive.
And for the grandchild he might never meet.
What am I supposed to do?

Ben sat in the departure lounge, tapping his foot on the floor. He checked his watch, got up from his seat to look at the information board, and walked over to the window. His head spun, so he returned to his seat only to start tapping his foot again. Ben reflected on all that had happened in the space of just twenty-four hours. He grimaced when he recalled his fraught confrontation with Mr Fogel.

A voice over the loudspeaker announced his flight. Ben picked up his backpack and joined the line to board.

Chapter 34

Zelig Fogel hovered at the gate. The lights were still on downstairs, but it was the middle of the night. Could he disturb him at this hour? Before he realised what he was doing, he had already tapped the knocker.

I should leave.

But it was too late. With the rattle of a chain, a click, a turn of the double lock, the rabbi himself appeared at the door. He was astonished to find Zelig Fogel standing on his doorstep at two o'clock in the morning. 'Reb Fogel, are you OK?'

'I'm sorry to trouble the Rav. I have a dilemma, and I didn't know where else to turn. Perhaps I should return tomorrow? I realise it's late –'

'No, please come in.'

He followed the rabbi into his private study which was lit by the warm glow of a desk lamp and cocooned on three sides by floor-to-ceiling shelves crammed with books. Several volumes, some old and parched, others new and pristine, lay across his desk. The rabbi sank into his high-backed swivel chair and motioned to the guest seat opposite. 'Please.'

'I apologise for disturbing you.'

'It's alright.' The rabbi clasped his hands together. 'Would you like to tell me what is troubling you?'

Zelig Fogel shifted on the chair. 'My second daughter, Miri, is of marriageable age.'

The rabbi nodded in agreement.

'In fact, the shadchen suggested a boy from an excellent family. But she turned him down.'

'It's natural for us as parents to be disappointed when that happens. But she is entitled to say no if she feels he isn't right for her.'

'Yes, I agree.' Zelig tugged at his shirt collar. His throat felt tight. 'The problem is, the real reason she refused him was that she had already met someone.'

The rabbi pushed up his glasses.

'Somehow, she met a boy herself. I'm not sure how,' he said in earnest. 'We found out she had been seeing him in secret.'

'I understand. This must have come as quite a shock to you and your wife. Do you know the boy or his family?'

'I spoke to him for the first time today. He's from the area, but not part of our community.'

'He belongs to a different *Chassidus*?'

'No. He isn't actually Chassidish.'

The rabbi looked at him expectantly. Zelig cleared his throat. 'He's, um ... Adeni.'

Zelig wasn't sure what sort of reaction he had been expecting. But there wasn't one.

The rabbi's face was expressionless. 'And?'

'I think he's frum. He mentioned he had been in yeshiva. But, they're not like ... us.'

The rabbi stroked his long, white beard. 'I agree, the circumstances are a little unusual. However, if your daughter seems set on this, perhaps you and your wife should meet his parents to see if they are a suitable family?'

'It's more complicated than that.'

'Go on.'

Zelig Fogel had difficulty looking his rabbi in the eye. What had he been thinking, coming here late at night to confess? He wanted to crawl under the broad, mahogany desk and hide there.

Suddenly the room had become stifling. 'I … it came to light … I mean … my wife found out …' He lowered his voice. 'Well, the thing is …' He contorted his face. What was the polite way to say this? 'She's … she is … with child.'

There was an uncomfortable pause.

That was it: this would be their ruin. They would be the talk of the town, walk the streets in disgrace, and no one would want to marry their other children.

It took a few moments for Zelig to summon the courage and raise his head. He couldn't read the rabbi's blank face. He appeared to consult a volume on the desk in front of him.

Several tense minutes passed. Zelig maintained a respectful silence and waited for the rabbi's response.

'Is the boy serious about your daughter?'

Zelig considered the question. Three times Ben had come round to their house and hadn't taken no for an answer. He'd begged and argued, said Miri meant everything to him and that he wanted to marry her. When his wife had suggested that perhaps this might be more than mere fun for Ben, he had dismissed her. But she had been correct in her assessment. She had been right about everything.

'Yes,' he said. 'I believe he is very serious about her.'

Zelig Fogel became aware of a ticking clock and his own irregular breathing.

Keeping his focus on the open page, the rabbi said, 'I am sure you are familiar with the story of Rebbe Akiva, who started out as a poor, illiterate shepherd. He couldn't even read until the age of forty. However, Rochel, the daughter of Kalba Savua, who was his wealthy employer, recognised positive traits in his character that others could not see. Despite her father's objections, she married him anyway. And we know how great Rebbe Akiva became.'

Zelig pondered on his words while the rabbi resumed his learning.

'So is the Rav saying … does that mean I should consider …?' Zelig ventured.

The rabbi glanced up and looked into his eyes. 'It's late, your wife must be concerned about you.'

'Thank you for your time. I apologise for troubling you at such a late hour.' Zelig Fogel rose from the chair and the rabbi stood up with him. 'It's fine, I can let myself out.'

The rabbi grasped his hand. 'Have a good night, and *hatzlocho*.'

It was after three in the morning when her husband tiptoed through the hallway. Zissy Fogel sprang from the sofa where she had been keeping vigil all night. He looked drawn, but managed a weak smile.

'Where have you been?' she said. 'I've been so worried.'
'Out.'
'Where to?'
'Walking.'
'What, all night?'
'Yes.'
'There's something I need to talk to you about,' she said.

324

'I also have a matter I want to discuss.'

'Alright, you first.'

He settled himself on the sofa beside his wife. 'I've given a great deal of consideration to the situation with Miri. It came as an enormous shock, to both of us. But perhaps I acted too hasty. If Ben returns, or if we can find out how to contact him again through his community, perhaps we should allow him to have Miri's details. Then, let's see what he does and how serious he truly is. What are your thoughts?'

Her mouth dropped open.

The captain's announcement that the plane had begun its descent roused Ben. At some point, he must have dozed off. He zipped open the pocket at the front of his backpack, felt for what he was looking for and relaxed.

He raised the plastic blind. Fiery beams flooded through the window, the rising sun chased away the darkness. Across the expanse of sky, ribbons of deep blue faded into pale pink and gold. Below him was the turquoise expanse of the Mediterranean Sea, and in the distance, the coastline of Tel Aviv, drawing ever closer.

He shut his eyes tight, taking a few breaths to steady himself, then opened them again.

Oh my God. This is real. I didn't imagine it.

When he'd left Miri's home, he slammed the door in frustration, thinking he had blown it. He had failed Miri. Failed their unborn child. He was no closer to finding out where she was, how to locate her, or had any idea what he should do next.

He didn't notice the door open after him.

'Ben!' He heard a low voice calling his name. He was sure he'd imagined it. But there it was again, uttered with even greater urgency. He spun around to see Mrs Fogel hurrying along the path to catch up with him. Without a word, she handed him a scrap of paper. Ben read the contents. He looked to her and back at the paper.

'Is this what I think it is?'

'Yes.'

'I don't know how to thank you!'

Her eyes welled. 'Just be good to my daughter.'

His eyes met hers and she nodded: they said all she needed to hear.

Ben startled Daniel as he hurled himself into the car. 'What on earth –?'

Ben was breathless. 'Can you please take me straight to the airport?'

'What, right now?'

'Yes! I have to get there ASAP to catch a flight tonight.'

'What happened over there?'

'You won't believe this –'

As Daniel drove, Ben described the excruciating encounter with Miri's father and the unexpected turn of events that followed.

'So you're saying, after all that, Mrs Fogel chased after you and gave you Miri's details? That makes no sense.'

'Yeah, I know. I don't understand what made her do it. But she did. It appears she's staying in Bnei Brak of all places. It can't be too far from Ramat Gan, where my late Savta's apartment is.'

'What's she doing there?

'Not a clue. All I have to go on is a scrawled address. Not even a phone number.'

Daniel pulled up outside departures and Ben leapt out of the car. Daniel followed. 'Good luck, Ben. I hope you find her.'

'Thanks, mate. I mean it, for everything. You've been a rock for me these past few days.'

Daniel gave him a brotherly hug. Then Ben hoisted his backpack and broke into a run.

'Keep in touch. I want to hear what happens!' Daniel shouted after him.

He gave a thumbs up with his free hand, the other glued to his backpack. 'I will!'

Zelig Fogel turned to his wife. 'You said there was something you also needed to tell me?'

'Yes.' She looked down at her hands and twisted her wedding ring. 'About giving Miri's contact details to Ben.' She swallowed hard, then sat up straight. 'Well, to tell you the truth ... I already have.'

He pulled back, and he studied her face. 'Oh.'

And then he nodded in tacit approval.

The aeroplane touched down on the tarmac.

Ben checked his bag again for the precious note before making his way off the plane. He entered the arrivals hall and headed towards his future.

Chapter 35

Ben stood outside a concrete apartment block supported on pillars – near-identical to every other on the busy street. He checked the address on his note. This was the one. He looked up at the windows. Somewhere in one of those rooms was Miri.

He checked his watch. It wasn't yet eight in the morning. Too early to appear unannounced at a stranger's door.

Ben paced back and forth, getting curious stares from passersby and growing restless knowing she was so close. He'd faced Mr Fogel's wrath and just flown two thousand miles through the night to find her.

Sod this! He was done waiting.

He swung open the door to the building, manoeuvred his way past the pile of pushchairs parked next to the drab stairwell and bounded up the stairs two at a time. On the second floor, he found the apartment. He paused at the door.

Then he knocked.

It was the sound of knocking that awoke Miri that morning, but at first, she tried to ignore it. She was in no rush to start the day. She'd spent the previous afternoon cooking and cleaning, followed by a meal with her great-aunt eaten in virtual silence. Miri had kept composure in front of her, but in the solitude of her bed, she'd cried herself to sleep.

Friday promised more of the same. Then a miserable Shabbat to look forward to with only her dour aunt for company. Even if she reached Raizy by phone later that day, as was her plan, it would not alter her wretched predicament in the short term.

The knocking persisted. She heard her aunt call out irritably as she shuffled through the apartment. There followed a muffled exchange in Hebrew between her and what sounded to be a male voice, but unable to understand a word, she didn't pay heed to it. The morning sickness had struck again. She lay still, eyes shut, hoping it would soon pass.

Her aunt's voice grew louder. She detected hostility in her tone and wondered what was going on. The man's voice had also become louder, more emphatic. Then she thought she heard her name. The voice had a note of impossible familiarity.

She listened closer.

'Miri!'

No, she hadn't imagined it. He was calling out to her.

Miri leapt out of bed and into the hallway. She froze. He stopped mid-conversation, eyes looking past her great-aunt towards her. He'd seen her too.

'Miri,' he said.

Her aunt turned and her eyes bulged. She took a step forward, away from the door, and gesticulated wildly at her. 'Pyjama! Pyjama!' she said, appalled to see Miri appear in a white, long-sleeved nightshirt in front of this stranger.

329

The woman's attention diverted for a moment, Ben seized the opportunity to push his way through into the apartment.

Miri took a step towards him but faltered, overcome by a wave of dizziness. She slumped against the wall for support.

Ben reached out, took her arms and steadied her. 'It's OK. I'm here. I've got you.'

At this, Miri's great-aunt became apoplectic and yelled a tirade of abuse at her in Yiddish about her lack of modesty.

Miri looked from Ben to her aunt and back to him, at a loss for words.

'I'm taking you away from here,' he said. 'Are you alright to get dressed and pack your things?'

She nodded.

'I'll wait here for you. I'm not going anywhere.'

Her heart thumped as she grabbed her clothes and wash bag from the guest room and headed for the bathroom. On seeing Miri again, her great-aunt had another fit, shouting at her in a mixture of Yiddish and Hebrew. Miri crept past, and Ben encouraged her onward with gestures as he silenced the woman's furious protests in rapid-fire Hebrew.

Once dressed, she returned to the bedroom, threw the last of her possessions into her case, and dragged it towards the door, but as soon as Ben saw her, he rushed forward to take it from her hands.

'Let's get out of here,' he said. 'I have a hired car parked down the road.'

Miri turned to her great-aunt. 'Thank you for having me. Goodbye.'

The woman yelled at them both in reply, and as Ben led her down the stairs, her shouts followed them down the stairwell.

Miri screwed up her eyes as they stepped into the bright

sunshine. 'Ben, how did you find me?

'Let's go somewhere quiet where we can talk.'

They drove in silence for about ten minutes, passing into a different neighbourhood where the roads grew wider and palm trees ran in a line through the central reservation. The windows of the stone-walled buildings shimmered in the morning sun. Every so often, Ben reached over to her and smiled.

He pulled up on the side of a small park and brought her to a secluded seating area bordered by vibrant, purple bougainvillea. They stood beneath a tree, and he gazed at her, taking her in. Then he placed his arms around her and covered her with kisses.

Ben gave a long sigh and raised his eyes skywards. She rested her head on his shoulder and could feel him trembling.

'I'm sorry,' he said. 'I'm so sorry for everything you went through because of me.'

She tried to speak, but the only sound that emerged was a sob. He held her tight and gently rocked her back and forth.

'Thank you for coming to find me,' she managed at last.

'Did you think I wouldn't?' He pressed his forehead to hers. 'I wouldn't leave you.'

'There is something you need to know.'

'About the baby?'

She studied his expression.

'It's going to be alright,' he said. 'We'll do this together.'

She smiled through her tears and he hugged her once more.

They took a seat on the bench nearby. He told her all that had happened since their parting at the airport up until he arrived at her great-aunt's door.

'One thing I don't understand,' Miri said. 'Why, after

everything, did my mother change her mind and give you my details?'

'I don't know. I don't get it either. But I'm so grateful to her that she did.' He withdrew the piece of paper which he'd stuffed into his pocket and showed it to her. 'How come your parents sent you here, though?'

'When my parents found out what had happened, it was terrible. I have never seen them so angry. Their biggest worry was that the news might get out, so they made hasty arrangements to send me away. I learnt that they intended to send me to Israel to stay with my great-aunt until they could make a more long term plan, so I didn't protest and went along with it. I thought it might be the only way I would ever see you again. My intention was to contact Raizy, tell her where I was, and somehow get a message to you.'

'I can't even imagine what you've been through these past few weeks.'

Miri drew a deep, quivering breath. 'There's something else you should know.' She wasn't able to face him as she continued, 'I hope you can forgive me for this. But I almost ended it. I was scared and confused. I visited a clinic and –'

'I know,' he said. 'Raizy explained everything to me. I understand why you felt pushed into that position. But I'm so relieved that you changed your mind.'

Ben rubbed his palms against his thighs and stood up. 'There is … one more … thing.' All at once, he seemed nervous.

She rose to face him, trying to read his thoughts. 'What is it?'

He took her hands in his and got down on one knee. 'Miri,' he said, 'will you marry me?'

'Yes.' She smiled, blinking back. 'Yes.'

His smile was radiant as he lifted her and twirled her around, and he kissed her.

'Mazal tov!' a woman called. They both turned to see an elderly couple walking arm in arm and waving at them. The plump wife blew them a kiss.

Ben waved back. '*Todah!*' He smiled proudly at his new fiancée.

'Do you know them?' Miri asked.

He laughed. 'Never seen them in my life. Welcome to Israel.'

Ben pointed to a building across from them. 'That's my late Savta's apartment where we're staying while my mum is sitting shiva. I left in a hurry on Wednesday morning and, except for a quick message to say I arrived in London, I haven't spoken to her. She must be frantic. My mum doesn't know anything about the situation yet and I need to break the news to her and my dad.' He studied her. 'I hate to leave you by yourself again. But it might be better if I speak to them first alone. Will you be alright out here for a little while? Or would you prefer to sit in the car?'

'I'll be fine here.'

'You must be famished.' He delved into his backpack, pulled out a plastic bag and handed it to her. 'I bought you some breakfast at the airport, just in case. A few pastries, a bottle of orange juice, a carton of chocolate milk. I wasn't sure what you'd be in the mood for.'

Miri laid her hand on Ben's arm and looked at him with adoring eyes.

'And this is the address,' he said as he pulled out a pad of paper and scribbled down a few lines. 'If you need anything in the meantime, come straight up.'

She cast her face towards the sun. 'Don't worry about me.

333

I'll be happy to sit here for a few minutes. I can't believe it's mid-December.'

'I promise I'll be back as soon as possible.'

She noticed the traces of apprehension he was doing his best to disguise. 'Good luck!'

He trudged along the path and started down the flight of steps that led out of the park.

'Ben!' she called.

He turned around at once.

'You've already faced my father. I'm sure this will be much easier.'

'We'll see.'

Chapter 36

'Ben!' said his mother as he wove his way through the crowded living room. He could feel curious eyes boring into him as the room fell silent.

'Hi, Ima.' He bent down to give her a hug and a kiss on the cheek.

'Ayuni, I've been so worried about you. You just took off without warning and you barely sent me a word since. What happened?'

'I need to talk to you and Abba,' Ben said. He turned to find he had an audience. 'Somewhere a little more private.'

She called across to Ben's father who was sitting on the other side of the room with his brother-in-law. 'Shalom!' And with a tilt of the head, she indicated he should follow them.

They retreated to the adjoining kitchen – not quite a closed-off space, but at least separated from the rest of the visitors.

'It might be better if you sit down for this,' Ben said.

They pulled out two metal stools which were tucked beneath the small kitchen table in the room's corner, his mother eyeing him all the while. Never in his life had he asked his parents to sit down.

'Alright.' He took a deep breath. 'Miri and I are engaged!'

335

His mother gasped, a hand over her heart. 'That was –'

'Unexpected,' said his father.

'Yes.' She glanced at her husband. 'Unexpected.'

But the hint of a smile emerged, blurring the indelible strain and grief of the last few days. 'Oh, Ben!' His mother hugged and kissed him. 'This is wonderful news.'

His father shook his hand. 'I'm happy for you,' he said, but he looked confused as if trying to figure out how he should react. 'Isn't it rather quick? You haven't been going out for that long.'

'Enough time to get to know her and be certain that I want to marry her,' Ben said.

Her husband's comments had tempered her joy with the reality of the situation. 'How did Miri's parents react? I take it you have spoken to them.'

'In a manner of speaking.'

Her eyes narrowed. 'And they agreed?'

'Kind of. It's a complicated story. I'll tell you all about it later.'

'So we have another wedding to plan?'

Ben smiled. 'Yes.'

'How exciting! Do you think Miri's parents would agree to hold it here in Israel? August would be a perfect time, during the holidays when it's easier for family and friends to fly out. Perhaps we can find a beautiful outdoor venue, in a garden, or even by the sea?'

'We'd rather make it sooner. I was thinking in about three weeks, at the end of the *shloshim* for Savta,' Ben had a vain hope his mother might agree without question, and they could keep their situation under wraps for the meantime.

'Ah! Is it because of Miri's family? They tend to have shorter engagements, no? If that's the issue, how about after Pesach? It's a little over four months away. Not long to wait, but enough time to make all the arrangements.'

'No, we'd like to get married sooner than that.'

'There's a lot of preparation involved in planning a wedding. Look at how much work went into arranging Davidi and Keren's.'

'Let's make it small and simple.'

'It's such a special occasion. A once in a lifetime celebration. Maybe you don't mind small and simple. But for Miri, I'm sure she'll want all the details planned with care to make it the perfect day. She needs to find a dress. She will want a makeup and hair trial. There are bridesmaids to think about. Flowers, colour schemes, selecting a venue, a photographer, the band, a caterer, the menu. There's a lot to consider.'

Ben frowned. It wouldn't be that easy to get away with this.

'You're a boy. It's different for you,' she said. 'You don't get these things.'

'Let Ima sort it out,' his father said. 'She's great at organising events. And I'm sure Miri's mum will also want some input as the mother of the bride.'

'Good point.' She waved her index into the air for added emphasis. 'I should speak to her straight after the shiva.' She turned to Ben. 'We can arrange an engagement party in three weeks. But not a wedding.'

'We don't want to wait that long.'

'The time will fly, you'll see,' she said. 'I don't understand why the big rush.'

He looked from his mother to his father. 'There's something else I need to tell you. Perhaps you should sit down again.'

337

His mother complied, but studied him with an expression somewhere between curiosity and concern. 'What is it?'

'The thing is ... we can't wait too long ...' He covered his face with his hands. 'Oh God!' he muttered to himself.

He shifted away to the kitchen counter, gripped it, and peered at them from the side.

'Ben?' Her patience was wearing thin.

'OK,' he said. 'The situation is ... we're ... going to have a baby.'

'What?' His mother's voice rose an octave.

'What?' repeated his father.

He turned to his dumbfounded parents. 'Miri is pregnant.'

His mother sprang up. 'She's what?'

'Tell me you're joking!'

'I'm not joking.'

He braced himself.

'Ben!' she screamed. 'Benzion! How could you?'

His father's lips moved but he couldn't form the words.

'*Yo! Shema Yisroel. Bor minan.* This isn't how we brought you up!' said his mother.

He decided the best course of action was silence. His mother wasn't having any of it. 'How could you?'

He cringed. 'It just kind of happened.'

'It doesn't just "kind of happen". How did it come to this?'

'We were afraid of being forced to break up, and one thing sort of led to another and we –'

His father held up his hand, signalling for him to stop. '*Ebb!*' It was the word his parents said to steer a conversation whenever they thought it was becoming too explicit. Ben didn't know where to put himself. This was beyond awkward.

'I warned you it was better to end it.' Hand to her forehead, his mother maniacally paced the kitchen. 'Shalom, I told him there would be trouble.'

Ben's father tried to placate her. 'You were right.'

She stopped pacing and turned to Ben. 'How far along is she?'

'A few weeks.'

'Oh my God! What are we going to do?'

'I'm sorry.'

'How could you have been so irresponsible?'

He looked down at his hands to avoid his mother's glare.

'Are her parents aware you've gone and got their daughter pregnant?'

'Yes. That's why I left in a hurry earlier this week. A friend of Miri's called to tell me because she suspected they had found out.'

'And how did her parents react to the news?'

'They were furious. They wouldn't let her see or speak to anyone. The following day, they sent her to stay with a relative in Israel until they could make permanent arrangements and find a place where she could have the baby in secret. I think they were planning on putting it up for adoption.'

'I can't believe what I'm hearing! So what happened, you went to see her parents? And then what?'

'At first, when her mum realised who I was, she told me to go away. She was angry.'

'I don't blame her.'

'I returned the following morning, and after some further persuasion, she agreed to let me meet with Miri's father.'

'And what was his reaction?'

'He was furious.' Ben quivered. 'It was the most difficult conversation I've ever had in my life. Then he threw me out of the house—'

'Good. You deserved it!'

She shook her head. 'What will people in the community think of us? What are they going to say?'

'Which is why I figured we should get married as soon as possible. The pregnancy isn't noticeable at the moment.'

'And you don't think people will have suspicions – suddenly this "quick-quick" wedding?'

'They might, but we can make up some excuse. And at least we will be married.'

'And before long, it'll be obvious what's going on.'

'So, we will have an early baby. It can happen.'

She sank onto the stool and placed her hands over her face while her body heaved with sobs.

Ben felt awful. Her outrage was one thing, but to see his mother crying … As if the strain of the past few days after losing her mother wasn't enough, now he'd sprung this on her.

'I'm sorry. I never meant for the situation to turn out like this or to make you upset. I'm sorry for disappointing you. But Miri and I love each other. We're happy. We want to be together and become a family. Please don't cry, Ima.'

His words just seemed to make her cry harder. But then she lifted her head, and he noticed a smile through the tears. 'I'm going to be a Savta! My first grandchild!' She looked to her husband. 'Shalom, we will be grandparents! Our first grandchild. A new baby in the family.'

Ben's father threw up his palms. Then he drew his wife and Ben towards him. The three of them held each other, crying and laughing through their tears.

'A Savta,' she murmured once more, digesting her imminent

status. 'Hang on. You mentioned her parents sent her here?'

'Yes.'

'How did you even know where to find her?'

'When I left the house, her mother came after me and handed me the address where she was staying.'

'Huh?'

'I'm not sure why she changed her mind. She sort of gave me her blessing and asked me to look after Miri.'

'So where is she now?'

'She's waiting for me in the park. I thought it better if I speak to you first, so I left her –'

'You did what?' Mazal pulled apart from the family hug. 'After all that poor girl has been through, you leave her sitting outside, in the park, on her own?'

Ben rolled his eyes. 'She's fine.'

'It's not fine, Ben. This is your fiancée. And in her condition. You must take great care of her.'

'It was only for a few minutes. I'm going to bring her up right now.'

But Ben remained by the counter, tapping on the surface with his fingers. 'Ima … would it be alright for Miri to stay with us? They sent her to the home of her great-aunt she'd never met before, and it was awful for her. She couldn't remain there.'

'I suppose that would be alright. But where will we put her? There isn't much space here.' She considered it for a few moments then a thought struck her. 'She can have your room.' She pointed a finger at him, her expression stern. 'And you'll take the sofa.'

Ben grew embarrassed under the force of her glare and he backed towards the door. 'I'll go fetch Miri.'

Faces turned to him and voices lowered as Ben passed through the living room. The visitors had heard the symphony of emotions emanating from the kitchen – surprise, cheer, shouts of anger, laughter, crying, then more laughing and raised voices.

He overheard one curious visitor ask Ben's uncle in Hebrew, 'What happened?'

His uncle shrugged and gestured towards Ben and back to the kitchen where his parents remained. 'English.'

The rest nodded in agreement, as if that somehow explained everything.

Miri was still sitting on the bench where he had left her. He could see the questions in her eyes and smiled in reassurance.

'Did you speak to your parents?'

'Yes.'

'And?'

'It's fine.'

'Even after you broke the news to them?'

'It's all sorted. Now.' They shared a look. 'I'll tell you later.' And he took her hand.

Ben's parents were upstairs at the entrance waiting to greet them. 'Miri!' his mother said. She held out her arms and enveloped her in an embrace. 'Mazal tov, ayuni! You have made us all so happy. Welcome to the family.'

'Thank you, Mazal,' said Miri.

'From now on, if you like, you can call me Ima,' she said. 'And next week, once I finish sitting shiva, we will plan your wedding. We have lots to do. We'll go shopping together and find you a beautiful dress.'

'Thank you so much. Ima.'

Her future mother-in-law smiled and kissed her on both cheeks, and Miri felt like she had come home.

Mazal Aharoni turned to her family and friends. 'Ben has just got engaged! This is Miri, our new daughter-in-law.'

The house of mourning erupted with cries of 'Mazal tov!' as Ben led her into the apartment, and they accepted their good wishes, blessings, hugs and kisses at every turn.

After the initial flurry of excitement, Ben took her into the relative calm of the kitchen.

'Ready to do this?' he said.

'Let's.'

He pulled out his phone, dialled the number, and held the phone between them.

'Hello, Mrs Fogel. This is Ben.'

'Oh, Ben…' Miri could hear the anticipation in her mother's voice.

'I have Miri here with me. She'd like to talk to you.'

'Mameh,' she said. 'I became a kallah!'

Miri heard halted breathing and the muffled tones of her mother saying, 'He got there already.' Miri wasn't sure whether she was speaking to herself, to her, or someone else at the other end.

'Mazel tov,' she said, and this time her mother was definitely talking to her.

'Ben told me about what you did. Thank you! Thank you for your help.'

'Miri, I'm so happy,' her mother's voice choked with emotion. 'For both of you.'

Chapter 37

Five months later

It started out like any other evening. One of those ordinary but blissful, relaxed evenings that Miri relished. They'd finished supper, done the dishes and shared stories about their day. A chill-out CD played in the background, Ben worked on his laptop at the table and Miri lounged on the sofa, drawing. Every so often, he would gaze in her direction and smile. He didn't realise how often she did the same, watching him, deep in concentration.

In about an hour when he finished for the night, he might suggest they go out for a walk or a drink, as he sometimes did. Or, if Miri was too tired, they'd curl up on the sofa, his arms wrapped around her as they watched a film. There were nights when an all-consuming tiredness washed over her. Next thing she knew, it was the following morning, and she'd wake up to find herself in bed, Ben having carried her there while she slept.

The sound of the buzzer drew their attention to the door. 'Expecting anyone?' he said.

'No.' She reached across the sofa for a cotton bandana and wrapped it around her long hair.

'You sit. I'll get it,' Ben said. He stretched out languorously and padded barefoot across the cool, tiled floor.

'Wow!' he said as he looked in amazement through the peephole.

'Who is it?' Miri asked.

Ben opened the door and stood aside to let the visitor enter. Miri placed a hand over her mouth and was on her feet at once.

'Oh my word!'

Raizy opened her arms wide and ran to her best friend.

'What a surprise! How come you're here?' Miri said.

'A last-minute plan. Naftoli's best friend from yeshiva is getting married here on Thursday. We got a cheap deal, so turned it into a mini-break. We arrived this afternoon.'

'This is amazing! Is Naftoli here too?'

'He's gone to visit his relatives this evening, and I wanted to surprise you.'

'I've missed you. It's been too long!'

Miri hadn't imagined when they parted at the bus stop it would be months until they saw each other again. Both their lives had since changed. That day seemed like a lifetime ago.

Raizy stepped back to study her friend who glowed with an air of contentment. A simple scarf covered Miri's hair, save for a few tendrils framing her face. Raizy's eyes travelled down to her neat bump concealed beneath a loose, white t-shirt.

'You look fantastic! How are you doing?' said Raizy.

'I'm great.' Raizy caught her glance towards Ben, who answered with a smile.

She was the same Miri, and at the same time, different. She had found what she had been looking for. It was clear she and Ben adored one another. Raizy experienced a warm rush of satisfaction for her part in bringing them together.

'You look stunning too!' Miri said. 'I like your *sheitel*. It suits you.'

Raizy accepted the comment with grace but suddenly felt a little overdressed in her elegant, custom-made wig and high heels.

'I can't believe I'm here in your home, at long last!'

'Shall I show you around?'

Raizy followed Miri on a short guided tour of the bedroom, bathroom and open-plan living and kitchen space, which comprised their tiny apartment. It made Raizy's three-bedroom home (a standard property for her neighbourhood) seem almost excessive in comparison. Yet Miri couldn't have been happier, or prouder, of their home. And they had done an impressive job decorating it.

Raizy wandered around the living room, admiring the original, framed artwork lining the walls. She liked the style and wondered about the artists. Most depicted Jerusalem with its winding alleys and stone buildings that reflected fantastic, golden sunsets, and a few were architectural studies of arched doorways or windows. There was also a beautiful painting – clearly an expensive piece of art – of a tender London scene of two figures entwined on a bridge over the River Thames. Raizy didn't recall Miri ever having an interest in art. She surmised this was Ben's influence. Like the two guitars she spotted, propped against the side of their snug, two-seater sofa. It brought to mind the time she had to stash away the questionable CDs he had lent Miri, in order to save her from being found out by her mother. But those times were behind them. She no longer needed to hide her CDs or the stack of novels on the bookshelf, or the TV which was positioned on a low unit on wheels, opposite the seating area. Raizy was a touch envious at the lack of societal pressure here. But not enough to wish trading places.

She moved closer to examine three wedding photos on their bookcase. In the centre was a night-time shot of Miri and Ben on the seafront, arms around one another, reminiscent of the London painting on their wall. Miri's hair hung in loose waves, framed by a diamanté tiara and veil. And the flared skirt of her simple, ivory dress billowed around Ben, who was wearing a plain white shirt and black trousers.

She compared it with the more formal wedding photograph she kept on the sideboard beside her silver candlesticks. Dressed in her flowing, custom-made gown, her wig styled in an updo with a tiara as a finishing touch, Raizy had felt like a queen. Her husband, too, looked regal in his new *streimel* and *bekishe*. Though not as intimate as Ben and Miri's pose, their comfortable stance as they leaned in towards each other reflected the closeness that had developed between them during their engagement. Although Raizy would be on the receiving end of some strange comments were she to display such a wedding portrait for visitors to see.

Her eyes lingered on the other two pictures which elicited her curiosity. She pointed to the image of Ben surrounded by a group of men holding candles.

'Why is Ben wearing white fabric around his head?'

'It's called a *Talbis*, a special ceremony for the chosson which takes place right before the chasseneh. It's an Adeni custom. The men hold candles and sing songs – you should hear how they sing – like singing you might imagine from the days of ancient Israel. It touches the soul. They tie a band around his head and place a *tallis* across his shoulder as a symbolic preparation for the wedding.'

'And in this one, why do you and the other women have mud on your hands?'

Miri laughed. 'It's henna paste. From the night of my hinnah.'

'Your what?'

'It's a pre-wedding party. We had ours two nights before.'

'You mean to say you saw each other so soon before your chasseneh?'

Ben chuckled behind his laptop. 'Why don't you take Raizy out for a walk around the neighbourhood and have a proper catch-up? Maybe stop off at our favourite café.'

'I'm up for that,' said Raizy.

'My love, are you coming as well?' Miri said.

'No, I'll stay here. I've still got work to finish. But I wouldn't say no to you bringing me back a slice of cake.'

She slipped on a pair of strappy sandals and he saw them to the door. 'Enjoy yourselves!' He brushed his wife's lips with his own.

Outside, the fragrant scent of pine permeated the balmy Jerusalem air, and in the fading light, stone buildings were bathed in gold. A chorus of birds chirped in harmony, and even the mellow shouts of children playing on the street didn't detract from the tranquillity. Across the road, an elderly woman acknowledged them from her plant-filled balcony. Miri knew her from her evening walks with Ben and waved back.

'Not quite Stamford Hill, is it?' Raizy said.

Miri chortled.

'But you seem settled.'

'Yes, I love it here,' Miri said.

'Listen, I must apologise for being so bad at keeping in touch the past few months. I guess you can relate. First, I was busy with the chasseneh preparations and then adjusting to married life.'

'Yeah, I understand.'

'And I'm sorry I had to miss your chasseneh. There was so much going on and my mum wouldn't let me fly out with just three weeks to go before mine. Yours was rather ... quick.'

'No choice. It was amazing how we pulled the whole chasseneh together in less than four weeks. All thanks to my mother-in-law. She was fantastic. It was a small wedding, but gorgeous. We held it at a hotel in Tel Aviv, right across the way from the sea. We had the hinnah party there too, and that was so much fun. Even my mother, who had some reservations, ended up enjoying it.'

'And your father?'

'No, he didn't come. Not his thing. *"Past nicht"* if you get what I mean.'

'Was he at your chasseneh?'

'Yes. He stayed on the sidelines most of the time, but he was there and wished us mazal tov. I imagine it has been hard for him to accept our marriage. But he sort of does. In his own way.'

'Does the situation with your parents upset you?'

'It has always been difficult. We've never been that close. It's different from the relationship Ben has with his parents or even you with yours,' Miri said. 'Though, my mother and I are starting to get closer. We speak on the phone a few times a week, and she's been giving me helpful advice about the pregnancy. Ben's parents are also wonderful, they treat me like their daughter. I miss them, but they are planning to come here again in time for my due date.'

Miri sensed Raizy's eyes on her baby bump. 'How far along are you now, is it already seven months?' she asked.

'Well,' Miri said with a twinkle in her eye, 'the official answer is five months. In reality, yes, seven.'

'It's lucky you're carrying small. You could pass for five. How do you feel?'

'Much better than at the beginning. Sometimes I still get so tired, but at least I'm over the morning sickness.'

'Did anyone make any comments to you about having such a quick chasseneh?'

'People were polite enough not to ask me straight out. I'm sure some wondered. My mother-in-law made the excuse we had been engaged in secret for a while, and that my parents hadn't been in favour of our relationship. And because they finally agreed to it and this was the only time they could fly out, we arranged the date to accommodate them. Perhaps they believed it. Kind of true, I guess.'

'Did anyone else come over for you?'

'My parents brought Ruchi and Eli, the youngest. The rest stayed with friends and family. It was far too expensive to bring everyone over. My sister Pessie wanted to come but she has her hands full with her baby girl and another on the way. Daniel flew in, which we both appreciated.'

'How is Daniel? We haven't been in touch since the morning I bumped into him and Ben down by the river.'

'Oh, that was the day after I left, right? He's fine. The same. He finishes his studies in the summer and then he'll decide what to do next.'

'Is he seeing anyone?'

'Not that I'm aware of. Nothing serious anyway. You know how he is.'

'Yes.' Raizy twisted a strand of her wig around her finger. 'It must have been hard not to have the rest of your family at your chasseneh.'

'I realised that's the way it had to be. It was a small price to pay. And I've become close with Ben's sister, Natalie, and my other new sister-in-law, Keren. So that made it easier. But I wish you could have been there. If it wasn't for you, Ben and I never would have met.'

'The most important thing is that you and Ben are together.'

'When I think back to what happened when my parents discovered my situation, and how different our lives could have turned out …' Miri's face clouded over, still haunted by that rocky chapter. 'I'll always appreciate what you did for us. Thank you for everything.'

Raizy's eyes met hers. 'You're my best friend, I'd do anything for you. It's great to see how happy you are. The two of you were meant to be. And thanks for not mentioning my involvement to your parents. I'm not sure how you found the strength under so much pressure.'

'I wouldn't have betrayed you.'

Miri pointed to a quaint café on the corner with an outdoor seating area decorated with coloured bulbs strung through the surrounding trees, glimmering between the branches.

'Do you want to stop here for a drink and maybe dessert?'

'I wouldn't mind. It is a kosher café, isn't it?' Raizy said.

Miri grinned, remembering how reluctant she had been to enter the café on the night she met Ben. 'Yes, don't worry. *Mehadrin.*'

They took a seat and browsed the menu.

'Oh gosh, I can't make head or tail of this. It's all in Hebrew!' Raizy said.

'Try the *hafuch.*'

'What's that?'

'It's like a cappuccino. And they do a delicious cheesecake too.'

When the waiter approached, Miri placed their order in her faltering Hebrew.

'I'm impressed. You've already learnt to speak Hebrew,' Raizy said.

'Not that well. But enough to order a coffee and cake.'

'The important things.'

'Naturally!' Miri said. 'Now, I want to hear all about your chasseneh. I'm sorry I had to miss yours too.'

Raizy spent the next hour regaling Miri with every detail of her wedding, the before and after, as well as the neighbourhood happenings she had missed.

'Do you miss anything from back home?' Raizy asked.

'You, most of all,' she said. 'I'm making new friends, but no one knows me like you do.'

'I miss you too. It's not quite the same without you. Do you ever plan to return?'

'We'll come for visits, but not for good. We want to make a life for ourselves here. A fresh start is the right thing for us. Ben has found a job building a company's website and is finding out whether it's possible to complete his degree here.'

'You mentioned in your last letter you're working too?'

'Yes. I have a part-time job as an English secretary at a nonprofit. The work is more interesting than my previous one, and the boss is kinder. After I've had the baby, I'm thinking of going back to study for a career, perhaps graphic or interior design. It's something I've always wanted to do. Ben is encouraging me to go for it.'

Miri took the last bite of her cake. 'I'm excited about the future and the new opportunities ahead. How about you, would you ever consider moving here?'

'No. I don't think I could ever do what you've done; leave behind everything familiar and start married life in a different country, almost alone. Stamford Hill isn't perfect, but it's home. I've got my parents and most of my sisters near me. I know where I am. It's comfortable. The situation changes when you're married. You don't have the same pressures as when you're single, waiting for that shidduch.'

This was the life Raizy had always expected.

'Except I see people eyeing me for signs I'm expecting. Perhaps I need to ask you for tips.' She playfully nudged Miri. 'By the way, what do you say to Devorah getting engaged?'

'I'm thrilled for her! And do you know who the boy is?' Miri said.

'I think his name is Bloch.'

'That's right, Lipa Bloch. Do you remember him?'

'Not sure. Should I?'

'He's the one my parents tried to set me up with on that shidduch.'

Raizy was open-mouthed. 'No!'

'Yes,' Miri said. 'He's a sweet and kind boy, just right for her.'

Raizy took a good look at her friend. 'Did you have something to do with it, by any chance?'

Miri smiled slightly as she said, 'I may have made a call or two.'

'I'm proud of you. That was very thoughtful,' Raizy said. 'You must have heard that her brother Tuli got engaged to our friend Yocheved as well.'

'Yes, fantastic!'

'He and Yocheved will be ideal for each other.'

'What makes you say that?'

'Well, Yocheved is more open-minded than many of our friends, what with her watching her parent's secret TV and so on. And Tuli is less sheltered than Devorah. After all, he was friends with Pinny Finer. He must have known what he got up to, especially after he had to go to that club to fetch him. He must be a loyal friend.'

'That never actually occurred to me. Did you play a part in introducing them?'

'Hmm ...' She mimicked Miri's expression. 'I might have made a call or two.'

'Strange how things work out. If I hadn't got mugged that night –'

Raizy startled her with a clap of her hands. 'I can't believe I still haven't told you this story. How could I have forgotten?'

From her excited expression, Miri could tell it would be a good one.

'You will love this! When I was at Devorah's engagement, about two weeks after your chasseneh, I overheard Mrs Finer talking to your mother. "It seems as if it was quite a sudden engagement and chasseneh. And an unusual shidduch too, if

I might add?" she said.

'Smooth as anything, your mother replied, "Yes, the suggestion also surprised us, but we made enquiries and found out he was a special boy from a fine family. Excellent yichus too. We spoke to the Rav, and he advised us not to pass up such a good shidduch, despite him not being Chassidish. He believed they were beshert for each other."'

'That's hilarious!' Miri said.

'Oh, there's more. She then tells Mrs Finer that the two of you were in fact engaged for several months but had to keep it a secret because Ben's older brother was getting married and his family have a *minhog* not to announce engagements until after the older sibling marries. Then, it was further delayed because his grandmother was *niftar*. "But they believe it's a segula to have a simcha at the end of the *shloishim*, so we agreed, despite the short notice," she explained.'

Miri raised an eyebrow. 'I'm not sure if Ben's family really have those customs.'

'Oh, I doubt they do. She made up the whole story! I'm sure Mrs Finer knew she was talking nonsense too and your mum was aware she did. But they both kept up the pretence. Mrs Finer just nodded politely and wished your mother much *naches*.'

Miri shook her head at the absurdity and Raizy let out a snort. Soon, they were both in hysterics.

Miri wiped the tears of laughter from her eyes. She sat back in her chair and savoured the moment. What a journey it had been since that October evening when Raizy dragged her along to the café in Islington to use her as an alibi. Who would have thought where it would lead them? This picturesque setting, a warm spring night, sitting with her best friend so far from the neighbourhood where they had grown up together.

Two friends, who at first glance may have appeared as though they came from opposite worlds, but in reality shared so much. Despite their different paths, there was an unbreakable bond between them.

'Your mum got one thing right in what she said to Mrs Finer.'

'What's that?'

'He is a special boy from a fine family. It was a good shidduch.'

Miri smiled with fond recollection of the night she first met Ben. 'But you could hardly call it a shidduch.'

'Of course it was!' There was a mischievous sparkle in her eyes. 'And Daniel and I were the shadchonim.'

Epilogue

Two months later

Miri stood between her mother and her mother-in-law. Every so often, they would lean across to give her a reassuring hug.

Zissy Fogel had donned her best wig for the occasion; Mazal Aharoni, an elegant black hat; and Miri, an elaborately wrapped, turquoise headscarf.

Three women. Three mothers. Standing side by side.

Miri had given birth to their son eight days ago. A sweet baby with a tuft of dark hair, his mother's mouth and his father's eyes.

The labour had been long and difficult, but Ben had been by Miri's side throughout and supported her. Now they were celebrating their son's *brit milah*.

In their discussions leading up to this day, Ben told Miri he felt she should be the one to choose the name of their first child. She suggested the baby should have two names and each of them would select one. Ben agreed but insisted she get the privilege to decide his first name, and he would give the second. It was a proposal that pleased them both.

No other family members knew the names on which they had decided.

Their little son lay on a satin pillow decorated with silver-embroidered Hebrew verses, cradled by Miri's father on his lap. Ben and Miri offered him the role of *sandak* – the person who would hold the baby for the ceremony. He accepted, saying he would be honoured to do this for his first grandson.

They had reached the naming part of the ceremony. Ben handed a slip of paper to the Rabbi.

Then he sought Miri where she stood watching and waiting for the return of their son, to nurse and comfort him. Wrapped in a *tallit*, Ben gazed at her adoringly with those deep, warm eyes of his that never failed to captivate her. They spoke of his devotion to her and their new son, his gratitude and his abiding love.

As she looked back at him, an image came to mind of the instant she first saw their baby's heartbeat. They had been through trials, but here they were, a family. Miri saw Ben unconsciously feel for his pendant, and she wiped away tears.

The Rabbi intoned the prayer, 'Preserve this child for his father and his mother, and his name in Israel shall be called ...' He paused, consulted the paper and read, 'Natan Shalom.'

Miri chose Natan, in memory of Ben's late brother, the uncle her son would never meet. The name's meaning: *He has given.*

And in deference to the Adeni tradition of naming a child in honour of his grandfather, Ben added Shalom, his father's name, meaning *peace*.

Mazal Aharoni couldn't conceal her emotion as she hugged her daughter-in-law. 'Thank you, ayuni. Mazal tov.' She

358

smiled through streaming tears.

'It's a beautiful name,' her mother whispered, and she kissed her. 'Mazel tov.'

Then her Mameh and her Ima embraced one another.

Shouts of 'Mazal tov!' resounded as Ben lifted his son, Natan, placed a tender kiss on his head and then handed him to Davidi. They had given his brother the honour of carrying him through the shul to his wife Keren, who would deliver him back to Miri. A segula, a good luck ritual, that they too may be blessed with a child.

Miri watched Ben's approach, walking behind his brother, accepting hugs, handshakes and congratulations at every turn.

She also kept her focus on their son, Natan, as Davidi passed him to Keren and she took the last few steps towards Miri.

And in that instant, as Miri held out her arms to take Natan from her, she lost sight of Ben for just a moment. But she was almost certain – out of the corner of her eye – she saw her father reach out and give a quick, tentative hug to his son-in-law.

Her husband and her love, Ben.

Acknowledgements

The writing of this novel was an incredible journey, a labour of love. I am so grateful for the experiences, the people I met, and the many wonderful friends I have made because of it. Thank you to all of you who helped or inspired a small part of this story.

To my dear parents for your encouragement, and my mother for being an early beta reader.

For your friendship, encouragement, advice, enthusiasm, suggestions, help with research, beta reading, feedback, and so much more: Nadine Adler, Natalie Arovo, Angie Attar, Benny Banin, Bernice Cohen, Dani Goldsmith, Yaniv Jacob, Laura Karp, Chedva Kleinhandler, Hadassah Levy, Uriel Messa, Limor Nassim, Sarah Pritzker, Orly Rafaelov, Sharon Rafaelov, Hadassah Sabo Milner, Leah Sheier, Rachel Velenski and Rachel Woolfson.

To the members of my writing group: Devorah Friedlander, Kibi Hofmann, Melanie Takefman, Suzanne Yantin and Deena Chava Haines, for your constructive input and enthusiasm.

Special thanks to the following for going above and beyond,

helping to make this book infinitely better, and for your treasured friendship.

Elana Abraham: for your encouragement, enthusiastically reading this novel again and again in its various draft forms, and sound advice. And Albert Abraham, for your encouragement and help at the start.

Helen Macabi: for the home-cooked Adeni food in your kitchen, enthusiastic beta reading, advice, help with research, and much more that helped make this book what it is.

Rifki Orzech: for your sound editorial advice, suggestions, research help, encouragement every step of the way, and your time. Thank you for helping me to shape this story by making me dig deeper.

Chen Yefet: for your insights, help with research, editorial advice, attention to detail, time and infinite patience. Thank you for helping me to go through revisions again and again as I honed this novel.

So much gratitude.

To our wonderful boys: for your enthusiasm, for your understanding when I needed space and quiet to write, and for sharing some of this adventure.

Shmuel: for your encouragement and constructive suggestions through the various drafts. Thank you for your support every step of the way, for your understanding, and for sharing this journey with me. Above all, thank you, ayuni, for your friendship and love.

Glossary

Key: A = Adeni AR = Arabic H = Hebrew HYP = Hebrew with Yiddish pronunciation Y = Yiddish

- **Abba** Father (H)
- **Adenim** Plural of Adeni (H)
- **Aveiro** Sin (HYP)
- **Ayuni** My eyes (A & AR)
- **Bas Yisroel** Daughter of Israel (HYP)
- **Bekishe** Long silk coat worn by Chassidic men for Shabbat and festive occasions (Y)
- **Beshert** Destined partner or destiny (Y)
- **Beshow** A Chassidish chaperoned Shidduch (Y)
- **B'ezrat Hashem** With God's help (H)
- **Bittul zman** A waste of time (H)
- **Borich Hashem** Thank God (HYP)
- **Bor minan** Keep away from me (A)
- **Brit milah** Circumcision ceremony (H)
- **Cappel** Skullcap (Y)
- **Challah** Plaited bread for the Sabbath (H)
- **Chasseneh** Wedding (Yiddish pronunciation)
- **Chassidish** Of a religious and conservative Jewish sect originating from Eastern Europe called Chassidism (Y)
- **Chassidus** Chassidism. Also refers to the individual

Chassidic sect that someone comes from (Y)

- **Chosheve** Important, prestigious (Y)
- **Cholent** A meat stew traditionally eaten for Sabbath lunch (Y)
- **Chossid** A Chassidic man (Y)
- **Chosson** Fiance, groom (HYP)
- **Chuppah** Wedding canopy (H)
- **Chutzpah/chutzpadik** Audacity, impudent (Y)
- **Drek** Rubbish (Y)
- **Ebb** Shame, disrespectful (A)
- **Eretz Yisroel** The land of Israel (HYP)
- **Erev Shabbes** Sabbath eve
- **Fahgarek fahgara** Woe is you, woe is me (A)
- **Frum** Religious (Y)
- **Gemach** Communal loaning or voluntary organisation (Y)
- **Git Shabbes** Sabbath greeting (Y)
- **Goyishe** Not Jewish (Y)
- **Habibti** My beloved (AR)
- **Hamsa** A hand-shaped amulet (H & AR)
- **Hashem** God (H)
- **Hatzlocho** Success, good luck (HYP)
- **Hinnah** Henna party (H & AR)
- **Ima** Mum (H)
- **Im yirtze Hashem** May it be God's will (H)
- **Inta magnoon** You are mad (A)
- **Kaddish** Mourner's prayer (H)
- **Kallah** Bride (i.e. just got engaged) (H & Y)
- **Kallah classes** Bridal classes to learn the laws of family purity and the physical relationship within marriage.
- **Kallah maidele** A girl of marriageable age (Y)

- **Kippah** Skullcap (H)
- **Kristallnacht** A pogrom against the Jews in Germany in November 1938
- **Kosher** Satisfying the requirements of Jewish law, especially regarding food (H)
- **Langer rekel** Black, knee-length jacket worn by Chassidic men aged 13 and up (Y)
- **L'chaim** Literally 'To life!' or 'Cheers!' (i.e. gathering for drinks to celebrate) (H & Y)
- **Loshen hora** Derogatory speech about another person (HYP)
- **Magen David** Star of David (H)
- **Mazel tov / Mazal tov** Congratulations (HYP / H)
- **Mehadrin** An extra stringency of kosher (H)
- **Meshugge / Meshuggener** Crazy (Y)
- **Minhog** Custom (HYP)
- **Mizrach** East
- **Mizrahi** Eastern / originating from the Middle East (H)
- **Motzei Shabbat / Moitzei Shabbes** Saturday night (H / HYP)
- **Naches** Pride (HYP)
- **Negel Vasser** The ritual washing of hands upon waking up (Y)
- **Niftar** Passed away (H)
- **Omein** Amen (HYP)
- **Past nicht** It isn't the 'done' thing (Y)
- **Pesach** Festival of Passover (H)
- **Peyes / peyot** Side locks (Y / H)
- **Pruste** Indecent, immoral (Y)
- **Rabbonim** Rabbis (H)
- **Rav** Rabbi (H)

- **Reboine shel oilom** Master of the universe (HYP)
- **Refuah sheleima** Complete recovery (H)
- **Saba** Grandfather (H)
- **Savta** Grandmother (H)
- **Sefardi** Jewish person with origins from Spain or Portugal (H)
- **Segula** Symbol for good fortune (H)
- **Sem** Abbreviation for Seminary - a finishing school for religious girls
- **Shadchen / Shadchonim** Matchmaker / Matchmakers (HYP)
- **Shabbat shalom** Sabbath greeting – literally: Peaceful Sabbath (H)
- **Shabbat/Shabbes/Shabboth** Saturday, the Jewish Sabbath (H / Y / A)
- **Shabbat Chatan** Celebratory Shabbat for the groom the week after the wedding (H)
- **Shacharit / Shacheris** Morning prayers (H / HYP)
- **Shaigetz** A man who isn't Jewish or doesn't appear to be (Y)
- **Shainkeit** Beauty (Y)
- **Sheitel** Wig (Y)
- **Sheva brachot** Celebratory meals for seven nights after the wedding (H)
- **Shidduch / im (pl)** Marriage match (H & Y)
- **Shiksa** A non-Jewish woman (Y)
- **Shiur** Bible lecture / lesson (H & Y)
- **Shiva** Period of seven days sitting and mourning after the death of a close relative (H)
- **Siddur** Prayer book (H)
- **Simcha/simches** Celebration (H) / Celebrations (HYP)

- **Shloshim / Shloishim** Thirty days of mourning after a close relative dies (H / HYP)
- **Shul** Synagogue (German and Yiddish term but used in almost all Jewish communities in the UK)
- **Shtreimel** Chassidic fur hat (Y)
- **Sukkot** Festival of Tabernacles which falls in autumn (H)
- **Tabla** A goblet drum, also known as a darbuka in Arabic and Hebrew. Adenim call this drum a tabla but isn't the same instrument as the twin drums called tabla from India (A)
- **Talbis** Adeni ceremony for the groom that takes place right before the wedding (A)
- **Tallis / Tallit** Prayer shawl (HYP / H)
- **Talmid chochom** Great Torah scholar (HYP)
- **Tashlich** Prayer said besides a river on the Jewish new year to symbolically cast away sins in the water (H)
- **Teshuvah** Repentance (H)
- **Todah** Thank you (H)
- **Torah** Bible (H)
- **Tzitzit** Four-cornered, fringed garment worn by men under their shirt (H)
- **Tznius** Modest (HYP)
- **Vort** Engagement party (Y)
- **Yachne** A busybody, a gossip (Y)
- **Yeshiva** An educational institution for Jewish boys that focuses on the study of traditional religious texts (H)
- **Yichus** Lineage (HYP)
- **Shema Yisroel** Hear O Israel – the first words of the main Jewish prayer (H – Adeni pronunciation & HYP)
- **Zeide** Grandfather (Y)
- **Zoinah** Prostitute (Y)

Stay In Touch

I hope you have enjoyed reading this book as much as I enjoyed writing it.

If you care to share your thoughts in a review on any online store, website or by word of mouth, it's very much appreciated.

And if you would like more stories, please sign up to the Readers Club on my website at:

www.sarahansbacher.com

There's no cost to join, and you'll get a free book to download, (a collection of short stories) as well as bonus gifts to follow. I care about your privacy, so if you want to unsubscribe at any time, it's simple to do so.

I look forward to welcoming you to the club.

Sarah

Also by Sarah Ansbacher

PASSAGE FROM ADEN: STORIES FROM A LITTLE MUSEUM IN TEL AVIV

When Sarah first walked through the doors of a museum that preserves the history of a little-known Jewish community, she only intended to do some research for a novel. But six months later she received their surprise job offer. She wasn't sure what to expect but accepted anyway.

She soon discovered its magic: a museum that came to life through its varied visitors. Among the remarkable people she met were Jews from Aden, Yemen, the Middle East and North Africa, children of Holocaust survivors, crypto-Jews, tourists from Germany, Poland and the Far East, Christians and Muslims. Those fascinating interactions served as a bridge between languages, cultures and generations, and shared stories about the past and present. She started writing them down

The result is this extraordinary collection of true stories. Amusing, poignant, insightful, they will take you to forgotten times and places and warm your heart.